BETTER THAN ME

KIMBERLY KINCAID

BETTER THAN ME

DEDICATION

To Elena Cuomo,
for some of the most powerful
words in universe.

Of course you can.

ACKNOWLEDGMENTS

A.K.A, the usual suspects and the wonderful, patient, kind people without whom none of my books are possible...

To my dream team, Jaycee DeLorenzo (cover goddess), Nicole Bailey (badass editor), Rachel Hamilton and Jen Williams (best betas ever), and Jenn, Brooke, and Sarah at Social Butterfly (who make me look good!) I love you guys so much.

All the gratitude in the universe to my SHoY family for keeping me centered, and Robin Covington and Avery Flynn for keeping me sane. If y'all cry at the end of this book, blame RC #herfault

And to my kids (who are too quickly becoming not-kids-anymore) and Mr. K...you are everything. I could not do one second of this without you.

1

There was a bathtub in Natalie Kendrick's living room. Which wouldn't be so bad, if she'd ordered a new one and it was awaiting installation, or even if she were living in a tiny little efficiency and had four hundred square feet to her name. But since the bathtub in question belonged to her upstairs neighbors, and it had arrived via the giant, gaping hole now turning her ceiling into a skylight, Natalie was less than pleased at the disaster zone in front of her.

And by less than pleased, she really meant internally freaking the fuck out, because from the look of things, the tub had been full to the brim when it had crash-landed on her couch.

"Whoa." Jonah's perfectly blue eyes went perfectly wide from where he stood beside her, amid the chaos of firefighters, utility workers, and absolute destruction. Having her best friend and fellow surgeon beside her usually went a long way toward calming Natalie in situations that had taken the handbasket route directly to hell. Right now? Jonah really had his work laid out in front of him.

"At least you weren't here when it happened," he said, and okay, she'd give him that. Still, this so wasn't the ending she'd anticipated from her Monday, especially since she'd preceded her post-work friends' night out with an eleven-hour shift at the hospital that had included three pediatric surgeries.

Natalie looked at her landlady, Agnes, and put her very best effort into a nice, calm inhale.

It didn't work.

"How *did* this happen, exactly?" All Natalie had to go on was the cryptic phone call Agnes had made fifteen minutes ago that had pulled her and Jonah away from their friends and colleagues at The Crooked Angel and into *Waterworld*.

"Well, you'll have to ask Max and Rebecca for the, ahem, exact particulars." She swung a gaze at the bathrobed couple standing sheepishly in the main hallway, and Natalie swallowed a groan. Max and Rebecca rented the second floor of the Victorian townhome, while Natalie lived on the first. Each floor had been renovated into completely separate, private apartments, but that had never kept the couple from making their highly active and wildly imaginative sex life audible from every corner of Natalie's space.

Oh, the irony.

Agnes continued, fluttering a birdlike hand over her floral housedress. "But it seems they were filling the bathtub for a night of relaxation when they became, ah, preoccupied with other endeavors. The tub overflowed, and well, you know how old the house is, dear. That tub is pure cast iron, and the hardwoods and plaster are part of the original construction. As soon as the floorboards got wet enough to weaken..."

She gestured upward with one arthritic hand, and Jonah's brows popped. "Wait," he said slowly. "So, they were, uh, preoccupied long enough to allow for a flood that made their bathtub collapse through the *ceiling*?"

"It appears that way." Agnes nodded.

"That's some serious stamina," Jonah murmured under his breath.

"You have no idea," Natalie said, very quietly, even though every last bit of her wanted to scream. She had to find the bright side. She always found the bright side.

Please, God, let there be a bright side. "Okay, so no one was hurt, but there's obviously a lot of property damage. What do we do now?"

Agnes blinked through her bifocals. "Well, I've called Wilfred to come take a look, but these nice firefighters here mentioned…oh, what was it?"

"Structural integrity," the nearest firefighter supplied.

Between Agnes's mention of her twin brother, who did all of the maintenance on the house at a pace that would make most snails look speedy, and the firefighter's ominous-sounding response, the smile that Natalie had manufactured slipped.

"Hi, Lieutenant…"

"McNamara," the guy said, tipping the brim of his helmet at her. "I take it you're the tenants?"

"Whoa, not me," Jonah said quickly, his hands hiking up as if he'd been scalded. "We don't…I mean, I'm not—"

"We don't live together," Natalie said. Under other circumstances, she'd laugh at how apoplectic Jonah looked at the suggestion, even though it wasn't nearly the first time a stranger had mistaken them for a couple. Right now? She had bigger fish to fry. "I'm the tenant. Natalie Kendrick."

She offered Lieutenant McNamara her hand, her manners having been sewn-in pretty much at birth.

"Wish I had better news for you, Ms. Kendrick. But with

how old this house is and the fact that there's damage from both the collapse and the flooding, there's really no telling how bad it is until a building inspector can take a closer look. It's definitely not safe to live in." He eyed her ruined living room with sympathy. "Not that you'd probably want to try. It looks like this thing took out part of your kitchen, too."

Natalie's pulse tripped. "Do you know how long repairs on something like this might take?"

"It really all depends on what the inspector finds once he or she gets in here," the lieutenant said. "But if I had to guess, I'd say you're looking at a minimum of four to six weeks."

Heat pricked in Natalie's eyes, her throat knotting over a hard lump that signaled imminent tears, but no, no. No, no, no, she would not cry. Not in front of Agnes or Lieutenant McNamara, and definitely not in front of Jonah. If she did, then he would know she was really upset, and if he knew *that*, he'd worry.

She had to put on a brave face, and she had to do it right freaking now.

Natalie closed her eyes. Counted to three. When she opened them again, her tears were gone and her silver lining was firmly in place. "Well. I suppose that's better than four to six months."

"Your bedroom looks like it was mostly undisturbed, and since it's on the other side of the house, you're okay to go in there to get some things."

Jonah must've sensed how close she was to flipping her pancakes despite her efforts to appear calm, because he stepped in and shook the lieutenant's hand. "Thanks, man."

"No problem." He fell back to supervise his crew as they

finished up their check of the place. Agnes shook her head, her stare all apology as she turned toward Natalie.

"I'm so sorry, dear. Of course, I'll have Wilfred start working on it right away, and we'll work with the insurance company to make sure they have everything they need to replace your belongings. But this is my only rental property. I'm afraid I can't offer you another place to stay."

Natalie nodded. "Thanks, Agnes. I'll figure something out."

What, she had no clue, but first thing was first. She needed to salvage what she could from her bedroom before the firefighters kicked her out of the house. "Okay," she said, looking at Jonah as Agnes moved toward the main hallway to talk with Max and Rebecca. "There are a couple of suit-cases in the closet at the end of the hall by my bedroom. If we—"

"Nat." Jonah stepped in her path, his body so close that she had no choice but to come to an immediate halt to avoid crashing into him. "Are you okay?"

"Of course I'm okay," she said. Jonah knew her better than anyone, so she had to put her back into the smile she'd forced out along with her answer, but come on. She'd conquered far thornier obstacles than this. For pity's sake, she'd beat *cancer* before she was even old enough to drive. A little household destruction should be a tropical island vacay, complete with flip-flops and umbrella drinks, compared to that.

Somehow, Jonah wasn't looking convinced. "You know, it wouldn't be totally outside the realm of normal for you to be a little freaked out right now."

"This isn't anything to freak out about," she said, and of course, the firefighters had to choose that exact nanosecond to confirm that yes, the water damage had extended into her kitchen. "Look at the bright side. No one got hurt, and at least my bedroom is intact."

The laugh that Jonah gave up was soft and chock-full of irony, but her argument had done the trick. He stepped back, letting her lead the way toward her bedroom. "You are the only person I know who would look at this mess and see the bright side."

"And what does the alternative accomplish?" Natalie asked, relieved to have an objective. She swung her bedroom door open and turned on the light. "Getting upset won't make my apartment any less wrecked."

"It might be cathartic," Jonah suggested.

"I don't need catharsis. What I need is a suitcase."

After a quick trip to her storage closet at the end of the hallway, Jonah rolled two empty, practically new suitcases over the threshold to her bedroom. "Not to ask a sticky question, but have you thought about where you're going to stay?"

Dread threatened to reclaim Natalie's belly, but she folded it neatly into the compartment where she kept all of her crappy emotions, far, far from her face.

"Four to six weeks really *is* outside the realm of a hotel stay," she mused. Even if her insurance company gave her an allowance for housing, it probably wouldn't cover a decent efficiency that was close to the hospital. And that was assuming one was even available on short (okay, fine. No) notice.

"You could ask Tess," Jonah said, prompting Natalie to give up a laugh.

"In case you haven't noticed, Tess has a three-month-old baby. And her marriage is already pretty strained. I'm not asking her to take me in for six weeks."

Their colleague and close friend was already under a

metric crap-ton of pressure. No way was Natalie going to add to the woman's stress. Even if getting to babysit Jackson from time to time *would* be pretty fun.

"Eh, you may be right," Jonah agreed. "What about Charlie, then?"

More laughter barged past her lips. "The same Charlie who literally announced her engagement *tonight* and lives with her fiancé, who, oh, by the way, is one of my interns? Are you nuts?"

"Okay. Your parents. I know they live outside the city, but they'd totally let you crash at their place."

For the first time tonight, actual fear took root in Natalie's chest. "No. *No.* My parents cannot know about this. Not today. Not ever."

"Jesus, Nat." Jonah's brows creased, but only for a second before he traded his confusion for a much more affable smile. "Your ceiling caved in. I know it's kind of whoa, but it's not a threat to national security."

"You're right. It's worse."

Jonah squinted across the bedroom at her. "What are you talking about? Your parents are two of the nicest people on the planet."

Okay, so that wasn't entirely inaccurate. Still... "They're two of the nicest, most *overprotective* people on the planet," Natalie corrected. Having a kid with cancer did that to otherwise lovely parents. The fact that she was about to celebrate her eighteenth remission anniversary from the acute lymphocytic leukemia she'd been diagnosed with at age ten made no difference, nor did the fact that she was a board-certified pediatric surgeon, and a damned skilled one, at that. They still worried about her. A *lot*.

She continued, "If I tell my parents this happened, they will lose their shit. My mother will kick things off with a speech about the two dozen ways I could've been brutally killed by that bathtub even though I wasn't even here when it fell, and I'd have seen the flooding long before the ceiling gave out if I had. Her diatribe will encourage my father to point out—for thirty minutes, minimum—that he knew when I moved in that this apartment is an ancient death trap, and it's probably violating, like, nine thousand sections of the Remington City Building Code right this very second."

"The building is pretty old," Jonah said, his Bahama-blue eyes moving over the admittedly creaky wide-plank hardwoods and the intricate molding around the doors and windows that had made Natalie fall in love with the place the second she'd clapped eyes on it five years ago.

She huffed out a frustrated breath. "So it's not a slick condo in an uber-trendy part of the city. But it's quirky and it's fun, not to mention all I can afford because I have medical school loans the size of freaking Kansas. But give me a little credit," Natalie said, and damn it, maybe she was going to go just a teensy bit thermonuclear after all. "I ran a check for building code violations online before I signed the lease, and Wilfred might be slow, but he's always fixed every-thing I've asked him to on the rare occasion that something fritzes out. Not that either of those things will keep my parents from worrying themselves sick if they find out about this bathtub thing, or keep them from helicoptering me to death if I stay with them for the next six weeks. So, no. Telling them is absolutely not an option."

She plopped down on her bed. She'd been so caught up with thoughts of gathering what few things she could that she hadn't realized exactly how few viable places she had to *bring* said things.

"I could camp out in an on-call room at the hospital, I

guess," she said, although her nose wrinkled involuntarily at the thought of flat mattresses and less than zero privacy. Plus, the hospital's chief of staff, Keith Langston, would probably kill-switch the idea once he got wind of it. The man took by-the-book to a whole new level.

"Ha, good one." Jonah cracked the sort of handsome, boyish smile that made most women fling their panties in his direction. "Next thing you know, you'll say you want to crash with me for six weeks." He laughed heartily.

Natalie didn't.

"Oh, my God, could I?" The idea sprang to life in her chest. Despite having been best friends for four years, she had never actually spent a night at Jonah's place, nor had he ever crashed at hers. He'd been in a serious relationship when they'd gone from colleagues to close friends, and after that had abruptly ended, he'd been in a thousand *not*-serious relationships. Both scenarios had made an overnight —even a platonic, I-had-one-too-many-can-I-face-plant-fully-dressed-on-your-sofa kind of thing—slightly awkward.

But beggars couldn't be choosers. Slightly awkward or not, she needed a place to live, and she needed it tonight.

"I…" Jonah's stare became very, very round before his smile reclaimed its place on his magazine-model face. "I was totally kidding, Nat."

"But I'm not." Natalie looked up at him. "I'm one hundred-percent stone-cold serious. Will you let me move in with you?"

2

―――――

Jonah Sheridan was screwed six ways to Sunday, and it was only Monday night. But he had exactly one rule for self-preservation, and that was to keep his dance space to himself. A large part of enforcing that rule was to never have a woman—*any* woman—in his apartment when the sun came up. Hell, if he could possibly swing it, he never even brought them back to his place at all, always pushing for option A when it came down to "your place, or mine?"

And now Natalie wanted to live with him for six whole weeks? As in, right there in his apartment, her dishes next to his in the sink, her bras in his washing machine, her toothbrush in his bathroom, *live* with him?

It didn't matter that their friendship was platonic, nor that her stay would have an expiration date. Living with someone, even as a roommate, meant commitment, and Jonah didn't do close.

He'd learned the hard way to keep his distance, and he wasn't going back down that road.

Ever.

He reached for the affable charm that got him out of ninety-nine-point-five percent of dicey situations. There had to be another viable alternative. He'd just have to help Natalie find it, that's all.

"Trust me," he said, giving up a carefully cultivated half-grin. "I'm the last person you want to stay with."

Funny, she looked entirely unconvinced. "Why?"

Natalie was tack-sharp, so Jonah went for logic first. "I don't even have a guest bedroom, for one."

"You have a den," she argued, not wrongly. "And as I recall, there's a futon in there."

"That futon dates back to when I was in medical school," he said.

"No matter how old it is, it's better than what I've got now."

Damn it, that was also true. But speaking of true... "My on-call schedule is crazy."

Natalie laughed, the cute, little kind that he'd always found so endearing. "I have one of those, too, you know. Anyway, I sleep like the dead. Unless you do a tap dance on my frontal lobe on your way out the door, I'll never even hear you if you get called in."

Jonah paused. According the nurses, Natalie was notoriously hard to rouse, and he'd had to wait for her on more than one occasion when they'd shared a ride to the hospital for a shift.

She must've taken his silence as consideration, because she stepped closer to the spot where he stood on the pretty blue and cream area rug placed neatly on the floorboards.

"Most of the time I'm there, I'll be sleeping, and when I'm not, I can give you your space. I'll kick in for food and utilities, *and* I'll split chores with you, fifty-fifty." Her stare glinted, the color of warm whiskey and full of hope.

It hit Jonah's chest, center mass. "I'm a terrible cook." Okay, so it was lame, but he was losing steam, fast.

"As luck would have it, I'm a great cook. You take dish duty, and we'll call it square."

"You and your parents are tight," he said, knowing it was a last-ditch, but that it was also her most feasible (and, fine. Only) alternative. "I get that they might hover a little, but they've got a nice, big house, and they wouldn't dream of asking you to do chores or pay for food. You'd be so much more comfortable with them than in my tiny shoebox of an apartment."

The breath Natalie huffed out couldn't decide if it wanted to be a laugh or a sigh. "My parents don't hover a little. They hover professionally and without remorse. Look"—her expression went soft and serious, something she usually reserved for the parents of a patient who were about to get bad news, and oh, shit, this couldn't mean anything good—"I know you've only lived with one other person, and that...didn't work out."

Leave it to Natalie to be polite about the eleventh-hour cancellation of his high-profile wedding to one of Remington's social elite. She'd been the only one to defend him after the whole thing had gone tango uniform, even though he'd never told her—or anyone—exactly what had happened that night.

Jonah needed his default, and he needed it right fucking now.

"I don't want to talk about Vanessa," he said quietly, and, to his surprise, Natalie nodded in agreement.

"I don't, either, because this wouldn't even be in the same hemisphere as that. You and I are just friends, and my living with you would only be temporary. I'm neat and fairly low-maintenance, and I really can cook like a boss. I know you like your space." It was a euphemism, and if the smile poking at the corners of her lips was anything to go by, Natalie knew it as well as Jonah did. He was a fucking island, and it wasn't by accident. "So I can totally stay out of your hair if you want me to. But please." In a blink, her smile disappeared. "I'm begging you. Don't make me stay with my parents."

Jonah's nice-guy propensity came out of hiding to pick a fight with his defenses, both of them quickening his pulse. His defenses didn't fight fair, though, reminding him that he had damn good reasons for not being a long-haul guy.

He opened his mouth to say he was sorry. To tell Natalie, rationally and with good reason, why he just couldn't let her move in with him for six weeks.

But what came out was, "Okay. You can stay."

Christ, his inner nice-guy was a sneaky son of a bitch.

"Really?" Natalie let out a gasp that quickly slid into an adorable ear-to-ear grin, and okay, Jonah was going to have to do some damage control here.

"With a couple of stipulations," he said, holding up his fingers to count them off. "If you want to watch rom coms or that channel that plays all those gooey holiday movies, you've got to do it on your iPad."

Jonah knew from experience that she loved both, and with Christmas only a month away, she'd certainly want to mainline them whenever she had down time. But while happily ever after might be on some people's agendas—and more power to them as long as they didn't try to convert him to coupledom—he sure as hell wasn't going to let it parade across his big screen TV.

"Come on! Not even *It's a Wonderful Life*?" she asked, but he stood firm.

"The only Christmas movie that flies in my apartment is *Die Hard*."

Her hands moved to her hips. "That is so not a Christmas movie."

"Take it or leave it, Kendrick. Yippie-ki-yay is all the holiday cheer you're going to get out of me."

Natalie frowned, but didn't push her luck, so Jonah continued. "I'll take that you cook, I clean bargain. I don't mind doing all the dishes, and I wasn't kidding when I said I can't cook. No complaining about football *or* hockey—the Rogues are kicking ass again this year on the ice and I want to watch every game that I can. And for the love of all that is sacred and good, no bras on the shower curtain rod."

"Done."

His surprise must have stumbled over his face, because she laughed and tacked on, "What? You know I love hockey, too, and after meeting Finn Donnelly over the summer at that fundraiser at The Crooked Angel? I'm all-in for the Rogues. I promised you I'd cook, and the other stuff"—she lifted one shoulder beneath her light pink sweater—"I can stipulate, even if it *is* kind of Grinchy. So, do we have a deal? I can come live with you until this mess is all fixed?"

Jonah exhaled. "Yes, we have a deal. My futon is your futon."

"Oh, my God, yay! This is going to be so much fun!"

At the look of pure panic he'd been unable to cage, she sobered and bit her lip. "Actually, no. It's not going to be any fun at all. It's going to suck. Hard."

Damn it, he laughed. "I don't think it's going to suck."

"Okay, whew, because I don't, either," she said, her grin returning in all its glory. Her happiness was practically palpable enough to grab hold of, and Jonah couldn't help but feel the tight knot of his shoulders release a bit in response.

"I'm just not used to living with anybody," he said by way of apology. "Guess I've got to get my head around it a little. But it's not you."

Natalie threaded a groan through her laughter, reaching for one of the suitcases Jonah had unearthed from her preternaturally tidy hall closet. "If I were a real girl, that 'it's not you' thing would be the kiss of death."

Grabbing the second suitcase, Jonah conceded, "Fair enough." He was certainly no stranger to expressing the sentiment in all of its various forms, and it rarely went over with enthusiasm.

"Can you take the drawers while I take the closet?" she asked, pointing at the white, vintage-looking bureau paralleling her bed, which was a king-sized brass affair loaded with pillows, and it occurred to him belatedly that he'd never been in Natalie's bedroom before.

"Sure." He shook off the weird, forbidden thrill that had just popped through his veins. Probably, he should've passed on that last drink at The Crooked Angel. "And for the record, you're totally a real girl. Woman," he corrected.

Natalie snorted. "You're really working that Jonah Sheridan charm over there."

She waggled her light blond brows at him as she turned toward her closet, but nope. He wasn't going to let her joke her way out of this one.

"Just because we're best friends, that doesn't mean I don't recognize you're pretty."

Natalie blinked at him from the threshold of her tiny walk-in closet. "What?"

"You sound surprised to hear me say that," Jonah said, and huh, looked like surprise was contagious. He'd certainly thought Natalie was attractive when he'd met her during their residencies, to the point that if he and Vanessa hadn't been together at the time, he almost certainly would've asked her out. But then their friendship had formed, fast and tight, and after everything imploded the night before his wedding, Jonah knew he'd never ask Natalie out, no matter how pretty he still thought she was.

He'd never trash their friendship over a one-and-done, just like he'd never sleep with the same woman more than a couple of times before he started looking for the door.

Natalie deserved better than him.

"It's just that pretty isn't usually the first word people use when they describe me," she said, the sound of her voice delivering him back to her bedroom. "Cute, smart, bubbly—"

"Modest," he interrupted (too good to pass up), and she rolled her eyes.

"Hey, I'm not the one looking like a freaking cover model over here."

Jonah selected his most charming smile and slid into it like the disguise it was. "Don't hate me because I'm beautiful," he teased.

"Exactly my point." Natalie took a sweater off the hanger in front of her and began to fold it with precise movements. "You're *you*. You've dated dozens of women who look like they've been Photoshopped. I'm just surprised that you, of all people, would put me in the pretty category. That's all."

Whether it was that last drink still lingering, or the residual adrenaline from the night's crazy events making him impulsive, Jonah couldn't be sure. But before he could stop himself, he said, "Well, you shouldn't be, because it's true."

"Oh. Ah, thank you." Her cheeks flushed, proving his

point in motherfucking spades, and yeah, he really shouldn't speak until he was certain he had full command of his brain to mouth filter.

Drawers. Suitcase. Something other than that forbidden thrill that not only didn't *take a hike, but is now headed directly for your Johnson, you great, big Neanderthal.*

Jonah cleared his throat. "So, did you want anything in particular from here, or...?"

Natalie looked at the dresser and shook her head. "I guess a week or two's worth of everything, since I can do laundry after that. The stuff on top is what I wear most."

Glad to have a task to keep his brain—and the rest of his anatomy—focused, Jonah tugged open the drawer in front of him, which happened to be full of socks. Having sexy thoughts about Natalie, even briefly, wasn't cool. She was about to come live with him for six weeks. He had to make sure to squash any errant feelings of attraction now.

And he knew one surefire way to do it.

"We didn't get to finish our conversation at The Crooked Angel," he said, taking four pairs of meticulously folded and paired socks out of the drawer and placing them in the suitcase.

"What, about finding true love?" she asked from the closet.

Jonah went for round two with the socks. "Yep." The conversation had been inspired by their co-workers, Parker and Charlie, announcing their engagement to the crowd at the bar. At the time, Jonah had wanted to change the subject. But now, it would work as a wet blanket on his over-eager libido, so he dove back in. "What was it you said? Something about cake and happiness?"

Natalie laughed. The blush on her cheeks had disappeared, and even though Jonah knew he should be glad, *was* glad, a tiny part of him wanted it back. "What I *said* was that I believe in the kind of love where you give the other person the last bite of cheesecake without thinking twice. Where you laugh when they're happy, and you ache when they're sad. Where you're not two halves making a whole, but two wholes making something bigger, that only the two of you can make. And if I remember correctly, you rolled your eyes."

"It's just not what I'm looking for," Jonah said, reaching for the second drawer and pulling out a few of the tank tops Natalie usually wore under her scrubs, then placing them next to the socks he'd accumulated. It was one hell of a euphemism, since he wasn't so much not looking for it as he was avoiding it like a land mine, but under the circumstances, it'd serve.

"I know," she said, all fact. "I don't think I'm necessarily *looking* for it, either. My dating apps all kind of have cobwebs on them because of work. But I do want to find it someday soon."

"Soon, huh?" That was a new development. Not that they talked about it frequently, but...

"Not for the reasons most people would assume. My mother talks about my biological clock far more than I do." Natalie had moved on to the jeans stacked tidily on a shelf in her closet. "I mean, I want to have kids, but I want to adopt. The reason I want to find someone to be happy with is that...well, I want to be happy."

So much to unload there. Jonah took a breath to temper the surprise that had made his pulse go momentarily haywire. "I didn't know you wanted to adopt."

"You never asked," she said. The brightness of her grin dimmed a level as she elaborated. "And to be fair, I only recently decided that it's what I want for sure. But I don't even know if I *can* have biological children, after having all that chemo and radiation when I was young. Plus, working with kids, and volunteering in the clinic, especially, has made me realize how many children there are without really good homes. In the U.S., abroad. It's really astounding. If I can make that difference to a handful of kids who need it, I feel like I should."

"A handful."

"Two. Three. Four." Natalie shrugged. "I'm probably not going to be able to be horribly picky."

A silence lapsed between them as they both continued packing for a minute. In truth, Jonah had never given being a father much consideration. His own family life had been less than stellar from the time his mother had left him and his old man behind. Jonah had been in kindergarten when he'd come home to an empty house and a hastily scrawled Dear John letter that he'd had to give to his father. Between that and the fact that the idea of a third date had him slowly easing toward the door, fatherhood just wasn't on his agenda.

Chalk up one more reason to steer clear of any dirty thoughts of his best friend.

Jonah opened the top drawer of Natalie's dresser and was greeted by an eyeful of lingerie, and so much for that fucking idea. "Oh, shit. I mean"—*smooth. Real smooth.* But come on, it wasn't his fault that she had panties in every color of the rainbow, each pair prettier than the last —"maybe you should, um, take care of this part?"

Natalie looked up. Saw which drawer he had open. And laughed. "And here I thought you were totally well-versed in women's undergarments."

"Not *yours*," he argued, the back of his neck going hot.

Her smile lost a little steam, as if the thought mortified

her, and Jesus, could he get any more ineloquent? "Of course not," she said, all business. "Here, why don't you finish up in the closet while I take care of that? Then I'll grab my toiletries and we can get out of here."

"Deal." Jonah switched places with her, adding a couple of sweatshirts and the pair of running shoes he knew she loved to the space left in the suitcase she'd been packing. Once it was full, he zipped the thing up, happily noting that she'd moved on to the toiletries. Her top drawer was firmly closed, and Jonah tried to convince himself that he hadn't seen the delicate lace. The soft silk and more functional, but somehow just as sexy, cotton.

The forbidden thrill reminded him that oh, yes, he had, and *hell* yes, he'd been turned on at the sight.

The next six weeks were going to last forever.

"Okay," Natalie said, reappearing from her adjacent bathroom, tote bag of toiletries in hand. "I think that should do it."

"Great." Jonah took a step toward the closest suitcase, but she stopped him with a hand to his sleeve.

"Thank you for doing this, Jonah. Seriously. You don't know how much I appreciate you letting me move in until this mess gets taken care of."

She looked so sweet, so honest and open and purely Natalie, that Jonah did the only thing he could do.

He gave up his biggest, most charming smile and said, "What are friends for?"

3

Natalie yawned into her hand and tried her level best not to fall asleep in the attendings' lounge. She hadn't stayed up particularly late, and Jonah's futon was actually far comfier than he'd let on. But he'd been pretty quiet on the way from her place to his, and the conversation, which usually flowed so easily between them, hadn't improved much when they'd gotten to his apartment. He'd given her a polite rundown of where everything was—sheets, extra blankets, the good cereal, that sort of thing—along with a quick tutorial on how to work the high-tech remote for the big screen TV mounted to the living room wall. He'd looked almost tentative when he'd taken the spare key off the hook inside one of the kitchen cabinets for her, placing it on the counter and sliding it over with a halting "I guess you'll need this" before punctuating the offer with a lightning-fast "well, goodnight."

Natalie had promised to stay out of his hair—a promise she'd meant, since he was doing her such a colossal solid and she knew he favored his space—so she'd made good use of the linen closet to cover the futon he'd unfolded for her, used the powder room in the hallway to wash up and brush her teeth, and turned in. But between the bathtub/ceiling disaster and the weird feeling of lying all pajamaed up in bed less than fifteen feet from where Jonah did the same, actual sleep had eluded her for hours. She hadn't been restless, exactly. At least, not in the usual toss-and-turn sort of way. No, last night, Natalie had been almost keyed up, like a current was humming, low and insistent beneath her skin. Like she was missing something—wanted it badly, even—but didn't know specifically *what* it was.

The whole thing sucked, because she couldn't say anything about it to the one person she'd normally bounce this kind of thing off of. Things between her and Jonah were unusually awkward, and that weird feeling she'd had? If she didn't know better, Natalie would say it had felt an awful lot like arousal.

Which was a joke, really, considering that there was exactly one thing she'd never told him about herself. One secret she'd just never been able to share that made their friendship far more ironic than he knew.

After all, the odds of Remington's only 32-year-old virgin and its most commitment-shy, sex-positive bachelor being BFFs had to be one in a million.

The fact that he'd treated her panties as if they'd been a time bomb with one tick left before detonation? Meant her V-card was safe, no matter *how* active Jonah's sex life might be.

Natalie took a long draw from the lukewarm coffee in her hand and chastised herself for being silly. Okay, yes, she'd always found Jonah attractive—just because she hadn't met a guy she wanted to give p-in-v privileges to yet didn't mean she was without a pulse. Between that tousled-but-not-messy blond hair, those inexplicably blue eyes, and the leanly muscled body that made Michelangelo's *David* look like a third-grade art project, Jonah was hotness personified. But they were best friends. Of course he didn't look at her that way. And normally, she kept her attraction to him firmly under the heading of an objective observation. She'd even built up an immunity to the preposterously chiseled abs she caught sight of every once in a while when he changed out of his scrubs in the attendings' lounge.

Or, at least, she *thought* she had...until she'd stretched out under sheets that smelled like Jonah, wondering how many times he'd slept under the very same ones. Whether the cotton wrapped around her had touched his bare skin. What it would feel like if *she* touched his bare skin...

Natalie released a nervous laugh into the empty room. Last night must have been a blip due to all the craziness. That was all. They'd get used to cohabitating in a few days, and everything would go back to normal. No problem. Easy-peasy.

God, his abs were really freaking chiseled.

The door to the lounge swung open, the sound of the two familiar female voices that followed grabbing Natalie's attention and depositing her back to reality.

"Hey, Natalie." Charleston Becker, their relatively new attending in general surgery, smiled in a warm greeting as she and Tess Michaelson, emergency department attending and Charlie's best friend, made their way into the lounge.

"Good morning! And, oh, my God, congratulations. You and Parker are getting married. Again!" Natalie found a genuine smile somewhere below her exhaustion, unfolding herself from the couch to give Charlie a big hug. Charlie had returned to Remington after a six-year absence, and been reunited with her ex-husband after a few bumps along the way, one of them being that Parker was now an intern at Remington Mem.

"I told you to get used to it," Tess teased in her blunt, no-holds-barred way. To Natalie, she said, "It took her, like, fifteen minutes to get through the lobby and the ED. Plus, Connor brought cake."

Natalie laughed. Their flight medic-slash-ICU nurse who sometimes filled in down in the ED was always looking for an excuse to eat cake. Not that his former Air Force medic physique showed it. "That sounds like Connor."

"Right?" Charlie asked, pausing in front of her locker for a smile that could light up lower Manhattan. "I don't mind getting waylaid a little. It's nice to have good news to share."

A pang of guilt squeezed through Natalie's belly beneath her dark green scrubs. "I'm so sorry I had to run last night before I got to congratulate you properly. I had kind of a, um, situation at home. But it's all fine now."

"Yeah, what happened?" Charlie asked, concern flickering through her green stare. "We just saw Jonah downstairs and he said a bathtub fell through your *ceiling*?"

Natalie bit back the weird hop-flip thing her stomach did at the mention of Jonah's name. By the time she'd dragged herself out of the few hours of dreamless sleep she'd finally managed to get, he'd been gone. He hadn't mentioned having to round early when they'd turned in last night, but she'd been secretly grateful not to have to deal with swapping turns for the only shower in his apartment.

"Oh, it's not nearly as bad as it sounds," Natalie said, dialing her smile up two notches. No need to worry her friends over something that was said and done.

Not that Tess seemed to buy her story for a single nanosecond. "Really? Because it sounds like a hundred-year-old cast-iron bathtub wiped out your apartment and a bunch of your stuff along with it, rendering you temporarily homeless."

"Okay, so that did happen," Natalie admitted. "But my neighbors' insurance company is covering most of my losses, and my neighbors have promised to pay for anything left over."

She'd spoken with Max on her way to the hospital this morning. He'd practically fallen over himself apologizing for everything that had happened. "And I found a place to stay while my apartment gets repaired," Natalie continued. "So it all worked out."

"Yeah, so we heard."

Charlie shared a smile with Tess, who tacked on, "So everyone heard."

Natalie froze. "What do you mean?"

Charlie bit her lip apologetically. "Jonah told Parker about it this morning when they did rounds, but I guess Don overheard them, and..." She trailed off, but the rest came through as if she'd shouted it through a bullhorn.

"Oh, no." Natalie groaned. Don might run the ED's intake desk like a drill sergeant, but he gossiped worse than a middle schooler. The entire hospital and half the patients must know that she and Jonah were sharing space by now.

"You know how it goes. The only thing that spreads faster than the flu around here is gossip," Tess said, shouldering her way into her scrubs.

The back of Natalie's neck prickled with heat. "There's nothing to gossip *about*."

"Do you have any idea how many women would commit actual murder to be you right now?" Tess asked, but only after she'd finished laughing at Natalie's claim.

"The number has got to be at least three digits," Charlie mused.

Natalie had to nip this in the bud before it got any worse. Things were already weird enough between her and Jonah, thanks. "Come on, you guys. I'm crashing on the futon in my best friend's den because my apartment needs repairs. I can promise you, there's no reason to commit a felony."

Tess looped her stethoscope loosely around her neck, waggling her caramel-colored brows. "And yet, you're the only woman in years who's actually slept in Jonah Sheridan's apartment until the sun came up."

Okay, so now that Natalie thought about it, that was true. Still... "I'm sleeping on his futon, not in his...you know, *bed*." The heat on her neck traveled down her spine, but ugh, this was crazy. "It's not even close to the same thing."

Charlie seemed to realize Natalie's discomfort, because she softened her voice and said, "We know, Natalie. And we told Don as much, too."

"Thanks," Natalie said, sinking back onto the couch. "I just don't want things to get uncomfortable for Jonah. He really likes his space, and he's doing me a huge favor by letting me stay. The last thing he needs is to have to field a bunch of weird rumors that aren't true."

Charlie tilted her head in thought as she poured coffee into a travel mug she'd taken out of her bag. "Forgive me if I'm being forward by asking, but you guys have been best friends for four years, right? Jonah is—and I say this objectively, because I adore my fiancé—hotter than homemade sin, not to mention, a pretty smart guy. You two have really never ever..."

She swung her index finger in a circular motion, but Natalie got the message, loud and clear. For a sliver of a second, she was tempted to tell Charlie that she'd really "never ever" with anyone, let alone Jonah. But even though she had a decent amount of experience with other intimate acts, admitting that she was technically still a virgin—even to friends as good as Charlie and Tess—was kind of embarrassing. Not that she was ashamed of it, per se. But it certainly made her the odd woman out in pretty much every social circle she belonged to, and even more of them that she didn't. For God's sake, Jonah didn't even know.

So Natalie settled on saying, "Nope," with as much ease as she could manufacture. "We're just friends. Always have been. Always will be."

"Well, you're a damn *good* friend for wanting to make sure Jonah doesn't get weirded out by the gossip mongers," Tess said. "Once they figure out there's nothing to talk about, they'll settle down, anyway. Don't pay them any mind."

Natalie knew Tess was right. "Thanks."

Realizing that it was too late to try for even a five-minute power nap to perk herself up, Natalie downed the rest of her coffee and headed to the nurses' station in the ED, along with Charlie and Tess. Parker was clearly on Jonah's service, the two of them Lord knew where, which left doctors Young, Boldin, and Vasquez up for grabs.

"Okay, people, what do you say we save some lives today? Or, at the very least, stitch some people up." Tess looked at all three interns, who—with three months under their belts now—knew just enough to be dangerous. But they were also eager and still mostly optimistic about medicine, and that made Natalie happy to coach them through the stuff they didn't know.

All three interns straightened, Vasquez speaking first. "Dr. Becker, I took the liberty of making sure the labs on all of your post-op patients were up-to-date per your overnight orders. And also, um, congratulations."

"Nobody likes a kiss-ass, Vasquez," Tess said, but Charlie

tugged an electronic chart tablet from the charging rack and passed it over to the intern.

"When she checks my labs, I do." To a smirking Vasquez, she said, "You'd just better hope your work is flawless, Dr. Vasquez. A kiss-ass, I can handle. Sloppy work, not so much."

"Yes, Dr. Becker," a more subdued-looking Vasquez replied as she scrambled to catch up to Charlie, who was already moving toward the elevators to check the woman's work.

Natalie looked at Young and Boldin. "I'm doing the workup and pre-op labs for an infant with biliary atresia today. Which one of you can tell me what that is and what the surgery to correct it is going to entail?"

Both interns' hands shot into the air—after all, Natalie had said the magic word (*surgery* was better than *please*, *pretty please*, and *abracadabra* combined)—but Boldin was a fraction of a second faster than Young.

"Biliary atresia is a congenital malformation that prohibits the liver from emptying bile," he said, and okay, he was one for two. Natalie looked at him in a wordless *keep going*, and so he did. Much to Young's dismay, if her expression was anything to go by. "To correct it, you'll have to surgically reconstruct the bile ducts, then reattach them to the liver."

"So cool," Young murmured, and Natalie lifted a brow at the woman.

"Not for the infant. Or his parents."

"Oh!" Young's eyes widened in trepidation. "Oh, God, no, of course not. I just, um. I meant…"

Natalie didn't have the heart to let the poor woman stew in her panic for more than a second. "I know what you meant. The surgery *is* really cool," she agreed. "But it's attached to a little person, and that little person is going to be pretty sick until I can get him into the OR for a very extensive procedure, so just keep that in mind."

"Yes, Dr. Kendrick." Young nodded.

"Tell you what," she said. "If there's room in the OR when I do the surgery tomorrow, you can scrub in, too, to see that firsthand. But you're going to have to earn it. Good?"

This time, Young's "yes" was a lot more enthusiastic.

Tess shook her head at Natalie, although her smile was obvious underneath all the tough-girl armor she wore even better than her scrubs and doctor's coat. "One day, I'll teach you to be a hard-ass."

"And steal your thunder? Never," Natalie said with a laugh. Turning toward Boldin, who had earned his way onto her service, she said, "Okay, doctor. Let's take care of some sick kids." She grabbed a tablet, tapping the thing to life and moving through a few of the screens to pull up a patient chart before starting for the elevators leading to the peds wing. "I want to go check in on Annabelle before we do rounds and start prepping for tomorrow's surgery."

Boldin's dark brows lifted toward his nearly shaved hairline. "Annabelle's back? Is she doing chemo this week?"

The intern had been on Natalie's service often enough to know the little girl and her general health history. Natalie had diagnosed the eight-year-old with non-Hodgkin lymphoma two months ago, and done the surgery to place a catheter into one of the little girl's arteries to lower the number of needle sticks she'd have to endure in chemotherapy. She was mostly under the care of a pediatric oncologist, now, but Natalie had formed a fast bond with the little girl and her mother. Whenever they were here, she always made it a point to make sure they had everything they needed.

"She was, but she's experiencing some complications. Here's her chart for this go-round." Natalie passed it over and remained quiet as the elevator cruised up to the third floor, letting Boldin get up to speed.

He frowned. "Belly tenderness, vomiting, dehydration, fatigue...do you think it's a reaction to the chemo, or something else?"

"I don't know," Natalie said. "I'm going to meet with her oncologist, Dr. Hoover, today to talk about it. It's possible it's just the chemo, but there could be a tumor in Annabelle's intestine causing a blockage. If there is, it's likely she'll need surgery to correct it."

Boldin asked a few technical questions that told Natalie he'd been doing his homework as far as peds *and* lymphomas went, and the medicine nailed both her calm and her focus into place.

This, she knew how to do. Examine the problem. Find the answers.

Make sick kids better, just as a team of doctors had once done for her.

"Knock, knock!" Natalie said brightly, rapping on the door in front of her even though it was partially open.

"Dr. Natalie!" Annabelle lay in the bed in the center of the room, her face pale even in contrast to the sheets and pillows. But Natalie chalked it up as a win that the little girl had at least perked up a little as she and Boldin came into the room.

"And Dr. B," Annabelle's mother, Rachel, added, pushing up from the recliner at Annabelle's bedside to greet them. "It's so good to see you."

"It's good to see you, too." Natalie paused to dose her hands in sanitizing gel before hugging Rachel, then—more carefully—Annabelle. "And good to see Mr. Flufferkins, as well." She hugged the stuffed fox that was pretty much never more than two feet from Annabelle's side. "I heard your stomach hurts and you're throwing up, too, huh?"

"Yeah." Annabelle frowned. "It feels a little better today, though, and I haven't thrown up since the middle of the night."

Natalie knew part of that relief was due to the poor kid being taken off all food and liquids by mouth, but she chose to look at the bright side, because there was one.

"That's really good." She turned toward Rachel, but made sure not to leave Annabelle out of the conversation. "The anti-emetics look like they're helping, and the IV fluids should continue to make Annabelle feel better."

"Anti-emetic is just a fancy name for the medicine that keeps you from throwing up," Boldin said to Annabelle, who nodded sagely.

"You have fancy names for everything," she said, and Boldin laughed.

"That's nothing. Try cholecystojejunostomy on for size."

Annabelle narrowed her eyes at him. "You made that up! Dr. Natalie, he made it up, right?"

"Nope. He's my student, so he's super smart. And the good news is, you won't be needing a cholecystojejunostomy."

Rachel still looked concerned, and as a single mom to a kid with cancer, Natalie didn't blame her. "So, you think this is all just a bad reaction to the chemotherapy? Her regimen *is* really aggressive."

"It's aggressive because it has to be," Natalie said gently. "It's possible that Annabelle's just reacting to the treatment. But it could be something else, so we're going to run some tests and scans and see if we can figure it out."

"More pinches?" Annabelle's brow furrowed, and she

looked at her mother. "I don't want more needles, Mommy. They hurt."

Natalie's heart used her sternum for batting practice, but she kept her expression dialed in to its happiest setting. "I promise we won't do any more than we have to, and I can even get Connor to come do your draws. You know he's fast, like a superhero, *and* he makes the best goofy faces." All true. For a big guy, Connor was one of the most laid-back people she'd ever met. "Once we get the scans back, we might even be able to let you have liquids, and you know what that means."

"Popsicles?" Annabelle asked, and there, *there* was the hope in her eyes that Natalie had been after.

"Yes, ma'am. Popsicles!"

"I heard we even got blue ones last week," Boldin said, and Natalie made a mental note to praise his bedside manner once they left the room. She ordered the appropriate scans and labs, with Boldin nodding and putting them all into Annabelle's chart, confirming the details before reaching out to squeeze Annabelle's hand.

"I'll page Connor for the blood draw and Dr. Boldin will take you to radiology as soon as we can get you in there without a ginormous wait. I'll talk to Dr. Hoover, and we'll let you know what we find." Looking across Annabelle's bed, she gave Rachel an encouraging smile. "If you need anything, have one of the nurses page me. Even if it's after hours, okay?"

"We hate to bother you after hours," Rachel said, shaking her head. "You must be so busy."

"You do look kinda tired today," Annabelle said, making her mother turn roughly the shade of a pomegranate.

"Annabelle! That's not very nice."

But Natalie threw her head back and laughed. "That's

okay, Mom. It's still important to be nice to other people," she caveated—her number-one rule was to honor a parent's word as much as she possibly could—"but in this case, you're right, kiddo. I look tired because I am. In fact, a very crazy thing happened to me last night."

"It did?" Annabelle asked.

Natalie nodded solemnly. "A bathtub came crashing through my ceiling and landed—*plop!*—right in my living room!" She embellished with a swooping hand motion and whooshing sound effects, and Annabelle giggled.

"Nuh-uh!"

"How could I make that up?" Pulling her phone out of her pocket, she showed Annabelle and Rachel the photo. They chatted for another minute before Natalie excused herself to finish her rounds, with Boldin right beside her.

"See if you can get her into radiology for those scans sooner rather than later? I want to try to rule out a tumor before I talk to Hoover."

Boldin nodded, but asked the glass-half-empty question a second later. "What if it is a tumor?"

Nope. Natalie wasn't going to think about it unless she had to. She had to tackle what was in front of her. What she knew for sure.

So she said, "Then I'll go in there and take it out. But one way or another, I'm going to do every single thing that I can to get that little girl healthy again."

4

Somewhere between a tracheostomy and a surgery to repair a gastrointestinal perforation, Jonah realized he was being an idiot. Yes, he'd had some wildly sexy thoughts of Natalie, and okay, yes again, he wasn't exactly wild about sharing his space with anyone, much less anyone in possession of a XX chromosome. But she wasn't some woman he'd met in a bar or on a blind date from some app. She was his best friend, the person who made sure he drank a glass of water and called an Uber after they did one too many tequila shots together, and who made fun of him when he ate his pizza crust-first (not that he could help it that she was wrong there). Surely they could cohabitate without the universe coming to an end.

Even if he had stayed up far too late last night thinking of the fact that she *and* her XX chromosome were snoozing away in the very next room.

"Okay," Parker said, tearing the surgical mask away from around his neck and slam-dunking Jonah back to the here and now of the scrub-in room where he was washing up, post-surgery. "Mr. Baumgartner is safe and sound in the post-anesthesia unit. His chart has been updated, and the PACU nurse is monitoring his vitals. She's going to page you when he wakes up."

"Great, thanks." Jonah gave in to the thought that had been flickering in the back of his brain all day. "Hey, I didn't get a chance to tell you earlier, what with how busy we've been today and all, but congrats on the, ah, you know." He held up his left hand, wiggling his ring finger.

Parker laughed, his dark eyes lighting unmistakably at the mere suggestion of his impending wedding. "Thanks, man. Second time's the charm."

"If you say so," Jonah said, keeping his expression intentionally laid-back and his cynicism far from his tone. "But really, I'm happy for you and Becker. Although, I guess we'll have to come up with a way of distinguishing between the two of you in conversation if she takes your name, since you'll both be Dr. Drake." He tilted his head. "He-Drake and She-Drake kind of have a nice ring to them."

"Oh, Charlie will love that," Parker flipped back with a snort. "We'll be sure to have throw pillows made. Or maybe monogrammed towels."

Jonah knocked back the irony of the fact that his one and only wedding registry had held a metric shit-ton of both throw pillows *and* monogrammed towels, along with hundreds of other high-end items he'd have never used. "Better than an electric wok or a set of cut-crystal brandy snifters."

"That, my friend, is the whole truth." Parker laughed for a second before his expression coalesced into something more dangerous. "Look, I know weddings aren't your thing, but...well, you were kind of instrumental in getting me and Charlie back together, so thanks. I don't know how I'd have made it if I'd lost her again."

Weddings aren't your thing. His mind flashed back to a night, three years ago, when he stood outside the empty ballroom at The Plaza hotel. The vintage silk of Vanessa's rehearsal dinner dress wrinkled from where she'd wrapped her arms around herself. The clack-clack-clack of her Louboutins as she'd paced on the marble floor. The wobble in her voice as she'd said things that had shifted his world on its axis. *I'm sorry, Jonah. I'm so sorry...*

He straightened, ignoring the combination of pain and bitterness threatening to expand in his gut. Everything with Vanessa had turned out for the best, and anyway, this wasn't the same. Parker and Charlie would last. They were the exception to the rule. Any fool could see that.

Just like Jonah would be a fool to go down that road again. Long-term relationships might work for some people, but for him, keeping it casual wasn't just smarter. It was self-fucking-preservation.

He just wasn't a long-haul kind of guy, and that's exactly how he liked it.

"No sweat," he said with a smile and a shake of his head. "And for the record, you did all the heavy lifting to get back together with Charlie, dude. All I did was offer moral support."

Parker grinned. "I still appreciate it."

"Enough to stick around to see Mr. Baumgartner through recovery?" Jonah asked, brows arched. He wouldn't normally cut out after a surgery, but the procedure had been textbook, and the patient had sailed through with near-perfect vitals. After sleeping like crap, leaving his apartment in favor of the gym at o-dark-thirty to avoid having to trade showers with Natalie, then spending all day on his feet in the OR, Jonah was beat.

"Sure," Parker said. "Danika's still here, too. Between the two of us, I'm sure we can hold down the fort."

At the mention of the third-year surgical resident who was as sharp as Parker would be when he reached his third year, Jonah's mind was made up. "Page me if anything changes. I'll round on Mr. Baumgartner first thing in the morning to see how he's feeling."

"You got it, boss."

Jonah made his way to the attendings' lounge to trade his scrubs for his street clothes, then aimed himself toward home. It was already late enough that he was sure Natalie had left, and a quick scan of the employees' parking lot confirmed that her car was indeed gone. He'd only seen her in passing today, one or both of them running in opposite directions. It had felt weird, to be honest—they usually grabbed lunch, at the very least, a cup of coffee at some point during a shift. He'd kind of missed her stories, the upbeat way she looked at all of her cases. The way nothing seemed to ever rattle her. Her enthusiasm was catching, always sneaking in to balance out his distrust. It had been his favorite thing about her from the minute they'd met as residents.

Yep. He'd been an idiot.

The trip back to his apartment was as quick as it was uneventful, both of them a win. He keyed his way over the threshold, the smell of something warm and hearty and goddamned delicious greeting him before he'd even made it three steps in.

"Oh, hey! You're out of surgery. Charlie said you and Parker caught a good one," Natalie said, looking up from the iPad and the empty bowl in front of her at the breakfast bar. She was dressed in a pair of leggings and a loose T-shirt that read *I Run On Coffee and Christmas Cheer*, her hair slightly wild and her smile bright.

Jonah laughed softly, unable to do anything but. "Perforated ulcer. But we fixed the guy right up. I left him with Drake and Brooks."

"Good hands, both of them." Natalie gestured to the bowl in front of her. "I didn't know how long you'd be stuck at the hospital, so I went ahead and made dinner. Nothing fancy, just some chicken and dumplings. It's probably still warm, though."

"It smells insane." Jonah's mouth watered at the prospect of a belly-warming meal that didn't take the direct route from his freezer to his microwave, and he shrugged out of his leather jacket to make his way to the pot on the stove.

She waved a hand in a no-big-deal motion. "Oh, that recipe is super easy. There's plenty left. I'll give you some privacy so you can eat in peace."

She shifted to get up and, presumably, head to his den... her room...whatever, but Jonah shook his head.

"You don't have to. I mean, unless you want privacy," he added, and oh for fuck's sake. This was *Natalie*. He needed to stop being an ass, once and for all. "Look, I know last night was a little bit..."

"Awkward and totally weird?" Natalie supplied, and Jonah laughed.

"I was going to say uncomfortable, but okay." He paused to toss a nearby dish towel at her, waiting out her laughter before turning to the pot on the stovetop to dish up some dinner. "Anyway, I'm not used to sharing space, and it just took me a second to get used to having you here. But everything's fine now."

"You sure?" Her expression marked the question as one

hundred percent genuine, and so he answered her the exact same way.

"Yep. Very." Jonah brought his bowl full of goodness over to the breakfast bar, parking himself on the high-backed stool next to hers. "So, what are you reading? Anything riveting?"

"Well, I guess that depends on whether or not you find research on alternative therapies for non-Hodgkin lymphoma riveting."

Ouch. "Patient?"

"Eight-year-old," she agreed with a sigh.

Familiarity flickered in the back alleyways of Jonah's brain, facts clicking against each other like dominoes, until —"Wait, the same one from a couple of months ago?" Anne-Marie? Annabeth?

"Annabelle Fletcher," Natalie said, and ah! Right. Annabelle. Natalie had been really subdued the day she'd confirmed the little girl's diagnosis, even though she'd bright-sided the situation with it being a fairly early catch and the fact that the best pediatric oncologist in the city had been able to take Annabelle's case.

"Isn't she Hoover's patient?" Jonah asked, taking a bite of the chicken and dumplings and fighting the urge to moan blissfully at the flavors turning his taste buds into goddamned Disneyland. "Jeez, Nat. This is delicious."

That earned him a smile. "Thanks. And yes and no. Hoover is treating her cancer, but Annabelle is at Remington Mem with belly pain. The scans show a partial blockage in her small intestine, and it looks like she's going to need surgery."

"Which also makes her your patient. You think it's a tumor?"

"I'm not sure what else it could be. I'm glad we caught it and that I can remove the thing, or at least part of it, but..."

"It sucks that you have to," Jonah finished. Managing adults with serious conditions was hard enough. Treating kids? God, she was made of better stuff than he was.

"It does." Natalie nodded, propping one elbow on the breakfast bar and pointing to the iPad with her opposite hand. "The chemo has been really hard on Annabelle already, and she's only done two treatments. I was just looking for a good clinical trial she might be eligible for, but so far, *nada*."

Jonah thought for a second. "I know a pediatric oncologist in Tampa—I operated on his sister a couple years ago after she was in a car wreck, and we still keep in touch every now and then. Want me to email him to ask if he's heard of any trials that might take her?"

It was kind of a long shot. Hoover was no slouch, and she probably had a pretty good line on trials her patients would benefit from. But Natalie still straightened fast enough for her T-shirt to slide off one shoulder, revealing the petal pink strap of her bra.

"Oh, my God. Would you?"

Jonah purposely kept his gaze fixed on Natalie's, even though a tiny, filthy part of him wanted to know if that strap was satin or lace. *It's just Nat, you ass. She's not for you.* "Of course. I'll do it as soon as I'm done eating."

"Did anyone ever tell you that you're the best?" she asked, her grin bright enough to light up a tunnel.

"Only you," he said with a laugh. He ate for another minute in comfortable quiet before looking at the stove and the countertop next to it. "Honestly, I had no idea I even had that many pots and pans."

Natalie rolled her eyes, but her smile marked the gesture

as far more playful than rude. "Okay, first of all, that's *one* pot and two mixing bowls. And secondly, you don't."

"I don't?" He was looking right at them, for Chrissake. Although, yeah, still not familiar.

"Nope," she confirmed. "After I dug through your cabinets for a minute or two this morning, it was pretty clear I was going to have to grab a couple things from Target or else we'd both starve. Seriously, you didn't even have a stockpot. Who lives like that?"

"People who have excellent taste in takeout?" Jonah asked, because it was better than admitting that he didn't know what a stockpot even looked like, let alone how to use one properly. "Anyway, let me pay you back for them."

She waved him off, her T-shirt staying put on her shoulder. *Satin. Nice.* "You wouldn't have needed them if I hadn't moved in. Don't worry about it."

He knew her better than to think she'd budge, so he said, "How about we split them, and I'll cover my half with takeout from the Thai place up the street this weekend? You shouldn't have to cook *every* night."

"Mmm. You just don't want to do the dishes every night."

"Okay, fair. But don't we both deserve a break?" Jonah loaded his smile with all the charisma he could spin up, and Natalie shook her head, her blond hair swaying over her shoulders.

"You know that charm thing doesn't work on me. Your logic, however...that, I will take."

"You don't give yourself much of a break, do you?" he asked. Now that he gave it some undivided thought, he realized just how many things she did for other people, and how little must be left for herself when she was done.

Her brows took a one-way trip toward her hairline. "Of course I do. I go to yoga twice a week, and have girls' night with Charlie and Tess on the third Friday of every month. I'm even reading one of those sexy romance novels Connor brought in."

Jonah bit back a laugh at the fact that their pro-wrestler-looking ICU nurse was addicted to romance novels, and he seemed to be converting everyone in his path to the language of love. Everyone except Jonah, that was.

"Okay, but I'd bet good money that you always bring the food or the wine to girls' night in, and that if one of the nurses asked to read the book you wanted first, you'd hand it over without a second thought."

The frown tugging at the edges of Natalie's mouth told him he'd hit pay dirt. "Well, yeah, but we all usually bring something to girls' night in, and the book thing is just courtesy. There are plenty of other titles to go around, and those nurses work hard."

"They do," Jonah agreed. "But so do you. When was the last time you took a vacation?"

"Last week. It was Thanksgiving, remember? Big holiday, everyone eats turkey."

Oh, Jonah remembered. He'd worked—voluntarily—but now wasn't the time to trot that little gem out. "Taking one of your days off for the week on a Thursday instead of a Saturday or Sunday so you can go to your parents' house for a couple hours, then come home to catch up on research doesn't count. I'm talking about a vacation, Nat. The kind where you went wherever you wanted and did whatever *you* felt like doing. Not what you should do, or what anybody else wanted to do."

The fact that she was quiet for a full minute was testament enough to the fact that her answer might well be never. "I don't know," she finally said, slowly, as if she were walking on icy pavement. "It's not like vacations are my norm. I was diagnosed with leukemia at ten, and with all the remission therapy, I didn't get a totally clean bill of health until I was fourteen. We couldn't exactly take a lot of family trips. You know the deal with cancer patients. The airport alone probably holds six billion different types of germs that could be hazardous to a person with a compromised immune system. Plus, time and money were kind of at a premium."

Jonah had known about Natalie's battle with childhood cancer for nearly as long as they'd been friends. Although she didn't tend to divulge the information to just anybody, and almost never to patients or patients' parents ("their own experience has nothing to do with my history or health. It should be all about what they need," she always said), it was common knowledge to those close to her. She treated it as she did everything else. Glass half full.

Still... "That's kind of a bummer," he said. Not that he'd gone on any childhood trips, himself. His dad's idea of a big vacation was to take Christmas Eve *and* Christmas Day off, and even then, he'd only done it sparingly. They hadn't been close then, and they weren't close now.

"Oh, it's no big deal," Natalie replied. "I can't miss what I never had, and anyway, I love my job. I don't mind not taking fancy vacations. I get to help kids be healthy. That's way better."

She said it so cheerfully that Jonah almost let it go. Almost. "That *is* great, but you can have both, you know."

Her laughter was of the don't-be-silly variety. "I don't need both."

Jonah couldn't be sure if it was the way Natalie always put herself last, or the fact that the *always* part was only just becoming so clear to him, but either way, something made him say, "But you deserve both."

Natalie blinked. A sound crossed her lips, too breathy for a simple exhale, but not something that qualified as a full-blown sigh, and Jonah recognized the error of his ways, too late.

Not that he'd have taken things back if he had, because fuuuuuck, whatever it was, that sound had been hot.

Jonah cleared his throat, mentally thumping himself on the back of the head for being a dumbass. "I mean, it doesn't have to be anything fancy or big-deal. Hell, you could check yourself into a hotel for a night and sit around in your bathrobe, ordering room service and binge watch those rom coms you love the whole time."

Natalie let go of a rare giggle, and Christ, it was just as appealing as the sigh. "Or eat cake for dinner."

"That's the spirit," he said. "But really, you should do *something* you've always wanted to. Just for you."

"I'll think about it," she said, her tone marking the words as genuine. "Anyway, I'm going to go do a little more research on lymphoma therapies before I crash. I'm doing a bile duct reconstruction on an infant in the morning, and I'm going to need to be on my toes to fix that little guy up. Will you let me know if you hear anything from your oncologist friend in Tampa?"

"Sure." Jonah nodded.

She grinned, unfolding herself from her bar stool and leaning in to squeeze his forearm. "Thank you. Call me crazy, but I have a really good feeling about it."

As Jonah watched her walk down the hall with her T-shirt off her shoulder and a happy little hum drifting up from her throat, he made a mental note to make sure she did more than think about having cake for dinner.

5

N atalie stood outside of Jonah's bedroom with a basket full of toiletries in one hand and her chest full of indecision. She'd waited as long as possible to get to this moment, brushing her teeth and choosing her clothes for the day and putting on a pot of coffee before stripping out of her pajamas and slipping her bathrobe around her shoulders. But she had to be at the hospital early for rounds, and with back-to-back surgeries scheduled after that, she needed to be in the shower like five minutes ago.

The same shower that stood on the other side of Jonah's bedroom door, and was the only one of its kind in his entire apartment. Which meant she was going to have to go *into* his bedroom and wake him up if she wanted to access the spray and suds.

Hence her indecision.

Squaring her shoulders, Natalie shook her head. This was stupid. Of course she didn't want to wake Jonah up, but she didn't have a choice. She needed to shower so she could go to work and save lives. Raising her non-toiletries-holding hand, she knocked softly on the door.

"Jonah? It's me. Natalie." *Suave stats: negative ten.* Who the hell else would be knocking on his door at six in the morning? "I'm sorry to wake you, but I need to take a shower."

A low, masculine murmur of acknowledgment sounded off from the other side of his door. It wasn't quite verbal, but it also wasn't a screaming "don't come in!", and Natalie couldn't be choosy. She cracked the door open, using the light from the hallway to tiptoe over the threshold without breaking her neck.

Jonah's bedroom was basically tidy, with the exception of the king-sized bed smack dab in the middle of it that was obviously unmade and rumpled because it was still occupied. He lay on his back on the side of the bed closer to the spot where she stood, one arm thrown over his head, his chest rising and falling in a deep, steady rhythm. He must've replied in his sleep, Natalie realized, but that wasn't the thing causing her heart rate to spike and her stomach to twist behind the sash of her bathrobe.

In the throes of sleep, Jonah had shoved the covers off his shoulders and all the way down to his waist, and he was beautifully, gloriously, completely shirtless.

Oh, shit, what if he slept naked?

Sweet baby Jesus, please let him sleep naked.

Natalie wrenched her eyes to the bathroom door even though they'd only been on Jonah long enough to register that he was A) still snoozing, and B) sans shirt. For the love of all things sacred and precious, he was her. Best. *Friend.* Not that it was okay to ogle a stranger, or anyone, in their sleep, because it most certainly was not. But now the split-second image of Jonah's bare torso was stamped across her mind's eye, and her imagination was doing triple-time wondering what the rest of him might look like. Whether or not his hips and legs were as tightly muscled as his chest. If his smooth, golden skin was as soft as it looked.

How far down that scattering of dark blond hair that started just below his belly button *really* went, and okay, that was it! Her imagination was officially a ho.

Straightening, Natalie moved to the bathroom door as fast as she could on her tiptoes, sliding past the threshold and closing the door with a near-silent *snick*. She locked the door—no sense in taking chances in case Jonah woke up groggy and auto-piloted his way to the loo like most normal people—and turned the water on, adjusting the temperature to a few degrees colder than normal, just for good measure.

She'd been having a whole lot of really steamy thoughts lately, to the point that it was obviously becoming a distraction. She didn't want to lose her virginity with just anybody, but maybe it really *was* time to start treating dating with less complacency. She'd meant what she'd said to Jonah about wanting to adopt one day, and the process could take years. True, she didn't need a partner in order to be a parent, but having a husband to go with her kids had always been her strong preference. Adopting aside, the longer in the tooth her virginity got, the more Natalie found herself just wanting to be rid of it.

She was curious. And ready.

Also, apparently hornier than a sailor on shore leave.

Brushing the thought—and the heat that had been mutinously growing between her legs—aside, Natalie forced herself to think logically. She couldn't exactly run her predicament by Jonah. The mere mention of monogamous dating gave him hives the size of silver dollars, and anyway, they'd just gotten over their rare hiccup of awkwardness. She was pretty sure that an "oh, hey, by the way, I've never had sex, but I'm looking to change that up if you've got any pointers" would send him back around the bend.

She'd have to ask Tess and Charlie for advice on the down low, at least about dating. Maybe if she actually *had* sex, she wouldn't be so hot and bothered all the time. At the very least, it would probably help get the image of Jonah's muscles out of her head. His chest. Those abs. That joyously happy happy trail arrowing down from his navel.

Natalie cranked the water as far over to the cold side as she could stand, vowed to talk to her girlfriends as soon as humanly possible, and forced herself not to spare so much as a millisecond's worth of a glance at Jonah *or* his muscles when she slipped out of his bedroom ten minutes later.

NINETY MINUTES after leaving Jonah's bedroom, Natalie's panties were in no less of a proverbial twist. She'd managed to slip out of the apartment just as the water had kicked back on in the shower, signaling that Jonah was up and at 'em, then channeled her energy into making sure everything was perfect for her upcoming surgeries. Boldin and Young—who, according to the hospital grapevine (a.k.a. Don) were "sheboinking like teenaged rabbits" (his exact terminology)—were both well-prepared for the bile duct reconstruction, each of them answering Natalie's questions and taking care of the pre-op lab results and patient prep with efficiency and care.

Their ambitiousness had allowed Natalie some time to check in on Annabelle, whose tumor resection was surgery number two today. The girl had been snoozing—a good thing, since rest had been few and far between for the poor kid with all that belly pain. But Natalie had been able to talk with Rachel for a few uninterrupted minutes, to do her best to reassure the woman and calm her understandably frazzled nerves, making sure she'd taken care of herself in the eat/sleep/breathe deeply departments, too.

After that, she'd had just enough time to track down Tess and Charlie for a quick cup of coffee and a covert looking-for-sex chat before she had to scrub in.

"Hey," Natalie said, relief spilling behind her breastbone at the sight of the two of them and no one else in the ED lounge. "Do you guys have a second?"

"Sure, but if you're looking for advice on that baby bile duct surgery you've got on tap for this morning, I'm probably not going to be of much help," Tess said. "My expertise in procedures is more crash-bang than slice-stitch."

Natalie shook her head. "Just because you're not a surgeon doesn't mean you're not a great doctor. But anyway, this is something more, um. Personal."

Charlie's green eyes lit with immediate interest. "Okay. What's up?"

For a second, she nearly balked. But really, how big of a deal could this be? It was just a casual question asked privately among good friends.

Natalie dug up every ounce of nonchalance she could find and said, "I was actually wondering if I could get your advice on some good places to meet single men."

Both sets of eyebrows skyrocketed up to the fluorescent lighting, and crap, it looked like this could be a *very* big deal.

"You want to meet a guy?" Charlie asked, forcing Natalie to nod.

"Yeah. I just...it's a long story, but yes. I'd like to start dating, and, ah. Doing some other things."

A soft laugh escaped past Charlie's shock-parted lips. "You mean having more sex."

Since Natalie's pride was nowhere to be found—the mutinous little shit—she just went with a simple, "Yes."

Tess recovered quickly, the whole thing seeming to make sense to her. "God bless the almighty orgasm. I say get them while you can. I'm sort of married, which puts me a bit out of the loop here, but have you tried any dating apps?" she suggested.

Charlie dismissed the idea with a snort before Natalie could ask Tess about the 'sort of' thing. "Take it from someone who was single up until recently. Those apps are for screwing, not dating. Which is totally fine if some probably-hot, no-strings-attached, one-night-stand sex is all you're after, but..."

She looked at Natalie to confirm that it was, in fact, *not* all she was after, and ugh, maybe this had been a mistake.

"No, I'd like to, um. Meet someone I actually see more than a time or two," Natalie said. She was all for sexual empowerment, but this was her virginity. A one-and-done felt kind of impersonal, as if it were more appropriate for ripping off a Band-Aid than for the maiden voyage of her maidenhead.

"Right. Today's PSA: Be selective about what you put in your body. From cheeseburgers to penises attached to douchebags," Tess said, making Natalie's cheeks flare with heat. "Sorry," she added with a matter-of-fact shrug. "I haven't been legally single in a while, but that seems kind of universal."

"No, that's...that does make sense," Natalie agreed slowly. "So, no on dating apps, then?"

"They're not all bad," Charlie said with a shrug. "You've just got to weed out the weirdos and the jackasses, so it's a lot of work."

"What's a lot of work?" came a cheerful voice from the doorway, and oh, no, no, no, no—

Tess looked at Connor and grinned. "Oh, Natalie's trying to find a man."

Well, shit. So much for a private conversation among girlfriends.

"Ooooh! For fun or for actual legit purposes?" Connor asked, his brown eyes lighting up as he crossed the lounge to park himself on the couch and kick his cross-trainers up on the coffee table in front of him.

"Both. Right?" Tess glanced at Natalie in question. There was no way she could back out now without drawing attention, and Connor was a good guy. It could be smart to get a single man's perspective, she reasoned.

"Yes. Definitely both."

"Both, what?" a different masculine voice asked, and sweet God in heaven, how was Emmett Mallory, their ortho attending, in here, too? And—Natalie fought the growing urge to flee—Jonah and Parker were hot on his heels.

"Oh, it's nothing, really," she said with a dismissive wave, hoping it would end the conversation.

No joy. "Nothing, my ass," Tess said. "Nat's on the prowl for a man."

"That's not what I said," she protested as Parker choked out a laugh and Mallory gave up a nonverbal *oh really?* Jonah, who was busying himself by filling his travel mug with coffee, remained impassive.

Mallory, however? Didn't. "I didn't know you were looking to date, Kendrick."

His interest wasn't creepy, but it was definitely present, and Natalie's pulse knocked at her throat. She liked Emmett —they'd known each other for a couple of years and hung out together after hours at The Crooked Angel from time to time. He was a great surgeon, handsome in a dark and slightly dangerous sort of way. But she'd never been attracted to him. No glimmer of longing. No spark to make her belly flip and her other, more southerly bits all giddy with anticipation.

Mallory must've realized that she'd connected the dots, because his slightly stubbled chin hiked upward. "Ah, not for me. I mean, nothing personal, but we work together, and just because Langston made an exception for these two"— Mallory gestured to Parker and Charlie, who had somehow convinced their ultra conservative chief of staff that they could work well together even though they were in a relationship—"doesn't mean I'm interested in testing his limits. But my brother is single, and he's a decent guy. He's a graphic designer. Lives near Landsdale Park, on the south side of the city. I could hook the two of you up for a drink, if you want."

"Oh." Natalie did a lightning-fast balance of pros and cons in her head. She *did* want to find someone to spend a little time with. If things didn't work out, there was a small chance of weirdness between her and Mallory, but she was getting ahead of herself, there. It was just a drink. If anything, it was at least worth a shot. Even if she did feel a weird pang of hesitation in her belly at the idea.

"Okay, sure. Why not?" Natalie said. "I'm in."

Jonah frowned from his spot across the lounge. "You're going to go on a blind date?"

"It's better than Tinder," Connor said, and Jonah's frown deepened.

"It's *exactly* like Tinder. They've never met and they're going to hook up for drinks."

His tone translated "drinks" to "an all-night fuck-a-thon", but before Natalie could serve up a fresh helping of what the hell, Tess beat her to the punch.

"No offense, Sheridan, but you're not usually uptight about this sort of thing. What gives?"

Just like that, Jonah's frown made way for an affable half-smile, so quickly that Natalie questioned whether or not he'd frowned in the first place. "Nothing gives. I just want to be sure Nat's safe, that's all. You can never be too sure."

Heat crept up the back of Natalie's neck, making her grateful for the long hair that covered what was surely an accompanying flush. She'd practically gone into spontaneous orgasm from one glance at his abs, and here Jonah was treating her like a kid sister. God, she needed to remedy this sex thing worse than she thought.

"I appreciate your concern, but I'm sure I'll be fine," she said lightly. Things had just gotten back to normal between her and Jonah (ogling aside). The last thing she wanted was for him to worry about her.

Mallory shot a hard stare across the lounge, the muscle across his jaw pulling just taut enough to signal his irritation. "My brother's not a knuckle dragger, dude. I wouldn't hook Kendrick up with an asshole, related or otherwise."

"Understood, man." Jonah lifted his hands, *mea culpa* style. "I'm sure your brother's great. Hey, did you get a chance to look at the patient in curtain three yet?"

"The guy who fell off a nine-foot ladder while putting up Christmas lights?" Mallory asked, blinking twice before following Jonah's change in direction.

Charlie looked up in surprise. "Who the hell puts up Christmas lights this early in the morning?"

"Who the hell puts up Christmas lights this early in the *season*?" Connor asked with a laugh. "Most people are still working on their leftovers from Thanksgiving."

"The guy in curtain three, that's who," Jonah confirmed. "Although, right about now, I'm betting he's questioning the hell out of his Christmas spirit." He looked at Mallory again. "His head and neck were clear, but he's still pretty banged up from the fall. Kelly was going to call you in for a consult."

Mallory nodded. "Yeah, I actually just saw the guy before I came in here. Vasquez is taking him up to radiology for a full set of films. I've got good money on his ulna being fractured, though. Maybe a bone or two in his wrist, too."

Relieved to have the topic be something other than her (lack of) sex life, Natalie dove headfirst into the subject change along with everyone else. "I'm sure Vasquez loved playing chauffeur," she said, punctuating the words with a smile to keep them out of mean-girl territory. Sofia Vasquez was a good intern—bordering on great in the skills department, actually. But she sure wasn't shy about her lack of affection for scut, and that included taking patients from point A to point B.

"I live to torture her with the mind-numbingly boring nature of ortho. Just ask her, she'll tell you," Mallory said, laughing. "But that's okay. One day, she'll learn we're not all splints and slings." Looking at Jonah, he added, "I'll let you know when the films are back."

"Sounds good. I'm going to head upstairs to do rounds. Drake, you in?"

"Always. I already pulled Mr. Baumgartner's chart," Parker said, grabbing the tablet he'd placed on the table in front of him and handing it over to Jonah. The group began to disperse, each of them saying their goodbyes and departing, and Natalie shifted her thoughts back to the surgeries in front of her.

It wasn't until nearly lunchtime that she realized she'd forgotten to ask Mallory for his brother's name and number.

6

J onah would give his left goddamned nut for an apartment with two showers. When he'd moved into the place a couple of years ago, he'd known beyond the shadow of a doubt that he wasn't likely to ever need an extra bedroom, let alone another full bath. With no close family and less than zero plans to have a relationship with a shelf life of more than forty-eight hours, the 1BR/1Bath route had been a no-brainer. Hell, the half bathroom that had come with the deal practically grew cobwebs for how little it was ever used. He had the futon in his den, true, but that was more sentimental than anything else. The old thing was a throwback from his med school days, the only thing he hadn't let Vanessa purge during their time together. She'd complained that it didn't go with any of the high-end, custom-made furniture she'd ordered for their loft, semi-sweetly enough that it had passed as gentle teasing, but with a layer of truth beneath that told Jonah in no uncertain terms that she'd have been thrilled to see the futon go. He'd never quite been able to pull the trigger, though.

In the end, that futon had been the only thing he'd kept from their relationship.

He hadn't even escaped with his pride, and fuck if that didn't make him a sucker, even after all this time.

At least the futon had staying power.

But Jonah had far more pressing issues at hand right now; namely, that the sun would be considering its Friday morning date with the horizon in the next half an hour, which meant Natalie's alarm was likely to go off at any moment. Their schedules had kept them separately busy yesterday morning, so trading up for the shower hadn't been an issue, and they hadn't talked about it as they'd shared dinner last night. But today, Natalie had a fairly early surgery on the schedule. She was going to need to take a shower, and *that* meant that for the second time in forty-eight hours, she'd be warm and wet and naked not ten feet from where he currently lay in bed.

He hadn't heard her come into his room the other morning, although that wasn't horribly shocking since he was a sound sleeper. Knowing Natalie, she'd probably gone out of her way not to wake him. But he'd surfaced from sleep a few minutes later in his usual state of drowsy arousal, his cock hard and his mind drifting along to the sound of the spray, and the suggestion of the very undressed woman enjoying it.

For one darkly sexy, half-asleep moment, his imagination had drawn the details of what Natalie looked like in the shower. Her hair glinting gold in the water, sliding between slim shoulder blades. Her high, pretty breasts covered in steam and spray, her nipples playing peek-a-boo with the bubbles as she washed her body, her hands stroking over her belly. Her hips. Her soft, smooth thighs...

And then Jonah had realized *who* he'd been thinking of,

his conscience dispatching his hard-on in a blink and his defenses forcing him to stay in bed and feign sleep until she'd tiptoed out of his bedroom ten minutes later.

No matter what his dick had told him in a moment of hazy impulse, the rest of him knew the truth. Natalie wasn't for him. She deserved better than the one-time joyride that was all he was willing to deliver. For Chrissake, she'd said she wanted as much in the lounge the other morning, in front of all of their co-workers, no less. Jonah's knee-jerk, fuck-no reaction to the idea of her going on a date with Mallory's brother had blindsided him, its presence and intensity so unexpected that he'd been unable to keep his mouth shut. He'd been able to duck and divert well enough —for every decent guy with decent intentions, there were a hundred dillholes, so, really, his unease wasn't horribly unfounded. Only a shitty best friend wouldn't want to ensure her safety. Still, the whole thing had left him on edge. He needed to blow off some steam and get Natalie and her soapy, sexy tits out of his head, once and for all.

"Damn it," Jonah muttered, throwing the comforter and sheets from his shoulders and stabbing his feet into the floorboards. He needed her at arm's length. All this proximity was killing him. The little suggestions of her—her shampoo in his shower, the dinner leftovers neatly packaged and labeled in his fridge, her car keys next to his on the table by the front door—were like tiny eye-openers, each one making him hyper-aware of all the things he'd never let himself realize when Natalie wasn't directly in his space.

For now, his best option was to get *out* of said space, at least until he could find someone willing to distract him properly and be done with this insanity. Grabbing his cell phone from his bedside table, Jonah shot off a text to Connor, Emmett, Drake, and a handful of guys from their circle of friends at Station Seventeen and the Thirty-Third District. **Drinks at that new club on Hanover at 8? First round is on me.** Then he took his toothbrush for a quick spin, thanking his lucky fucking stars that his gym had good showers.

Jonah reached for the drawer where he kept his workout clothes, cursing under his breath when he realized a second later that it was empty. He'd shoved a bunch of stuff into the dryer last night, then promptly forgotten about it. Padding down the hall, he tugged open the bi-fold doors keeping his washer and dryer neatly tucked from view and clicked on the light...

And found himself standing in a jungle of Natalie's unmentionables.

Jonah's pulse flared, his eyes going fuck-me wide as he took in the sight in front of him. Red satin, teal silk, the pale pink lace from the other night, all of it was draped over the retractable laundry line spanning the space over the appliances, making the tiny closet look like a lingerie factory had exploded inside of it. He watched his hand reach up as if the arm attached to it was completely on auto-pilot, his brain telling it to cease and desist while his dick—the treasonous bastard—cheered the move on. His fingers brushed over the closest item (which was the petal pink bra, because of *course* it was), his blood heating and his imagination shoving the image of Natalie wearing it and a smile and nothing-freaking-else front and center.

"Mmm, morning."

Her sleepy voice floated up from the spot beside him, damn near sending him into A-Fib.

"Shit!" Jonah whipped his hand back to his side, jerking his chin to look at her. *Get it together. Right. Now.* "I mean, uh, good morning."

"I didn't know you'd be up so early," she murmured past a yawn, thankfully oblivious to his sort of startled, definitely aroused state. "Sorry for the mess. I'll just get this stuff out of your way."

She nudged closer to him, her forearm brushing his as she reached up to the line for a pair of red lace panties like nothing-doing. Her blond hair was sleep-mussed and loose around her shoulders, the very nipples Jonah had just banished from his imagination pressing against her tank top in the world's most provocative good-morning-to-you, and sweet Christ, he needed a way out of this, fast.

"I thought we had an agreement about...this stuff," he said, waving a hand at her ridiculously large collection of lingerie. But the joking nature with which he'd intended the words fell sadly flat.

"I promised not to put them over the shower curtain rod," Natalie reminded him, dropping her pink bra—his favorite, apparently—into the laundry basket beside her feet. "But I have to hang them up to dry *somewhere*."

Jonah exhaled, grasping for logic or air or, okay fine. Anything that would work to keep her thongs out of his brain pan. "Can't you just put them in the dryer like normal clothes?"

"If I want to ruin them." Brows creasing, she stopped what she was doing in favor of turning to look at him. "Come on, Jonah. It's not as if you haven't taken hundreds of bras off hundreds of women."

"Not you," he croaked. *Do not look at the thong in her hand. Do not think of all the ways you could remove it from her hips with your teeth. Do not collect two hundred dollars.*

But Natalie's brow crease *in*creased. "I know this might be a shock to you, but I am, in fact, female. I wear bras. I also wear thongs, and have ovaries, and get my period. It's kind of what we do. It's also something you knew about me when you said I could move in with you."

"I do know," Jonah said, the irony of exactly how much he'd begun to realize her femininity not lost on him.

"Okay, so what's the big deal, then?"

He opened his mouth to tell her that the big deal was that now that she was living here, he was *too* aware of her bras, of how sexy her tousled hair was when she'd just rolled from bed, of how much he'd liked sitting down and talking with her this week over dinner instead of eating silently on his own. But then he stopped himself short.

He didn't just want to tell her. He wanted to *do* something about it. He wanted to kiss her, to lift that tank top over her head and taste those nipples that plagued his imagination until she moaned in pleasure. He wanted to yank off her pajama pants and lift her onto the dryer and do unspeakably filthy things to her pussy with his tongue.

And she wanted a boyfriend. Someone to fall in love with, who would marry her someday and adopt a horde of kids with her.

Jonah would not—absolutely could not—be a long-haul guy. For fuck's sake, he had *reasons* for that, ones he'd known forever and that had only been hammered farther into place over time. But they were the only thing he'd ever kept from Natalie, so he gathered up a devastating smile, dialed his voice to its most easygoing setting, and said, "Ah, I'm just giving you a hard time, Kendrick. No worries. I'm headed to the gym, so the shower's all yours."

Then he grabbed his laundry and ran.

THE VELVET CURTAIN was exactly what Jonah had expected

it to be. Although he'd never been to the club before, he knew the prototype like he knew his last name. Low lighting punctuated by pops of red and gold coming from strategically placed fixtures. Tall, plush booths designed for privacy, yet still visible enough not to encourage anything highly illicit or illegal. The gigantic, black-lacquer bar stocked to the nines with top-shelf liquor and staffed by stunningly beautiful bartenders of both sexes, and yep, Jonah could've drawn a detailed map of the place, sight unseen.

It was perfect for what he needed tonight; namely, a nice, stiff drink and a pretty partner willing to trade a few hours of her life for a couple of screaming orgasms.

"Hey, Sheridan. How's it going?" Kellan Walker, one of the firefighters from Station Seventeen, stepped in to greet Jonah with a steady handshake and a genuine smile.

"Walker. Hollister," he said to the auburn-haired detective standing next to the guy, who also happened to be Kellan's fiancée's partner at the Thirty-Third. "Good to see you guys."

"Hell, if you're buyin', I'm in," Hollister said with a laugh.

"I'm a man of my word." Jonah lifted a hand to get the bartender's attention, ordering a trio of beers. "After this week, I could use a drink."

"Don't let Sheridan fool you," came Mallory's voice from behind Jonah as he and Connor walked up to join them at the bar. "His week wasn't all *that* bad. After all, he landed a pretty roommate."

Jonah's heart thumped faster, but he kept his expression neutral and his smile in place. "Dude. Kendrick's place was totaled. I'd be a pretty crappy friend not to let her crash with me for a few weeks."

"I hear you, man. You two have always been tight. Ah, could we get two more of those, please?" Mallory asked the bartender as she brought the beers Jonah had ordered over with a smile.

"Sure thing." Her big blue eyes landed on Jonah's and held. "Did you want to start a tab..."

The lead-in was so obvious, he couldn't *not* fill in the blank. "Jonah."

"Jonah," she purred, leaning in to put her admittedly spectacular cleavage on display. "It's nice to meet you. I'm Celeste. I'll be taking care of you tonight."

His brain knew that she was A) gorgeous, and B) very likely to take care of him in more ways than one if he showed interest. But the rest of him remained oddly non-committal about her dark-haired, overly made-up beauty, even though he tried to convince it otherwise. "It's nice to meet you, too. I've got this round, but after that, these guys are on their own, so I'll pass on the tab."

"Are you sure I can't get you anything else?" Celeste asked, her bright red lips curving into the slightest pout, but Jonah shook his head.

"Maybe later. But for now, just the check, please."

Jonah took care of the bill, then turned back toward his friends, all of whom were—ah, hell—looking at him with varying degrees of disbelief.

"Are you feeling alright?" Mallory asked. "Because in case you've gone both blind and stupid in the last two minutes, that woman is smokin' hot and totally into you."

"She's pretty," Jonah agreed, because objectively, she was. "But what kind of friend would I be if I asked you guys to hang out, only to ditch you before we've even had a drink?"

"The kind of friend who got laid with all of our blessings?" Connor suggested. The conversation thankfully paused as Celeste brought Connor and Mallory their beers, and Jonah was able to shrug off his unease at not being into her.

"The night is still young, and she's clearly not going anywhere." Maybe after he'd had a drink, he'd be able to loosen up a little bit. After all, finding someone exactly like Celeste was what he'd come here for in the first place.

"So, how's it going living with Kendrick?" Mallory asked, taking a long draw from his beer. "Is familiarity breeding contempt yet? You do like your space."

Jonah's face got hot at the thought of Natalie's bras hanging in his laundry room and the way her shampoo made his bathroom smell all flowery and nice. Familiarity was breeding something, alright, and by *something*, he meant unrequited lust.

"Nah," he said, stuffing the thought back and dousing it with beer. "Everything's fine. It's actually pretty cool."

Mallory's brows went up, his beer halting halfway to his lips. "Now there is something I never thought I'd hear you say about living with a woman."

Jonah fought to keep his pulse in check, but before he could work up a reply, Kellan beat him to it.

"I don't know," he said, smiling as he leaned back against his bar stool. "Isabella and I have lived together for a year now, and I think it's pretty okay."

Hollister laughed. "Seeing as how you two are getting married in a month, I sure as shit hope so."

"Okay, I might not be the most unbiased example," Kellan admitted, and funny, he was still smiling. "But still, cohabitation isn't all bad."

An odd feeling expanded in Jonah's gut. "Natalie and I are just roommates. Temporarily," he added for good measure. "It's a very different thing than what you and Isabella have going on."

"That may be. All I'm saying is that it's not all bad to have someone to go home to. Even if you're just roommates."

The conversation drifted to other topics, like the Rogues season and all of their mutual friends and what they'd been up to lately with work and cases and calls. It was a carbon copy of pretty much every guys' night out in the history of man, the sort of thing Jonah almost always enjoyed. And he wasn't having a *bad* time—he didn't get to see Hollister or Kellan all that often, so the fact that they'd come out was cool. But the longer they all sat there, with one beer turning into two and Connor and Hollister breaking off to flirt with a blonde and a brunette who had settled in at their end of the bar, the more restless Jonah became.

He'd come out in search of something to get his mind straight, but the more he looked for a distraction, the more he missed Natalie. For every woman all decked out in a form-fitting dress, he wondered if she was still in whatever jeans she'd put on after work, or if she was already back in those cute plaid pajama pants she'd been wearing this morning. He wondered what she'd had for dinner, whether she'd made a quick meal or if she'd actually indulged in cake, like she'd joked about the other night. And the more he thought about her, the more distracted he became from *finding* a distraction.

Which was dumb as shit, not to mention counterproductive. He needed to get his head really, truly screwed on right, once and for all.

Turning toward the bar, Jonah leaned in until he caught Celeste's eye, motioning the beautiful brunette over so he could settle up for his second beer and get the hell out of there.

7

Natalie cuddled up with a mug of soup in one hand and the TV remote in the other. She'd overheard Jonah and Connor talking about some guys' night thing in the lounge this morning, so she knew better than to expect to see him until he rolled out of bed at o-noon-thirty tomorrow. Or maybe that was when he'd roll *in*, she thought with a pang. After all, he was single and stupidly hot, not to mention pretty notorious for hooking up with someone new whenever he went out. Common sense dictated that there was a more than decent chance he'd spend the night in someone else's bed.

"Don't be silly," she chided herself, clicking the TV on and scrolling to the cable menu. The activeness of Jonah's sex life was hardly a news flash, *or* any of her business. She was taking steps to get her own personal life in gear, having finally asked Mallory for his brother's number yesterday. True, she hadn't actually put it to use yet, but she'd been slammed with cases, plus, she'd had to juggle a bunch of phone calls to her insurance company and Agnes.

Between the bathtub, having to do another surgery on

Annabelle, and all the other insanity that went with a busy, high-pressure job, Natalie should be grateful for a quiet night in, she knew. And while she did usually enjoy having a rare evening to herself—her favorite station was even doing a rom com movie marathon of classics like *When Harry Met Sally*—something about tonight felt odd and stiff. Jonah had told her to make herself at home, and she *did* feel comfortable in his apartment after having spent a whole week here. But the place was so quiet without him in it, sharing a laugh with her over dinner or busting her chops over her laundry or helping her try to find a clinical trial for Annabelle.

As crazy as it seemed, especially since she'd seen him a mere nine hours ago when they'd grabbed a quick lunch between surgeries, Natalie missed him.

Badly.

Her cell phone buzzed out a familiar ringtone, and her heart squeezed uneasily at the sight of the smiling face on the screen. Normally, Natalie didn't mind chatting with her mother, but the woman had a freakish sixth sense for picking up on her moods when they were less than one hundred-percent healthy and happy. Since she knew from experience that not answering would only make her mother worry, she paused the movie and swapped her soup for her cell phone, tapping the icon to answer the call.

"Hey, Mom. How's it going?"

"Oh, I caught you! I wasn't sure if you'd be home."

Natalie bit her lip, artfully dodging the *home* thing as she settled back in against the couch cushions. "I had a long week, so I decided to stay in tonight."

"That sounds nice and relaxing. I'm glad you're taking care of yourself. How have you been feeling? You sound a little tired."

While the comment might come off as backhanded from

anyone else, her mother laced it with enough genuine concern that Natalie took no offense.

"A little. I've just had a crazy couple of days," Natalie admitted, turning up the wattage on her tone to make sure the next part stuck. "But I'm completely fine, plus, I have all weekend to relax, so it's all good."

Her mother's murmur wasn't quite a concession, but it was close. "Well, don't forget, your annual remission check is coming up. Just because it's been eighteen years doesn't mean you should put it—"

"Already scheduled, Mom. I'm a doctor, remember? I know how important the checkups are." The peace of mind was just as crucial to her parents as it was to Natalie herself. No way would she skip the re-check, plus, it was only a blood draw. Easy like Sunday morning.

"Hmm. Just because you're a surgeon doesn't automatically mean you'll take care of yourself," her mother said, but Natalie laughed.

"Yes, it does. At least, in my case it does. Anyway, I've knocked the last seventeen of these checkups out of the park. I have a very good track record. You don't have to worry."

"I know, but you just said you're tired."

Natalie's heart gave up a hard twist at the concern in her mother's voice. "I work twelve-hour days at a pretty demanding job," she said softly, because to deny her fatigue would have meant straight-up lying to her mother. "I promise you, being tired is normal." Clearing her throat, she swerved the subject. "How's Daddy? And Mark and Trish?"

Her younger brother and sister were close, both in age and to each other. The gap was bigger with Natalie in regard to both, too. Logically, how tight they were made sense. They'd been stuck together with various babysitters and family friends while Natalie had undergone nearly four years' worth of tests and chemo and radiation. Not that she could blame them—she doubted the rift had even happened consciously—but still. Emotionally, it stung that they were close with each other and only spoke with her a handful of times a year. She got nearly all of her updates on their lives either from their mother or Facebook.

"Oh, they're all fine," her mother said, falling for the redirect hook, line, and update. She filled the next ten minutes with happy chatter about Natalie's father and siblings, which Natalie punctuated with some well-timed mmm-hmms and a few easy questions. She ended the call by promising (again) that she'd get some extra sleep this weekend and make sure she took her vitamins.

She hated lying by omission about the bathtub thing, but it was still far better than the alternative. After her cancer had gone into remission, her mother had insisted on not returning to her job at a lucrative marketing firm, choosing to home school her all the way through the twelfth grade, instead. Her parents had been equally adamant that she live at home for all four years of college, plus most of medical school, and even though Natalie hadn't wanted to do either, she hadn't been able to refuse after all they'd been through on her behalf. The mental stress. The mountains of insurance claims. The financial black hole caused by what hadn't been covered. She had finally stood firm on getting her own place when she'd begun her residency, but her parents still worried. True, she'd told Jonah she couldn't fess up about being temporarily homeless because they'd get even more overprotective and drive her bat-shit crazy. But putting them through more stress over something as little as a housing mishap wasn't on her agenda.

She'd already been the cause of a lifetime's worth of

worry. Bending the truth and staying with Jonah was by far the smartest choice.

Even if she *was* still fantasizing about his abs.

The thought had her shoving up from the couch, grabbing the soup mug that she'd drained in between comments while she and her mother had talked. She'd text Mallory's brother first thing tomorrow. For now, she needed to find something to get her mind good and busy and far, far away from her best friend's anatomy.

Making her way into Jonah's kitchen, Natalie rinsed her mug and put it in the dishwasher, then reached into a nearby drawer in search of a dishtowel to dry her hands. The drawer was stuffed with paper napkins (good enough), a haphazard stack of takeout menus, and an overly large collection of condiment packets, many of them of questionable quality. Cleaning out the drawer seemed as good a thing as any to distract her before she went back to her movie, she decided as she pushed the sleeves of her thermal pajama top all the way up to her elbows. Plus, she had promised to split all the chores with Jonah right down the middle.

Natalie was five minutes and fifty ketchup packets into the job when the front door opened, sending her heart halfway to her throat.

"Hey," she said, her surprise turning into something much more forbidden at the sight of Jonah in his perfectly broken-in jeans and black button-down shirt that seemed tailor-made for his lean, muscular frame.

His blond brows lowered in confusion. "What are you doing?"

"Cleaning out your drawers." Natalie's face flushed at how unintentionally dirty her reply sounded. She needed to recover, and fast. "Did you know that you had ketchup packets in here that expired three years ago?"

"Those expire?" he asked, waving his question away before she could answer it. "You know what, never mind. You seriously don't have to clean anything out."

She couldn't exactly tell him why she'd decided to get wrist-deep in his condiment drawer, so she settled on, "Oh, it's no big deal. Really."

"Fine. Then move over."

"What? Why?"

Jonah stepped in to nudge her hip with his, and good Lord, how could he smell even better than he looked? "Because if cleaning out the kitchen drawers is good enough for your Friday night, then it's good enough for mine."

"I thought you were going out with Mallory and Connor," Natalie said.

Jonah shrugged. "I was. I mean, I did. But I decided to come home early."

"Are you feeling okay?" She was mostly teasing, but it was pretty unusual for him to cut a night out short at—she glanced at the clock on the microwave—nine thirty.

"Yep." His lips upturned into the charming smile Natalie had seen no less than a million times, but somehow, *this* time, she felt it slide beneath her breastbone as he looked at her. "What can I say? I missed you."

At that, she had to snort. "Right. Because the whole pajamas on a Friday night thing I have going on is so glamorous."

"Hey, you never know. Plaid flannel might just be the new black."

The easy back-and-forth soothed the unease that had been building in Natalie's chest all evening, and she tidied the stack of takeout menus before placing them on the counter. Jonah opted to toss all of the ketchup packets, and they worked side by side for a minute to clear the rest of the drawer.

"So, how's Annabelle?" he asked after a minute of amiable quiet, and Natalie gave up a smile designed for optimism.

Always lead with the good news. "Her recovery went as well as we could've expected. The tumor was kind of a bear." The surgery had taken longer than Natalie had planned, partly because she'd wanted to be as careful as possible, and partly because the tumor had been larger than the scan had indicated. "But it's out now, and I was able to release her this morning, which are both good things. Have you heard anything from that oncologist in Tampa?"

Jonah nodded, closing the drawer and leaning back against the counter to look at her. "He was caught up in a pretty big case this week, but he finally got back to me this afternoon. He was pretty sympathetic—he's treated a couple of kids who have the exact same type of cancer and agreed that it's pretty brutal. He didn't know of anything offhand, but he promised to dig around a little to see if he could find a trial she could apply for."

"Oh, thank you!" Natalie pressed both hands over her heart, unable to cage her grin. She knew it was a massive long shot—clinical trials for cancer patients had notoriously strict guidelines and mile-long wait lists. Annabelle's history would very likely preclude her from being eligible for most, if not all, of them. But Jonah's contact clearly had knowledge and influence that Natalie and Dr. Hoover didn't, and the right clinical trial might make all the difference in Annabelle's treatment if she was a good fit. "Really, Jonah. You're the best."

An odd look flickered over his face, something Natalie

couldn't categorize and was fairly certain she'd never even seen before, and she stepped toward him with concern.

"Hey, are you okay?"

"Sure. Of course," he replied, his voice as smooth as melted butterscotch. The look that had triggered her worry was gone, replaced by a smile dazzling enough to suggest it had never existed. His shoulders were loose, blue eyes crinkling just enough at the edges to match the rest of the easygoing ensemble, just like always.

God, she must be losing it. "Okay. Well, I was about to continue the trend of my wild and crazy Friday night and watch a movie, if you wanted to..."

She hooked a thumb toward the couch in invitation, and Jonah shook his head after a pause. "Nah, that's okay. You've probably got some love story for the ages queued up. I don't want to crash your party."

Well, hell. He had her dead to rights on the love story thing. Still... "For the love of God, Sheridan. You can run a trauma from stem to stern without breaking a sweat. Are you seriously trying to tell me that two teensy hours of romantic comedy are going to break you?"

"No," he said automatically, and ha! She had him.

"Great. Then go change into your sweatpants while I make the popcorn, and watch a damned movie with me."

Jonah rolled his eyes, but his accompanying laughter took all the heat from the gesture. "You're a pain in my ass, you know that?"

"Yep. Now hurry up. Harry and Sally aren't going to wait forever."

"You do realize I don't even know who that is, right?"

Natalie tried his eye roll/laughter combo on for size. "Go, or I'll eat all the popcorn myself and leave you with nothing but crumbs."

A few minutes later, they were shoulder to shoulder on the couch, with Jonah hogging the popcorn, as usual. He eyeballed the movie description on the TV menu that had popped up when Natalie had paused it to talk to her mother, then eyeballed her with doubt.

"I hate to be the bearer of bad news, Nat, but these movies are complete fiction."

"Uh-huh," she said, her lips twitching into a wry smile she couldn't help. "Because all of those action movies you love are so realistic."

"They're more believable than this." Jonah pointed to the TV just in time for Natalie to laugh out loud.

"Jonah, please. The last action movie you dragged me to go see had the main character *literally* taking on a star fleet of aliens all by himself." It had been entertaining, she guessed, although she'd totally have added a better love story—which was to say, there hadn't been one in the movie at all. "How is that more believable than *When Harry Met Sally*?"

"It's a love story, right? They meet, overcome some obstacle, then ride off into the sunset together, all happy and perfect as long as they've got each other?"

"That's one hell of an abridged version, but yes," Natalie agreed. "That's the idea."

Jonah scooped up a huge handful of popcorn. "Which is exactly why it's not believable. That's not how real relationships work."

They were veering toward touchy territory for Jonah, she knew. He never talked about Vanessa, or what had made him walk away from his wedding the night before the ceremony, even though, of course, Natalie had asked him about it more than once. She'd sensed that there was far more to the story than the "it just didn't work out" he'd given up, but

Jonah had always refused to elaborate, so eventually, she'd stopped asking.

Still... "It's not believable because they actually end up in love at the end of the movie?"

"It's not the love part I'm disputing. People fall in love all the time. Well, people other than me, I guess," he caveated with a shake of his head. "It's when you start talking about it lasting forever that I call bullshit. Love ends in heartache, not happily ever after."

Natalie blinked. Tried to process his theory. Annnnd nope. "So, you're saying that love can exist, it just can't last?" she asked doubtfully.

"Yep." God, he hadn't even hesitated. "That's exactly what I'm saying."

"Okay, but what about those couples who have been married for fifty years?" Natalie asked by way of argument, because no way was she going to concede this crazysauce without a fight.

But Jonah simply shrugged. "Just because they're married doesn't mean they're in love. My parents are a prime example."

Natalie's gut panged behind her pajama top even though she'd known Jonah's basic family history for years. "They might have loved each other once," she tried, but his sardonic smile told her she'd never make the argument stick.

"I appreciate the sentiment, but not even you can brightside the fact that my parents were married seven months before I was born and my mother only stuck around for six years after that before taking off for parts unknown," Jonah said, as pragmatically as he'd relay a patient's vitals in the ED. "My father never got over it. He's sitting in a retirement community in Charleston, pining over a woman who left him twenty-seven years ago and never loved him for a single day."

"Okay, but what about my parents?" Natalie asked gently. She hated that Jonah's mother had left both him and his father, and that his father had ended up alone, but surely, there was a flip side to this coin. "They've been together for thirty-five years and they're still happy. And Parker and Charlie found their way back to each other. Now they're more in love than ever."

"They are, and that's great." Jonah's expression softened enough to make the words genuine, but not so much to slow his argument. "But they're rare exceptions. Love works for them, I guess, but as far as I'm concerned, the whole thing is overrated, at best. With the odds that it'll end up in a dumpster fire or a messy divorce rather than happily ever after? I'll pass."

"That's cheerful," she said, although her tone was all sarcasm. "Come on. Can you honestly tell me that you can't come up with one *single* scenario in which you fall head over heels in love with someone?"

"Sorry. I know happily ever after is your jam. But yeah, I can honestly tell you it's never going to happen for me. Flying solo is safer and smarter."

His matter-of-fact delivery twisted sharply beneath Natalie's breastbone, prompting her to put the popcorn bowl aside. "But you should end up happy. You're a great guy, Jonah. I know things between you and Vanessa didn't work out, but—"

"You don't know the half of it."

The way his eyes had briefly widened told Natalie he hadn't meant to let the words escape, and a not-small part of her knew she shouldn't push. But for Chrissake, this was *Jonah*. They'd traded manners for brutal honesty ages ago.

"Okay, then enlighten me. What is it that I don't know that's making you so jaded when it comes to the idea of a relationship that actually works?"

Jonah laughed, although the sound held no joy. "Because I never left Vanessa at the altar. She left *me*."

8

Jonah had spent three fucking years keeping his mouth nailed shut on the topic of his ruined wedding. He'd crafted dozens of non-responses and slanted truths, not to mention an entire lifestyle to match the story that he'd been the one to leave Vanessa the night before they were supposed to pledge their undying love to each other in front of God and five hundred of Remington's most elite socialites. The fact that neither he nor Vanessa had ever flat-out said who had left whom didn't matter. People believed what they wanted to believe, especially when she'd left the country on a one-way ticket less than a week later, and Jonah had sworn to himself that he'd never correct them. After all, staying mum was far less painful than having to admit the truth he should've known. Yet all it had taken to undo his vow of silence was one single no-bullshit question from his very beautiful best friend.

Make that his very beautiful, very *shocked* best friend, and damn it, Jonah was screwed.

"Wait," Natalie said, blinking as if she were getting her head around the information in degrees. "Vanessa left you the night before your wedding, and she let everyone think it was the other way around?"

The very un-Natalie-like sting that sharpened the words were a testament to how deep her allegiance ran—actual anger, with its harsh edges and barbed words, wasn't usually in her wheelhouse. But since Jonah had long since gotten over any hard feelings (or, okay, any feelings, period) he might've had for Vanessa and the way their relationship had ended, he went with the straight-up truth.

"In her defense, I let everyone think it, too, and she wasn't here to elaborate. It's kind of a long story."

One that, by the look on Natalie's face, there was no way he was going to get away with not telling in full now that he'd impulsively opened his trap. Better to just get it over with. At any rate, it proved his argument about love in spades.

"I knew something wasn't right between me and Vanessa for a couple of months leading up to that night," Jonah said. "She was distant, just one step out of reach. But we were both working a lot of hours, and you know her parents. The wedding planning was pretty extensive. I thought all of that was just making things crazy between us, and I didn't press."

Vanessa's parents had made the list of Remington's top ten wealthiest business owners for decades, having founded an incredibly lucrative brokerage firm together during the first year of their marriage. As their only child, Vanessa had taken a position at the firm after she'd graduated with her MBA and was being groomed to move all the way up the career ladder until she eventually took over as CEO one day. Marrying an ambitious trauma surgeon had really been the cherry on top of her parents' sky-high expectations. Or, at least, it would've been, had she actually pulled the trigger.

"Vanessa finally came to me the night before the

wedding and said we needed to talk," Jonah continued, his tone as non-committal as the rest of him. "She said she'd tried to love the family business, living in Remington. Meeting the expectations her parents had set for her. All of it."

"Including marrying you," Natalie said, finally starting to connect the dots.

Hindsight really was the meanest bitch Jonah knew. "We'd been together for two years. We started out happy. In love with each other." On second thought, maybe irony was meaner. "Everyone assumed we'd get married, including us. But somewhere along the way, Vanessa realized she wanted something else."

"Oh, my God," Natalie said, and who knew her eyes could get so big? "She chose the Peace Corps, didn't she? *That's* what she wanted."

And there it was. "Yeah. She'd always hated all the social obligations, the lifestyle, pretty much everything that went with the business she'd have inherited if she hadn't found a way out of Remington. It was everything her parents had ever worked for. She felt trapped here, in this life. She was just too afraid to tell her parents the truth."

"That can be pretty overwhelming," Natalie admitted, but then she shook her head. "Still. She was the one who wanted out, but you took all the blame. That hardly seems fair."

Jonah bit back a bitter laugh. Fair was just a four-letter f-word. "She told me *before* we made the biggest mistake of our lives, and I know it was hard for her."

He'd been hurt at the time—duh—but not so much that he hadn't been able to see that trying to convince her to stay would've been a lost cause *and* a colossal mistake. There was no fixing what could never work.

And he'd known far before she'd left him that love never worked.

"We didn't ever say I was the one to leave her, and Vanessa never made me out to be the bad guy to save face with her family," Jonah said, carefully keeping his emotions far from the words. They didn't belong here, mingled in with the truth. "The story just kind of unfolded that way, and we both let it. Then she left for Nicaragua a few days later."

"Okay, but why didn't you ever *say* anything?"

He shrugged, his shoulders shushing against the couch cushions. "Because Vanessa had a lot to lose if the truth came out, and I didn't. Because I stupidly thought I loved her. Because it was easier to let people jump to the natural conclusion that I left her at the altar rather than her leaving me."

Natalie leaned in, her brown eyes glinting with something Jonah couldn't name, but that slid all the way through him, regardless.

"No," she whispered. "I meant, why didn't you ever say anything to me?"

His pulse stuttered. "I guess I didn't think it would really matter. Airing it out wouldn't have changed what happened, and the truth is, Vanessa did me a favor."

At Natalie's shocked exhale, Jonah continued, "I didn't realize it at the time, but that doesn't make it any less true now. Relationships just aren't for me." His emotions reared up, threatening to spill over, but he kept them in check. This was just the truth. He'd known it forever. All Vanessa had done was give him proof.

"I'm not a long-haul guy. But I'm also not sad about it." Jonah shrugged. "I don't want to end up divorced and heartbroken like my old man, or in a loveless relationship like

Tess and her idiot husband, and millions of other couples. Better that I know now. Even if my reputation took a hit for it three years ago."

Natalie took a minute to process everything, opening her mouth, then closing it, then finally saying, "I still can't believe you never told me any of this."

The regret in her tone arrowed right to his solar plexus. He needed some levity, and he needed it fast. "Oh, come on. Like there aren't things you've never told me before."

He edged the words with just enough teasing to make the corners of her mouth hint at a smile. "Not things like that," she said. But the smile didn't fade, so Jonah worked up one to match it.

"You don't have one secret? One thing about you that I don't know?"

Her chin dropped toward her chest as a blush tore over her cheeks, and good Christ, she was pretty. "Maybe one. But it's not a *secret*. It's just something I've never told you."

"Let me guess." He turned toward her on the couch, his knee brushing hers. "You're a spy."

She rolled her eyes and huffed out a laugh. "No."

"You know who really killed JFK."

"Seriously?"

"Hey, I'm just trying to cover all my bases," Jonah said, tapping a finger against his chin before feigning enlightenment. "Ah! I've got it. You're going to *literally* take on a star fleet of aliens and save the world all by yourself."

Natalie shook her head, her laughter taking over. "Oh, my God, no! I'm just a virgin. That's all."

For a second that lasted for roughly a month, Jonah couldn't breathe. "You're...what?"

"It's not a big deal. I'm not, you know...defective, or

anything," Natalie said, her shoulders stiffening just slightly beneath the thin cotton of her top.

"God, no. Of course not," Jonah replied, looking directly into her eyes so she'd know beyond the shadow of a doubt that he meant it. But holy shit. The aliens thing might've shocked him less. "I just, ah. I'm surprised."

Her brows winged up. "Why?"

"Because you're"—*Smart. Genuine. So pretty it hurts*—"thirty-two," he managed, and Jesus, he needed to get a grip. "That's just a little unusual."

"It's not *that* unusual once you consider my history." She shrugged. "I was diagnosed with leukemia at ten, and didn't finish remission therapy until I was fourteen. I was home schooled, and even though my parents had all the best intentions, I was pretty sheltered. It's not like I went to football games or homecoming dances or any other things normal teenagers do when they shed their virginity. I lived with my parents all the way through college, so that was more of the same, and by the time I got to medical school, I was pretty much the last virgin standing."

Jonah had to admit, it did make more sense when she parsed it all out like that. "I get that everyone's focused on the work in med school," he said, because he knew it first-hand. His social life had been a frigging wasteland during those years. "But you weren't in classes and labs twenty-four/seven, and there's no way guys weren't interested in you. You must've dated at least a little."

"I didn't say I didn't hook up or get pretty close to sex a handful of times," Natalie pointed out with a tart smile. "I'm a virgin, not a nun. But I don't want to look at sex like taxes or a flu shot."

He couldn't help it. He laughed. "No offense, but I sure as hell hope not."

Natalie laughed, too, scattering any awkwardness or tension the moment might otherwise carry. "What I mean is, I don't want to just get it over with. Which isn't to say that I *don't* want to do it. I actually do. But *when* I do, I want to do it right. Especially the first time."

"So, you're not waiting for marriage?"

"God, I hope not," she said. "I don't have to lose my virginity to the person I'm going to spend my whole life with. I just don't want to have sex with someone for the sake of having sex. It doesn't have to be hearts and flowers and I love yous, but it does have to be with someone I like and really trust. I guess I haven't felt like I've met the right guy for that yet, you know?"

Jonah's mind spun back to the handful of men she'd dated, a few of them at the boyfriend level, over the last couple of years. "Okay, but what about that computer programmer guy...Billy—no. Brian. You two were kind of serious for a while."

"Brian was great. But there wasn't a whole lot of chemistry there. Kissing him was like kissing my brother."

Natalie shuddered, and okay, yeah, Jonah had to admit, lack of chemistry was a deal-breaker for him, too. "There was the sous chef. Micah, right?" he tried again, and this time, Natalie laughed.

"Come on, Jonah. You met him. Would *you* have given your virginity to that guy?"

"He was a little, ah, high-strung," Jonah allowed, trying to go easy.

"Please. I might not have realized it until we'd gone out for a month or two, but he was so uptight that I was tempted to order an MRI to confirm that the world's largest stick was, indeed, lodged up his ass," Natalie said. "But all of the guys

I've dated aside, really, is it that hard for you to believe I've never had sex?"

"No. Yes." Jonah shook his head, trying to clear the stupid thing once and for all. "It's not hard for me to understand why you're waiting. To be honest, I think it's pretty badass."

She snorted. "That's me. The badass virgin."

Something odd broke free in Jonah's chest, making him lean toward her enough to erase the space between them by half. "It *is* you, though. I don't know anyone else who would stick to what she believed in, even if it put her in the minority, rather than say fuck it at some point and settle for something less than perfect."

"Oh." Natalie's eyes widened, her lashes sweeping up to frame them as she blinked. "But you said yes, too. So, it does surprise you?"

"The part that surprises me has nothing to do with you," Jonah said, the truth pouring out of him as if it had been shaken up and set loose. But it *was* the truth, and, God, right now, in this moment, she deserved to hear it. "There's nothing wrong with you being a virgin, Nat. What I don't get is how none of those idiots you dated ever realized how great you really are. I mean, at least a couple of them could've been your guy, the one you liked and trusted enough. But none of them ever figured it out. I just don't understand how no one ever bothered to uncover you."

Her lips parted, a soft sound moving past them, and fuck, it undid something in places he didn't even know he had.

"You did," she whispered.

"That's different," Jonah said a second later, when he'd recovered the breath she'd just knocked clean out of him. "I'm your best friend."

But in that moment, he realized how close they were. Registered that his knee was still touching hers, the connection firm and warm and not enough. Recognized how much more he wanted, that the glint in Natalie's stare and the way she'd shifted even closer toward him, her mouth only inches away now, said she wanted it, too.

"It doesn't feel different," she said, her chin lifting toward his. "Right now, it feels—"

Jonah closed the space between them out of pure impulse, capturing whatever word she'd planned to use with his lips. She exhaled against his mouth, not in surprise, he realized as the exhale coasted into a sigh, but in want. Pressing closer, he cupped her face between both palms, tightening his fingers in her hair and keeping her exactly where he wanted her as he eased into the kiss.

Not that there was anything sweet about it. No. The way Natalie had wrapped her arms around his shoulders and eagerly parted her lips, then—ah, *fuck*—darted her tongue out in search of his made Jonah's cock jerk beneath his sweats. He answered with a bold move of his own, slipping his tongue over hers for a suggestive taste, then another. Natalie arched into the contact of his chest on hers, her breasts sliding against the front of his body with just enough friction to make him temporarily insane, and he lowered his arms to haul her into his lap.

Oh, hell yes. "That's better," Jonah murmured, a bolt of dark, dirty want moving from his breath to his balls as Natalie settled against him from hips to shoulders to mouth. Her kiss was all agreement, another sigh drifting up from her chest and knocking his already tenuous composure down a peg. Somewhere, from the way, way, *way* back of his brain, came the warning that this was Natalie, and that anything that happened in the heat of the moment couldn't be undone. But it *was* Natalie, beautiful, smart, kind-to-her-toes Natalie, who didn't just know him, but got him.

And the only thing about this moment that Jonah wanted undone was her.

Slow and hot and more than once.

Jonah pulled her closer, his heart thundering in his chest as he poured every ounce of intention and want into kissing her. Each glide of his tongue grew more purposeful, every taste more intense. Yet, rather than letting him dominate the kiss like he usually did, Natalie met each ministration, balancing out his greedy need not by giving in, but by giving back. The equal back and forth, the concession, then control, was the hottest thing Jonah had ever felt, so different than the laundry list of motions he'd gone through for years—shit, maybe forever.

Desire, sharp and hot, flooded through him, locking his fingers over her hips to hold her flush against his aching cock, crushing his mouth to hers so he could take and give and take some more—

Her cell phone went off like a grenade.

"What? Oh," Natalie murmured, blinking twice before turning her chin to stare at the thing in confusion, and good Christ, was he out of his *mind*?

He'd been one sweet sigh from stripping his best friend naked and fucking her senseless on his couch, taking her virginity and destroying the only relationship he'd ever had that actually worked in the process.

Well. At least that answered the question.

"You should get that," Jonah said, loosening his grasp on her hips and sliding his hands up to a far more respectable place on her waist, but damn it, *damn* it! The damage was done.

"I don't want to get it," Natalie said. "Jonah—"

"Nat," he interrupted, lifting her out of his lap and setting her on the cushion beside him. Jesus, he was the worst sort of deplorable for putting that look of confusion on her face, but even that was better than what he'd have been if they hadn't been interrupted. "Answer your phone."

The confusion on Natalie's face slid from realization to hurt, but only for a beat before she blanked it and reached for her phone. "Hello?"

Her brows tugged sharply downward, sending a frigid shot of worry between Jonah's ribs. "Rachel?" Natalie said. "Slow down. Slow down and tell me what's wrong."

Jonah didn't know who Rachel was, but any idiot could see that whatever she was saying to Natalie wasn't of the hey-how-are-ya variety. Torn between wanting to give Natalie privacy and offer support, he made the executive decision to keep his ass parked on the couch, but he also stayed quiet so he didn't distract her from her call.

A few beats later, Natalie—who had gone stick-straight on the couch beside him—said, "Okay. And she hasn't kept down any of the fluids you gave her? Is she complaining of specific pain, like at the incision site or anywhere else? Okay. No, that's probably good. Do you think you can get her to the ED? Alright, don't worry. I'll meet you there. Yes, I'm leaving in a minute."

"What's wrong?" Jonah asked, because at this point, asking *if* anything was wrong was just plain duh.

Natalie blew out a shaky breath and lowered her phone to the coffee table. "That was Annabelle's mom. Annabelle spiked a fever of 101.9, and she's vomiting and lethargic."

Oh, *hell*. "You think she's got a post-op infection?" Those could range from aggravating to acute, depending. In a case like Annabelle's...

"I don't know. It could be that, or it could be one of a

half-dozen other things," Natalie said. "I'm going to meet them at the ED, and I guess we'll find out."

Natalie paused, pinching the bridge of her nose between her thumb and forefinger. It was a brief showing of vulnerability, her fear there and then gone as she pushed to her feet, but to Jonah, it might as well have been a billboard.

Not once in the whole time that he'd known her had he ever seen Natalie anything less than one million percent a-okay.

His feet found the floorboards before his brain had any chance of catching up to the command to move. "I'll drive you."

"Don't be silly. I could be hours," she pointed out after a brief hitch of surprise. "Plus, I'm perfectly fine to drive to the hospital on my own. I do it every day, remember? It's no big deal."

Nope. Not one fucking chance Jonah was budging on this. "If the situation were reversed, there isn't even a snowball's chance in Satan's backyard that you'd let me drive myself to the ED. So, go on. Get changed, and I'll meet you out here in a couple of minutes."

Natalie hesitated, her teeth clamped over her bottom lip in a way that shouldn't make his pulse race, under the circumstances, but since he was already batting a thousand in the jackass category tonight, it so did.

"We should talk about...what happened before Rachel called."

For a single breath of a single second, Jonah wanted to agree. He wanted to tell her that he hadn't been able to stop thinking of her ever since she'd moved in, that he'd meant every syllable of what he'd said about her exes being morons of the highest order for not seeing how beautiful she really was. He wanted to say that he'd been an idiot himself for not fully realizing it until she'd landed under his roof, and now he couldn't *un*-realize it. But Jonah could not, under any circumstances, say any of those things, so instead, he went with, "There's nothing to talk about. I was out of line, and you deserve better. I apologize."

"So, it was a mistake," she said, hurt flashing through her stare again.

"It was an error in judgment," he corrected, and yep. Idiot. For Chrissake, he had *one* rule. No emotions. No attachments. No exceptions. "Mine, specifically. Let me make it up to you by being a better friend. Let me drive you to the hospital."

Before Natalie could argue—and her expression said she was primed and ready to—Jonah took a step toward her. "Look, I know you're capable, and I know you're tough. But would you please let me do this so I can also know you're okay?"

She exhaled, her lips pressed together in what wanted to be a frown, but didn't quite make the grade. "I *could* use the drive time to log into the system and review Annabelle's chart," she said. "Five minutes?"

"Done," Jonah said.

The feeling in his chest as she walked away should have been relief, he knew. After all, his impulsiveness would've had their friendship on the chopping block if they hadn't been interrupted. But as Jonah stood there, with the taste and feel of Natalie's mouth still fresh on his, the feeling in his rib cage wasn't relief at all.

It was regret.

9

N atalie sat back against the passenger seat of Jonah's Lexus and tried not to feel like a fool.

Considering the circumstances, it was an uphill battle.

She hadn't meant to tell him she was a virgin—God, her ears still burned at the thought of his handsome face so caught up in shock—and she definitely hadn't meant to let whatever girlish fantasy she'd been having lately come to life by *literally* throwing herself in his lap. But all it had taken was a little laughter to go with that special brand of Jonah Sheridan charm, and a few well-meaning compliments later, bam. She'd tried to climb him like a fucking jungle gym.

If Rachel hadn't called when she had...

Straightening, Natalie shook herself back to reality. Rachel *had* called, and Natalie really needed to focus on that. Jonah had flat-out said that the kiss had been a heat of the moment mistake, plus, Annabelle's fever was troubling, and far more important than Natalie's personal life. The little girl's condition could be serious. She was Natalie's patient, someone Natalie had promised to take care of. The truth was, she was worried, not just more than she'd let on to Rachel on the phone—that was a given; making the poor woman panic without a clear and concrete reason to wasn't on Natalie's agenda—but even more than she'd shown Jonah.

Or, at least, more than she thought she'd shown him. She must be slipping. She'd pulled out her most shiny "totally fine, nothing to see here", only to have him insist on playing chauffeur.

And instead of feeling guilty that she'd put him out on a Friday night and made him worry that she wasn't one hundred percent okay, she found herself grateful for the comfort of his presence.

Wanting to kiss him *and* wanting him, security blanket-style? Ugh, she was definitely slipping.

"You okay over there?"

"Yep," Natalie said, just a shade too emphatically. She cleared her throat and gave herself a fleet-footed mental kick. "I'm fine."

Jonah slid her a glance out of the corner of his Bahama blues. "Did anything jump out at you from Annabelle's chart?"

"Unfortunately, no."

Natalie had used her staff access to pull up Annabelle's chart on the secure hospital system via her cell phone a few minutes ago, and it was exactly as she'd thought it would be. She had discharged Annabelle herself, reviewing the orders with Rachel thoroughly no more than twelve hours ago. "I mean, she's clearly brewing something with a fever that high. But until I can get a look at her and run labs, I'm just shooting rubber bands at the night sky, you know?"

Jonah nodded. "I do. But I also know she's in great hands."

"Thanks," Natalie said.

He pulled into the hospital's employee parking lot, swinging into a space marked *Physicians Only* before turning to pin her with a devastating smile. "Oh, I meant mine. I don't hang out at this place for grins, you know. If I'm coming out to the hospital on a Friday night, it's because no one else's expertise will do."

Natalie laughed, just as he'd probably known she would. "Oh, my God. I honestly don't know if there's enough room in this car for the three of us."

"Three?" Jonah asked, killing the engine.

"You, me, and your ginormous ego," Natalie said sweetly.

Of course, his grin only got bigger. "Hey, size matters, sweetheart."

As if he'd recognized the sexual innuendo too late, he straightened against the Lexus's driver's seat, palming the key fob and averting his eyes. "So, are you ready to do this?"

Natalie fought the flush that wanted to creep over her cheeks. Of course, he probably wanted to steer clear of anything suggestive enough to remind either of them about their impulsive-as-hell (*hot*-as-hell) lip lock. "Absolutely. I told Rachel to meet me in the ED, so let's go see if they're here yet."

She hadn't wanted to text Rachel as she and Jonah had gotten close to the hospital in case the woman was still driving. But a quick trip across the parking lot and past the main entrance to the ED revealed her sitting in the waiting room, her face drawn and pale and her arm wrapped around Annabelle's shoulders.

"Oh, thank God," Rachel said, relief spilling into her expression as soon as she saw Natalie, and Natalie's heart lurched against her ribs despite everything she knew about staying one step removed from any medical situation, be it a paper cut or the plague.

Rachel looked from Natalie to Jonah, her eyes going momentarily wide. "I'm so sorry to bother you. You said to keep an eye out for things like fever and vomiting, and I didn't know what else to do."

"You did exactly the right thing, Rachel. I wouldn't have given you my personal number if I didn't want you to use it in an emergency. This is Dr. Sheridan. He's a trauma surgeon here at Remington Mem. Jonah Sheridan, Rachel Fletcher." Natalie stepped back to let them shake hands and exchange a pair of brief hellos before turning toward Annabelle. "Hey, kiddo. Dr. Sheridan is a friend of mine. Would it be okay if he helped me figure out what's making you sick?"

"Uh-huh," the little girl said weakly, and the concern on Rachel's face edged toward panic.

"You think she needs a trauma surgeon?"

Shit. Natalie shook her head. "Not at all. Dr. Sheridan is a very accomplished physician, and a good friend, who I trust. Sometimes having another set of eyes can make all the difference in a case. Plus"—she worked up a reassuring smile—"he gave me a ride here, so we're kind of a two-for-the-price-of-one tonight."

"Oh. Okay," Rachel said, clearly relieved. Jonah turned toward Annabelle, who was curled up in her chair and hugging her stuffed fox to her chest. He didn't normally handle pediatric cases unless it was necessary during an ED shift, and while Natalie still trusted his knowledge one million percent, she also knew that dealing with the under-ten set on a person-to-person level wasn't smack in the center of his comfort zone.

"Why don't I get a wheelchair so we can move you into an exam room. How does that sound?" he asked, and she gave up a small nod.

"Mkay."

After going through the logistics of getting Annabelle checked in and gowned up, and alerting the night-shift attending that they were treating her, Natalie pulled up the little girl's chart for Jonah to review while she took her vitals.

"Okay, kiddo. Your mom gave me a little bit of the scoop on the phone, so now it's your turn. What's going on?" she asked, and ugh, Annabelle's temperature was still 101.

"I don't feel good. I'm tired and I feel sweaty."

"Yeah, a fever will do that. How about your stomach? How does that feel?" Natalie asked, murmuring Annabelle's temperature, blood pressure, heart rate and sats to Jonah, even though she barely broke eye contact with the little girl.

Annabelle hesitated. "Mommy gave me some chicken noodle soup and the medicine that's supposed to make my fever go away, but I threw up."

"Just that one time?" Jonah asked Rachel, who nodded.

"Yes. I thought it might just be residual from the chemo meds and everything she had here this week, but then her fever jumped from 99.4 to 101.9, too. I was scared to give her anything else to eat or drink after that. I didn't want her to compromise her sutures or get dehydrated if she threw up again, and I figured you'd give her fluids once we got here."

"Good thinking, Mom," Natalie said. God, she hated that Rachel knew all of these protocols by heart. "Alright, Annabelle. I'm going to feel your belly and take a look at your incision. But before I get to that, is there anything else you can tell me and Dr. Sheridan that might help us figure out what's making you feel bad? Does anything hurt, or not feel like it normally does?"

Annabelle bit her lip, hugging Mr. Flufferkins a little tighter. "My incision hurts."

"What?" Rachel asked, straightening against the chair at Annabelle's bedside. "Why didn't you tell me that?"

A familiar pang worked a path between Natalie's ribs, quickening her heartbeat beneath her long-sleeved T-shirt. "That *is* pretty important, kiddo. Did it just start hurting?"

"No." Tears formed in Annabelle's eyes, wobbling on her dark lower lashes. "It's been hurting since we got home. But I knew that was bad, and after I threw up, my mom looked really worried." She looked at her mother. "I thought if I told you, you'd just get more scared."

"Oh, sweetheart." Rachel shot off a few rapid-fire blinks and scooped up Annabelle's hand, clearly fighting tears. Natalie wanted to say something, *anything* to bright-side the situation at least a little bit, but the whole thing was so close to home that her throat just refused to work.

Thankfully, Jonah broke the silence. "So, your incision site hurts, huh?" he asked gently, and when Annabelle nodded, he added, "Can you rate that pain on a scale of one to ten, if one is only a little bit of pain and ten is the worst you've ever felt?"

Natalie hated that Annabelle's ten had probably been far more painful than what most people experienced in their entire lives, let alone in their first eight years. But she hated it even more when Annabelle whispered, "Six."

Jonah looked at Natalie, his expression translating what she already knew. Low immunity from chemotherapy. Pain at the surgical incision site. Fever. Vomiting.

Post-op infection, Jonah's eyes said.

I know, hers replied. Now, they just had to stop it before it got worse.

Natalie cleared her throat. "Okee doke. First things first. I'm going to take a peek at it. Then we'll figure out why it's hurting, and do our best to make it stop."

"Okay." Annabelle nodded. Natalie slathered her hands in antibacterial gel before grabbing a pair of nitrile gloves from the dispenser on the wall. Shifting the blanket over Annabelle's legs, she made sure to only expose the part of her torso covered by tape and gauze, removing both as carefully as possible. Her heart climbed into her windpipe at the sight of the angry red incision, now clearly infected, and she took a deep breath.

"I know that hurts," Natalie said, even though Annabelle's clenched jaw said she was trying to brazen it out. Natalie looked at Jonah, who was clearly cataloguing everything he saw with care. "I'll go as fast as I can."

As gently as she could while still getting the job done, she did a quick exam, palpating the rest of Annabelle's belly and starting to formulate a strategy in her head. She conferred with Jonah on what tests to run and meds to order, and in less than a few minutes, they came up with a strong, steady treatment plan.

"Okay, you two, here it is," Natalie said. "Annabelle's got a pretty nasty infection. We won't know specifically what kind or how bad it is until we run some tests, but the good news is that nearly all infections like this one get treated in the same way."

"So, we can start now," Rachel said, and Natalie nodded.

"Yes. Which is good because that means that Annabelle will probably start to feel better pretty soon."

Of course, Rachel read right between the lines. "But it's bad because...?"

Natalie hesitated, and Jonah said, "We have to re-admit her."

A sound of frustration crossed Annabelle's lips, mirroring the look on her mother's face, and Natalie cobbled together every ounce of calm she could find.

She touched Annabelle's arm. "I know you just got released, and that you want to be at home, with all your toys and books. But we have to give you some pretty strong medicine and make sure it works, and we can only do that here. I promise, I wouldn't make you stay if I didn't need to. But in this case, I really do."

Toughness slowly took over for the girl's resignation, and she nodded. "Okay."

"And hey"—Natalie's heart squeezed, but she forced her expression to remain as untroubled as possible—"you don't ever have to be scared to tell your mom or me if something hurts, or doesn't feel right, okay? We can't make you feel better if we don't know those things. I promise, if your mom gets scared or worried, I'll be here to help her, okay?"

She lifted her pinkie, and Annabelle hooked her little finger around it with a solemn nod.

"I promise."

"Good deal." Shifting back, she looked at both Rachel and Annabelle. "Our next step is to run some tests to see how bad the infection is and get some fluids and medicine going to make Annabelle feel better. I'll see if we can get her settled into a room upstairs as soon as possible. I know you're both probably exhausted." The sooner both mom and daughter could rest, the better.

"I'll grab an IV kit and have a nurse come in to do the draw for the labs," Jonah said, turning toward the exam room door.

"Can Connor come do the IV? Please?"

Crap. *Crap.* "I'm afraid not, sweetie. He's not here tonight."

Annabelle's voice wavered. "It really pinches when other people do it."

Dread formed a heavy ball in Natalie's gut. She hated the idea of hurting the kid, who was clearly needle-phobic and already a little dehydrated, but the IV had to be placed, so she said, "If you want, I can do it."

Jonah cleared his throat from the spot where he still stood, a few feet away on the linoleum. "I'm pretty good at placing IVs, if you want me to give it a go."

"Are you really?" Annabelle asked, doubt tinging her voice, and Jonah lifted a hand like he was taking an oath.

"I promise. Sometimes I have to do it really fast, so I practice a lot."

Her eyes went wide. "Can you do mine fast?"

"As fast as I can and still get it right," he said.

Annabelle seemed to consider this. "Do you have any bubbles?"

"Any...what?" Jonah blinked, as if Annabelle had asked for a trip to the moon with a side order of world peace.

"Bubbles," she repeated, and the laugh that Natalie had been trying to cage popped out.

"They help with the deep breaths," she told him. "Plus, they're really fun."

Jonah nodded slowly in understanding. "Oh. No. I'm sorry. I don't have any bubbles."

Annabelle's face fell. Rachel opened her mouth, probably to reassure her daughter and remind her that she'd had plenty of IVs without bubbles, but Jonah's eyes lit with sudden charm.

"I do have this really cool lidocaine spray, though."

One of Annabelle's dark brown brows arched suspiciously. Not that a little eight-year-old doubt was going to dissuade him. "We usually use it on people with minor burns to make them feel better." He turned to look at Rachel. "It's a topical pain reliever, but it's got some short-term numbing qualities. It might take some of the sting out of the needle stick."

"So, it's *magic*," Annabelle murmured.

Between the bubbles and the magic, Jonah had clearly been thrown for a loop. "It's, um…"

"It's a great idea," Natalie said.

Looking grateful for the save, Jonah said, "I'll go grab everything, then."

Before he could fully pivot on his cross-trainers to turn the words into action, Natalie caught his eye and mouthed, *thank you*. His no-problem smile in return sent a thread of comfort through her, and she found herself able to fully exhale for the first time in over an hour.

She did have one piece of business to attend to, though, and it was one that couldn't wait.

"Hey, Annabelle, would it be okay if I talked to your mom for a second out in the hallway? Boring grown-up stuff," she added with an exaggerated eye-roll.

Annabelle nodded, and a few seconds later, Natalie and Rachel stood just outside the exam room doorway, although they left it open in case Annabelle needed anything.

"Thank you so much for all of this," Rachel said. "You've done so much for me and Annabelle, and your boyfriend was great with her, too."

"My what?" Natalie sputtered, her heart thwacking her rib cage at the suggestion.

Rachel's brows lifted, and she gestured down the hallway in the direction in which Jonah had disappeared. "Dr. Sheridan. Aren't you two…"

Natalie shook her head, prompting Rachel's brows to inch even higher. "Oh, God, I'm so sorry," she said. "You got here together, then you said he was a good friend. I thought that was for Annabelle's benefit. Plus, you two have some seriously crazy nonverbal communication skills. You read each other like the *New York Times*. I just assumed you're a couple."

"We're roommates. Temporarily," Natalie added. "Just friends."

Rachel tilted her head. "Oh. He's very, ah. Good-looking."

Natalie's libido gave up a game-day cheer in agreement. "He is."

"He looks like a Disney prince," Annabelle called out from her bed.

"Annabelle," Rachel warned, her cheeks turning pink. "Eavesdropping on adults is rude."

"Sorry. But you don't whisper very quietly."

Natalie laughed, because it was that or let her embarrassment burn a giant ring of fire in the floor. Dropping her voice to a true murmur, she said, "Anyway, I just want to check in to see how you're doing."

"Me? I'm fine. Well, I will be once this infection is under control," Rachel whispered back. "It's just...difficult to be the only parent."

"I'm sure it is," Natalie said, although it took effort to keep the emotion from her voice. "You shouldn't have to shoulder all of this alone. We have some great staff members who are specifically trained to help the families of our pediatric cancer patients cope with the stress."

"Like therapists?" Rachel asked, her brows drawn in question, and Natalie nodded.

"Yes, but you don't have to think of it as anything so

formal. It can be extremely beneficial to talk to someone who's familiar with what you're going through, just to bounce your thoughts off of them in case they can help, or even if you just want someone to listen."

"Sort of like how you did with Dr. Sheridan tonight? Another set of eyes on the case?"

Natalie's pulse rattled in surprise, then again in realization. "Yes. Exactly like that, actually."

Looking through the open doorway and into the exam room, Rachel exhaled and gave up a small nod. "I'd really like someone like that."

"I can have someone come to Annabelle's room tomorrow, and we'll have a nurse keep an eye on her for as long as you need during your appointment. If you think it would help her, we can have someone chat with Annabelle, too."

"Oh, could we?" Rachel asked, and Natalie didn't hesitate.

"Of course. I want you both in tip-top shape so we can kick this cancer's butt." Stopping for a breath, she considered her next words very carefully. But if the right trial came along, Rachel needed to be prepared. Natalie didn't want to offer false hope, but *some* hope was always a good thing. "I'd also like to see what we can do about getting Annabelle into a clinical trial, maybe at UNC or Collins General."

Rachel's brows flew upward. "But Collins is in Alabama."

"It is," Natalie agreed. "It's also a state-of-the-art cancer center, where they have pediatric oncologists who are very well-equipped to tackle Annabelle's specific type of cancer."

"They're also not you and Dr. Hoover."

Of course, Rachel didn't want to take Annabelle out of her comfort zone. Still, Natalie said, "No, but these trials are run by incredible doctors. They can provide huge breakthroughs for some patients. I've talked to Dr. Hoover about it, and we both think it's worth looking into."

"Oh." Rachel nodded slowly. "Well, I'd hate to move Annabelle to a strange city and a new hospital, and to leave you, especially, but if you think it's a good idea, then yes. Let's look."

Relief spilled through Natalie's chest. There was an answer out there. She just had to find it. "We can talk more about it in the morning, after you've had some sleep. But for now, I'll go see about getting a bed ready in the peds wing. It's been a long night."

As Natalie replayed Rachel's words about Jonah, then all the events of the last couple of hours in her head, she felt the fatigue that usually followed a good, hard shot of adrenaline settle in, realizing only then exactly how big of an understatement that was.

10

Jonah spent his Wednesday afternoon up to his wrists in a patient's chest cavity. Since it had followed a morning spent removing not one, but three bullets from a robbery victim's extremities, then repairing the extensive damage each one had left in its wake, to say that he was spent was definitely a euphemism.

After three straight days of wall-to-wall surgeries, none of them uncomplicated, plus just as many shifts covering the ED in the tiny pockets of time in between, Jonah was balls-out wrecked.

Double-checking the post-op update Dr. Young had put in their last patient's chart to make sure the intern had covered all of her bases, Jonah headed to the attendings' lounge to finally lose the scrubs that had felt like a second skin this week. He'd even outlasted Charlie and Tess today, both of whom were serious contenders for the Workaholic of the Year award, as well as Natalie, who had finally been able to discharge a fever-free and stir-crazy Annabelle early yesterday morning. She'd erred on the side of caution since Annabelle's immune system was so compromised from the chemo, but in the end, the heavy cocktail of antibiotics Natalie had ordered had done the trick to knock out Annabelle's infection.

Jonah was looking forward to getting all the details about her recovery and release from the hospital, actually. He wasn't really used to being around kids, either as their physician or otherwise, but he had to admit it. Annabelle was pretty cute. Watching Natalie interact with the girl and her mother? Was pretty damned endearing, not to mention impressive as hell.

All that, and she's the best kisser you know, whispered an unbidden, unruly voice he'd been trying—unsuccessfully, thanks—to snuff out for the last five days. Things had returned to business as usual between him and Natalie, with neither one of them mentioning the kiss they'd shared again. Yet despite the fact that he damn well knew he shouldn't, Jonah hadn't been able to stop thinking about it any time his mind wasn't immediately and fully occupied. The kiss was imprinted in his memory as if it had just happened, the smell of Natalie's skin right there in his nose, his mouth tingling from the press of her lips, parting over his in a flawless give and take. No matter how much Jonah tried to remind himself that kissing her had been a reckless impulse he'd *known* he'd had no business giving in to, and that he needed to just forget about this crazy attraction to Natalie, the more he ended up wanting her.

Problematic, really, since they were sharing space at home *and* at work.

Shaking his head and shouldering his way into the grey Henley he'd stashed in his locker at o-dark-thirty this morning, he stamped out the thought, once and for all. Yes, he and Natalie had kissed, and fuck yes, it had been hotter than the inside of the sun. But they'd agreed to forget it. She wanted all sorts of things Jonah could never give her, and what's more, she deserved them.

No matter how surly his inner voice was about not kissing her again.

Jonah finished up with his change-and-get-out-of-here routine, realizing that he hadn't tended to his stomach since lunch, and even that had been a grab and go. He had just enough time to pick up some takeout from his favorite Thai place, which was—bonus—on his way home. It would give Natalie a breather from having to cook, besides. Tapping off a quick text to tell her he had dinner taken care of, Jonah made his way from Point A to B to C, finally crossing the threshold of his apartment about twenty-five minutes later.

"Hey," he said to Natalie, who had changed into an infuriatingly cute pair of sweatpants and—God help him and his traitorous dick—tied her hair into two loose braids to frame her pixie face.

"Hey!" she said, looking up from the half-dozen medical journals, plus her laptop, that she'd slathered over his coffee table. "Oh, my God, that smells divine."

"You're not the only one who can whip up dinner around here." Jonah moved into the kitchen, placing the bag full of takeout on the counter by the sink and starting to unload the cartons. Natalie wasn't wrong. Everything smelled freaking delicious.

Her eyes lit at the sight of a clear plastic container full of soup. "Ohhhh, Tom Kha Kai is my favorite."

"I remember." Jonah preferred Tom Yom Goong, personally, the spicier, the better, but he knew Natalie loved the milder, chicken in coconut soup. "It's all yours, plus, I got shrimp lettuce wraps, pad Thai, and green curry. Oh, and mango sticky rice," he added, because really, it was a given.

"Did you invite a hockey team over or something?

Maybe Finn and some of his buddies from the Rogues?" Natalie asked over a laugh. "These portions are huge. There's no way you and I can eat all of this."

Jonah snorted, taking the last of the plastic containers from the bag. "Clearly, you underestimate me. Plus, whatever we don't eat today, we can have as leftovers tomorrow. Then you'll get a whole two days off from kitchen duty."

The beginnings of a frown built between her brows. "But I promised you I'd cook."

"And I promised *you* we'd get Thai food over the weekend, remember? I know Annabelle's case kept you pretty busy, so we didn't get a chance to do it, but consider this my rain check."

"Hmm." She reached into the utensil drawer for spoons and forks, keeping one spoon in reserve as she placed the rest on the counter, then picked up the container of soup. "You're lucky I'm hungry enough to give in."

"You're tough as hell, Kendrick. Did anyone ever tell you that?"

Natalie shrugged, but he could see the smile brewing beneath the non-committal expression she'd worked up. "Hey, a deal is a deal. I'm just trying to be a woman of my word."

"Yeah, yeah," Jonah teased. Christ, she was probably one of the most honest people on the planet, *including* nuns. "So, what are you working on?"

She followed his gaze through the open-concept kitchen to the pile of journals she'd been perusing when he'd walked in the door. "Ah. More alternative therapies and possible options for Annabelle. I know Hoover's a great doctor, and the aggressive chemo regimen she prescribed is the best way to treat Annabelle's cancer, but..."

"As Annabelle's surgeon, you want to do all that you can

to send that cancer into remission," Jonah finished, an odd tightness blooming somewhere in the vicinity of his chest. Grabbing a fork and the container of curry, he said, "Well, come on. We'll make better headway if we work on it together."

Natalie blinked. "But you just spent all day working. Parker even said you and Young had to pull bullets out of someone. Plural."

"I did, but you worked all day, too. Something about a mishap at an indoor skate park?"

"Yeah." She grimaced. "A platform to one of those skateboard ramps collapsed. It was only five feet above the ground, but there were eight kids on it at the time."

Well, that probably explained the collapse. "Mallory said you two were doing films and scans for hours. I bet you're exhausted."

"Exhausted goes with the job, remember?" Natalie teased, sock-footing her way back to the coffee table, soup in hand. "But Annabelle is my patient, no matter how tired I get."

Jonah pulled out a charismatic smile to try and win her over. "Ah, but after Friday night, she's my patient, too."

"You're pushing it, Sheridan."

"Yeah, but you're going to let me. Come on."

"Fine." Natalie laughed. Settling in on the couch, she removed the lid from the container of soup. "In truth, I really *could* use the help."

She paused for a bite of soup, then another. A blissful moan crossed her lips, causing Jonah's brain to let out an *oh shit* and his cock to wake up with an *oh yesssss*. Her eyes drifted closed, her lips turning upward into a wide-open smile, and fuck, he was either going to spontaneously combust or kiss her until he ran out of air.

"So, um, Annabelle," Jonah said, his voice rough in his ears. *Focus on the medicine. Facts. Figures. Anything other than Natalie's sugar-and-sin mouth.* "She responded pretty well to the treatment protocol for that infection. Does Hoover think the setback will impact her chemo schedule?"

Natalie opened her eyes, looking at the research in front of her. "We'll have to re-check her white cell counts and keep our eye on things, but I hope not." Pausing, she tilted her head, one corner of her mouth lifting. "Rachel mentioned that you checked in on them Monday morning."

"Yeah, I had a few seconds. Figured I'd say hi in between surgeries." He checked in on lots of patients whose cases he'd been called to consult. Usually, he just touched base with the primary physician, but he'd already been on the third floor on Monday, taking out someone's gallbladder on the fly. Peds had only been a handful of steps away.

"Mmm." Natalie swirled her spoon through her soup. "She said you brought Annabelle bubbles."

Well, shit. "Oh, yeah." Jonah capped his no-big-deal tone with a shrug, busying himself with the container of curry. "I saw them at the drugstore when I stopped for a couple of things over the weekend. They were an easy grab."

Funny, Natalie's wry smirk didn't budge a millimeter. "Right. Because I'm sure they were right there next to the shaving cream."

"You're just mad I beat you to it," Jonah teased by way of distracting her, since the bubbles had been halfway across the store, not to mention the primary thing he'd gone in for. So he'd felt bad for the kid. Sue him.

"Maybe a little," Natalie said, surprising him with a wistful glance. "You were really good with her. I can't believe I never thought of using lidocaine spray before placing an IV."

"To be fair, that's not its primary use, which is probably why you didn't think of it," Jonah said between bites. "And the bubbles thing is pretty smart, too. Annabelle really seems to like them."

Natalie's nod equated to a nonverbal *I guess*. "I didn't get a chance to say this the other night, but thank you for going with me when Rachel called. Having you there really helped."

"Of course. Any time."

A burst of laughter flew past her lips, surprising Jonah into asking, "What's so funny?"

"You'd better be careful, or people might start to think there's more to you than all that cocky, one-night-only charm."

His pulse tapped in warning, steady and insistent. "Who, me? Never."

"Deny it all you want," Natalie said. "But I know the truth. There's a good man lurking beneath all that dazzle."

"Why do you believe in me so much?"

The question had popped right out of Jonah without thought or permission from his brain, but somehow, its brutal honesty didn't bother him the way he'd expected upon realizing what he'd said.

Not even when Natalie's whiskey-colored eyes glinted as if he'd issued a challenge. "Why don't you?"

Jesus, there was some irony there. The charming smiles, the borderline arrogant pickup lines he could recite if he were halfway to a coma. The litany of one-night stands that had been his default setting ever since Vanessa had boarded that flight to Central America. They were all deceptions in their own right, carefully designed to keep everyone at arm's length and to keep *him* from being in any sort of a committed relationship.

Yet, somehow, Natalie clearly saw far enough past them to believe he was truly, deeply decent.

"Because," Jonah said. "I'm not ever going to be in a relationship. Most of the city thinks I left my ex at the altar. *All* of the city knows I'm not a long-haul guy. That doesn't exactly make me quality material."

It was a reality he'd come to terms with years ago. He didn't love it, no, but it beat being a sucker, that was for damn sure. True love, with all the hearts and flowers and commitment, just wasn't built to last. *Especially* not for him.

"Oh, bullshit."

Natalie said it so cheerfully that Jonah was certain he'd misunderstood. "Sorry?"

Without breaking stride with her soup or her smile, she repeated, "Bullshit. Just because you don't want a relationship doesn't make you a degenerate by default, and anyway, what everyone thinks isn't even close to what actually happened. It's also no one's business but yours and Vanessa's."

Jonah processed her words. Tried to pick his jaw up off the floor. Didn't even come close. "Have you forgotten that you're happily-ever-after's biggest cheerleader?"

"For me," she qualified. "But it's clearly not what you want. Although, I have to admit," she added after a second, "I still don't understand exactly why not."

And there it was, that Natalie-like enthusiasm that seemed as unshakeable as the Rock of Gibraltar. God, he hated to bust her bubble.

"You mean, other than the fact that my one and only attempt at love ended with my fiancée leaving the country instead of saying 'I do'?" he asked, trying to paint the words with enough levity to flirt his way out of the thorny truth behind them.

But Natalie was far too smart for that. "I get that what happened with Vanessa makes you hesitant. But she was one person. Tons of people move on from bad breakups to end up in happy relationships."

"And tons end up going from dead-end relationship to dead-end relationship for their entire lives," Jonah pointed out matter-of-factly. "People leave their partners and spouses all the time. They start out crazy in love and swear they'll never feel any other way. Then something happens to change one or both of their minds, and bam. Splitsville. And before you go blaming my feelings on what happened with Vanessa, let me assure you, my not-a-wedding nightmare is really just one of a billion reasons why I'm not a long-haul guy."

"A *billion*." Natalie's frown outlined her words. "Hyperbole much?"

Eh, she might have him there. Still... "Melissa McGee."

"Who?"

"Melissa McGee," Jonah said, shifting on the couch cushions to look at Natalie more fully. "The prettiest girl in the seventh grade. Broke my heart after two dates."

Natalie bit her lip in sympathy, but it didn't last. "Paul Sanchez." At Jonah's questioning look, she added, "He was my lab partner in biology class, freshman year of college. My first real kiss. Sweet guy, but ultimately, there wasn't enough chemistry between us. No hearts broken."

"Yeah, but you didn't end up together, either," Jonah pointed out, after pausing to wonder if this Sanchez guy was insane to not feel chemistry with her. "And neither did the thousands of couples who filed for divorce last month alone."

"How about the thousands who didn't?" she countered, but oh, this was too easy.

"There's always next month. Look, I'm not saying I think you should ditch your aspirations for love or marriage or... what was it? Someone who will buy you a cheesecake?" he teased.

A smile flirted with the corners of her mouth even though she looked like she was trying to cage it. "Share the last *bite* of cheesecake," she corrected. "And who will laugh when I'm happy, and ache when I'm sad."

"Exactly. You want to be more than two halves making a whole, and that's cool. But as far as I'm concerned, the odds of that actually happening are practically nil. Casual is smarter."

Vanessa. Tess, whose marriage to her douche canoe of a husband was hanging on by the barest of threads. More than half of the married people in the country. His own mother, who he and his father had never heard from again. People left people they'd promised to love and cherish every single day. Christ, somewhere, someone was doing it right this very second while he sat here and ate takeout. Relationships weren't meant to last. Period. Hard stop.

"In fact, I'd bet that the average person is probably far more likely to see Bigfoot riding a unicorn than to find happily ever after," he said.

"That's a really jaded way of looking at love, you know that?"

Jonah shrugged, although, funny, the rise and fall of his shoulders was starchier than he'd expected. "I'd rather be jaded than burned."

"Okay," Natalie said, putting her soup down on top of one of the journals on the coffee table and turning to look at him. "But are you happy?"

Her question screeched across his ears like the needle of

one of those vintage record players, slamming his thoughts to a halt. "What?"

"It's a fairly straightforward question," Natalie replied softly. "Are you happy—really happy—with the idea of never settling down with someone? Because if you are, then there's no reason you shouldn't have one-night stands until you're ninety, and stand up to anyone who says otherwise. But if not..."

One-night stands until he was ninety. Jonah's stomach took a full-gainer toward his knees.

And wasn't *that* just stupid as hell, because as unappealing as an endless stream of one-night stands suddenly was, the idea that he'd find a relationship with real, God's honest staying power was just as impossible.

He wasn't a long-haul guy.

"Of course I'm happy," he said, his most charming smile locked tightly over his mouth.

"Good." Natalie smiled back. "I'm glad."

But as they turned their attention toward the rest of their dinners and the research in front of them, Jonah realized that for the first time in his life, he'd told her a lie.

11

Natalie stared at the cardboard cup of coffee in her hand, certain she was going crazy. Seven days had passed since she and Jonah had shared that insanely hot "error in judgment" kiss. On the surface, they'd gone back to normal. Researching alternative therapies for Annabelle a couple of nights ago. Ride-sharing to work when their schedules were in sync. Sneaking in lunch or coffee in between surgeries and shifts in the ED. He'd even asked her if she was up for staying in to watch the Rogues game tomorrow night.

Everything should be the same. Everything *was* the same.

Except that was a load of crap.

Exhaling in frustration, Natalie placed her coffee—which was her fourth of the day and now cold, anyway—on the coffee table in the attendings' lounge and slumped back against the couch cushions. Things between her and Jonah were far from normal. They weren't bad or awkward or uncomfortable; in fact, the happy ease she'd always felt around him was still right there, front and center. But ever since they'd kissed, Natalie had been hyper-aware of every suggestion of him. The sight of his leather jacket hanging on the stand by the front door of the apartment on the nights he'd beat her home. The cadence of his voice as she overheard him giving the interns advice on a case in the ED. The smell of the soap he used, and how it mingled with the scent of his skin to become something uniquely Jonah.

The way she wanted him to kiss her again, this time slow and deep and without interruption, and oh God, she was in over her head here on so many levels.

Time for the Bat Signal, a.k.a. Girls' Night In.

Need to talk. Girls' night a week early? I'll bring the wine and queso, Natalie added to her text. After two hell yeses and a bit of back and forth on logistics, she and Charlie and Tess agreed to meet at Charlie's apartment. Relief spilled through Natalie's chest behind her scrubs, but it quickly turned to resolve. She had just enough time to do the routine tonsillectomy on her afternoon schedule, then check in with Vasquez to make sure their post-op patients were status quo and their cases in the ED were turned over to the night-shift attending before she'd have to run to the grocery store for wine and snacks.

She turned her To Do list into action, taking all the appropriate time to reassure the parents of the now tonsil-free six-year-old that the procedure couldn't have gone more smoothly, then reviewing the rest of her cases with her (thankfully, ambitious) intern. Swapping her scrubs for a sweater and leggings, Natalie grabbed her cell phone. Her fingers hovered over the icon of Jonah's smiling face, her heart doing an involuntary pirouette as she tapped out a quick text to let him know she'd be home late. She might be on her way to confess her snowballing attraction to him to two of their colleagues and friends, but there was no sense in making him worry.

Right. She was going to need extra wine.

Bags in hand and her heart taking up residence in her esophagus, Natalie knocked on the door to Charlie's apartment. Her heart relocated to her throat, proper, when Parker answered the door.

"Hey, Dr. Kendrick. Come on in," he said, reaching out to take the two reusable grocery bags from her grasp before stepping back to usher her inside. Of course, Parker was here, she chided herself. He *lived* here, for pity's sake. Normally, Natalie wouldn't care one whit if he hung out with her and Charlie and Tess during their monthly girls' night in, but since she was kiiiiiind of going to explode if she didn't tell Charlie and Tess about crushing on his freaking mentor badly enough to want to lose her virginity to him... yeah. Tonight might be just a teensy bit awkward.

"We're not in the ED," she said, in an effort to recover her wits. "You can call me Natalie, you know."

Parker paired his nod with an easy smile. "I know. Charlie and Tess are in the kitchen."

"Really?" Natalie asked in surprise, her cheeks burning as soon as the word slipped out.

But Parker just laughed. "You don't have to worry. They're not cooking anything. I think they're looking for wine glasses. Come on, I'll take you back."

"Thanks."

Following Parker through the apartment, they arrived in the kitchen a few seconds later, just in time to catch Tess unearthing a trio of wine glasses from a cupboard and Charlie snuggling Tess's three-month-old, Jackson, while singing the Baby Shark song in a silly voice, much to the baby's delight.

"You're going to scar that kid," Parker warned, putting the bags on the small island in the center of the kitchen before turning to kiss Charlie and take the baby from her grasp. "C'mere, little man. Let Uncle Parker save you from your crazy aunt."

"Hey, Natalie!" Charlie said, her green eyes sparkling as she gave up a warm hug to go with her greeting. To Parker, she said, "That song is very popular, I'll have you know."

Tess waved to Natalie, then rolled her eyes heavenward. "Also, the biggest earworm in the galaxy." Turning toward Parker, she added, "Are you sure about tonight?"

"One hundred percent," he said, holding up one of Jackson's chubby little hands and waving it at Tess. "Say 'bye to Mom for a little while."

At what must have been Natalie's perplexed expression, Charlie told her, "You called an emergency girls' night, so I called in reinforcements."

"I'm on cool-uncle babysitting duty," Parker elaborated, waiting until Tess kissed Jackson three times, then taking the baby over to the car seat carrier in the corner of the kitchen to buckle him in with care. "A-shift is on at Seventeen, so I'm going to take the little man out for a while. Give you ladies a chance to relax with no XY chromosomes around."

Natalie's belly panged with guilt. "You don't have to leave just because I asked for a girls' night in."

"I don't mind," Parker said, his tone marking the claim as entirely genuine. "Plus, those guys might talk a mean game, but you should see Hawk with babies. He freaking loves them. Quinn, too, and Slater practically raised his little sister, Hayley. I promise, Jackson will be in great hands—probably literally—all night."

Tess softened at the mention of the rescue squad lieutenant and Parker's former paramedic partner and her boyfriend/current paramedic partner, all of whom were part of the large circle of first responders and doctors who hung out at The Crooked Angel in their non-working hours. Still, she said, "Just be careful, would you?"

"I'll be in a house full of firefighters and paramedics, Tess. Come on." Parker shouldered the diaper bag Tess handed over like a boss. "You deserve a few hours off."

"Okay. But text me if you need *anything*."

"You know I will. Okay, dude." Parker picked up the car seat carrier. "Me, you, and pizza night at the fire house. Baby sharks optional." He winked at Charlie and kissed her quickly before turning back to the baby. "Let's do this."

As soon as the front door thumped shut, Natalie shrugged out of her jacket and looked at Charlie. "Parker is such a good guy."

"Yeah, he's totally getting laid later for that," Charlie said, her laughter mingling around Tess's snort.

"Like you wouldn't be having wild monkey sex with him tonight even if he hadn't taken my kid out for a couple of hours."

Charlie tilted her head in concession. "Fair enough."

Under normal circumstances, Natalie might have shifted the subject away from sex, or even dished up a smile and nod that implied that she wasn't, in fact, still hauling around her V-card. But tonight, she was all about not avoiding the topic.

Tess glanced at the door through which Parker had disappeared, her expression oddly wistful. "Well, I'm grateful Parker was willing to take Jackson for a little while. Alec is..."

Natalie's radar pinged full bore as Tess trailed off and Charlie made a rude noise in the back of her throat. "Is everything okay, Tess?" She knew things between Tess and her husband had been rocky lately, but she'd never seen her friend look anything other than completely fierce.

Tess squared her shoulders. "Well, shit. I guess people are going to find out about this sooner rather than later, and I'd rather the people I actually like hear it from me." She looked at Natalie. "Alec and I are separating."

"Oh, Tess." Natalie's breath rode out on her shock, and she crossed the kitchen to hug her friend. "I'm so sorry."

"Don't be," Tess said sensibly. Charlie looked unsurprised, so she must've already known, and Tess capped her words with a shrug. "I've been unhappy for a while now, and I've tried everything I can to get happy again, but Alec isn't interested in helping my cause. It's really the best option, for both me and Jackson, so...anyway. You sent up the Bat Signal. What's up?"

Natalie blinked. "Oh. I, uh. It's no big deal."

She couldn't possibly unload her to-sex-or-not-to-sex predicament on Tess and Charlie now. It would make her the worst friend ever.

But not only did Tess see right through her, she also wasn't having it. "Oh, no, you don't. You've never sent out a cry for help in the three years I've known you, and anyway, I've been doing nothing but thinking about my crummy soon-to-be-ex and diapers for the past month. You're doing me a favor by distracting me from The Jackass Formerly Known as My Husband. Trust me."

Well, when she put it that way... "Maybe we should, um, have some wine?"

"I'll drink to that," Charlie said. She busied herself with the corkscrew and one of the bottles of Malbec that Natalie had grabbed on her way over. A minute later, they all had nice, full glasses in hand, and Tess—being Tess—got right to it.

"Okay, Pixie Stick. Spill."

Right. Natalie was smart. Articulate. Honest. How hard could this be?

She took a gulp of wine and blurted, "I think I want to have wild monkey sex with Jonah. Like, *badly*."

Charlie and Tess froze simultaneously, both of their mouths falling open in very obvious surprise.

"Okaaay, this conversation is going to require more liquor," Charlie finally said, reaching for the second bottle of wine that Natalie had brought.

"And chips," Tess declared, tugging them free from the grocery bag.

Charlie nodded. "Don't skimp on the queso, Michaelson."

Tess raised a brow while Natalie gulped more wine. "You insult me." Popping open the chips and queso, she finally smiled at Natalie. "So, you want to do the deed with Sheridan, huh? What prompted *that* after all this time?"

So, so much to unpack there. "It's, um, kind of a long story," Natalie said.

"We have time. And wine." Charlie nudged a nearby bar stool in Natalie's direction, then slid into another one while Tess did the same. "And this is a no-judgment zone."

Natalie bit her lip and engaged in a giant game of chicken with her nerve, which won by a hair. "Oh, good. I guess this is a great time to tell you guys I'm still a virgin, then."

"You're a virgin? As in..." Tess's eyes widened across the kitchen island.

"I've never had actual sex with anyone."

She dove into the same story she'd given Jonah a week

ago, telling them both about her sheltered teen years and her work-focused college experience. The words tumbled out with more ease than she'd expected, both of her friends listening genuinely, and by the time she'd loosened all the details, her pulse had returned to normal.

"That makes perfect sense," Charlie said, reaching across the island to squeeze Natalie's hand. "And honestly, I think it's pretty cool that you didn't just have sex for the sake of having sex. Most people wouldn't have stuck to their principles."

"Well, yeah, but I still haven't ever *had* sex," Natalie pointed out. "And I'm thirty-two."

Tess eyed her over the rim of her wine glass. "So, why now? I mean, I'm not knocking your choice to take the plunge. Believe me, I'm all for it if you want to consensually trade orgasms with someone like baseball cards. But something's got to be behind this desire to finally go for it."

"You mean, other than the fact that I'm horny and curious and so, so ready?" Natalie gave up a wry smile, but it didn't last. "All this time, I've just been waiting for someone I trust. I guess I feel like Jonah is that guy. And living with him made me really realize that I'm attracted to him on top of that trust."

"Familiarity breeds temptation," Charlie said, lifting her wine glass in salute.

"Okay, but I'm not quite sure how to ask him," Natalie said. "I can't exactly pop off with, 'great weather we've been having lately, and, oh, by the way, I'd really love it if you'd let me take off your pants.'"

Tess pulled the bowl of chips closer and laughed. "Probably not your best tactic, although, not the worst I've ever heard, either. Still, this is you and Jonah. He's not some random guy. He knows you're still carrying your V-card, right?"

Natalie thought of the conversation and the kiss that happened afterward, her skin prickling with involuntary heat. "Yeah."

Charlie nodded. "So, maybe honesty is your best policy. He's not going to want you to give it up to some cretin on Tinder, and he's not exactly shy when it comes to sex. If you tell him what you just told us about being curious and ready, and you legit ask him to help you out, he might be game."

"That makes it sound like a business transaction," Natalie said.

"Do you want to lose your virginity or not?" Tess asked, and okay, she had a point.

"Under the right circumstances, I do."

"And you obviously find Jonah attractive enough to make that work."

Tess had barely finished her sentence when Charlie choked on her wine. "Have you gone blind recently? Of course he's attractive enough."

Natalie's brain chose that moment to cough up the oh-so-vivid memory of Jonah's abs, and she fought her blush for the second time in as many minutes. "I am attracted to him, yes. But more importantly, I trust him. I don't need him to love me, or anything, and I'm not in love with him," she added quickly. "I don't want a relationship with him. But we, um, kissed last week, and—"

"Wait." Tess held up a hand. "You *kissed* The Orgasm Whisperer? Jesus, Nat! You could've led with that, you know."

"I was getting to it. And the what?" The *Orgasm* Whisperer?

"Nothing," Charlie said, shooting a warning glance at Tess.

Who promptly ignored it. "It's just that Jonah kind of has a reputation. What?" she asked Charlie, whose glance had grown into a frown. "It's not like she doesn't know that Jonah totally gets around."

"I do know," Natalie said. The thought, which had never bothered her before, made her feel a little queasy now that it was front and center. But she had to be sensible about this. "And yes, Jonah and I kissed, and yes, it was..."

"Dreamy?" Charlie asked.

"Steamy?" Tess asked.

"Really, really hot," Natalie admitted, unable to keep her smile under wraps. "There was definite chemistry."

Tess waved her hand in a gimme motion. "Oh, my God, woman. I have cobwebs in my pants! Details. I need details!"

"There's not a whole lot to tell other than that. We were talking, one thing led to another and we kissed, but we got interrupted. Then he kind of pulled back."

Both women groaned on her behalf. "There's nothing like coitus interruptus," Tess said, a rare flush moving over her cheeks as she added, "Or maybe just interruptus. Sorry."

"Honestly, I don't really know that it wouldn't have gotten there if we hadn't been interrupted. It was *that* hot," Natalie said.

"But now Jonah's acting like it didn't happen? Like a friend zone kind of thing?" Charlie asked, and Natalie shook her head. She'd given this a shit-ton of thought over the past couple of days. She knew Jonah. Could read his facial expressions from a nautical mile away. His body language, too. There was no denying that what he said he wanted and what she saw beneath the surface didn't add up.

He was feeling *something* about what had happened

between them, and whatever it was, he was going to great lengths to hide it.

"See, that's just it. I don't think Jonah wants me in the friend zone. I think he's attracted to me, too," she said. "I mean, he's trying to act like business as usual. But there's this heat between us now that was never there before. He looks at me just a beat longer than he used to, even a couple of weeks ago. If we touch by accident, like the other day when we both reached for the coffeepot at the same time and our hands bumped? He lets out this breath like he's trying to fight the same attraction I feel. You couldn't cut the sexual tension in his apartment with a hacksaw, and I'm telling you, that kiss was..."

"Dreamy," Charlie murmured.

"Steamy," Tess murmured.

"Like a promise," Natalie said, making her friends give up twin happy-sighs. "And even though he's trying to be all status quo with me now, there's no *way* he didn't feel it, too."

Charlie reached for the bottle of wine and topped off everyone's glasses, her head tilted in thought. "Jonah might have a hell of a reputation for being a serial bachelor, but he's also a good guy."

"That's true," Tess mused. "Even if he's into you—and it sounds like he totally is—if he thinks it would wreck your friendship to screw around, I bet he'd try to fight it."

Oh. Natalie had to admit, it made sense. Sort of. "Okay, but I haven't made any secret about the fact that I've been wanting to, um..."

"Find someone to punch your V-card?" Tess volunteered, and both Natalie and Charlie laughed.

Charlie chided, "Tess."

"Fine." Tess took a sip of wine and waggled her brows at Natalie. "Tend to your lady garden."

"Have sex with," Charlie said.

"Yes," Natalie told them both. "I mean, I got Mallory's brother's number and everything." Not that she'd used it, or that he'd texted her, either. "It seems pretty obvious that I want to get it on with somebody."

Tess shook her head. "You said you wanted to date, though. That's very different than casual sex, *especially* to a guy like Jonah."

Natalie opened her mouth. Closed it. Then opened it again to utter a very eloquent, "Fuck."

Charlie giggled. "If that's your goal, then I think Tess is right. You're probably going to have to be straight with him. But if you're both attracted to each other and you're both honest about your expectations, and all you want is casual sex..."

"Then there's no reason not to get any," Tess finished. "Or at least give it a shot."

Natalie's heart beat faster at the thought, then faster still as she realized they were right. She and Jonah had always been honest with each other. It was a huge part of what made their friendship work so well, and an even huger part of why she genuinely liked him.

She did trust him. She did want to have sex with him. She knew she wasn't imagining all the signs that he wanted her, too.

Putting everything out on the table made sense.

"Okay," Natalie said slowly. "So, let's just say that, hypothetically, I tell him all of this and he's on board. Then what?"

"Like, logistically?" Charlie asked, and Natalie gave up a semi-hesitant nod.

"I'm not horribly inexperienced, and obviously, I know what'll happen in the anatomical sense." She'd delivered more babies by emergency C-section than she could even count, for cripes' sake. She knew darned well how each and every one of them had gotten in there, even if she'd had to take them out. "But there *is* the Orgasm Whisperer thing, and I'm not exactly brimming with firsthand knowledge, here. I don't want to look like a complete idiot. So, hit me. What do I need to know?"

Tess's snort was all irony. "You might not want to ask me. I have far too many weeds in my lady garden to be giving out decent advice."

"Okay, but at least you've *had* sex. Which means you have a whole lot more to go on than I do," Natalie pointed out. "So, really. Help me out."

"Condoms," they both said simultaneously, and Natalie nodded.

"Given." She'd at least gotten that far, having swiped a few from the clinic across from the hospital, where she volunteered a few times a month. "For Jonah, too, I'd imagine."

"I think the most important thing other than that is to try to relax and let things happen naturally," Charlie offered. "You're into him, he's into you. Unless you accidentally knee him in the hey-nannies or something, you're not going to screw it up."

Natalie swallowed hard. She thought she'd be worried enough about her vagina. Now she had to worry about her knees accidentally connecting with Jonah's balls, too?

"You could always try reading one of Connor's romance novels for a few tips," Tess said, and Charlie brightened.

"I have a new one in my room! Hang on."

Okay, so this wasn't a bad idea. Natalie did enjoy romance novels, and it had been a while since she'd been able to sit down with a pleasure-read.

"Here you go," Charlie said a few seconds later, handing over a book with a photo of a very ripped, very tattooed shirtless guy on the cover.

"Holy crap. Is this guy even for real?" Natalie let her eyes take an appreciative second trip over the front of the book.

Tess grinned. "Who, Muscles Marinara? Apparently, he's very real. He and Connor are, like, best friends. They were in the Air Force together."

"Wow." The guy might not be Natalie's usual cuppa, but he was definitely cover-worthy.

"Right?" Charlie said. "Anyway, all the good scenes are dog-eared. I'm pretty sure you'd have to be a professional gymnast to do the thing in Chapter Eighteen. I mean, the heroine in the book *is* a professional gymnast, so there's that, but...anyway, all I'm saying is maybe don't start out there."

"But the Chapter Seven thing is hot," Tess said, prompting Charlie to nod.

"And the Chapter Thirteen thing? Works like a charm."

"You dirty bitch!" Tess laughed. "You did the Chapter Thirteen thing?"

Charlie gave up an angelic smile. "Twice."

Natalie couldn't help it. She opened the book. Found Chapter Thirteen. And... "Whoa. I will never look at Drake the same way again."

As if she could sense the layer of hesitation beneath Natalie's joke, Charlie took the book and put it on the island. "Natalie, look. You don't have to use the book, or anything else, as a checklist. Having a great experience in bed with someone is all about doing what feels good for the two of *you*. You know yourself, and you trust Jonah. He'll have your back."

"And your front," Tess said with an encouraging smile.

"As far as finding the right person to take your virginity, I don't think you could do any better."

"Really," Charlie agreed. "Don't worry about anything other than that."

Natalie nodded. "Okay."

Although she knew Charlie and Tess were right, and she also had no reservations about what she wanted, she also knew it was going to be tough not to worry at all. The Chapter Thirteen thing seemed a little over-zealous, and now she was going to be overly cautious about keeping her knees far, far away from Jonah's anatomy. Plus, now there was this Orgasm Whisperer thing to contend with. Jonah had a metric ton of experience, and she had a whopping none.

But their kiss had worked out just fine on its own (okay, if by fine, she really meant warning-label hot). The rest would probably happen the same way.

Now, all Natalie had to do was ask him to take her virginity.

12

Natalie stared at the door to her/Jonah's apartment and damn near balked. The courage from her one and only glass of wine had long since evaporated, even though the rest of her evening with Tess and Charlie (during which they'd both repeatedly assured her they'd never once knocked a potential bedmate out of commission by accidentally kneeing him in the nuts) had actually been fun and relaxing. But now that she was home, her pulse kicked a rapid rhythm against her throat.

No. *No.* She couldn't walk away. She'd made up her mind. She wanted this. She wanted Jonah. It was now or never.

And never wasn't an option.

Taking a deep breath, Natalie put her key in the lock and made her way inside the apartment. The sight of Jonah sprawled on the couch, casually watching a basketball game, did nothing to calm her racing heart, and the way his T-shirt hugged his lean, well-defined muscles with just enough suggestion for her to picture them sans cotton did everything to make the space between her legs turn hot and damp.

"Hey," he said, reaching for the remote and muting the TV. "I didn't think you'd be home so early."

Natalie slid out of her jacket and rummaged for a smile, semi-surprised when it came easily. "Yeah. Tess had the baby with her, so she had to get moving to get him to bed, and I wanted to give Parker and Charlie at least *some* of their Friday night together, so here I am."

"You want to watch some hoops? There are leftover wings in the fridge," Jonah offered, pushing up to standing. Oh, God, he was in jeans *and* barefoot? How much freaking sexier could one man be?

It's just Jonah. You can do this.

She sent another deep breath down the hatch. "Actually, I was hoping to talk to you about something. But you have to promise to hear me out."

"I'm not budging on those rom coms, Kendrick. I mean it," he said, giving her a smile that said he really didn't.

Natalie's nerves released another ounce of their grip on her as she smiled back. "A) you're giving rom coms a bad rap. And secondly, that's not what I wanted to talk to you about."

"Okay. Shoot. What's up?"

Her heartbeat pressed against her ears, but still, she said, "It's about what happened last Friday night. When we kissed."

Jonah froze to his spot beside the couch, his easygoing expression turning instantly serious. "Nat, I'm so sorry. I know I already said it, but I was way, way out of line, and—"

"No, Jonah. You really weren't."

His blond brows traveled up. "What?"

"You weren't out of line." Natalie stepped toward him,

the truth taking precedence over the last of her butterflies. "We're two single, consenting adults. You kissed me, and I kissed you back, and it was...well, it was a really good kiss."

"It was," Jonah agreed slowly, and Natalie continued before her newfound calm could have a chance to recede.

"Which brings me to what I wanted to talk to you about. You and I are close, and we're obviously"—*hot together. So. Very. Hot together*—"physically compatible," she managed past her blush. "I'm really comfortable with you, and just as importantly, I trust you."

Now or never, came the whisper from her brain as she paused for a breath. But oh, Natalie didn't just want him.

She wanted him now, so she said, "You're kind of everything I've been looking for when it comes to losing my virginity, so I was hoping that you might consider having sex with me."

JONAH WAS as stunned speechless by the question Natalie had just asked him as he was the internal *fucking-A, YES!* that had just taken the slingshot route from his cock to his brain. He took a second—or maybe it was a year—to try and displace some of his shock, but yeah, no. Just not happening.

"You want me to take your virginity," he finally said, and she nodded, her cheeks flushed to a perfect, pretty pink that didn't help his resolve.

"Yes. I do."

Despite her blush, she seemed completely unequivocal, her answer clear and concise. But this was her first time they were talking about. There would never be another one.

"I've never done that before," Jonah said. "Not even

when I was a virgin." Even in high school, his girlfriends had always been older, and more experienced.

"Okay, so it would be something new for both of us," Natalie said, her bright-side enthusiasm tempting him to smile.

He could *not* be considering this. "It's not even close to the same thing."

"Okay, maybe it's not," Natalie agreed. "But I've given this a lot of thought, and I meant what I said last week. I don't need a whole bunch of hearts and flowers in order to have sex with someone, even for the first time. But I do want to do it with someone I trust, and I'm ready. God, it's why I told Mallory I'd meet his brother in the first place."

A feeling Jonah couldn't describe and didn't quite recognize snapped through his chest. "You want to have sex with Mallory's brother?"

Her laughter shocked the hell out of him, and damn, she was beautiful. "No, dummy. I want to have sex with *you*. My point is, I'm looking for someone who I like and trust, not some random stranger. I'm curious, and ready, and for the love of God, I've been a virgin for*ever*. I'm ready to not be one anymore, and I want to not be one with you."

Jonah opened his mouth to argue that he wasn't the right guy for the job, but somehow, he couldn't. He thought of Mallory's brother—sure, Mallory was a decent guy, a little bit cocky, maybe, but then again, that was probably a pot/kettle situation, coming from Jonah. The guy's brother was probably cool enough, and probably the kind of man Natalie *should* be propositioning with this sort of thing. One who she at least had a shot of ending up with, happily ever after, like she eventually wanted.

But the thought of her giving up her virginity to Mallory's brother made Jonah want to slice the guy's nuts off with a ten blade. Which was honestly insane, since he'd never even clapped eyes on him. But as irrational as the emotion was, Jonah recognized it as jealousy, and he knew it could only stem from one thing.

He wanted to have sex with Natalie. He'd wanted her the night her bathtub had caved in, although he hadn't been able to admit it. He'd wanted her when they'd kissed, and he wanted her now. He wanted to know what other parts of her flushed when she was aroused, and what the spot between her neck and her shoulder tasted like. He wanted to know what she sounded like the second she was done coming, and he wanted to be the one who got her there. In fact, he'd never wanted anyone so much.

And he was tired of trying to fight it.

"Okay," Jonah said.

"Okay," Natalie repeated. "As in, yes?"

She looked at him, her gold-blond lashes fanned upward in surprise. But then she smiled a big, beautiful, wide-open smile of happiness, and okay, yeah, Jonah was going to need to get a handle on this, quick.

"I have a couple of conditions, though," he said, and her forehead creased in confusion.

"I already told you, I don't expect a relationship or anything. I just want—"

Jonah shook his head. "I know what you want, but if you want *me* to give it to you, I'm going to do it right."

"Okay." She drew the word out like a question, and he didn't hesitate to answer it.

"First, let's get the obvious out of the way. If you change your mind at any point—"

Now it was her turn to cut him off. "I won't."

"*If* you do, you need to tell me," he insisted. "No matter what."

Her frown became that sweetly fierce thing that he found so fucking appealing, it was damn near unfair. "Do you really think I'd have propositioned you if I didn't want to have sex with you? It's not like I haven't thought this through."

"Promise me, Nat. Or we're not even having a conversation, let alone sex."

"Okay, okay. I promise. If I change my mind, I'll tell you."

Her tone labeled the words as genuine, but it was really just an added bonus. Jonah knew she'd never lie about something this big.

"Good," he said. "Next, we should talk about birth control." Not the sexiest topic, he knew, but also not one he was leaving up in the air. Or, worse yet, for the heat of the moment, when his upstairs head would want to show far less restraint than the situation required.

Apparently, Natalie wasn't leaving it to chance, either. "Oh, no, we're good. I have condoms. Just because I'm not sure if I can get pregnant doesn't mean I want to go testing the theory."

"That makes two of us." Jonah paused. This last one was the biggest of his three deal-breakers, and even though they'd already touched on it, he needed to be one hundred-percent sure she understood.

"This has to be completely casual," he continued. "No promises, no commitments, like you said. It has nothing to do with you. I'm just not a long-haul guy. So, if you think us having sex would ruin our friendship or get weird for you, I need to know that, Natalie."

His heartbeat sounded off like thunder in his ears. Jonah knew that sleeping with her wouldn't mess with things on his end. In fact, it would probably solve a thing or two by getting the unexpected attraction he'd been feeling for the last two weeks out of his system, once and for freaking all. But if having sex with her would unravel their friendship— or, hell, make her want more than their friendship—he couldn't say yes. No matter how badly he wanted to.

Fuck. He *really* wanted to.

After what felt like an eon, Natalie said, "I never would've asked if I thought for a second that it would change a thing. Our friendship means more to me than that."

Jonah exhaled the breath that had been spackled to his lungs. It took mere seconds for his body to get the message, his blood quickly tearing a southerly path to his cock.

"Okay, then." He looked at her from across the living room, the soft light filtering down from overhead making her eyes glint like whiskey in a cut-crystal tumbler. "Come here."

Her bow-shaped lips opened on a soundless gasp. "You, uh. You want to just, like, go for it right now? Is that how it works?"

Good Christ, she was adorable. "Sometimes," he said, although, really, for him, it was damn near always. He'd honed the whole thing down to a science—the flirting, the foreplay. The fucking and the farewell, all within a span of hours. But Natalie trusted him to take her virginity. Yeah, it was no strings attached, but he was still going to do it properly.

She wanted pleasure, and that's exactly what she was going to get.

"That's not how I want it to work with you, though. Not tonight."

"Okay." Her expression eased, just as Jonah had intended it to. "Then how *do* you want it to work?"

He tilted his head at the couch, waiting until she crossed

the room and sat down on one side before he clicked off the basketball game and sat beside her. "I'd like to get to know you a little before we actually have sex."

Natalie laughed, long and loud. "You already know me. Maybe better than anyone." Kicking off her boots, she tucked her sock-feet beneath her and looked at him.

"Not like that. Like this." Jonah moved closer, lifting a hand and trailing his fingers over her sweater-encased arm. The fabric was thin and soft, gliding under his fingertips with just enough friction to make them both shiver. "I want to know what you like. What you don't like. What you need."

"Oh." The word collapsed past her lips on a sigh. "I suppose that sort of getting to know each other is probably smart."

"You weren't wrong about that kiss," he told her. His fingers traveled higher now, to her shoulder, then the spot where the sweater surrendered to warm, smooth skin. "It was pretty hot."

"I haven't been able to stop thinking about it." Natalie leaned in to his touch, subtly, but it was enough.

Score one for the things she likes category. Jonah let the contact with her collarbone linger, partly because she liked it, and partly because *he* liked that she liked it, and wasn't that just one more thing he hadn't expected.

Damn it, he needed to focus, and not on himself or any of his freaking feelings. He might want this to be good for her, but they were still just motions. Anyway, this wasn't about *him* at all.

"So, if I kissed you again, maybe this time, like this"—he hooked his index finger beneath her chin, tipping it up and brushing his mouth over hers, just for a beat—"you'd think about that, too?"

"Mmm hmm," Natalie murmured, all throat and breath.

His cock jerked to attention, but he took a steady inhale to counter the urgency with which it wanted to work. "And this?"

Another slide of his lips across hers, this one equally soft but lasting a little longer, allowing him to taste her just enough to draw a sigh out of her before he pulled back.

Natalie nodded, her whispered "yes" filling the barely there space between their mouths hotly.

Oh hell, it was going to take all the self-control Jonah had—along with some he didn't—to make it through this without exploding.

Especially when she fanned her lashes up to look him right in the eye. "Yes, but..."

Every last one of Jonah's muscles froze until she finished with, "I want more."

And that was it. Three tiny words, a half a breath's worth of syllables, and something inside of him snapped like a thread. Pressing forward, he covered her mouth with his, pushing past her lips to slide their tongues together. But Natalie angled up at the same time he moved, their bodies crashing into one another gracelessly before their arms ended up in a tangle and they both started to laugh.

"I'm sorry," Jonah said, his lips still on hers even through the laughter. "That didn't exactly go the way I envisioned it."

"Me, either." Natalie kissed him, soft and quick. "But it's okay. I guess it's all part of the learning curve."

Readjusting, Jonah slid his hands beneath her arms, guiding her back over the couch cushions. "Let's try this," he said, lying on his side next to her. The new positioning gave his mouth fantastic access to hers and his hands the opportunity to roam, and oh *hell* yeah, he took both.

"This is good," she murmured as he kissed a path over her neck, and he couldn't help it. He laughed again.

"Just good?" He nudged higher to taste the delicate hinge of her jaw. Trace her outer ear with his tongue. Follow with the slightest hint of his teeth, and there. *There* it was.

Natalie moaned. "So good."

Her spine bowed up, and Jonah met her rising body with his free hand. The playfulness between them grew into something deeper, the same back-and-forth that had made their first kiss so sexy resurfacing as if it had just been waiting for the chance. He returned to her mouth, exploring with his lips and teeth and tongue, memorizing her replies. His fingers, which had settled in at her hip, slid up to the indent of her waist, her sweater soft but her skin softer as he lifted the material just enough to bare the bottom of her rib cage.

Jesus, she was killing him with those little sighs. But when she reached out with *her* free hand to push her fingers beneath his shirt, holding him close in return? Yeah, he didn't even have a name for what *that* was doing to him.

But he did know a feeling that deep, strong enough to rattle his bones in less than a breath, was dangerous as fuck.

The realization made Jonah freeze. Natalie stilled in turn, her fingers tightening over his lower back.

"Are my hands cold?" she asked, and he shook his head.

"No. I like it when you touch me." He pressed his hips against her thigh, just hard enough for her to feel the proof of his honesty, then reached back to grasp her fingers and return them to her side.

"Wait, I'm confused," Natalie said. "If you like it, then why do you want me to stop?"

He dipped his head to kiss her for a long minute before replying. "So I can concentrate on you."

"But what about you?"

"I'm right here," Jonah told her.

She frowned, just a tiny downward tilt of her kiss-swollen lips. "No, I mean, I want to get to know you, too. I want to learn what *you* like."

Jonah was tempted to let the irony in his chest emerge on a laugh. God, she wasn't like anyone he'd ever been with, the scores of women who were more than happy to lie back and let him pleasure them sixty ways to Sunday. But Jonah had to make this about Natalie.

It couldn't be about him, and it damn sure couldn't be about that feeling that had shot through him when she'd held him close.

So he went with an approximation of the truth. "We'll get to me soon enough. But for tonight, what I like, what I want"—he paused to kiss her—"what is turning me on more than you will ever know, is learning you."

Natalie nodded, albeit tentatively. "Okay. As long as you promise I'll get a turn to make you feel good, too."

A dark smile twitched at the edges of his mouth. "I promise I'm going to enjoy every second of being with you."

Now *that*, he fucking meant. After all, she was gorgeous, and if there was one thing Jonah was good at, it was pleasure.

Starting with hers.

Kissing her with renewed purpose, he moved his hand back to the sliver of skin he'd bared over the waistband of her leggings. He stroked higher, mapping her navel—a ridiculously hot cross between an innie and an outie—her rib cage, and her side with his touch. Natalie moved right along with him, arching into the contact and exhaling her approval when he reached the lacy fabric of her bra.

Make that the *pink* lacy fabric, and fucking hell. He

should've known the damned thing would look a trillion times sexier on her than hanging over his dryer.

"Off," Jonah demanded, his voice emerging from his throat as if it needed a good sanding. "I want to look at you."

Wide-eyed, Natalie complied without pause. She reached down to hook her fingers over the hem of her sweater, and Jonah helped her remove it in one economical tug. The lace cradled her breasts, and the sweet suggestion of her darker pink nipples showing from behind it made his cock throb behind the fly of his jeans.

"Like this?" she asked, glancing down at herself dubiously.

Jonah kissed her, maybe harder than he would've otherwise. But he wanted her full attention. "You don't know how beautiful you are, do you?"

"I..." She trailed off, and he shook his head.

"You are. And I want to show you, so keep your eyes wide open and watch."

To his surprise, Natalie did. Propping her chin to her chest, her gaze followed his fingers over her body, widening as he cupped one breast, then fluttering closed as he slid his thumb over the peak of her nipple.

"Watch," he demanded. It was bossier than his usual sexy talk, but his cock jumped as she opened her eyes and did as he'd said.

"So pretty." Another pass of his thumb had her moaning, her spine arching up to work in rhythm with his touch. "Do you see how pretty you are?"

"Yes," Natalie murmured. Her eyes were fixed on his fingers, as if she was powerless to look away, and Jonah took full advantage of her attention. Pulling the lace aside, he freed her nipple, his heart pulsing in anticipation of taking a taste.

He trailed a line of kisses from her neck over the flat of her chest, even though the slowness damn near slayed him. Natalie seemed to catalogue every move, her exhales growing in intensity until he finally, blessedly, closed his lips around her tightly peaked nipple.

She cried out at the same time that he groaned, and truly, he had no idea which one of them was more turned on. Her fingers found the back of his head, knotting in his hair in encouragement. Not that Jonah needed an ounce of the stuff. Nope.

From the second he'd put his mouth on her, he'd known he wasn't going to stop until she came.

"Ohhhh." Natalie's sigh was more vibration than actual word, and Jonah let it move all the way through him before tightening his lips and letting his tongue in on the action.

Her sigh became something else entirely, some sound he'd never heard her make. It seemed to surprise her for a second, lifting upward into a gasp before she punctuated it with a bite of her lip.

Well, they couldn't have that. "I can't learn you if you don't let me," Jonah said, the words rumbling over her skin. Her nipple was flushed and glistening from his ministrations, the contrast of pink on pink with the surrounding lace so sexy, he knew he'd be thinking of it later, when he lay in bed with his fingers wrapped hard around his cock.

Not yet. "So, if you like something. Like this," he said, tracing the edge of her nipple with the very tip of his tongue, and bingo. Another sigh. "You don't have to let me know with words. But I *do* want to know."

"I like that," Natalie said, her sudden boldness taking him by surprise.

But oh, it turned him on. "Let's see what else you like."

Returning his mouth to her nipple, Jonah tested out

everything, from soft glides of his tongue to far more purposeful tugs with his lips. His fingers joined in, freeing her other breast from its triangle of lace to give it the same treatment, steady and hot, and Natalie arched into every move. Jonah committed each murmur and moan to memory, until finally, she lifted her hips in a wordless search for contact that he couldn't help but give.

He slid his hand from her breast to her belly, then to her hip. Her leggings surrendered to her modest curves—she wasn't built like a pinup girl, but there was far too much strength in her sweetness for Jonah to worry he'd break her.

"Yes. Please, yes," she whispered, her head thrown back, her golden hair a wild frame for her angelic face. Her knees widened in clear invitation. "Please touch me, Jonah."

His name in her mouth was like sweetness and sin, and no force in the universe could keep him from complying. Curling his fingers over her waistband, he moved past the stretchy fabric, then past a swath of lace that—ah, fuck him —matched her bra.

But then he reached the soft, wet skin beneath the fabric, and he forgot the panties, his name, and how to goddamn breathe.

"Jesus." Jonah's cock jerked in pure envy of his fingers, his heart beating insistently as Natalie moaned and canted her hips in search of more contact.

He gave it. Sliding his index finger over the seam of her body, he pressed upward, until her heated intake of breath told him he'd found exactly what he'd been looking for.

"There," she gasped. But he was already ahead of her, reading her body and stroking slow circles over the firm knot of her clit.

"Keep showing me," he told her, his forearm firm over the flat of her belly. His hand was covered by cotton and lace, his fingers shielded from view even as he moved them more wickedly through her slickness, and a forbidden thrill shot through him at the suggestion of what he couldn't see. A shard of worry cut through Jonah's chest as Natalie reached down to grab his wrist, but the feeling became something else entirely when he realized she hadn't done it to stop him.

She'd done it in encouragement.

"More." Her fingers moved from his wrist to the clothes that, while sexy, were hindering what she clearly wanted. Jonah didn't break contact with her body—he wasn't fucking crazy—but he did shift to let her lower her leggings and panties far enough to give him better access and her the freedom to move.

God, she was unbelievably sexy, laid bare like this. She flushed and looked away as if he'd spoken out loud, but oh no. *Hell* no. He wasn't about to let her believe anything other than the truth.

"You are beautiful," he told her. He circled her clit, his fingers sliding with ease, and she sighed in proof. "See?"

Her whiskey-colored stare caught his and held. "You make me feel beautiful."

Jonah gave in to the dark part of himself that had wanted to make her come since the minute she'd moved into his apartment. This, he was good at. This, he knew how to do.

This might be all he could give her, but he *would* give it.

"By the time I'm done with you, you're going to feel like a fucking goddess," he said. Stroking firmly, he adjusted the pace of his fingers to the cadence of her sighs, slow at first, then increasing in speed. Natalie moved with him, lifting her hips and seeking his touch, her thighs falling wide. Jonah slipped his index finger lower, letting his thumb take its place over her clit as he pushed slowly deeper, into her pussy. Her inner muscles clasped his finger with wet heat, and Jesus, she was so tight, the feel of her was going to end him.

"Oh, God." Her voice was like gravel and silk, both sultry and sweet. For a split second, instinct dared him to yank off his jeans, to bury his cock inside of her and fuck her until they were both good and sweaty and spent. But this wasn't about him—it couldn't be about him—so instead, he focused on Natalie. He circled her clit with steadfast pressure, pulling back with his finger only to push back inside a fraction deeper, then repeating the movement again, and again. She thrust up to meet every forward push, quickly creating a rhythm between them. When he added a second finger, she let go of a pleasured cry. When he turned his wrist in search of the hidden spot deep in her pussy that would take her over the edge—right...*there*—her breath caught on a keening sigh. Her inner muscles went even tighter, making Jonah's cock throb in demand, but he didn't stop.

"That's it, Natalie." He thrust again, reading her and daring her and pleasuring her all at once. "Let me make you feel good. Let go for me."

Her hips jerked up, locking his fingers deep inside of her as she came undone around him. Her pussy clenched and released, squeezing him in waves that made his cock so hard, it nearly hurt. Need flew through Jonah, dangerous and dark, and it took all of his power to deny it.

He had to stick to what he was good at. What he knew.

What would keep him safe.

So he took Natalie through every wave of her pleasure, making sure to maximize each sensation and tremor. He scaled back on his touches second by second, until finally, her sighs had turned to slow, soft exhales.

And then he gently righted her clothes, kissed the top of her head as he wished her goodnight, and pictured her face in the shadows of his bedroom as he made himself come harder than he ever had with only three swift strokes.

13

Natalie was dreaming. She knew, because she was floating, her body warm and weightless. Jonah was there, his face hard to see, but his voice right there in her ear, velvety and thick, like honey, calling her a goddess. She wanted to laugh. Her brain knew she should— the thought was crazy, the stuff of fantasies. But this *was* a fantasy, a dream where she was as beautiful as Jonah had said, her name in his mouth like a prayer. Only, when his face came into view, his blue eyes were dark with some emotion Natalie couldn't name, and he tumbled out of her reach, falling further and further away as her body grew heavier, weariness creeping in and taking over as she reached for Jonah, then reached again...

And woke with a start, face-down on his futon.

"Uggggh." She released her groan into her pillow, not wanting her voice to filter through the wall she shared with Jonah, in case he was still sleeping. Her eyes were heavy with the remnants of deep sleep, her body still pressed so firmly against the sheets that she'd be shocked if she hadn't left a weary outline imprinted in the cotton. A tiny thread of soreness squeezed between her legs, heating her face and sending a very big, very involuntary smile across her mouth.

Orgasm Whisperer, *indeed*.

Burrowing deeper under the blankets for a stolen second, Natalie let herself relive everything that had happened between her and Jonah after she'd gotten home from Charlie's last night. Despite the fact that she'd been certain her fledgling attraction to him had been mutual, part of her had been stunned he'd said yes when she'd asked him to take her virginity. Of course, she *had* been both logical and convincing, and his stipulations had covered all the potential sticking points. Natalie hadn't expected a trial run on his couch, and while she trusted Jonah enough to know he'd do all that he could to make her first true sexual encounter a positive one, she definitely hadn't expected the intensity that had accompanied their little getting-to-know-you session.

The transition from the man who'd been her best friend for three years to the man who'd agreed to seduce her had been more seamless than Natalie had expected, she mused from under the covers. Nothing awkward between them. No urge to giggle or get shy when he'd leaned in to kiss her mouth. When he'd moved lower, sparking a need deep in her body that she'd never known could exist. When he'd touched her so intimately, yet so hotly that she'd flown apart —God, even when he'd set her clothes back into place after she'd come, it had all been so easy and familiar and *Jonah*.

And she'd liked it.

No. That wasn't quite right.

She'd wanted him so badly, it took her breath away.

Welcome to the part she really hadn't expected. Yes, she was curious, and definitely yes, she was turned on. But when Jonah had touched her, Natalie's want had been more profound than simple arousal. She'd needed...something, although she still wasn't sure how to quantify it. She'd gotten close to it, oddly, not when Jonah had made her come (more intensely than she ever had in her life, BTW), but when he'd talked to her. He'd called her sweetheart and said she was beautiful, and they might have just been terms of endearment, all part of the process designed to give her the pleasure he'd promised, but in that moment, Natalie had felt them. She'd felt cared for. *Seen.*

Which was completely whack-a-doo. Yes, she was attracted to Jonah. Yes, she trusted him, and dear sweet Jesus, yes, he came by that Orgasm Whisperer thing honestly. But they'd agreed it would just be sex.

And if last night was any indication, it was going to be seriously *great* sex. She'd get what she'd asked for, then she'd be able to move on and find someone to date with the experience under her belt (so to speak), and without the weirdness of her virginity hanging over it all.

You are beautiful...see...

Natalie rolled over, taking one last minute to savor the warmth of the covers and the chance to rest. But then the light trying to poke past the window blinds registered, the ripple of confusion running the length of her spine quickly turning to alarm as she grabbed her cell phone and checked the time.

"Shit!" Natalie's heart thwacked against her breastbone. How could she have slept this late? She might sleep like the dead once she crashed, but her body had a flawless internal clock. She never overslept for something important, *ever.*

Except, apparently, today.

Whipping the covers back and stumbling out of futon-landia—ugh, her muscles were achy, too?—she flew across the hall to grab her toothbrush, then hustled toward the kitchen in search of the caffeine jolt she obviously needed. Jonah stood at the kitchen counter in a pair of sweatpants and a compression T-shirt that suggested he'd already been to the gym, his brows lifting up as she rapidly brushed her teeth with one hand and reached for a coffee mug with the other.

"Whoa, where's the fire?"

"I oeuhflap."

"Okay, that can't be English," he said, reaching for the coffeepot and filling the mug she'd taken from the cupboard.

Natalie rolled her eyes, mostly at herself, and used the kitchen sink to rinse her mouth and toothbrush. "I overslept."

More shock moved over Jonah's handsome face. "For your Saturday?"

"I'm volunteering at the clinic. There's a free flu shot drive today, and they're already understaffed on normal days. Plus, Annabelle's coming in for a post-op check this afternoon, too."

"Yeah?" Jonah's expression brightened. "Want company?"

"Are you serious?" she asked, and hey, look at that. Now they were both surprised.

Jonah recovered first. "No, I'm totally kidding. Jeez, Nat, of course, I'm serious. You just said they're understaffed, right?"

They were underfunded, too, if the lack of decent equipment and supplies was anything to go by, but it wasn't a detail Natalie had time to add. "Well, yes. It seems like there are never enough doctors or PAs on the clinic schedule to tend to the people who come in seeking care."

"Okay, then. I've been meaning to put in some volunteer

hours, and this way, I can spend a little time with my favorite patient while I'm at it."

"You're not poaching my patient," Natalie said, burying her involuntary smile in her coffee mug.

One corner of Jonah's mouth ticked up into the half-smile that fully charmed its intended target far more often than not. "Too late. I'm a Disney prince, remember?"

Before she could pop off with a tart reply—and oh, how she wanted to—he jerked his chin toward the hallway, his smile still firmly in place. "Go take the first shower, and while you're getting dressed, I'll take mine. I hit the gym, so I can't skip it, but I'll go fast. In the meantime, I'll put more coffee in a travel mug and run a bagel through the toaster for you. Sound good?"

An odd feeling, adjacent to guilt, perked in Natalie's chest. "Oh, you don't have to do that. I'll just make my own breakfast after I get dressed. Or if there isn't time, I'll grab something when I get a break. I'll be fine."

His expression remained completely affable. His words, however? Wouldn't budge despite the charisma with which he delivered them. "Come on, Kendrick. It'll take me two minutes, and I have to wait for you to shower, anyway. I know you're the Energizer Bunny, but you've got to eat."

She frowned, but also didn't have time to argue with him. "Fine. I'll be out of the shower in ten, tops."

The hot water eased the weird ache out of her muscles easily enough, and between her adrenaline and the caffeine boost, she made quick work of getting ready. Grabbing the roll of snowman stickers she'd picked up on her last trip to the store and stuffing it into her bag, she returned to the kitchen, where Jonah was waiting, as promised. It was unfair, really, that he could look so good with so little prep, blond hair tousled, five o'clock shadow looking far more sexy than sloppy, jeans and Henley fashionably broken-in and flawlessly molded to his body. For a second, Natalie considered the shower-damp knot she'd twisted her hair into, the lightning-fast combination of powder/lip gloss/fuck it she'd applied to her face. But she'd be administering flu shots and throat cultures all day, for God's sake, not heading down a runway. Plus, Jonah had seen her look far more bedraggled than this, after twenty-four-hour shifts and hellish on-calls that had felt like they'd lasted a month.

You are beautiful...

"Ready?" he asked, handing over a travel mug and a sesame seed bagel, split and toasted and slathered with cream cheese.

Her stomach rumbled, even though she hadn't realized it was so empty. "Yep. Ahhh, thank you." She took as big a sip of the coffee as the heat of it would allow. "I guess you're right. Even the Energizer Bunny needs fuel."

"I can drive if you want to eat on the way," he offered, tacking on, "and you don't have to worry. Your secret need for food is safe with me."

"Ha-ha. You're hilarious. Really."

They both laughed as they made their way out of the apartment, then down to the spot where he'd parked his Lexus. Natalie spent a minute devouring the bagel—sesame seed was her favorite—then going to work on her coffee, before Jonah broke the comfortable silence.

"Did you sleep okay?"

The question arrived innocently enough. Hell, he'd probably asked her the exact same thing hundreds of times, all part of the friendly small talk they shared whenever they rode to work together or hooked up on a break in between procedures and patients. But somehow, this time, it carried a layer of concern, as if maybe she'd slept poorly from unease.

She laughed, both in an effort to reassure him and because it couldn't be helped. "I slept *too* okay. Last night was..."

"Good?" Jonah supplied, his smile cocky.

Her cheeks heated. "I'm never living that down, am I?"

"Nope," he told her with glee. "But I'm glad you think it was."

"I really do."

Natalie's ear-to-ear grin slipped when her cell phone buzzed with a text, then disappeared as the words on the screen registered.

Don't forget your re-check! Love you.

She met Jonah's quizzical look with a sigh. "My mom, reminding me for the seven hundredth time to go get my blood drawn for my annual checkup. But I'm seriously fine. I wish she wouldn't worry."

"That's a good one," Jonah said. When he realized Natalie had given him the brows-up treatment, he elaborated, although somewhat sheepishly. "It's just that you not wanting anyone to worry about you is a little ironic, since you go so far above and beyond for everyone else."

"Lots of people do that, though. Caregiving is a huge part of both our jobs," she pointed out. They were surgeons, for God's sake. They couldn't exactly take care of people halfway.

Jonah countered. "Okay, but that's work. I'm talking about the rest of the time. Take today, for example. Of all the attendings—hell, of all the staff at Remington Mem, including Langston, who's in charge of everybody—who volunteers the most hours at the clinic?"

Shit. "The clinic is way understaffed, and the people who go there need care," Natalie said.

"I agree. But that's not what I asked."

She frowned. She didn't hate the time she volunteered there, but she did hate that she was on her way to losing this argument. "Fine. I do."

"Mmm. And who spent over an hour the other day calling around to find a contractor who specializes in restoring older homes when the current one ran into all those snags with the plumbing in your apartment?"

Damn it, she was oh for two. "Come on, Jonah. Agnes has had to hire four different contractors to fix that mess, plus a structural engineer. The poor woman is in her eighties. She's frazzled enough as it is trying to juggle them all."

"I'm not saying your kindness is a bad thing, Nat." Jonah coasted to a stop at a red light, then turned to look at her, his eyes backing up what he'd said. "You take care of a lot of people, and that's great. I'm just wondering who takes care of you."

"I do," she said with a laugh. "It's called adulting."

He arched a brow as if to say *really*? "Not like that. For Chrissake, you're one of the most intelligent, independent people I know. I'm fully aware that you can pay your taxes and go to the grocery store and get your oil changed. I'm talking about the other stuff. The kind of stuff that you do for Tess and Charlie and Annabelle and Agnes. Even me."

Natalie paused. They were getting into dicey territory, she knew. But still, something made her say, "Well, my parents are very caring, and we're obviously close." She held up her phone, the text message from her mother still emblazoned across the screen.

"But you don't let them take care of you. Medical reminders aside."

"They've already done that. A *lot*." Her heart tapped in stern warning, and for the first time ever, she didn't heed it. "Do you remember last weekend, when Annabelle didn't tell Rachel that her incision site hurt, even though it clearly did?"

"Yeah." His expression grew serious, and he stared through the windshield. "The poor kid must've been in some serious pain. I don't know how she didn't say anything."

"I do."

The admission slipped out without the consent of her better judgment. But now that she'd aired it, she might as well follow through. "Being a cancer kid is hard. I mean, the physical challenges are a given, but...it's tough emotionally, too. There were times I would've given anything to be well, not for me, but for my parents."

"Most pediatric cancer treatments are pretty brutal for everyone involved," Jonah said quietly, and Natalie nodded.

"My cancer was really hard on my parents, even though they tried their best not to show it." She doubted either one of them would admit the struggle, even now, eighteen years after the fact. "We couldn't be like normal families. Everything hinged on how I was feeling, what my white cell counts were. Chemo treatments, scans, procedures. My mother even quit her job, a job she *loved*, to take care of me."

Jonah shook his head. "I'm sure she loved her job, but you're her kid. You're close." Another beat passed, his voice growing strangely tight. "She loves you more."

"I know she loves me," Natalie said, because she really did. "But she and my dad, they both went without vacations, new cars, a bigger house, pretty much everything that wasn't absolutely necessary because the cost of the treatments was exorbitant, even with insurance. My brother and sister missed out on a lot, too. No travel baseball teams, no hosting sleepovers. They barely got to spend time with either of my parents one-on-one for four whole years."

"You didn't choose to have leukemia, Nat. You can't blame yourself for having been sick," Jonah said, and Natalie laughed at the irony.

"I might not have chosen it, but that doesn't mean it didn't happen anyway, and it damn sure doesn't mean I feel any less guilt for what my family went through because I was sick. They worried all day, every day, for years. I hated it." She broke off for a breath, even though she knew it would do nothing to firm her voice when she continued. "I hate it still. Not because my parents hover, although that can get frustrating at times. But...I hate that they still worry that something might happen to me, no matter how much I insist that I'm fine. I just want them to be happy. Like, *really* happy, the way they should've been when I was growing up. The way they would've been if I'd never had leukemia."

"Wait." A V formed over the bridge of Jonah's nose, growing deeper with each passing second, and her heart pounded as she watched him mentally connect the dots. "Is *that* why you do that thing you do? Where you always say you're fine?"

"I don't always do it," Natalie said. Old defenses died hard, apparently.

Just as old friends called bullshit when it was warranted. "You're not really going to go with that, are you? I can count a dozen times that you've gone the 'I'm fine' route, this week alone."

She exhaled slowly. "Okay, but a lot of the time, I really *am* fine."

"And other times, you're not, even though you tell everyone you are."

Leave it to Jonah to get right to the heart of the matter. Natalie had spent her entire life looking at the bright side. Caring for other people, sometimes at the expense of her own needs. Trying to atone for guilt that logic told her she shouldn't have, but life had placed directly into her chest, regardless. So she had no choice but to say, "Yes. Sometimes I'm not, even though I tell everyone I am."

"So, the answer is no one."

Natalie replayed the last minute of their conversation in her head, but still came up empty. "The answer to...?"

Jonah pulled into a parking spot across from the clinic, putting the Lexus in *park* before turning to look at her. "Who takes care of you?"

"I'm f—" She bit down on the default an instant before it launched. Damn it. "Trying."

If his expression was anything to go on, the reply surprised them both. "You are?" he asked.

"Maybe not with my parents," she admitted. After all, not wanting to be smothered was only half the reason she'd begged Jonah to let her stay with him when that bathtub had one-wayed into her living room, even if she hadn't been able to tell him that at the time. "I don't know that I'll ever be able to not do everything in my power to assure them that they don't need to worry about me. But maybe..."

Natalie had to give him credit. Jonah waited out her silence patiently, without pressing. It made it all too easy for her to say, "I know you think it's stupid, but maybe that's why I'm looking for someone to eventually get serious with. I don't need saving, or anything." She paused to snort, eking out a smile when she realized Jonah had made the exact same sound at the exact same time. "But it would be nice to find someone to have my back. To give me the last bite of cheesecake, and laugh when I'm happy. To feel sad when I'm sad. Maybe losing my virginity so I can actively date without having to worry about it is my way of saying I'm ready to find someone who will take care of me like that."

"I don't think that's stupid in the least," Jonah said.

The emotion that Natalie had seen in her dream flashed over his face, there and then gone in the same breath, and she realized with a start that she hadn't invented it at all. She'd seen it last night, too, darkening his eyes and then disappearing with the same swiftness, as if he were so well-practiced at covering it up, it barely lasted long enough to register with most people.

Natalie wasn't most people.

But before she could say so much as a syllable, he was dishing up that dazzling smile of his, winking at her in a way that only he could get away with as charming over cheesy and making her wonder—yet again—if she'd been seeing things, after all.

"In fact, I think that's perfect for you, and I really hope you find it. Now, did you want to head in and start taking care of some patients? There's already a line of people waiting at the door, and I have a feeling today is going to keep us on our toes."

14

J onah lowered himself into the chair behind the clinic's intake desk and exhaled a long, slow breath. If he never saw another flu shot again, it'd be too freaking soon. They'd been slammed with patients from the second they'd opened the doors, fielding complaints of everything from contusions to chest pain, and he'd treated as many of those patients as he'd been able to, as well. Easier said than done, with the shortage of supplies and the outdated or even absent equipment necessary for some of the tests and procedures he'd wanted to perform. Jonah had needed to get creative in a few cases—lucky for him, his experience dealing with traumas made him fast on his feet.

Make that his *aching* feet. Still, he didn't regret spending the better part of his Saturday administering a metric ton of flu shots and basic healthcare for two reasons. One, the people who received the shots had a far lower chance of becoming sick with an illness that could be potentially serious—always a win. Secondly, getting to work side by side with Natalie and watch her in her element, caring for people and making silly faces at all of the little kids as she handed out stickers and calmed their tears, was quickly becoming one of Jonah's favorite pastimes.

Something neighboring on tenderness unfolded in his rib cage, and he ran a hand over the front of his scrubs in an effort to snuff it out. Of course he felt affection for Natalie. They were best goddamned friends. Feelings like that were normal, just like the way his gut had twisted when she'd fessed up about her guilt over having cancer as a kid was to be expected, especially since she was always so cheerful that it had never occurred to him that she *had* vulnerabilities, let alone hid them.

Jonah's pulse pushed faster in his veins. He couldn't tell what he hated more—that Natalie felt guilty over something she hadn't chosen and couldn't have controlled, or that he'd never realized it before.

That he'd felt an impulsive, unexpected urge to be the one to care for her? Yeah, that had only added to the pile of emotions he had no business feeling about her, let alone showing her.

How had he not recognized her remorse?

Not like you don't know a thing or two about covering your shit up, his sneaky little inner voice reminded him, and okay, point taken. He hadn't realized it because Natalie had kept it close to the vest and covered it with genuine kindness, and his concern over who cared for her when she needed it was a perfectly natural, perfectly best-friendly reaction.

The way he'd wanted to kiss her all morning, then again all afternoon? Was not a best-friendly reaction. But that was just attraction. Physical. Sexual. Jonah would get it out of his system soon enough.

And then she'd move on and find someone who could give her what he couldn't, just as she deserved.

"Dr. Jonah!" A familiar, little-girl voice dropped him back to the clinic, sending a wide, warm smile past his tumbling thoughts.

"Well, if it isn't my favorite patient," he said, Annabelle's ensuing giggle taking his mood a little further into happy territory. He dosed his hands with a quick shot of anti-bacterial foam before leaning over the counter to give her a fistbump, then smiled a hello at Rachel. "Let me get you two into an exam room. We don't want to risk exposure to any nasty germs. Once you're settled in, I can go track down Dr. Kendrick."

Rachel's smile was all gratitude, the worry lines that had bracketed her eyes last week mostly a memory. "Thank you."

"No problem at all." Using his ID badge for access, Jonah ushered them past the set of automatic doors separating the lobby from the rest of the clinic, then walked the pair back to one of the clinic's six private exam rooms.

"I see you brought Mr. Flufferkins," he said, pointing to her stuffed fox.

Annabelle nodded seriously. "Of course. I can't leave him at home alone. I'm his person."

"His person, huh?" Jonah helped her (and Mr. Flufferkins) up to the exam table, taking a plastic bag holding a crisply laundered hospital gown from one of the cabinet drawers and placing it next to her.

"Well, I can't be his mommy. I'm not a fox." Her tone tacked on the word *obviously*, and Jonah bit back a laugh. "But he needs someone to help take care of him, and he makes me feel better when I have to get IVs and stuff. So, I'm his person, and he's mine. Even though he's a fox."

More *obviously*, and this time, Jonah did laugh. "You

asked for it," Rachel murmured from the corner of her mouth, and okay, yeah. He supposed he had.

"Smart thinking to have a person," Jonah told her. "Tell me, does Mr. Flufferkins like Jell-O?"

"He likes *green* Jell-O," Annabelle said, breaking into a gap-toothed grin. "Very much."

God, she was full of hustle, this kid. "Lucky for Mr. Flufferkins, I know a guy who can make that happen. Go ahead and put on your gown, and I'll find Dr. Kendrick. After she checks you out, we'll have ourselves a Jell-O party. Okay?"

"Okay!"

Turning on the heels of his cross-trainers, he headed back to the main room in the clinic, swiveling his gaze from curtain area to curtain area until he caught sight of Natalie. She stood a few beds away, chatting animatedly with a pregnant woman as she finished up an ultrasound. Jonah stepped toward her quietly, but stood on the periphery, not wanting to interrupt.

"Well, Marta, I know this isn't a fancy 3D machine, but your baby still looks fantastic," she said, capturing a grainy photo image from the ultrasound screen and sending it to the printer at the bottom of the machine. "He's perfectly healthy and snug as a bug. And you are one smart momma for coming in for your prenatal well check."

"Thanks, Dr. Kendrick."

"I'm sorry you had to wait so long," Natalie said, trying on a bright smile. "But the management here is still figuring out the best way to schedule well visits and handle all the patients who need more immediate care for illnesses and injuries."

She looked up from the patient, and even though her eyes locked with Jonah's for the briefest of beats, she seemed to know what he'd come to tell her. "I'm going to let our physicians' assistant, Sara, finish things up here. She can answer any questions you've got and let you know when to come in for your next checkup, okay? In the meantime, keep up the great work."

Passing the woman's chart over to the PA, Natalie excused herself and took a few steps toward Jonah, a smile twitching at the corners of her mouth.

"Let me guess. You've already given Annabelle and Rachel the star treatment."

"I can neither confirm nor deny that there will be an invite-only Jell-O party after the appointment," he teased.

"You're terrible."

"There goes your VIP pass."

Natalie laughed. "Not a chance. You might be a Disney prince, but I'm a goddess, remember?"

Did he fucking *ever*.

Seeming to remember the exact circumstances under which he'd made the reference, Natalie's cheeks pinked, her spine going straight beneath her scrubs and doctor's coat. "So, ah, let me pull Annabelle's chart, here."

She was all business as she went through the motions of grabbing a tablet from the nurses' station and reviewed Annabelle's chart. The clinic had closed its doors to incoming patients for the day, and even though a handful of people still lingered in triage, none were emergent. The staff nurses, ever-capable, had them well taken care of, so Jonah asked, "Is it okay if I tag along?"

"I think Annabelle would be disappointed if you didn't," Natalie said. "She's not as immune to your charm as I am."

Jonah smiled reflexively, but he also didn't budge. "Maybe not, but you *are* her doctor. She's no longer emergent, so if you'd rather take the re-check solo, I understand."

Natalie looked up from the chart, her blond brows disappearing beneath the wisps of hair that had made a jail-break from the knot at the crown of her head. "I appreciate the courtesy," she said softly. "But you were there when I needed the help with her case, and you did help me treat her for this infection. Anyway, I'm not in the practice of disappointing my patients, so...are you ready?"

"Absolutely."

They made their way to the exam room, all four of them talking easily as Natalie took point and examined Annabelle. The girl had recovered well, under the circum-stances, and it lifted Jonah's mood past the natural fatigue setting into his muscles after the long-ass day. He hung back as Natalie did all the honors, answering Rachel's questions and checking Annabelle's incision site and proclaiming her infection-free. Jonah delivered on the Jell-O party (hello, he was a man of his word), then promised to visit Annabelle when she returned to Remington Mem in a week for her next round of chemo. Natalie's eyes sparkled, and even though he could see the weary shadows hinting beneath them, she looked purely happy. Her mood was infectious, and by the time they walked Rachel and Annabelle out to the waiting room for their goodbyes, Jonah was grinning right along with her.

His grin slipped, however, at the sound of an authorita-tive throat being cleared from behind him.

"Sheridan. Kendrick." Dr. Keith Langston, a highly-regarded physician, the hospital's chief of staff and, oh, by the way, their uber-conservative boss, regarded them from the spot where he'd been standing by the intake desk.

Jeez, the guy was stealthy. "Dr. Langston," Jonah said, quickly realizing the man wasn't alone. A tall, willowy woman in an expensively cut navy blue suit stood beside him. She reminded Jonah of Vanessa; or, at least, the Vanessa her parents had wanted her to be, pretty in a look-but-don't-touch sort of way, with a heavy air of authority to go with her high cheekbones and fair, flawless skin. Her platinum-blond hair was pulled into a tidy twist, her ice-blue stare shrewd and assessing as she sent it first over the clinic's now-quiet main space, then over Jonah and Natalie.

Langston nodded. "This is Harlow Davenport. She was recently appointed to Remington Memorial's board. Her family has been very generous to the hospital over the past year and a half."

"I'll say. They funded the entire clinic," Natalie murmured, extending her hand with a very Natalie-esque smile. "I'm Natalie Kendrick, peds attending. It's nice to meet you, Ms. Davenport."

"Pleasure," the woman clipped out, her tone putting frost on the claim. She was equal opportunity with her all-business manner as she shook Jonah's hand, too, although she did manage a polite smile as she gestured to the curtain areas with an impeccably manicured hand. "I wanted to come down and thank you both for volunteering your time today. We've been quite understaffed here in the clinic, of late. Your participation in today's flu shot drive was rather helpful."

"Oh." Natalie blinked. "Well, thank you, but really, the preventive care will help to keep them out of the ED this season, so it's kind of a win for everyone."

"Well, it's a win we certainly needed." Harlow turned toward Langston. "I'd like to see the rest of the facility more closely. Then we can review some of the numbers. I want to be fully prepared for Monday's budget meeting."

"Of course." Langston acknowledged him and Natalie with a lift of his chin. "Doctors," he said, leading Harlow toward the exam rooms. When they were out of earshot, Natalie looked at Jonah, lips parted in surprise.

"What was that all about, do you suppose?" she asked as they moved to the small employee room where they'd stored their street clothes.

"I don't know. I mean, the clinic is named after her mother, and she's been on the board for, what? Four months or so?"

"Yeah. I overheard Don talking about it the other day. The details are kind of hazy—you know Don." Natalie paused to grab her jeans and sweater from the locker where she'd left them, taking everything into one of the two curtained-off changing areas at the back of the room. "He's got a master's degree in gossiping. But I guess Harlow has taken some sort of new, hands-on interest in the clinic recently."

"Most people who give the hospital a chunk of money big enough to have a clinic named after them have a vested interest in the facility," Jonah agreed. He grabbed his own clothes, trying like mad to block out the rustle of fabric that said Natalie was less than dressed only a few feet and two flimsy curtains away from him.

"I guess," she said. "Whatever her newfound motivation is, I'm glad for it. This place might be state-of-the-art in terms of the actual structure, but between the ancient equipment and the lack of good management, they sure can use the help."

Jonah couldn't disagree. The clinic had only been open for about six months, but it was rumored to have seen a whole lot more failures than successes. The demand for qualified staff to run the facility on both the medical side *and* the business end was overwhelming, and the misman-agement was really beginning to show.

"She certainly seems to have the steel for it, but more power to her," Jonah said.

He made quick work of getting changed, running a hand through his hair a time or two before just deciding to give up and call it good. He and Natalie dodged a few snowflakes on the way to his Lexus, and her kid-in-a-candy-store grin made up for the cold weather in spades. The ride home was filled with an easy mix of laughter and quiet, during which she tried to convince him to let her decorate the apartment for the upcoming holiday (no), she renewed her argument that *Die Hard* wasn't a Christmas movie (more no), and she tried once again to convince him that rom coms were at least plausible (big, fat fuck no). Jonah made his way into the apartment, tossing his keys onto the table in the foyer and slipping out of his jacket, hanging it on a nearby hook before turning to look at Natalie.

"Did you still want to watch the Rogues game?" she asked. Her cheeks were flushed from the cold, the handful of snowflakes that had caught in her hair on the way upstairs now melted into glassy droplets. The effortless happiness that seemed to follow her everywhere rang through her smile, and God, how had Jonah never realized how truly beautiful she was?

His step toward her was more automatic than breathing. "Not really."

"Oh." Her smile faded, but only for a second. "Okay. If you're tired, or you just want to relax on your own, we can totally call it a night."

"I'm not tired, and I don't want to relax on my own," Jonah said. His pulse pounded in an equal mix of anticipation and desire, and he was done denying both. He closed the space between them—not that there was much of the stuff to begin with—his breath growing thicker and his cock twitching as Natalie's pupils flared, her eyes glinting with unmistakable heat.

Reaching out, he pressed the pads of his index and middle fingers under her chin, tilting it gently upward until their gazes caught and held fast. "I made you a promise last night. And if having sex with me is still what you want, then I'd like to spend tonight making good on it. If you don't, that's okay, too," he said. "But make no mistake, Natalie. The only thing I want tonight is you."

15

"I want you, too."

Somehow, Natalie managed to get the words past her thundering heartbeat, but she couldn't deny the pure truth of them. The need she'd felt last night rushed through her like a tide, and she answered it the only way she knew how.

She moved closer.

A smile broke over Jonah's impossibly handsome face. It wasn't one of his usual smiles, designed to captivate or charm. No. This smile was something entirely different, wide open and wanting at the same time, and it sent a shot of wild heat directly between her thighs.

"Guess we should do something about that," he said, lowering his mouth at the same time she lifted hers. The kiss started out simply enough, just a brush of their lips, then another. But all too quickly, Natalie's need for more surfaced. She parted her mouth, pressing harder in search of more contact, and oh, Jonah gave it. Sliding his tongue over her bottom lip, he deepened the kiss in one unrelenting stroke. His hands lifted to frame her face, his palms firm as he held her exactly where she wanted to be, the blunt edges of his fingertips knotting in her hair.

Heat blazed through her body—how could desire feel so *intense?*—and she kissed him back, just as deeply. Their give and take didn't feel like a back and forth so much as an equal meeting, each of them reading the other the way they always did, and the next thing Natalie knew, her arms had moved around Jonah's shoulders, his around her rib cage, and he was lifting her off her feet to haul her in close.

An appreciative groan drifted up from his chest. With the way the move had brought their hips into perfect alignment, her legs wrapped around his waist and the seam of her body pressed against his fully erect cock, it was all Natalie had not to fly apart, right there in the foyer.

"Jonah," she said, although the word poured out as mostly a sigh. Her pulse hammered, the rhythm rapid and erratic in her ears. After taking a second to presumably get used to the shift in balance, he tightened his arms around her torso, flattening his palms over the curve of her ass and starting to move toward his bedroom. Every step provided friction that made her breath catch and her clit throb, and by the time they crossed the threshold, she was desperate.

"Mmm." As soon as Jonah lowered her to her feet, she reached for the hem of his shirt.

He caught her fingers just shy of contact. "No."

Confusion wound a path through her lust in a chilly thread. "But—"

"I want you, Nat." He kissed her hotly enough to prove it. "I want *you*. Please. Let me make this good for you."

For a single beat, Natalie was tempted to argue. Not that she wasn't dying for him to touch her and kiss her and make her come, because sweet God in heaven, she was. But Jonah had slid around letting her touch him last night, too, and the truth of it was, she *wanted* to.

But then his mouth was on her neck, kissing and testing and tasting her hypersensitive skin, and any argument— hell, any coherent thought that wasn't *please don't stop*— disappeared from her mind like snowflakes melting on the pavement. His tongue traced a long, delicate path from behind her ear to the base of her neck, where he switched to a pair of more purposeful open-mouthed kisses. When he ran into the blockade of her sweater, he pulled back with another sort of smile Natalie had never seen before.

This one was pure seduction, dark and dangerous and scorching hot. And even though she'd thought it impossible, that smile made her want him even more.

Jonah's hands curled over the bottom of her sweater, lingering there as he turned his chin to look at his bedroom door, which was still open wide. "Can I keep the light on?"

Surprised, Natalie turned her eyes to the soft light spilling in from the foyer and the hallway. As if her expression telegraphed the *why?* from her brain, he added, "It's easier for me to know what you like when I can see you, and I want to be sure you're a hundred percent, every step of the way. Plus"—he reached up to close his thumb and forefinger around a lock of hair that had tumbled free from the knot on her head, sliding them slowly down the length of it until he reached the end—"you're goddamned gorgeous. I can't help but want to be selfish with you."

"Oh," she whispered. "Well, when you put it like that..."

Still, Jonah paused, and she realized with a start that he was waiting for the actual words. "Yes," Natalie told him. "The light is okay with me."

"Okay." Sliding his hands lower, he returned his attention to the edge of her sweater, lifting it slowly over her head. She sent up a silent prayer of thanks that she'd had the wherewithal to leave her most threadbare bra in her suitcase, although the functional, cream-colored cotton she'd hustled her way into this morning was only a notch better. Ugh, maybe she hadn't *quite* thought the whole sure-you-can-leave-the-light-on thing all the way through.

And then she saw Jonah's face. "Gorgeous," he said again, the same way he'd spoken to her last night. The truth in his stare made Natalie believe him, and she squared her shoulders.

She might be a virgin in a plain-Jane bra who was about to sail into some seriously uncharted sexual waters, but with Jonah's eyes on her body, as soft as a caress and as sexy as the promise of so much more, Natalie felt like a fucking goddess.

"I want to see you, too," she said. When Jonah opened his mouth—to protest, if his shift in expression was anything to go by—she continued. "You said you want me to be a hundred percent, every step of the way, right?"

"Yes."

"And that you want me."

"Yes." His voice gripped the word, making Natalie even bolder.

"Then take me, Jonah." She stepped back, but only far enough to open her arms to him fully. "But let me see you while you do it. That's what *I* want."

To her surprise, he deferred. Reaching down low, he pulled his shirt over his head, dropping it beside her sweater on the floor.

"*Oh.*" Natalie's heart kicked a hard rhythm against her breastbone as she took in his tightly muscled shoulders. Ridged abs that were a testament to all that gym time. The dusting of golden hair creating a path from his navel to his waistband, then to the impressive erection pressing against his jeans, and okay, yeah. She'd never been so happy she'd stood her ground.

Jonah reclaimed the space between them with a step. He took a quick second to kick off his cross-trainers, giving Natalie the chance to do the same with her own before he guided her to his bed to maneuver them both over the tousled covers. His skin was warm under her fingers, and Natalie spread them wide over his shoulders, parting her knees to accommodate his body against hers. He balanced enough of his weight on the palm he'd planted under her arm not to crush her, but gravity kept them connected enough for her to recognize how right there with her he was.

She arched up into his body, fitting her mouth to his, the kiss growing just intense enough to double the need in her belly before Jonah broke it. Trailing lower, he kissed her jaw, her earlobe, her collarbone—places that, before now, she'd have called ordinary, but in this moment, were on fire. Natalie tightened her fingers over his shoulders, the play of his muscles rippling in return making her smile.

But when he moved lower still, to the space between her breasts, her smile turned into a moan.

"Yes?" Jonah asked, looking up at her. His eyes glittered, nearly navy blue in the dim light spilling in over his shoulders, and she nodded without thought.

"Yes."

He was moving before her voice had fully faded into the quiet of his bedroom. With a deft twist of his fingers, he undid the front clasp of her bra. A few small movements from both of them had the thing on the floor with the growing pile of their clothes, and Natalie's nipples peaked in anticipation. Jonah—thank *God*—didn't make her wait.

Lowering his head, he closed his lips over one nipple, making her cry out. The pleasure of the wet friction warred with the ache pulsing between her legs, and she gave in to one while trying to ease the other. Jonah worked her with perfect strokes of his lips and tongue, moving from one nipple to the other, then back again. Finally, when she was certain she'd combust, or at the very least, lose her mind, he shifted lower, his fingers resting on the button of her jeans.

At his pause, Natalie nodded. "Yes," she said again. In that moment, she realized then that while Jonah might be the one dishing up the pleasure, she still held every ounce of control over it. The understanding turned her on even more, and she reached down to undo her jeans, sliding them from her body even though it left her in nothing more than her light pink cotton panties, her damp, aching pussy just one layer and a few scant inches away from Jonah's touch.

"Jesus." His throat worked over a swallow, the flash of raw emotion in his eyes there and then gone.

The dark, dirty confidence that took its place made Natalie's breath hitch.

"Have you ever been kissed here?" he asked, his mouth hovering just over the spot where her panties gave way to bare skin.

"Twice," she said. While both men with whom she'd had the encounters had been nice enough, she had to admit she'd been left wondering what all the fuss was about.

Jonah traced a finger over her hip. "Did you like it?"

"It was...fine?"

His laughter rumbled over her, leaving goose bumps in its wake. "Do you remember how I said you'd feel like a goddess by the time I was done with you?"

All Natalie could do was nod.

"Good." Jonah pinned her with a stare that sailed all the way through her. "Because I'm just getting started, and I'm going to show you so much more than fine."

Hooking both hands over her panties, he slid them down, over her knees, then off completely. It occurred to her that she should feel vulnerable in her nakedness, especially when Jonah was still partially dressed in his jeans, and if she were with anyone else, she probably would have.

But this was Jonah, who she trusted. Jonah, who she wanted right now more than anything.

Jonah, who was looking at her not just like she was a goddess, but like she was *his* goddess.

"Fuck, Natalie," he said, settling back between her parted thighs. His stare said the rest, making her feel beautiful. Strong and in control.

She opened her knees wider to give him both permission and access, and he took it. Kissing a soft path from her belly to the top of her hip, he pressed his palm to one inner thigh while letting the fingers on his opposite hand stroke over her sex.

"Oh, my *God*." The touch, as light as it was, had her arching off the mattress, her inner muscles clenching with need.

"Easy," Jonah murmured, the pressure on her thigh constant and steady, grounding her. "I'm right here with you."

"You're driving me insane," she said, and he huffed out a laugh.

"Under the circumstances, I'll take that as a compliment. Now let me give you what you need."

This time, he didn't wait. Edging his shoulders securely between her thighs, he dropped his head, dragging his tongue over her pussy in one long, slow lick, then reversing the movement to focus on her clit. Natalie didn't even have the air to breathe, much less sigh or moan or cry out, so she simply gave in to the sensations ripping through her. Jonah kissed and tasted and took, testing out different rhythms until he found one that—*ah*—turned the need between her hips desperate. Keeping his attention on her clit firm, he slid his fingers lower, pushing one inside of her with ease.

Her muscles squeezed in pure pleasure, drawing a sigh past her lips. He moaned in reply, the vibration against her hypersensitive skin bringing her that much closer to the edge, adjusting his touch in accordance with her breath. Jonah added another finger to stretch her slowly, sweetly. The pressure of his fingers, now sliding back and forth as he circled her clit with his tongue, was both too much and not enough. Natalie chased his movements with her hips, greedy pleasure filling her more and more, until finally, he twined his fingers together to find that spot hidden deep inside of her—the one she'd have said was a myth before last night—and she was lost. Her orgasm shockwaved through her, gripping her tightly before sending her flying. Jonah was right there with her, his touches gradually growing slower and softer, until he shifted back to look up at her.

A few beats later, she regained command of her lungs, the hold tenuous, but there. "Come here," she whispered.

He didn't hesitate. Pushing forward, he realigned their bodies from shoulders to hips, settling in at her side.

"You're wearing too much." Natalie ran her fingers over his chest and torso—damn, his abs felt even sexier than they looked, which would be unjust if it weren't so fucking hot—pausing when she got to the top button. Jonah surprised her by arcing into her touch, his gaze locked on her hands as she undid the button, then the zipper, then pushed the denim away to reveal a pair of snug black boxer briefs. Her heart tripped at the outline of his cock beneath the cotton, and for a sliver of a second, she felt self-conscious. They were fast approaching the part of things where she had no experience whatsoever. She wanted him, but...

"What?"

Of course, he'd seen right through her. "I don't just want this to be good for me," Natalie whispered.

Surprise darted through her at his laugh. "Believe me, you have nothing to worry about."

"But you're doing everything, and—"

"Do you still want to do this?" he asked, the question level and devoid of anything other than the want of an honest answer.

Desire swirled and rebuilt in her belly at the thought. "Yes. I'm sure."

"I want it, too, Nat. I promise."

The intensity Jonah had banked earlier returned to his eyes, only this time, he didn't hide it. He kissed her, slow and deep, as if the two of them alone were in charge of time. Natalie kissed him back instinctively, sliding her hands down low to finish undressing him. Her breath caught when her fingers grazed his cock, but want quickly took over, cutting through her nerves. She wrapped her fingers around him firmly, her arousal flaring as she started to stroke.

"Natalie," he hissed, his hand closing over hers.

She didn't give in. "I like touching you," she said, sliding the circle of her fingers from base to tip in proof.

Jonah's eyes flashed in the shadows. He relented, but kept his fingers curled tightly against hers as she began to move again. The glide of their hands, pressed together and working as one, was completely erotic, the strokes growing longer and gaining purpose, until finally he broke off with a groan.

"You're not going to get what you want if you keep that up," he said, enough of a smile hanging in his words to make her concede. He took a handful of seconds to get a condom from his bedside table drawer, getting it into place with a few economical movements. It hit Natalie that she was about to lose her virginity, and a tiny wave of adrenaline splashed through her, speeding up her heart.

"Still yes?" Jonah asked, returning to her side. The move put their faces level, and she answered him with all the honesty she owned.

"Still yes. It's just that I've never done this before. Obviously." A nervous laugh bubbled up. "I'm a little out of my depth."

"I'll go slow," he promised. "Just do what feels good."

It sounded easy enough, so Natalie nodded. Jonah returned to the cradle of her hips, angling over her and splitting his balance between one palm and both knees. Her thighs fell wide, and he used his free hand to brush his fingers over her sex.

"Oh," she breathed, her body coming alive. His fingers moved freely through her slickness, the blunt head of his cock nudging over the same skin. Pressing. Stretching. For one split second, Natalie wondered if this would actually work—she'd seen enough penises to know Jonah's was impressively big. But then it *was* working, with him pressing deeper and her body accommodating, and she let out a breath. There was a spot of discomfort at the halfway point, an odd pressure that bordered on pain, but Jonah pushed past it swiftly, gliding gently deeper until it became an afterthought.

And then they were completely joined.

"Oh, my God," Natalie blurted, her smile impossible to cage.

One corner of Jonah's mouth lifted. "Yes?"

"Yes." She nodded, her hair rustling against the pillow it spilled over. "Definitely yes."

"Good."

She opened her mouth to make a smart comment— she'd known she was never going to live that *good* thing down—but then he started to move, and Natalie forgot her name.

A sound flew past her lips, part sigh, part something else she couldn't label. Jonah's slow in-and-out slide made every nerve ending between her hips come to life. Sensations flew through her, nearly too fast for her to register them, save one.

Pleasure.

"Christ, Natalie," Jonah said, his voice like gravel as he withdrew just an inch, then pumped slowly to seat his cock all the way inside her again. "You're so fucking tight."

The look on his face erased any worry she might have that that was a bad thing, and she eased even further, her inner muscles sparking in reply.

Oh. "Jonah," she murmured. Sliding her hands over the back of his rib cage, she held him close as he began to thrust into her pussy. The rhythm started slowly, but just as he had with everything else, he measured her breaths and sighs, testing out what worked and reading her to change what didn't. She adjusted to each wicked feeling just in time for him to heighten it and draw it out, and release teased, low and deep at the base of her spine.

Natalie gasped at the unexpected sensation. She'd already had one Richter-scale orgasm. No way could she have *another* one.

But the way her pleasure had brightened was too strong to deny. Need coiled tighter within her, building with each forward press of Jonah's hips, and when he leaned forward to bring his cock in direct contact with her aching, swollen clit, her exhale started to shake.

"Please, don't stop. Please, please." Her orgasm was right...there, and oh, God, she'd never felt anything like this need, so close to pleasure and yet also bordering on pain.

"Natalie, open your eyes."

She hadn't quite realized she'd squeezed them shut. When she did what Jonah had said, his gaze was right there, waiting.

"I'm right here, sweetheart. I won't stop."

He didn't. Jonah's motions stayed exactly the same, guiding her to the edge only to tumble her over. Natalie's climax left her breathless, caught for a moment between everything and nothing, and she let it, let *Jonah*, have her. His movements began to slow, but she reached up to touch his face.

"You promised you wouldn't stop." She lifted her hips, rocking suggestively against his cock until he'd filled her completely. "So don't."

His eyes glittered, midnight blue and more intense than she'd ever seen them, and for a breath, she thought he'd refuse, the way he had when she'd wanted to touch him. But his grip on her hip tightened, the motion he'd just scaled back on growing faster and gaining intent. Jonah's thrusts became harder, sending pleasure through Natalie that she couldn't explain, but oh, oh *God*, she wanted it as badly as she'd wanted her own release. Finally, his muscles went taut, his body stilling for only a second before he started to shudder. Her name spilled out of him, over and over like a mantra, making her heartbeat quicken.

"Natalie," he whispered, dropping his forehead over hers. They lay there for...well, hell, Natalie had no clue because time honestly felt as if it didn't apply to her universe right now. Jonah's body was a warm weight on hers, their damp chests pressed together and their legs tangled in the bed sheets. She had no clue what was supposed to happen now, but she felt too good to care, so she did what Jonah had told her to.

She did what felt good, and started to laugh.

"Oh, my God, that was..." Yeah, there was no fucking chance she was going to find a way to accurately describe the sex they'd just had. "Can we do it again? Like, the deal is for all night, right?"

Jonah chuffed out a laugh. "You're going to have to give me a couple of minutes, sweetheart. But, yes. The deal is for all night."

"So, it was good?" Natalie asked, and yeah, she really needed to expand her vocabulary unless she wanted him to tease her for the rest of their *lives*. "I mean, for you?"

"Yeah." He laughed again, leaning in to place a kiss over her mouth. "It was good." His stare, which had been soft, turned wicked in an instant, making Natalie's breath catch. "Now, let's get some food in you. If all night is what you're after, you're going to need it."

16

Of all the ways Jonah had envisioned the moments after sex with Natalie, the fact that they might be filled with genuine, balls-out laughter had *not* crossed his mind. He'd never once had a partner laugh, happily or otherwise, post-coitus, and he'd damn sure never felt the sort of ease that had followed the whole untangle/wash up/get dressed routine he and Natalie had just gone through.

Not worrying about how long he had to lie there before he could feasibly slip away had been a relief. The fact that he hadn't wanted to slip away at all?

He'd deal with *that* little emotion later.

"Okay," Natalie said, the light from the fridge combining with the glow from the overheads to put the sexy flush of her cheeks on full display. "I think we've got enough here for me to get a couple of omelets together. There will be greens," she warned, holding up a bag of spinach. "But we've got some ham in the deli drawer, too, so that'll balance things out a little."

Jonah stepped in next to her, nodding. "Fair enough. How can I help?"

"Oh, you don't have to." A wisp of hair that had never made it to the loose knot on top of her head drifted forward to frame her face as she waved him off. "Omelets are easy. Especially now that you actually own a skillet," she teased.

Annnnd nope. "If they're easy, then you can teach me," he said, moving to the sink to wash his hands. "After today, I've discovered that I like working side by side with you."

"Smooth talker." Her arched brow made the word an accusation. Her sugar-sweet smile? Made it something else entirely. "You really don't have to help me."

"For someone who's trying to let other people take care of her a little, you kind of suck at seizing your opportunities."

Natalie pressed her lips together, but her smile still peeked out at the edges. "You are no longer charming."

Ah, the disguise he could wear in his sleep. Jonah dished up his best chin lift/quick wink combo. "Oh, yes I am. If it makes you feel any better, I'll let you split the dishes with me when we're done," he said, taking the carton of eggs and the bag of spinach from her.

"We're using paper plates," she argued.

Not that it made him budge. "Great. Less work on the back end for both of us."

"You're a pain in my ass."

"Yep. I'm also still helping."

Seeming to see that she was in a no-win situation—good Christ, she was tough—Natalie laughed. "Fine. Grab the cutting board from that drawer. And as much as I enjoy the view"—she paused to send an appreciative gaze from his face to the sweatpants he'd slung over his hips for the sake of decorum—"you should probably put on a shirt, just in case the oil pops."

"Party pooper."

Natalie's smile was angelic even though her wild hair and tissue-thin tank top made him think nothing but purely wicked thoughts. "Trust me when I say it hurts me more than it hurts you."

One minute and one T-shirt later, Jonah was back in the kitchen. Natalie put him on chopping duty ("you're a surgeon," she'd pointed out) while she put together the egg mixture. They worked comfortably together even though the tat-tat-tat-tat of the whisk against the bowl and the snick of the knife on the cutting board were the only sounds in the kitchen, and soon enough, there was nothing left to do but construct the omelets.

"I'll just give the onions and spinach some quick heat first," Natalie said, sight-measuring a turn of olive oil around the skillet she'd placed on the burner in front of her.

"Huh. You can't just throw them into the egg mixture, like you did with the ham?"

"I could." She shrugged. "But then the onions taste kind of harsh and the spinach gets unruly. It's easier to cook them first. See how the spinach wilts down to less than half its volume?"

Jonah eyed the skillet, surprised. "Hey, that's pretty cool. Who taught you how to cook?"

"Both of my parents, actually." She stirred the onions and spinach, which were starting to smell freaking delicious, then added a pinch of salt. "For as sheltered as I was, they did teach me a lot of life skills. That, and I pestered them out of sheer boredom." She paused to grin. "But they always split everything right down the middle, from cooking dinner to mowing the lawn. They were equal opportunity about teaching me to do both."

"Yeah, not so much in my house."

Shit. Shit, shit, *shit*. The residual high from all the great-sex endorphins must be making him loose-lipped. How could he have let something like that slip out? And in front of Natalie, no less, who was looking at him with those curious brown eyes and that kind, wide-open expression that made him want to do the opposite of clam the fuck up, like he should.

"I know you said you and your father aren't close. Has it always been that way?"

She kept cooking as she spoke, tapping the wooden spoon against the edge of the skillet and turning off the burner like nothing-doing. Jonah's heart thundered against his ribs, his defenses screaming at him to deflect her question and one-eighty the subject with a flirty smile. He could make Natalie come, and he could take her virginity, but he could not let himself feel for her. Definitely not enough to tell her this, the one thing no one else, not even Vanessa, knew.

Except you already do.

He considered the devil's advocate that had clearly taken up residence in his grey matter. Okay, so he did have feelings for Natalie. Not in a falling in love sort of way—Christ, he knew better than *that*. But he did like her, and what's more, he trusted her. They'd never really gone the pour-your-heart-out route, and he wasn't keen on changing that. But she'd been straight with him about her cancer guilt. If she could spill something she'd kept that close to the vest for years, the least he could do was cough up a little family history.

"Pretty much," Jonah said, the words not sticking in his

throat the way he'd expected them to. "I mean, we never had a fallout or a fight over anything big. It's not like that."

"That's good, right?"

Natalie passed him the bowl full of the egg mixture to hold while she slid the spinach and onions into it. Whether it was the nonchalant way she worked or the ease in her expression, he couldn't be sure. But something made him keep talking.

"My old man has just never been a really emotive guy. Even before my mother left, he was always pretty quiet and reserved. He worked a lot of long hours—he was a foreman at a steel mill—so all the parenting fell to my mother. At least, it did until she left."

They were quickly veering into territory Jonah didn't want to touch, so he was relieved when Natalie stuck to talking about his father. "I didn't know that's what he did for a living. That's a pretty labor-intensive job. He must have one hell of a work ethic."

Surprised at both the thought and the fact that it had never occurred to him before now, Jonah nodded. "He does. Or did, I guess. He's been retired for four years now. No, five." Had it really been that long? "He didn't want to leave, but the plant where he'd worked for most of his career had grown pretty automated. The company didn't want to let him go, but they also didn't need him anymore, so they nudged him into retirement. To be honest, I'm not shocked he hung on until the very end. That job was everything to him." More than Jonah ever had been, that was for sure.

"Sounds like that's where you get your dedication from."

Natalie continued to cook while Jonah continued to be whammied by her words. "I guess, but he and I aren't really that much alike. It's not that he doesn't love me in his own way. I never doubted that there would be a roof over my head or plenty of food to eat, and he was there for the big stuff, like when I graduated from college and med school. But we were never close. I always..."

He broke off. But Natalie was right there, listening without a shitload of emotion or wah-wah sympathy, and the next thing he knew, he kept talking. "I always got the feeling I reminded him of my mother, and how much he missed her made it hard for him to be close to me. He'd always been a man of few words, but after she left, the distance between us grew bigger."

"If he's a quiet man and he didn't do a lot of hands-on parenting stuff before your mother left, maybe he didn't know how to bridge it," Natalie offered.

"Maybe. But he also might not have wanted to."

Jonah could see the desire to get defensive on his behalf was right there on Natalie's face. She was his best friend—of course she'd argue that his father not wanting a close bond with him was crazy, even though Jonah knew it was entirely probable, given how one-sided his father's love for his mother had turned out to be.

But, to Natalie's credit, she acknowledged the possibility by way of pragmatism. "Did you ever ask him about it?"

"No. At first, I was too young to really grasp anything other than the fact that my mother wasn't coming back." He'd spent years, really, grieving the loss of a woman who had never died. Well, she might be dead now, he reasoned. She'd never once tried to contact him, so he had no way of knowing, and he damn well knew he shouldn't care.

He stuffed the emotions that went with that part of things back into their hole, where they belonged. There was a difference, after all, between sharing and skewering himself over shit he couldn't change. "After that, I guess I figured the damage was done. Things weren't picture-perfect, but they weren't so bad. Now we talk a few times a year, just to check in. But the conversation is always pretty short."

For a minute, Natalie said nothing, busying herself with getting the first omelet, now done, out of the skillet and the mixture for the second one into place. "You could try asking him now. Just because you aren't close doesn't mean you can't ever be."

"I don't think that's a good idea." The answer escaped with sharper edges than Jonah had intended, and he sanded over them with a smile. "He seems happy living in Charleston. The retirement community he moved to is one of the best in the area, with lots of activities and things like that. I don't want to disrupt his routine by bringing up a bunch of painful things better left in the past."

Natalie frowned, her bright side/happy ending tendencies made of some seriously strong stuff. "But Christmas is in two weeks. Maybe you could take a few days off and go see him," she tried.

"Maybe," Jonah said, and even though he hadn't technically lied with the evasion, it still made his gut pang. Damn it, this was supposed to be a night full of sexy fun. He'd already had a hell of a time keeping his emotions out of his head and off of his face when they'd been in bed. He didn't want to have to worry about it on a whole new level. "So, once you get the egg mixture into the skillet, you just do that flip-thingy to cook the other side?"

Natalie looked at the spatula in her hand as if she'd forgotten she'd been holding it. "Oh. Well, yeah, there's a bit of technique to it, but it's easy enough with practice."

Jonah pulled together a grin to seal the subject-change deal. "I'm here to learn, Obi-Wan."

Even after he'd massacred the omelet (which Natalie

had, of course, then salvaged), conned her into watching *Die Hard* while they ate, then carried her back to his room for another round of mind-altering sex, Jonah couldn't quite shake the feeling that he didn't just want Natalie. He felt safe with her.

Which meant he needed to tighten the knot on his emotions, because after this weekend, they were going back to business as usual.

NATALIE ROLLED over to turn off the alarm on her cell phone even though she'd been awake for over an hour. No, scratch that. She'd been awake for most of the weekend. But it wasn't her fault, really, that she'd never had a nooner, or that she'd never been the recipient of gloriously good oral sex in the shower, or that Jonah had decided she *really* should experience both before their time together was up. Their one night had turned into all weekend, and all weekend, Natalie had felt startlingly good.

She took an extra second to burrow beneath the covers, the scent of laundry detergent mingling in with something distinctly more masculine sending a pang through her belly. She hadn't been surprised by the fact that Jonah was highly attentive in bed, nor had she been terribly shocked that there had been very little awkwardness between them after they'd first done the deed. After all, they were best friends, and they'd agreed to the terms of their sexcapade (Tess's word, not hers) ahead of time.

What *had* thrown her for a hey-now was the way he'd opened up about his father. Although the conversation hadn't been particularly lengthy or earth-shattering, the details had been far more than he'd ever shared before. The emotions banked way down deep in those Bahama blues had told her it was the tip of the proverbial iceberg, and even though neither of them had brought it up again for the rest of the weekend, Natalie knew there was a whole lot more there that Jonah had been keeping under wraps.

How had she never noticed it before?

Blowing out a breath, she sent her gaze to the ceiling in Jonah's bedroom, hating how empty the bed felt without him. He'd been on call starting at midnight, and sure enough, he'd been paged a couple of hours ago to tend to a nasty MVA. He'd kissed her gently on top of the head when she'd stirred, and Natalie knew it was a true kiss goodbye. Yes, their promise of all night had turned into all weekend, but now that it was Monday morning, she knew she had to face facts.

Her between-the-sheets experience with Jonah had been incredible. Even more than she'd hoped it would be. But now it was over.

No matter how badly she wanted to relive it one last time.

Throwing the covers from her body, she planted her feet over the floorboards and padded to the bathroom. She had a jam-packed day, and an even more jam-packed week, ahead of her. Now that Annabelle was infection-free, she had another round of chemo on tap, and until Natalie could find an alternative, they had to move forward as planned.

After a quick run through her get-ready/get-out routine, Natalie made her way through the morning rush, heading toward Remington Mem. Although traffic wasn't horribly bad, she still dragged herself from her car into the building, then to the lounge to get changed so she could start her day. Her muscles were achy and her eyelids felt far heavier than normal, but she only had herself to blame for losing far too much sleep.

Oh, how it had been worth every. Single. Toe-curling second.

"Good morning, Dr. Kendrick." Parker's voice tugged her from Fantasy Island, depositing her back in the staff lounge in the ED, lickety split. "I'm on your service today."

"Great," Natalie said, far too brightly. Ugh, she needed to stop thinking about the sex she'd finally had and get a grip. Life was still normal, for pity's sake. Just as it had been last week and month and year. She really had to start acting like it.

"Go ahead and check the board for emergent cases, then pull the post-op patient charts and get up to speed so we can round. Annabelle Fletcher is coming in today for her next chemo session, and unless there's an emergency in the ED that requires our attention, I'd like to be in the peds ward to get her settled in when she arrives."

"Already on it," Parker said, holding up a tablet with their first patient's chart, locked and loaded.

"Perfect. We've got a busy day ahead of us. Let's take care of some sick kids."

17

N atalie was living on bad coffee and dry shampoo. She hadn't showered in days, thanks to a huge influx of back to back (to back to back to...) peds cases that had required her full and immediate attention in both the ED and the OR. The one time she'd been able to escape long enough to head home, she'd spent every possible second on her futon, face planted, eyes shut. That had been two days ago. *Before* Annabelle had started suffering from adverse reactions to her chemo regimen.

Although they were wildly rare, there were days when Natalie wondered why she hadn't aimed herself at a nice, low-stress, eight-to-five job, where things like bathing and meals involving more than half a protein bar were a daily occurrence.

Leaning more heavily on the counter at the nurses' station than she normally might, Natalie lifted her cup of coffee to her lips, making a face when she got a taste of the cold, murky contents. Before she could turn to toss the cup into the nearest trash bin, where it well and truly belonged, her cell phone buzzed in the pocket of her doctor's coat.

Hi, sweetheart! Nine days to go Just triple-checking that you're coming for Christmas Eve dinner. Dad is making his famous twice-baked potatoes.

Natalie couldn't help but eke out a weary smile. Her father's signature side dish was a ridiculous combination of carbs, butter, and crack cocaine (okay, fine. Technically, there was no crack in them, but Natalie still swore they should be labeled a Schedule 1 narcotic for their addictive qualities). Plus, she'd been so busy over the past few weeks that she hadn't been able to visit, or even really talk with either of her parents at length, and she missed them.

Of course. What can I bring? Natalie thumb-typed in reply.

Just your holiday spirit, sweetheart. Love you!

Natalie held on to her smile and slid her phone back into her pocket, making a mental note to try and squeeze in a cookie-baking session this weekend so she could at least bring *something* to her parents' house besides presents and Christmas cheer. But since it was...she counted backward on her fingers...shit, Thursday morning and she and Dr. Hoover still hadn't found a way to keep Annabelle comfortable or a better way to treat the cancer that was slowly making her sicker and sicker, the chances she'd get cookies made from scratch looked slim enough to be a runway model. Natalie picked up her coffee, getting it to her lips again before realizing it was—ugh—still cold, and a new cup of fresh, hot coffee appeared in front of her like a mirage.

"Thought you might need a caffeine fix," Jonah said, leaning in next to her, and Natalie let out a happy moan.

"Oh, my God, I could seriously kiss you on the mouth right now."

The words flew out before she could stop them, and sweet Lord in heaven, could she *be* any more graceless?

Jonah froze, but to his credit, it lasted for less than a second before his camera-ready smile made an appearance. "I doubt the coffee is *that* good. But you've been here all night. At least it's a little boost." He nodded toward Annabelle's room. "How is she?"

Natalie had seen Jonah in tiny pockets of time over the past four days, just long enough to realize that she was A) comforted by his presence, and B) still missing his kisses. Since she couldn't do anything about her residual desire except wait for it to wane, she focused on what she *could* get; namely, the comfort.

"Truth?" Natalie asked, her stomach sinking even as she plied it with fresh coffee. "Not great. The treatment is aggressive because it has to be, but it's making her so sick that we had to admit her last night."

"Yeah, Young was on my service yesterday and I heard Boldin telling her you were going to keep Annabelle at least overnight. He seemed pretty concerned, but Young reminded him that it's a marathon, not a sprint."

Natalie managed a tiny smile at that. The two interns were proving to be a pretty good support system for each other. Sheboinking aside.

"Well, it's a marathon that's kicking our asses right now," she admitted quietly, even though it was early enough in the morning that the nurses' station and the hallways surrounding it were still pretty empty. "The chemo is making her so weak. It's like the thing we're giving her to fight the cancer is making her as sick as the cancer itself. I just wish there was another way."

"She's tough, plus she's getting the very best care possible," Jonah said, although his expression looked as concerned as Natalie felt. "Is Rachel still doing her coun-seling sessions?"

The one bright side, albeit a very small one. "She is. They seem to be helping. She's still really worried, of course, but she's treading water, for now."

"How about Annabelle?"

Natalie bit her lip. "She's, um. Fine," she tried, but Jonah shook his head, stepping in closer.

"You want to try that again?"

Shit. Shit, shit, shit. Natalie wanted to say something optimistic, to find some bright spot of hope to offer up. But the truth was, the little girl's morale was flagging, her strength along with it, and Natalie's heart ached more for her with each passing minute.

She'd tried everything she could think of. Researched dozens of alternative therapies. Looked into at least that many clinical trials. Nothing was working to make Annabelle better.

Natalie was tired and smelly and frustrated.

And *scared*.

"I..." She blinked, startled to realize that tears had filled her eyes. Gently, Jonah scooped up her elbow, guiding her to a nearby vacant room and closing the door. She shuttered her eyes in vain, willing her tears to disappear—for God's sake, she couldn't cry. She had to find the bright side, here. She *had* to.

But then Jonah shut the blinds and moved in close and said, "It's me, Nat."

And that was all it took.

"She's struggling so hard," Natalie said, her voice waver-ing. "She's trying, but the meds are *so* potent and her body won't cooperate. I don't know how to help her."

Her traitorous tears breached her bottom lids, coursing

over her cheeks, and her words poured out, equally unchecked. "Hoover's doing all the right things, I'm doing all the right things. God, I'm doing everything I can possibly think of! Annabelle's fighting as hard as she can. Rachel's right there to support her. And still, it's not *enough*. At this rate, I don't know how much longer she'll be able to fight. I want to hold out hope, I really do. But I'm so scared that nothing will work."

All the exhaustion and emotion of her week ganged up on her then, and her words gave way to tears. Jonah's arms were around her in an instant, and the pure comfort made her cry even harder. He didn't say anything, just gave her the space to bawl it out, and she did, even though she hadn't realized how badly she'd needed to.

Finally, once the hitch in her chest began to subside, Natalie was able to breathe. She didn't want to let go of Jonah, and she damn sure didn't want him to let go of her. He wasn't making a move to do so, no awkward pat on the back or tension in his muscles that suggested his desire to withdraw—if anything, he held her tighter—so Natalie gave in and leaned on him.

"I know it's hard to see her so sick," Jonah murmured into Natalie's hair. "But if anyone has this kid's back and can find a way to help her, it's you."

She sniffled against his doctor's coat. "I want to believe that, but—"

He pulled back, stunning her momentarily until his hands reached out to frame her face. "Then do. Believe it. You're an incredible doctor, Natalie. You're doing all that you can to help Annabelle fight her cancer."

"That's true," she said slowly. "I mean, the part about doing all that I can, anyway."

One corner of Jonah's mouth lifted in a smile that made

her smile a little by default. "We'll work on your ego later. In the meantime, let's tackle the first obstacle in our path. We need to get Annabelle's spirits up so she feels stronger. I spent all day in the ED yesterday, and I don't want to risk inadvertently carrying something nasty into her room, but I can FaceTime with her once she wakes up."

"She would like that," Natalie admitted. They hadn't allowed anyone into her room who wasn't purely necessary for that very reason. Even then, they'd stuck to protocol with gowns and masks.

"I'll get Connor in on it, too. Lord knows he's goofy enough. Is Annabelle on a restricted diet?"

Natalie's heart beat faster, a thread of hope uncurling in her chest. "No, but her nausea is pretty overwhelming, so her appetite sucks." It had been a huge challenge just to get her to nibble a few Saltines and drink some apple juice yesterday.

Jonah nodded as if to say *challenge accepted.* "I'm going to see if I can grab some green Jell-O from the kitchen. Also, do we still have those ginger-flavored lollipop thingies that drug rep had with her last week? There was a box of them in the lounge."

"The ones from the prenatal vitamin company?" Natalie laughed. "They're for morning sickness."

"Nausea is nausea. And, for the record, they also work like a charm on hangovers. Anyway"—he shook his head —"I'll grab some of those, too, along with some of that kickass chicken noodle soup from the bistro on Shelton Street."

"Okay, wait. You're going to go to Shelton Street for soup?"

Jonah's brows gathered over his impossibly beautiful eyes. "Don't be silly. Of course not. They deliver. And have you *had* that soup? It's fucking delicious—the best in the city. Hopefully it'll perk Annabelle up enough to let her rest and heal a bit while we figure out the next steps. Now, for you."

"What about me?" Natalie asked, confused.

"I mean this in the kindest way possible, Nat, but you look like shit."

A laugh popped out of her, her first in days. "Wow. I'd hate to hear the meaner version."

"Sorry, but if you want a best friend who will lie to you, you should probably start shopping around," he said, his affable smile turning slightly more serious as he continued. "You can't take care of Annabelle if you don't take care of yourself. Do you have any surgeries scheduled this morning?"

"Well, no. Not unless there's an emergency," she clarified. She'd cleared her schedule to try and do more research on clinical trials, and Vasquez was on her service, taking care of whatever cases came into the ED.

"Good." Jonah pointed to the door. "Go find an empty on-call room and get some sleep."

"But—"

He stepped in so swiftly that Natalie didn't have time to react until his fingers were on her lips and his body was ohhhhhh so close. "Do you trust me?"

"Yes," Natalie whispered against his fingers. For a split second, his eyes darkened with that unnamed emotion she'd struggled to identify.

But then he lifted his fingers from her mouth. "Good. Then you know I mean it when I say I've got this. I'll have Parker cover me in the ED and Danika can take my surgeries. If a major trauma comes in and I have to go, I'll have a nurse page you. If something changes with Annabelle's condition, I'll page you myself. I know you have her back, Natalie. Now do me a favor, please, and let me have yours."

Natalie's pulse raced, her breath growing tight as she waited for the argument she knew she should want to launch to pop out of her mouth.

Only instead, she nodded. "Thank you."

"You're welcome," Jonah said, his smile moving all the way through her as if it belonged there. "What are friends for?"

"No way. You beat me *again*?"

Jonah sat back in the chair beside Annabelle's bed, looking at the six *Uno* cards still left in his hand, then glancing pointedly at the one she'd just placed face-up on the pile between them.

She nodded sagely, her face pale but her smile firmly in place. "Yep."

"I told you she's a shark," Rachel said from her spot in the recliner on the other side of Annabelle's bed.

"That's the last time I play cards with you," Jonah said, prompting Annabelle to let out a weary giggle.

"You said that when I beat you just after breakfast, too."

He pulled an exaggerated frown, scrunching up his face until she giggled again. "Well, this time, I mean it."

Jonah collected the cards, his muscles reminding him that he'd gotten five hours of broken sleep on a flimsy on-call mattress. The last twenty-four hours had been pretty grueling, but they'd also been worth the effort. It had taken more than a little doing, but Natalie and Hoover had been able to find just the right treatment plan to make the anti-emetics play well (fine. As well as possible) with Annabelle's chemo meds. The ginger lollipops had ended up working wonders, too, settling her stomach enough to let her get some much-needed rest. She was still exhausted and in need of IV meds and monitoring that would keep her at Remington Mem for a little while longer, but at least now, the chemo wasn't making her sicker than her cancer.

Provided that it worked.

Jonah smacked the thought square in the face. He'd told Natalie to believe this would work. Of course, it would take good medicine and a lot of time to go with that hope, and none of it was a guarantee. But the despair on Natalie's face when she'd broken down and cried in his arms yesterday had gutted him. Her optimism wasn't just a sometimes-thing. It was her defining thing. Her *everything*. And as jaded as he was, he couldn't let her lose that, not even for a minute.

He might not be a long-haul guy, and there were damn good reasons he never would be. Ones he'd never told anyone. Ones Natalie could never know. But he could still be a good friend.

Even if he missed her in his bed far more than he wanted to admit.

"Okay, you two." Rachel's voice interrupted his thoughts —thank God—before they could linger on the image of Natalie with her head thrown back on his pillow, her face caught up in pleasure. "It's time to rest. Anyway, Dr. Jonah has other patients. We've kept him long enough."

"Ah, I don't mind," Jonah said. "I'm just glad I made it past the doorway today." He'd reached the official twenty-four-hours-removed-from-the-ED mark at dinner last night. He and Natalie had switched off keeping watch over Annabelle as she'd slowly started to respond. "But your mom is right. You need to rest, kid."

Annabelle's nod was a testament to her fatigue. "Okay. Will you come back later, though?"

"Of course." He held up the cards with a grin. "I want a rematch."

Pushing to his feet, Jonah said his goodbyes and made his way through the door. He paused for a second by the window, his heart giving up an unexpected squeeze at the sight of Rachel smoothing Annabelle's thinning hair. She tucked her in so carefully, her eyes full of nothing but pure love even in the face of all the adversity they'd both endured, and Jonah's hand auto-piloted to the cell phone in his doctor's coat pocket.

Just because you aren't close doesn't mean you can't ever be...

His fingers paused over his father's name and number. God, maybe it was crazy for him to call after all this time. The gaping space his mother had left when she'd torn out of their lives couldn't possibly be bridged *now*. His father had never gotten over her, and all Jonah would do was serve as a reminder of what the old man had lost.

Or maybe you'll remind him of what he still has.

Before he could stop himself, Jonah tapped the icon and raised the phone to his ear. It rang three times before going to voicemail, and shit, this had been a bad idea. But his father would see that he'd called regardless, so Jonah scraped together all of his nonchalance as he waited for the beep.

"Hey, Dad, it's Jonah. It's been a while, so I'm just checking in. No need to call me back or anything. Okay, bye."

Fuck, he was an idiot, he thought, sending one last look at Rachel and Annabelle before lowering his phone. Their parent-child relationship was nothing like Jonah's. Yeah, he and his old man had been through their own brand of hell together when Jonah's mother had left, but that was where the similarities ended. Thinking things could change now wasn't just stupid. It was dangerous.

It didn't matter if the love was romantic or familial.

It never, ever lasted.

Jonah's cell phone vibrated in his hand, startling the crap out of him. Ah, hell. He'd shuffled a lot of cases to Parker and Danika in the last twenty-four hours. Most of them hadn't been urgent, but that didn't mean they couldn't turn on a dime and leave nine and a half cents change in their wake.

But then he saw the name on his caller ID, and he realized in an instant that the person on the other end was calling about something far more urgent than anything the ED could throw in his direction.

18

Natalie looked at the text on her cell phone for the fortieth time in the hour since she'd received it, right after her last surgery of the day. Although Jonah had prefaced his cryptic message with "don't worry, nothing is wrong", then punctuated it with "*really*...nothing is wrong", he'd also asked her to come back to the apartment ASAP after her shift. They hadn't had a private conversation since her semi-embarrassing, totally cathartic meltdown yesterday morning, and now that she'd had sleep, a shower, and several meals (that soup really *was* the best in Remington), she was no less uneasy about how she'd cried like an infant with his arms around her.

That was the second time she'd been vulnerable in front of him in as many weeks. Even worse?

She'd felt so good with Jonah holding her that all she wanted was for him to do it again. This time, without the tears.

Natalie shook her head. She needed to focus on right now, and the fact that Jonah was clearly up to...something. Now that she was in the elevator, headed up to the apartment, her heart fluttered with an odd cross between curiosity and—okay, fine—concern (old habits, and all).

"Don't be silly," she whispered to herself. She knew everything with Annabelle was status quo. Hell, she'd spent the better part of the day checking in on her and Rachel in between other cases and a few routine surgeries, and now that Annabelle was far more stable, Natalie knew she'd be in good hands with the night-shift staff, who would call her immediately if something went south. Likewise, if something had happened to one of their friends, Jonah never would've told her nothing was wrong. But his request for her to leave the hospital as soon as her shift was over hadn't sounded run of the mill, either. It was hardly a "hey, let's hang out and order a pizza."

What the hell was he up to?

Natalie stepped off the elevator, her curiosity/concern becoming full-blown shock as she registered the sight of Jonah standing in the hallway, leaning against the doorframe to the apartment.

"Hey," he drawled, as if none of this was bat-shit crazy. "There you are. I was starting to think you'd gotten lost."

"First of all, I kind of live here," she reminded him, unable to keep her wry smile in check. "Secondly, what on earth is going on?"

"It's a surprise."

"A what?" Natalie asked, and Jonah shook his head, pushing off the doorframe.

"A surprise. You know. Something unexpected, where if I tell you, it's no longer a surprise?"

She laughed, because it was either that or scream. "I'm aware of what a surprise *is*. I'm just not sure why you called me here for one. And how long have you been standing out in this hallway, waiting?"

"About thirty seconds," Jonah said, elaborating when her brows shot upward. "I bribed Don to text me when you left."

"You bribed Don," she repeated, more and more convinced this was some sort of practical joke. "With what?"

Jonah looked at her as if she'd just asked what color the sky was. "Donuts. Anyway, now that you're here, I won't keep you in any more suspense. Close your eyes."

Before she could argue (and oh, she was *totally* ready to argue), he gave up that million-dollar smile she'd always thought she was immune to. "You still trust me, right?"

"Yes," Natalie heard herself say. God, it flew out so easily.

"Then close your eyes."

Jonah took her bag, and waited for her to do as he'd asked. When her eyes were firmly shut, he took one of her hands in his, then used the other to shush the front door open. They made it only eight steps in before he stopped, and she felt him move beside her, presumably to lower her bag.

"That ought to do it," he said. "Okay. Open 'em up."

Natalie fluttered her eyes open, blinking once, then twice, before her mouth fell open in shock. A Christmas tree stood in the corner by Jonah's bookshelf, blazing with hundreds of tiny white lights that illuminated the otherwise shadowy room. The fireplace—which Natalie would bet good money Jonah had probably never once used before now—was on, the orange flames dancing merrily behind the glass front, and oh God, there was even a shiny gold star on top of the tree.

"What...why did you do this?" she blurted, her face heating at her extreme lack of elegance.

But Jonah just laughed. "Because we're celebrating."

"Christmas is still a week and a half away," Natalie pointed out, but he shook his head.

"What we're celebrating is better than Christmas. Do you remember that pediatric oncologist I called a couple of weeks ago?"

Natalie's mind spun. Caught, and wait... "The one in Tampa, whose sister you treated a while back?"

"That's him. Dr. Kazinski. He called me this morning," Jonah said. Natalie's heart began to pound, her brain filling with a billion questions, but she clamped down on her lower lip so he could keep talking.

"One of the bigger drug companies he does a lot of research with is putting together a trial for some pretty cutting-edge stuff to treat pediatric non-Hodgkin lymphoma. He remembered that I had someone who might be a good fit for a trial, so he reached out."

Oh, my God. Natalie realized she'd let the words slip out loud, and Jonah nodded.

"It turns out Annabelle's not just a good fit. She's a *great* fit. So I hooked him up with Hoover at lunchtime, and they compared notes via Skype." Jonah held up a hand, likely to stave off the protest he had to know she was working up. "We didn't want to tell you because nothing was a lock. But after they talked, Kazinski went to the doctor running the trial, and they agreed. Annabelle's in."

Natalie's breath whooshed out of her in a rush. "She's in. Like..."

"They formally accepted her and want her in Tampa as soon as possible."

Tears sprang to Natalie's eyes, her pulse racing so fast, her thoughts couldn't keep up. "Oh, my God. Does Rachel know? Does Annabelle?"

"Hoover should be giving them the good news right

about now. I told her I'd tell you. I know you've got lots of questions, so I had Kazinski email me everything. And, of course, he'll want to confer with you at some point over the weekend, too. But for now, I figured we should celebrate."

Natalie pressed a hand over the front of her sweater, trying—and pretty much failing—to process it all. Annabelle was accepted into a trial. One that had some serious potential to help her manage her cancer, if not guide her toward full remission.

She flung her arms around Jonah and started to laugh. He held her back and laughed, too, and the next thing Natalie knew, he'd tugged her off her feet to swing her around, both of them laughing like crazy people.

It was the best she'd felt in ages. And it was all because of Jonah.

"I thought you said no Christmas tree," she finally said, after he'd lowered her back to the floorboards.

Funny, he still held on to her, his arms firm around the back of her rib cage, his chest pressed against hers. "I'm still not caving on those holiday rom coms. Anyway, I didn't have time to do more than put the lights and star on it. This barely counts."

Natalie shook her head. "This totally counts."

"It might count a *little*," Jonah conceded. "But it is Christmastime, and you're nuts about all the decorating and holiday cheer. You're stuck here instead of being in your own apartment, so it only seemed fair to at least have a tree."

"I don't feel stuck here." Her words emerged on little more than a breath, her heart beating faster even though they were true. Here, in Jonah's apartment, in his arms? She felt far from stuck.

She felt *right*.

Jonah's pupils flared, his bright blue eyes glinting in the

soft light spilling around them from the tree. "I don't feel stuck with you here."

His mouth hovered inches from hers, so close, Natalie could feel the heat of him. "We said we wouldn't do this again," she whispered, although, God, she wanted him so badly, she was practically shaking.

He held steady enough for both of them. "We did," he agreed, cupping her chin in one hand and running his thumb over her bottom lip.

"Okay. Well, as long as we're both on the same page..." Natalie murmured. But everything else she meant to say, from *thank you* to *I want you*, got lost when she pressed up to kiss him.

NATALIE ARCHED up at the same time Jonah lowered to meet her, their mouths crashing together in a tangle of tongues and pure, raw, want. He knew—God damn it, he fucking *knew*—that this was a bad idea. He hadn't wanted the same woman more than once in over three years. He was ripping back the cover on a huge tangle of dangerous emotions, and it was getting harder and harder to hide them.

He knew, and he didn't care.

He wanted Natalie too badly for that.

"Christ, you feel so good," he said, placing the whisper in the silky spot behind her ear as he breathed her in.

"Just good?" came the sassy reply, and Jonah gave in to the rumble of laughter building in his throat.

"Spectacular." He kissed her neck, sliding his tongue over the juncture where it met her collarbone until she sighed. "Incredible." His hands slid up, splaying wide across her shoulder blades to pull her flush against him from chest to belly to hips. "Stunning."

Jonah lifted his chin, making sure he held every ounce of her warm bronze stare before he finished with, "Beautiful. You're so goddamned beautiful, Natalie."

He meant to kiss her with tenderness. God knew she'd been through the emotional wringer over the last couple of days. But then her lips were right there, parting beneath his, her hot little mouth and those sexy as fuck sighs begging him for more, and his composure slipped, his own want darkening. He pressed into Natalie's mouth, kissing her with deep strokes of his tongue, knotting his fingers in her hair and giving her everything he could muster.

But she didn't just take it. No, Natalie took it and gave it back with equal measure. She didn't *just* let him push past her lips or slide his tongue over hers to give her pleasure she clearly wanted, if that moan she'd just let out was any indication. She let him give, but then she gave right back, kissing him and finding all the things that drove him crazy —holy fuck, if she nipped at his lip again, they weren't going to make it past the couch before he ripped off every stitch of her clothing. Natalie even discovered some new things Jonah hadn't known would turn him on, like when she kissed *him* on that soft spot behind *his* ear, just as he'd done to her. All too soon, he was holding her tightly, kissing her hard and desperate for so much more, and he walked her backward toward the couch.

"Wait." He hated parting from her, even for the nanosecond it took to grab the blanket he kept draped over the back of the couch. But then he saw her kiss-swollen mouth, her mussed blond hair framing her face like a wild halo, and okay, yeah, that nanosecond was suddenly so freaking worth it.

Not that he wanted to waste any time getting his hands back on her, though. Turning on his heels, Jonah scanned the softly lit room, and *ah*. Perfect.

He spread the blanket out beside the fireplace, just close enough to enjoy the ambiance of the pretty light and take advantage of the heat it gave off without posing a safety threat. Reaching for Natalie, he pulled her close for one slow kiss before waiting for her to toe out of her cute little ballet slipper-like shoes so he could guide her over the blanket.

They didn't speak, but then again, they didn't really have to. Jonah could read her with ease, the happiness in her eyes mixing in with provocative desire. She was such a perfect combination of sexy and sweet, and watching her here, in the glow of the Christmas lights, seeing the nuance of every emotion so wide-open on her face, Christ, it turned him on like nothing else. His cock ached in demand, but he pushed down on his own need by moving to fulfill hers.

"Let me see you," he said, his breath catching when she didn't hesitate to pull her sweater over her head and toss it aside. Today's bra was dark green satin, and—ah, *hell*—her panties matched. Jonah knew because Natalie had just slid her jeans over her hips, discarding them just as she'd done with her sweater, without pause. Her bra was one of those low-cut affairs, the sort that showcased her cleavage and made him want to rip it off of her with his teeth. The top edge barely covered her nipples, and Jonah couldn't decide if he loved it or hated it for driving him mad.

Natalie took a half-step back to look at him, a smile hooking at the edges of her mouth. "I want to see you, too."

His defenses squalled. Of course, he knew he'd have to undress. He couldn't fuck her fully clothed, and he *so* intended to fuck her. But this couldn't be about him, and seducing her was a far cry from letting her pleasure him in exactly the manner her tone suggested she wanted to. The way that would make him invested. Emotionally connected to her. Too vulnerable.

And yet, this couldn't be about her and not also be about him, too. Try as he had to keep his emotions banked since the first minute he'd touched her all those weeks ago, they were there, simmering and swirling and searching for her. So Jonah did the only thing he could do.

He took off his damned clothes and let Natalie look her fill.

"You're beautiful, too," she whispered, skimming her fingers over his shoulders. His muscles twitched in the wake of the contact, his heart beating faster, then faster still as her touch slipped over his arms, then back up again to cover his chest, then his abs. His control redlined when Natalie got to the top of his boxer briefs, which he'd kept on even though they were doing a piss-poor job of masking his raging hard-on. But if her fingers had reached their destination, if she'd wrapped them around his cock and started to pump, or, Christ forbid, if she'd gotten her mouth on him, he wouldn't have been able to make her stop. He'd already let her too far in as it was.

Fuck, she felt so good there.

Jonah grabbed her hand, swiftly scooping up the other to clasp both wrists between his fingers before she could protest. "I'll show you beautiful."

Yanking her panties down, he dropped to his knees in front of her, not pausing for so much as a sliver of a second before slanting his mouth over her pussy. A noise crossed Natalie's lips, some combination of surprise and pleasure, and oh, it only made him want to give her more.

"*Ah*," she moaned, hinging slightly forward, almost as if

the sensation were too much. But Jonah didn't scale back. He swept his tongue up, finding her clit with ease. He read her like a map that he knew by heart, easily rediscovering what he knew while exploring new places he hadn't before. Natalie widened her stance to grant him better access, her hands landing on his shoulders, then sliding up to knot in his hair and hold him where she wanted him, and the brazen encouragement made his cock jerk even harder in demand.

Shifting forward, he quickened his movements, hyper-aware of her response. The sounds she made. The play of her muscles, the rhythm of her breath. The way she tasted on his tongue. Everything about her filled Jonah up, stamping itself into his memory and pushing him to give her what she needed.

"Oh, God." Natalie's breath hitched over the words. Her head tipped back, and he wrapped his arms around her hips to bring her closer. She thrust against his lips and tongue, which he was now using to work her in firm, fast strokes, until finally, she stilled on a sharp cry. He carried her through her orgasm, greedily wringing every moan and shiver and shake out of her before reaching up to lower her to the blanket. The firelight flickered over her body, illuminating some places while casting others in shadow, and Jonah stole a second—just one—to memorize the glint in her hair and the surrender of dark green satin as it cradled the perfect curve of her tits.

He'd been wrong before. Beautiful didn't even touch this woman.

She was something else entirely.

Natalie propped herself up on her elbows, her bottom lip finding purchase between her teeth. "Come here, Jonah."

He was moving before she'd even finished the request.

Pausing only to rifle through his discarded jeans for the condom in his wallet, he closed the space between them, parting Natalie's knees to settle himself just shy of contact. Jonah's heart raced, his composure fracturing as he took her in. Flushed. Wet. Wanting, and when she lifted her hips in invitation, he was powerless to resist. One tug had his boxer briefs low enough to free his cock from the cotton, another seamless move had the condom in place. He thrust into Natalie in one fluid stroke, the inner muscles of her pussy gripping him so tightly that he nearly lost both his breath and his goddamned mind. Her pleasure-soaked cry did nothing to help him regain his composure. Jonah struggled to stay level, to hold back the intensity brimming brightly inside of him. But then Natalie looked up at him, wrecking every last ounce of his control with one tiny word.

"Please."

Something snapped deep in his chest. Levering forward, Jonah gripped Natalie's hips, pulling back by an inch only so he could find home, again and again. She arched her back, her eyes squeezed shut and her face caught up in pure pleasure as her knees fell wide, the sight turning Jonah on like nothing ever had. Sliding her forward to keep his cock fully seated inside of her, he shifted to kneeling, the change in angle allowing him a perfect view of how deeply he filled her pussy.

Natalie murmured her approval, lifting up to meet every thrust. Quickly falling into rhythm, they moved together like waves, rising up to meet each other and crash back down, only to roll upward again. Her breath caught, and yes, fuck yes, *this* was what he wanted. Jonah slid his thumb to her clit, pressing circles there just the way she liked, smiling darkly when her exhale collapsed on a moan that turned into his name. Her slick inner muscles grasped and released, and he didn't think. Christ, he *couldn't* think. Pushing back over her, Jonah thrust deeper, covering her body from shoulders to hips. His movements raced along with all the emotions pulsing through him, his climax rushing up so hard and fast, it caught him by surprise. For a split second, he tried to hold back, or at the very least, scale down. But Natalie looked up at him, her eyes glittering in the firelight, and holding back became as impossible as moving a mountain range.

Please, her gaze said. *Let me make you feel good.*

So he did.

And as he gave in to the best orgasm he'd ever had, Jonah knew he was dangerously close to a bridge he couldn't cross. The problem was, he felt too good to care.

❮

19

Natalie was having the best dream. Annabelle was laughing, holding her stuffed fox and running toward her. Her cheeks had a rosy glow, her hair braided elaborately over her head like a crown, and Natalie's heart swelled. Then, Annabelle faded and Jonah was there, holding her hand and giving her a Christmas tree, laying her down in front of the fireplace and making her mindless with pleasure. He picked her up and carried her to bed, kissing her hair and stroking her back as she drifted further into the dream. The darkness around her grew blurry and soft, shapes fading into the background and gravity pulling her down. Her body was tired all of a sudden—God, she was *so* tired, surely she'd never be able to open her eyes. She commanded herself to wake, to move, to shout, to breathe, but her traitorous body refused to comply, too tired to do anything other than drift. A bubble of panic rose in Natalie's chest, trapping her voice and cementing her limbs. Her body refused to cooperate, floating deeper into the darkness, her exhaustion pulling her under, holding her down, trapping her...

Natalie woke with a start. Reality returned in clips and scraps, fatigue and residual sleepiness making it a slower process than usual. The text from Jonah. Annabelle getting accepted into the trial. The Christmas tree, the mind-blowing sex that had gone with it, the way Jonah had carried her to bed afterward. All of that had been real, she realized as her heart began to stutter. Annabelle had gotten into a clinical trial. One that could very well save her life.

And Jonah had made it happen.

She sat upright, her vision tilting from the sudden movement. She recognized a beat later that she was wearing only a tank top, her panties, and Jonah's bed sheets around her legs, and that he was sitting in a chair a few feet away. Daylight streamed through the blinds, drawing an involuntary groan from her chest.

"Oh, hey." He looked up from the laptop he'd propped on a pillow, setting it aside a second later. "You're up."

Natalie winced against the daylight, her eyes still heavy with sleep. "What time is it?"

"Just shy of one."

What the—"In the *afternoon*?" She blinked. They'd fallen asleep well before midnight, for God's sake.

He nodded, completely unfazed. "Yep."

"Jeez, Jonah! Why didn't you wake me?" Natalie's pulse went from zero to warp speed in less than a breath. She flung the covers off her legs, but Jonah held up a hand to stop her movements, then used said hand to tick through his responses, one by one.

"Because it's your day off. Because you've worked a ridiculous number of hours over the past few weeks. Because you needed the sleep. Clearly." He indicated the rumpled sheets with a charming half-smile that made her worry slip despite her panic, but only for a second.

"But Annabelle—"

"Is totally fine," he promised. "I've been in contact with Hoover, Kazinski, and Rachel all morning. Of course, Kazinski still wants to confer with you, and Rachel and Annabelle said they'd very much love to talk with you when you're ready. They're both very excited. But as far as the logistics go, you don't need to worry. Everything is taken care of. Really."

Oh, God. This was really happening. It hadn't been a dream. Annabelle really *was* going to Tampa for this trial.

Gratitude filled Natalie's chest. "Thanks to you."

Shaking his head, Jonah set his laptop aside and got up to sit in front of her on the bed. "I believe that honor goes to you. You poured every ounce of your energy into caring for that little girl. All I did was make some phone calls."

"Phone calls that worked," Natalie insisted, and he conceded as far as he was probably going to with a shrug.

"Guess we just make a good team."

Memories of the night before flashed through Natalie's mind. His mouth on her sex. His cock buried deep inside of her. The want that had burned so hotly under her skin, want that was rebuilding again, even now, and God, *good team* felt like the largest euphemism ever to be uttered.

They were fucking spectacular together.

Natalie's cheeks flushed. "Guess we do."

Jonah paused for a heartbeat, flicking a glance over the bed where they'd spent the night (again) as if he'd read her thoughts (again). "Look, I know we said sleeping together was a one-time thing, and then..."

"It wasn't?" she supplied.

"It wasn't," he agreed. "And I don't regret that. Last night was really good." His eyes crinkled over the word, making Natalie press her lips together over her smile. "But as true as that is, nothing about what I told you a couple of weeks ago has changed. I'm not a long-haul guy. I also know you're looking for something serious in the long run. You want the cheesecake, the two halves. The whole deal."

"I do," she said slowly. She couldn't, and what's more, *wouldn't* deny that, even if the time she'd spent with Jonah had felt better than she'd ever expected. He'd never promised her anything other than short-term, and she'd never expected more. But she did want it with someone, eventually. "You were clear from the beginning that whatever happened between us would be strictly casual. I would never ask you for anything other than that."

Jonah looked at her, his blue eyes full of honesty and all the things that had always given her comfort.

"And I would never stand in the way of you finding what you need, Nat. But this"—he paused to gesture between them—"right now, this feels good. I don't want it to mess with our friendship. I would never risk that—"

"But it's not," Natalie interrupted. "I mean, yes, we had sex, and that's more than friendly." She paused to roll her eyes at the understatement. "But we also worked together to help Annabelle. We took coffee breaks at work and watched *Die Hard* last weekend. Aside from the really great sex, everything else felt totally normal. Just like it always does."

He nodded. "It did."

"So, you want to keep doing...this." She repeated the gesture he'd just made, swinging her finger in a circle to encompass them both. "Like friends with benefits, emphasis on staying friends?"

"Yeah," Jonah said. "Do you?"

Natalie paused. She'd meant what she'd said about their friendship still feeling exactly as it had before they'd slept together. If anything, she and Jonah had gotten closer since she'd moved in, and nothing about their sexual encounters had been awkward. If they'd slid into things seamlessly, there was no reason to believe they couldn't slide out in the exact same manner once she moved back to her own place in a few weeks. Yes, she still wondered about those emotions he kept so carefully hidden—after last night, she was certain she hadn't been imagining them. But she couldn't deny that she felt better with Jonah than she had in...well, maybe ever.

He might not be a long-haul guy, but what could a few weeks hurt? Especially if they were going to feel like this?

"Well, I guess that depends," Natalie said, running a finger over the back of his hand. "Does friends with benefits involve breakfast in bed?"

Jonah smiled, and God, she felt it all over. "I think that could be arranged. What do you want?" He flipped his hand over, lacing his fingers between hers, and oh, yeah. If this was how friends with benefits worked, she was *definitely* on board.

She threw back the bed sheets and grinned. "Why don't you come back to bed and I'll show you?"

JONAH EYEBALLED the shopping cart in front of him, unable to help his laughter. He and Natalie had only been in the superstore for ten minutes, and yet the thing was more than half-full with everything from fuzzy socks to travel snacks, not to mention the two big red and green gift bags and glittery tissue paper to hold it all.

"Oh!" Natalie exclaimed, reaching up for a value pack of coloring books. "Annabelle will love these. She's going to need a lot of things to keep her busy in the car."

"The drive will take nine hours, not nine days," Jonah teased. "Plus, you've already got four books, two movies, more snacks than she and Rachel can eat in a week—"

Natalie slid one hand to her hip, although her great, big smile kind of took the sting out of the move. "Do you have any idea how stir-crazy an eight-year-old can get? Anyway, they're going to be in Tampa for a while, and living in an efficiency—even a nice one—is a far cry from home. Trust me, a few extra goodies won't hurt."

A pang spread out beneath the center of Jonah's sweater at the reminder that Natalie knew what she was talking about, firsthand. "Well, in that case," he said, reaching for a giant bottle of bubbles and dropping it into the cart, then adding a plastic princess tiara from the next shelf for good measure. "Let's spoil the hell out of her."

Natalie's smile settled in as she murmured her agreement, pushing the cart farther down the aisle. Now that she'd spent the morning catching up on some seriously overdue sleep and the afternoon catching up on all the details of the clinical trial, the shadows beneath her eyes had nearly disappeared. Of course, she'd insisted on cooking an early dinner for both of them before they'd headed out to grab bon voyage/Christmas presents for Annabelle and Rachel, who were headed to Tampa bright and early tomorrow morning. But Natalie had let him help —okay, at least, she'd let him put the salad together—and do the dishes, just as she hadn't argued when he'd offered to upload Annabelle's latest scans and complete medical history to the database in Tampa so she could use the time to talk to Hoover and Kazinski. As small as they were, those things were also more than Natalie had probably ever allowed him to do for her, and *definitely* more than she'd ever asked for help with, outright.

But ever since she'd broken down and cried in his arms the other night—ever since she'd moved in with him, really —Jonah had started to see her differently. She was still the same sweetly fierce, endlessly kind woman he'd always known. Nothing short of a complete personality transplant would change that. Only now, he saw *why* she cared so much for other people, the deep-seated reasoning behind her bright-side, everything's-fine disposition. He saw how ingrained it was, how she'd set aside her own needs and comfort and even her health in order to take care of other people.

And just for a little while, he wanted to take care of her in return.

Jonah's phone buzzed in the back pocket of his jeans, quickly depositing him back to the reality of the games and puzzles aisle.

"Work?" Natalie asked, a tiny furrow of worry appearing between her brows as he reached for the thing.

"Shouldn't be. I'm not on call." He slid his phone into his palm, his confusion turning to a cold trickle of unease. "It's my father."

Natalie's eyes went round. "It is?"

Holy shit. "Yeah, I, ah. Called him the other day and left him a message, but..."

"Go." She nudged his shoulder, pointing toward the empty customer-service alcove by the front of the store. "Find a quiet spot and take the call. Go."

Jonah nodded, pressing the icon to answer the call before it could go to voicemail. Something had to be gravely wrong. His father would never reach out to him otherwise. On the rare occasion that they did touch base, Jonah always, *always* made the call.

"Hello?"

"Oh." A thread of surprise colored his father's voice. "You picked up the phone."

Jonah made his way to the front of the store, his heart beating faster in concern. "Yeah. Is everything okay?"

"Yes. Everything is fine."

Okay, that couldn't be right. "You're not hurt or sick or anything?"

"No." Silence extended over the line. "I'm calling you back."

"Oh."

There was no masking the shock in his response, so Jonah didn't even try. It was on the tip of his tongue to remind his old man that he'd said he didn't have to return the call, but he bit the words in half just shy of launch.

He was glad his father had called back.

"So." His father cleared his throat. "How have you been?"

Not knowing what else to do, Jonah followed the script of the conversation. "Good. You?"

"Good."

This was the point where Jonah usually had mercy on the old man and started to wrap things up. But it struck him suddenly that, while his father never actively participated in their conversations by asking questions or being particularly chatty, he never moved to end things, either.

Could Natalie have been right? Was it possible that he *wanted* to talk to Jonah—or at least listen—only he didn't know how?

"I've been working a lot," Jonah offered. "I just helped a friend of mine, another doctor, with a pretty big case she was working on."

His father paused, but only for a breath. "Oh, yeah?"

His voice lifted, just slightly at the end of the question, but it was enough. Hell, it was more interest than Jonah had heard from him in years, maybe even decades. Or maybe it was the first time Jonah had thought to dig deeper, to nudge a little and read between the lines.

To look for the bright side.

IN THAT MOMENT, Jonah knew he could do one of two things. He could default to his defenses and guide the conversation to an end, keeping the carefully cultivated arm's length between him and his father intact. Or, he could keep talking, even though it was a risk.

Fuck it. The bright side looked pretty good from here.

"Yep," Jonah said. "We got a little girl placed in a clinical trial. Looks like it's going to be a happy ending."

Settling into one of the plastic chairs in the deserted customer service area, Jonah launched into the story. His father mostly listened, but he never tried to steer the conversation to a close, and by the end, he was peppering his mmm-hmms and oh, reallys with a handful of short but genuine questions.

"Well, that does sound like a happy ending," his father finally said when Jonah had relayed the whole thing. "I hope it helps Annabelle into remission."

"Me, too. She's a pretty great kid," Jonah said.

The topic lulled to a gentle halt, and he knew this was where the conversation would really end. They'd already shared more words tonight than they had in the last decade combined. Of course, it couldn't last. Love, familial or otherwise, never did.

Out of the corner of one eye, Jonah caught sight of Natalie, and his heart tripped faster against his breastbone.

The neatly bagged items in the cart beside her said that she'd finished shopping, yet she stood far enough away to give him the space to finish his conversation without the pressure of hurrying, or even letting him know she was waiting. Although she was looking down at her phone, Jonah could still see her face, and when she gave up a big, unabashed smile at whatever she'd just read, he didn't think. Just spoke.

"So, I've got a little time off for the holidays. Just a couple of days," he added. "Maybe I could drive down for Christmas. We could spend the holiday together. If you want."

After a startled pause, his father said, "I...yes. That would be nice."

"Okay." Jonah's hard exhale made him realize he'd been holding his breath. They agreed on a few logistics, then hung up with the promise of seeing each other soon. Putting his phone back in his pocket, he walked over to the spot where Natalie stood waiting.

"Hey." She looked up at the sound of his footsteps on the linoleum. "Is everything okay?"

Jonah slipped his arms around her, pulling her in for a quick kiss and loving the taste of surprise on her lips.

"Actually, everything is great."

20

Natalie made her way into the staff lounge in the ED with three dozen donuts in her hands and a whole lot of dirty thoughts in her head. To be fair, the dirty thoughts *were* the product of a group effort. After all, she might've participated (enthusiastically) in the quickie that had made her run late this morning, but Jonah had inspired it. In fact, he'd inspired lots of things over the last thirty-six hours. Hot things. Wicked things. Multiple things.

Friends with benefits was better than chocolate and martinis and sleeping until noon combined.

"Good morning!" Natalie sing-songed, grinning hello at both Tess and Charlie as the door to the lounge bumped shut behind her. "I brought breakfast."

"Holy shit, you and Sheridan totally had sex," Tess said.

Natalie's grip went thermonuclear over the pastry boxes, her gaze whipping around the—*whew*—otherwise empty lounge. "Oh, my God, are you psychic now? Or does it, like, *show*, or something?" Dropping the donuts to the table in the center of the lounge, she reached up to skim both hands over her face.

Tess laughed, not unkindly, and got up from the couch. "Neither. I was bluffing. You, my friend, are an easy mark. So honest."

"That, and the donuts and pure happiness on your face were kind of a dead giveaway," Charlie said, tucking a strand of red-gold hair behind one ear and following Tess over to the table to help take the lids off the pastry boxes.

Tess nodded. "Sooooo. How was it? I mean"—she raised a hand—"I have to work with the guy, so I don't want all the gory details. Just like, on a scale of one to ten."

Natalie flushed, feeling equally torn between not wanting to kiss and tell and wanting to laugh her fool head off. "Okay, you have to remember that I have nothing to compare it to."

"But...?" Charlie prompted, leaning in.

Natalie bit her lip. "Would a thousand seem like an overstatement?"

"No," both women said in unison, and Tess let go of a wry smile. "Guess he lives up to his nickname."

Charlie reached for a cake donut and laughed. "A thousand seems about right for a great experience. Especially if you two were that into each other."

"We really are," Natalie admitted.

Tess's chin lifted, her hand freezing to a halt over a double-glazed cruller. "*Are*? As in, present tense? I thought the deal was for him to take your virginity. You can kind of only do that once."

"Oh." Shit. Shit! Why hadn't anyone warned her that great sex would turn her brain into tapioca? "Um, well, he did. But we're sort of...still sleeping together."

"Okay, stop right there." Tess exchanged a glance with

Charlie that lasted for roughly a nanosecond, yet frighteningly, both women began to move with purpose. Charlie guided Natalie over to the couch as Tess grabbed two Boston cream donuts and put them on a paper plate, then marched out of the lounge. She returned less than a minute later, and Charlie dispensed the three cups of coffee she'd poured in Tess's short absence.

"Not wine, but desperate times," she said, looking at Tess. "Are we set?"

Tess nodded, and in that moment, Natalie had never been so grateful for the two women sitting on either side of her. "Don has been bribed with donuts, and the interns have been threatened with scut. The residents have the floor, and Mallory's out there doing a consult, just in case. So unless a bus literally crashes into the ambulance bay or a massive epidemic of some long-dead disease breaks out in the next couple of minutes..."

"You know that only happens on TV, right?" Charlie asked, and Tess arched a brow.

"I once had to remove a toilet plunger from the ass of a man who was trying to home-remedy his severe constipation. You'd be fucking shocked at what happens in real life around here."

"On that highly pleasant note..." Charlie looked at Natalie, who had no choice but to laugh. "Please, for the love of God, change the subject, Natalie."

"Okay." Cradling her cup of coffee between her palms, Natalie gave up a concise and basically non-explicit version of the events of the past week and a half. She included her brief meltdown of frustration over Annabelle's treatment, as well as the support Jonah had given her to try and find a resolution, and their decision to keep sleeping together casually, for now.

"So, that's everything," Natalie said, sitting back against the couch cushions.

"God, no wonder you've got that smile on your face," Charlie mused. "You're having Chapter Thirteen sex with the Orgasm Whisperer."

"*And* you two are into each other," Tess added, popping the last bite of her cruller into her mouth. "I always knew someone would come along to make an honest man out of him."

A nervous laugh popped out of Natalie. "Okay, so Jonah and I *might've* done the Chapter Thirteen thing," she said, giving the memory of it an internal happy-sigh before continuing. "But we're not serious. We agreed it would be just sex."

"Lots of it," Tess pointed out.

"Well, yes." Natalie couldn't deny that. But come on, she had lost time to make up for.

"And you're living together," Charlie said.

Natalie's gut squeezed. "That's still temporary."

Tess hmmmed. "*And* there's the whole you-cried, he-held-you,   you-worked-together-to-treat-a-kid's-cancer thing," she added, but Natalie shook her head.

"Okay, but we're best friends. We'd have done that for each other regardless."

"Would you, though?" Tess asked, matter-of-fact. "I mean, I know you guys have always had each other's backs. Ride or die, and all that jazz. But can you really say that things between you and Jonah are exactly the same as they used to be, only now you're having sex on top of it?"

Natalie opened her mouth to say of course things were the same...but then an image of Jonah, his eyes loaded with emotion and his hands on her, wild and intense, spread out in her mind's eye. But that was just the sex, she reminded herself. It was what they'd agreed on. Yes, she card for Jonah, and yes again, she knew he cared for her. But they always had. This wasn't any different.

It couldn't be.

Before she could say so, though, the door to the lounge opened, and Connor ambled in. "Hey, ladies. Oooh, donuts!" he said, rubbing his hands together with glee.

"I should've known Don would only do his job for so long," Tess muttered, while both Natalie and Charlie clamped their lips shut.

Connor stopped, mid-step. "Whoa, girl talk." At Tess's arched brow, he tacked on, "What? I can smell the estrogen from here, and Dr. Kendrick has, like, zero poker face. I take it you three need privacy."

He edged toward the door—which was kind of comical, considering that he was roughly the size of a small nation— but Natalie shook her head.

"No, it's okay." It didn't seem fair to shut the guy out of the lounge. It was the only place for the nurses to take a break, and anyway, she and Jonah had agreed to keep things completely casual, and that meant treating the fact that they were sleeping together like no big deal.

"Are you sure?" he asked, descending on the donuts before she'd finished nodding. "You know, Dr. K, if you're interested in a guy's perspective, I'm always happy to trade advice for carbs."

Natalie had to admit, getting a man's insight on the whole friends-with-benefits thing might not be such a bad idea. Still, she and Jonah hadn't really talked about whether or not they would go the full-disclosure route with their colleagues and co-workers, so she'd have to get creative with some of the details.

"I, um, slept with someone," she said. Connor didn't

seem to find this news earth shattering, so she continued. "It was someone I know. A friend." Funny, the word suddenly seemed so standard and insufficient when she applied it to Jonah. "We agreed ahead of time that it would be completely casual, and it was...it *is*..."

Connor looked up from the pair of jelly donuts he'd balanced over the napkin on his palm. "But?"

"But now they're both into each other and neither one of them wants to admit it because they're worried it's going to fuck things up," Tess said.

"We are not *worried*," Natalie argued. Ugh, why hadn't she just kept her mouth shut? "And we're not into each other. Not like that. There is no 'but'. We're just two friends who like and respect one another, and we also happen to be having great sex for the short-term. That's all."

"Huh." Connor took a bite of his donut, chewing thoughtfully for a minute. "Well, it's about damned time you and Sheridan did the deed."

Natalie's jaw unhinged. "How did you know I was talking about Jonah?"

An ear-to-ear grin appeared amid the auburn stubble on Connor's face. "Ha, I was bluffing, but awesome. It really is about time."

"Connor," she warned, and he took a deferent step back.

"Okay, okay. Don't worry, I'm not going to tell anybody. So, what's the big deal? You both agreed to keep it casual, right?"

"We did."

"And is it?"

"Yes. Sort of. Yes," Natalie said, and God, it was official. She was never opening her yap about her personal life again. "Of course things aren't *entirely* casual. We've been best friends for years. You can't have that without some sort of depth."

Okay, so there was lots of depth between her and Jonah, along with respect and trust and a great, big boatload of sexual chemistry, but that wasn't a hair she was going to split right now. They'd agreed on keeping things casual, and that was the safest way to ensure that their friendship remained intact. "Jonah and I want different things from different people in the long-term, but for right now, we're on the same page, so yes. We're sleeping together, and we're friends, but it's really not a big deal. We're just enjoying it while it lasts."

Charlie and Tess exchanged a glance so brief, Natalie couldn't be certain she'd seen it. But then Charlie gave up a genuine smile. "As long as you're both happy, that's all that matters," she said, and Tess agreed with a nod.

"Truth? I think it's great," Connor said, sliding his second donut to the table and reaching out to give Natalie's shoulder a friendly squeeze. "I mean, it's far better to sleep with a friend than an enemy, right?"

Before Natalie could tell him that only happened in romance novels—after all, she might be new to the game, but who really slept with someone they hated?—the door to the lounge opened again.

"Seriously, Don is fucking fired from guard duty," Tess muttered under her breath. The words fell prey to a precise clack-clack-clack of designer footwear pretty much never found in the ED, making Natalie turn in complete confusion.

The woman belonging to the—yep—very expensive-looking four-inch heels and the immaculate dark gray sheath dress looked at Natalie without smiling. "Dr. Kendrick."

"Ms. Davenport?" Natalie pushed up from the couch in surprise. What the hell was Harlow Davenport doing down here in the ED?

Harlow nodded with a single, brisk lift of her chin. She cleared her throat expectantly, and Natalie's cheeks flushed in realization.

"Oh. I take it you haven't met Doctors Becker and Michaelson," she said, gesturing to Charlie and Tess, who stood closer to Harlow than Natalie and Connor. "This is Harlow Davenport. She was recently appointed to the hospital's board, and obviously has a vested interest in the clinic."

"Your name does precede you," Tess said, and Harlow smiled, an entirely polite gesture that didn't consider lasting any longer than it had to.

"It usually does. Doctors," she said, shaking both of their hands, then turning back toward Natalie, who gestured to Connor.

"And this is Connor Bradshaw. He's one of our very best nurses. We're lucky enough to have him come down from the ICU and help us out in the ED from time to time."

Harlow's ice-blue eyes narrowed slightly as they traveled over Connor's huge frame and brightly inked arms. "Bradshaw," she said slowly, as if she were turning over some puzzle in her mind.

"Yes, ma'am," he said stiffly. "That's what my dog tags say."

"Oh. I see." Harlow blinked once, then shook her head and returned her attention to Natalie. "Well. Dr. Kendrick, I've been looking for you."

"For me?" They'd only had that one exchange in the clinic a few weeks ago. What could they possibly have to discuss that couldn't have been done via email?

"Yes. I'd like a word." She paused. Looked at Tess, Charlie, and Connor pointedly. Then added, "In *private*."

"I believe that's our cue," Connor said, although Natalie couldn't help but notice he'd put a little un-Connorlike frost to the words to match Harlow's all-business tone. Natalie said a quiet goodbye to her friends, who shuffled out of the lounge in various states of curiosity (and in Connor's case, irritation), and Natalie had to admit, she was overflowing with the stuff, herself.

"How can I help you, Ms. Davenport?"

"We're both intelligent women with very busy jobs, so I'm going to get right to the point. The clinic is failing. *Badly*. As a director for Davenport Industries and a member of this hospital's board, I've recently taken over all of the clinic's operations in an effort to change that. I need someone to run the facility on a permanent, hands-on basis, and I'd like for that person to be you."

Natalie's breath whooshed from her lungs. "I'm...sorry?"

"I realize this may seem abrupt," Harlow said, and it took all of Natalie's control not to blurt *no shit, Sherlock* in reply. "But after reviewing the business and management plans currently in place, it's become very clear that we need someone in charge of the clinic who understands protocols as well as infrastructure. Your experience as a physician and your history of volunteering your time speak for themselves, and Dr. Langston highly recommends you. The board feels you'd be a strong asset."

Dear Lord, the amount of jargon in that one sentence alone made Natalie's head hurt. "Okay, can we just skip the formalities and speak plainly, here?"

A tiny smile, the real kind, twitched at the edges of Harlow's mouth, but only for a blink before disappearing. "Fine. The person running the clinic right now is an idiot.

You, Dr. Kendrick, are not an idiot. In fact, I think you'd be perfect for the job, and the clinic is losing an astronomical amount of money every day. I need a director in there who doesn't have their head in their ass, and I need it right now."

Natalie had to give the woman credit. She could speak plainly like a *boss*. "Okay, but I already have a job. I'm a surgeon. And I've never directed anything in my life."

"You mentor interns and residents, and you've got an impeccable track record coordinating treatment plans with other doctors. In fact, Dr. Hoover was quite effusive with her praise for your dedication to the case you just worked on together." Harlow lifted a perfectly penciled blond brow. "Annabelle Fletcher, was it?"

"Well, yes," Natalie said. "But that was a team effort."

"Precisely. You already know how to direct plenty. Plus, you and I would be working very closely to start, so whatever you don't know, I can teach you."

Natalie plucked the next question from the huge pile growing in her mind. "But my job is to help patients, not manage other medical professionals."

At that, Harlow paused. "You'd still be able to treat patients, of course, although the parameters would change. But with a good management team in place, the clinic can treat thousands of patients who need care. With you as the director, you'd have a hand in *all* of their wellness and care. Also"—she slid a folder out of the slim, leather bag on her shoulder—"the salary and benefits are quite competitive. This would be a big advancement in your career."

Natalie flipped to the top page, her heart climbing all the way up her windpipe. "Ah, okay," she managed. Holy shit, that decimal point had to be in the wrong spot. "This is a really generous offer, but one I really wasn't expecting, at all. I'm grateful for the consideration," she added, because holy-shit factor aside, she really was. "But it would be a huge change. I'm going to need some time to go through the particulars, and to talk to Dr. Langston, in order to make a decision."

Harlow didn't look pleased, but she also didn't look shocked. "Understood. I'll need to know as soon as possible. We'd like to make an announcement before the end of the year."

Natalie swallowed. "That's less than two weeks away."

"It is," Harlow agreed. "But you'll soon find that when I set my sights on something, I stop at damn little until I get it. This clinic *will* be running successfully six months from now. You can take that to the bank. In the meantime, let me know if you have any questions. I'd be happy to answer them."

And then she walked out of the lounge, leaving Natalie to wonder what the hell had just happened to her career.

21

"And that was it? She just walked out of the lounge?"

"Yep," Natalie said, leaning her head back against Jonah's leg. They were sprawled out over the couch in his apartment, with him sitting at one end and her stretched out on the cushions, at his insistence. Her back *had* been killing her today, but, then again, three pediatric surgeries plus a whole raft of ED cases would do that to a girl. "That was it."

The ten hours that had passed since Harlow had offered Natalie the director's job at the clinic hadn't made things any less whoa. The fact that Natalie had needed to wait this long to tell Jonah about it had only made her edgier, but they'd both been up to their eye teeth in patients all day. She hadn't even seen him since they'd rolled out of bed this morning.

"Jesus, Nat." Jonah looked down at her, his shock paving a path for his smile and his handsome face lit by the soft glow of the Christmas tree. "This is huge. Just think of all the things you'd be able to do as a director."

"It is huge," she agreed, biting her lip. "And it is possible that I'd be able to make a lot of strides for wellness and health care awareness, especially for kids, which is great."

Jonah read her mind in less than a breath. "But?"

"But for all the things I *could* do, there's one really big thing I'd have to give up."

"Surgery," Jonah said after a beat, and all the unease that had been pricking at Natalie's belly came bubbling to the surface.

"What I do now is already a full-time job and a half. Add the day-to-day management of an entire urgent care clinic to the mix? There's no way I'd still be able to perform surgeries, even if I limited my schedule. I just wouldn't be able to give any of my patients the sort of one-on-one care they'd need and deserve. It would be a huge change."

"And you're not sure you want to make it," Jonah said.

Natalie huffed out a sound that wanted to be a laugh, but fell just the tiniest bit short. "Am I that obvious?"

"That's not a fair question." Jonah traced his fingers through her hair, and although the contact was slight, still, it soothed her. "This is me we're talking about."

He had a point. He might be the only person in the world who knew that she kept any negative feelings she might have hidden from the rest of the world, and he was definitely the only person who knew why. But he *did* know that sometimes, her glass wasn't half full. Natalie had trusted him with that. She could trust him to see her uncertainty now.

"It's not that I don't understand how huge this opportunity is, or that I don't recognize that I could potentially have a lot of chances to make a difference in peoples' health and wellness. But for as much influence as the position might carry, the work is nearly all administrative. I'd never get to personally treat the patients."

She knew, because she'd asked Langston point-blank today when he'd performed his last surgery. He'd taken so long to come up with the answer that the fact that it had been months ago had been a given. "There are meetings and committees and more meetings, and I get that they're necessary. We do need stronger plans and policies in place at the clinic in order to provide strong health care."

"You're just not sure you want to be the person in charge of facilitating that," Jonah finished.

"I don't know that I'm the *right* person to be in charge of facilitating that. I'm a surgeon. I want my name on the OR board, not a bunch of budget meeting agendas." Natalie exhaled, her indecision riding out along with her breath. "Does that make me a horrible person? It does, doesn't it? If those budgets are allocated properly, it could help a lot of people, too." Ugh, she hated this!

But Jonah just laughed. "Sweetheart, I can think of a thousand words that accurately describe you. Horrible is not on the list."

"I shouldn't be putting what I want ahead of the needs of all the people the clinic could help if it were run more effectively," she argued. "Yes, directing the clinic is a huge job, and yes, that's probably a *really* huge understatement. But what sort of person would I be if I said no?"

"The kind, smart, caring sort who loves the career she's already got," Jonah replied, his fingers still moving gently through her hair, and God, all of her conversations about life-changing decisions should happen like this. "Look, I hear what you're saying, and I'm not trying to downplay the fact that, yeah, you'd have a shitload of opportunities to make a difference in patient care if you took this job.

But you already do that as a surgeon. Just look at Annabelle."

The death grip Natalie's lower back muscles had put around her spine eased a notch at the thought. "I guess that's true."

"You *guess*?" Jonah snorted, scooping her up and turning his body to bring them face to face. "Try again."

This time, her laugh was more genuine. "Okay, okay. I do."

"You do," he agreed. "Every day. And while you're obviously Harlow's first choice for the director's job, you're also not the only person who could make those changes happen at the clinic. So, saying no, *if* that's what you choose"—he paused to lift one hand—"wouldn't necessarily deny anyone care."

"Well, yeah, but with the wrong person as director, the clinic won't help people, either," Natalie hedged.

Jonah paused. "That's true. But it's still not selfish to choose a career that you love over one you know you won't."

"The trouble is, I don't *know* that I won't. Not for sure. If I took this job and was able to make strides..." She broke off, completely frustrated, her brain spinning like one of those pop-up carnival rides her mother always warned against. "I just don't know."

"You have time to think about it, right?" he asked, and at least here, she had the luxury of a yes. Even if it came with a caveat.

"A little. Harlow said she wants to make an announcement by the end of the year."

A frown hinted at the edges of Jonah's mouth. "She's pretty intense, huh?"

It was his way of asking Natalie if she really wanted to work with the woman, she knew—a topic to which Natalie had given a whole lot of thought on her drive home. "She is really intense, and if I took this position, it's something I'd have to get used to. But she's clearly passionate about her job. Even if she has a super prickly way of showing it," Natalie added. "But I can't really fault her for wanting the clinic to be successful. I want it to be successful, too."

"I guess if there's going to be a shark in the water, it helps to have them on your side," Jonah said, and Natalie knew it was true. Or, it *would* be true, if she and Harlow agreed on how to run the clinic. If not...

Natalie sat back against the couch cushions, lacing her fingers through his. "All of this is making my head spin. Tell me something good about *your* day."

"My old man wants to take me fly fishing."

Although he delivered them with enough seriousness for her to know he wasn't kidding, the words still sent a smile over Jonah's face.

Which sent one over Natalie's by default. "For the record, I *so* want pictures of that."

"Yeah, it's not exactly in my wheelhouse," Jonah agreed with a laugh. "But I guess it's his thing now that he's retired. He's really into it, and he told me a couple of stories when we talked on the phone yesterday. I don't mind giving it a go."

Natalie's heart squeezed at the thought. Now *here* was something to be glass-half-full over. "You two have talked a lot over the last week," she ventured, and to her surprise, Jonah answered openly.

"We have. Well, a lot for us," he amended with a tilt of his head. "But it's good, you know? I tell him about work, and he tells me about fly fishing. He's even made a couple of good friends who also live in the retirement community, and the staff there makes sure he's got everything he needs. We don't talk about...anything else." Now came the pause Natalie had expected, and the squeeze in her heart along with it. "But we don't really need to, I guess."

"Well, I'm really glad you're connecting again." Tightening her grasp on Jonah's fingers, she snuggled in closer, his body feeling warm and solid and so, so good against hers. "I know I grumble about my parents being overprotective, but I love them, and I love that we're close. Even if I *am* going to get my ass royally kicked by my father in Pictionary on Christmas Eve."

"Speaking of things I want pictures of," Jonah said with a laugh, and the idea that unfolded in her mind skipped right past her brain-to-mouth filter.

"Oh, my God, you should come with me! You're not leaving for your dad's until Christmas morning, and my parents would love to see you."

Her parents had met Jonah years ago when they'd come to visit her at work, and she talked about him all the time, so it's not as if they were strangers. Plus, her parents probably wouldn't hover nearly as much if she brought a partner in crime, and then Jonah wouldn't be alone on Christmas Eve. Talk about a win-win.

He stiffened beside her, his smile slipping before turning into the charming version he used on everyone else. "Ah, I wouldn't want to intrude on your family gathering. Plus, it'll give me some time to rest before my drive to Charleston."

Natalie's gut dropped, and she gave herself a gigantic mental kick. She'd been so brain-drained by this whole job offer, then so happy hearing about the conversations he'd been having with his father, that the invitation had just barged out. Of course she wanted Jonah to come with her to her parents' house. But of course *he* saw it as something she'd ask him to do if they were a couple. Something seri-ous. Together indefinitely.

God, she really *did* want him to go with her.

"Oh, right. That makes perfect sense," Natalie said, covering up the thought with a bright smile. They'd agreed to keep things casual. She'd been impulsive to ask him, even on a no-big-deal level. "I'll probably be there super late, anyway."

Jonah nodded, and after a beat that felt like forever, he gave her a dazzling smile. "So, should we watch a movie? There's a *Die Hard* marathon on."

"Sure," she said with a grin. "You make the popcorn, I'll grab the blankets?"

"Deal."

But even after he'd kissed her and gotten up to head for the kitchen, the funny feeling in Natalie's gut remained.

JONAH HAD the sneaking suspicion he'd acted like an idiot. Three days had passed since Natalie had asked him if he'd go with her to her parents' house for Christmas Eve dinner, and while she'd acted one hundred percent normal after he'd declined, he'd seen the flash of disappointment in her eyes in the moment. To be fair, it was the exact *same* moment that he'd been clutching in dread at the impromptu invitation to the sort of event usually reserved for someone who'd achieved boyfriend status. But the more Jonah had thought about it, the more he'd realized that A) Nat had agreed to keeping things casual, and if her feelings had changed, she'd just freaking say so, and B) as much as the idea of Dinner With the Parents had been a hard no for him over the past three years, now that he'd gotten over the knee-jerk shock of her asking, he didn't exactly hate the thought of going with her.

For Chrissake, this was *Natalie*. His best friend. The woman he'd been having more fun with over the past month than he'd had with anyone since...well, shit. Ever. He'd already met her parents ages ago. Yes, he had a serious aversion to anything even hinting at commitment—and for good goddamn reason—but this was totally different than if anyone else had asked.

She was totally different than anyone else, period.

"Damn," came a familiar voice from beside Jonah, reminding him that he was leaning against the nurses' station in the surgical unit, probably looking like he'd seen better days. A ten-hour shift with multiple trauma surgeries would do that to a guy, even without all the mental fuckery. "Long day, Sheridan?"

Jonah looked up at Mallory, who was handing a chart over to Parker. "Aren't they all?" he asked, aiming for a nonchalant smile.

"The guy whose hip we just replaced would say yes," Mallory replied, and Parker nodded.

"It was a pretty cool procedure, though."

Mallory arched a dark brow. "You say that about all the surgeries you get to assist on."

Parker arched a brow right back, although he paired the move with a smile. "I'm an intern. With all due respect, you're damn right I do."

"Fair enough." Mallory turned back toward Jonah, his eyes narrowing in concern. "So, what's got you making that face? Rough surgery?"

"Nah." Jonah reached for the easygoing demeanor he attached to everything from work to women, his shoulders tightening when it wouldn't come. "It's nothing, really. I just..." Oh, fuck it. He wasn't making himself feel any better by stewing in his thoughts. He might as well air them out and see if that helped. "If you're friends with someone of the opposite sex, doing the stuff you'd do if you were *more* than friends is different, right? Like, it's not as big a deal as if you were actually a couple."

Mallory laughed, although he dropped his voice to keep the conversation away from anyone who might be passing by. "It's so fucking cute that you think you and Kendrick aren't more than friends."

"We aren't," Jonah protested. "I mean, we are, but we're not, like, *together*." His heart rate skated higher as he realized, too late, what he'd admitted. "And who said I'm talking about Kendrick?"

"Um, you just did." At least Parker had the good grace (and the good sense) to look semi-sheepish as he pointed out Jonah's error, and shit. *Shit*. "But if it helps, we kind of put two and two together before this. You two have just had a different vibe around each other lately. Not a bad thing," Parker added swiftly. "It's just pretty obvious that you're into each other."

"Of course we're into each other. We're friends," Jonah said, caving a second later at Parker and Mallory's twin looks of *annnnd?* "And we also might be sleeping together."

"Might be?" Mallory asked, painting the question with a healthy dose of good-natured sarcasm.

Jonah swiveled a gaze around the nurses' station to make triple-sure no one was within earshot before he bit the bullet. "Fine. We're definitely sleeping together. But we totally agreed to keep it casual."

"Good Christ, it's about time," Mallory said. At the pure WTF that must have broken loose over Jonah's face, he added, "What? You two have been attached at the hip for freaking ever."

"It does seem like a logical step up," Parker agreed with a shrug so matter-of-fact that the unease in Jonah's chest took a breather.

"It's no big deal, though. Everything is the same as it's always been. Okay"—Jonah rolled his eyes at Mallory's knowing look—"everything except the sex."

"Which is...?" Mallory let the question hang, and Jonah couldn't help the reflexive smile that took over any time he thought of Natalie in his bed...or his shower...or bent over his couch with the soft glow of Christmas lights illuminating her skin...

"Even better than the friendship," he said, leaving it at that out of respect *for* said friendship.

"Okay," Parker said, after blinking twice in what appeared to be surprise. "So, you're having great sex with someone you also like hanging out with, and you're both on board with keeping things casual. This is a problem why, exactly?"

"She asked me if I wanted to go to her parents' house for Christmas Eve dinner. I don't think she meant it as a thing," he emphasized at Mallory's *oh boy* whistle. "Like I said, we agreed to keep things low-key, and Natalie doesn't have a manipulative bone in her body."

"That's definitely true," Mallory agreed, and Parker nodded to make it unanimous. "Still, holiday dinner with the parents is usually a pretty big deal."

Parker tilted his head in dissent. "Not necessarily, though. I mean, this is a woman who spent a decent chunk of her last shift making sure we had a stash of presents wrapped and ready for any kids who had to spend Christmas in the peds ward. You two are tight, and you've been spending even more time together lately. Maybe she didn't want you to be alone."

Well, shit. Parker just had to go and make fucking sense. "That does sound like Kendrick," Mallory said. "Could be that she just wanted to hang out with you."

He hadn't even finished speaking before Jonah realized they were both probably right. He hadn't meant to take Natalie's request out of context, or—worse yet—turn it into something she hadn't intended, but damn it, that was exactly what he'd done, and he'd disappointed her on top of it.

At least one of those things, he could fix. "You wouldn't happen to know where she is right now, would you?" Jonah asked, and Parker nodded.

"Actually, yeah. She was over in oncology when we passed by after we got out of the OR. Sitting in the waiting area, of all things."

Ah, right. She'd mentioned that her annual blood draw was today. Just in time to appease her mother for Christmas, she'd joked. "Got it. Thanks."

Turning on the heel of one cross-trainer, Jonah aimed himself toward oncology. He made the trip quickly, just in time to see Natalie coming down the hallway, a cotton ball/gauze tape combo peeking out from beneath the sleeve of her scrubs.

"Hey," he said, his heart speeding up in a way that had nothing to do with the fact that he'd fast-tracked his ass across two entire hospital wings to find her. Without think-ing, he pulled her into a hug. "I was looking for you. How did it go?"

"Uhm, fine," she laughed, although she let out a breathy sigh as she hugged him back. "It was just a blood draw. I get one every year. Is *that* why you were looking for me? Because really, I'm—"

He dropped his mouth to her ear, close enough to ensure privacy, yet with enough distance between them to remain respectable. "Natalie Kendrick, so help me God, if you utter the word *fine*, I will have no choice but to spank you."

She flushed, but didn't look away. "Well. That does make it tempting. But it was just a tiny needle stick. Still, I'm grateful that you have my back."

"I do," Jonah said, and hell if it wasn't why he'd come to find her in the first place. "Speaking of which, I wanted to ask you something."

His cell phone chose that exact moment to sound off in the pocket of his doctor's coat. He was tempted—not a little —to ignore the damned thing. But Natalie dropped her eyes to the sound of the ringtone so expectantly that he had no choice but to at least check to see who it was.

Wait... "That's weird," he said, squinting at the screen to be sure he was reading it correctly. "We didn't call anyone at Saint Elizabeth's Hospital for a trial for Annabelle, did we?"

"Saint E's?" Natalie asked, her nose crinkling in confusion. "The one in Charleston?"

"Yeah, I..." Jonah tapped the icon to take the call, an odd feeling pricking somewhere deep in his chest. "Jonah Sheridan."

"Dr. Sheridan?" came a voice over the line, changing his world with just one breath. "My name is Dr. Christina Reyes. I'm an emergency physician at Saint Elizabeth's Hospital, in Charleston. I need to speak with you about your father."

22

Something was very, very wrong.

Natalie's heart hammered against her breastbone, her fingers itching to reach for Jonah. His entire demeanor had one-eightied in less than a breath, from the titanium stiffness now commandeering his shoulders and spine to the clinical chill that had replaced the happiness in his voice.

"Yes, I am," he said, his eyes focused straight ahead even though he didn't seem to see a thing. "I understand. When was he brought in?" Another pause. "And you're taking him to CT right now? Okay, good. Have the radiologist call me at this number as soon as the scans are up. I'll be there as soon as I can."

"What is it? What's wrong?" Natalie asked as soon as Jonah lowered the phone. He looked at her, his brilliant, blue eyes loaded with so much emotion that, for a split second, she couldn't breathe.

But then the emotion disappeared, as surely as if he'd slammed a steel door over it to lock it out. "My father was brought in to the ED at Saint Elizabeth's about fifteen minutes ago. The doctor didn't have a lot of details. He's altered, but the staff at the assisted living facility insisted they call me immediately. It"—Jonah paused, but his tone remained flat and unchanged—"looks like he might've had a stroke."

Oh, God. *Oh, God.* "Okay." A thousand medical questions crashed through Natalie's brain, each of them screaming to be asked. She obliged none of them. "Come on," she said instead, threading her arm through Jonah's and starting to walk briskly toward the attendings' lounge, which was thankfully on the same floor of the building as the oncology unit they'd been standing in front of. They made the trip quickly enough, Natalie's heart pressing faster against her ears as she caught sight of Tess looking at them in wide-eyed surprise from the couch.

"Hey, Tess. Can you do me a huge favor?" No time to fuck around with pleasantries, but if anyone would get that, it was Tess. "Can you find Langston and tell him Jonah and I have to take care of a personal emergency? Boldin is on my service, and Vasquez"—she looked at Jonah, who nodded absently in confirmation—"is on Jonah's. They should both be up to speed on surgical patients."

"You got it," Tess said, her feet already in motion. She slowed for the briefest of seconds, just long enough to shoot an empathetic glance at Jonah and a knowing nod at Natalie before she disappeared through the door.

"Okay," Natalie said softly, reaching for the handle to her locker. "We can stop by the apartment to grab some things on our way out of town, or we can go directly and figure it out once we get to Charleston. It's entirely up to you."

Finally, Jonah found his voice. "Nat, you don't—"

"I do." Turning to look at him, she grabbed both of his hands, not really giving a shit that anyone could walk in and

ally see them. He needed her. She would damn well
e, just as he'd been there for her when she'd needed
him. "You can't get updates and drive at the same time, and
it's a three-hour trip. You need to focus on this." She let go of
his fingers to press one hand over his chest, the rapid *thump-
thump-thump* of his heart pressing back. "So let me focus on
you. Okay?"

The pause that followed was like an electric charge, the
magnetic force of it a living, breathing thing.

Let me in. Please, let me in.

Finally, Jonah nodded, his voice quiet and his expression
unreadable. "Okay," he said.

But as Natalie lowered her hand and began to change
out of her scrubs, she couldn't tell if that magnetic force had
pulled them together or yanked them apart.

~

Saint Elizabeth's Hospital was a beautiful building, all
stately lines and Southern charm. The details registered in
Natalie's brain—the elegant brickwork set off by just
enough glass to lend a modern air to the place, the tidy
landscaping that was flawless despite the chill of late
December. She didn't really see them, though, other than to
recognize that they did, indeed, exist. As she put the Lexus
in *park* and quieted the engine, the only thing that truly
registered was Jonah.

He sat beside her, staring through the windshield and
into the dusky shadows surrounding the brightly lit hospital. Natalie had done her best to read him in an effort to do
what he needed, fully prepared to provide solace or take
care of details or, hell, dance an Irish jig if it would help.
And yet, Jonah had been nearly impossible to decipher,

answering her questions in polite yeses and nos, holding her hand when she'd offered it but not seeking it out when she didn't. She knew he was likely still in shock and trying to process—God, they saw it all the time with both patients and their families.

Still, Jonah had been so quiet on the drive (which Natalie had made as swiftly as possible without committing a felony—thank you, GPS). The only non-yes/no words he'd uttered were when he'd spoken to both the radiologist and the head of neurology at Saint Elizabeth's, then when he'd relayed the scant clips of information to her upon ending the calls.

Yes, the diagnosis was that his father had suffered a stroke. No, they didn't know how much time had elapsed between the onset of symptoms and when his neighbor and a nurse from the facility where he lived had found him on his kitchen floor and called nine-one-one. Yes, that meant they'd likely lost critical time. No, his father hadn't been a candidate for tPA as a result. Yes, he was still unconscious.

No, there was no guarantee he'd ever wake up.

"You ready to go in?" Natalie asked, and Jonah inhaled slowly, as if unfolding himself from a dream.

"Yeah." His nod was clipped, his voice perfectly even. "Dr. Aronson is the neurologist. He said to come directly up to the third floor and have him paged when we arrived."

"Okay." They both got out of the car and headed inside the hospital, navigating their way to the third floor easily enough. A large nurses' station stood to the right of the elevators, and although it was brightly lit and festively decorated with all manner of sparkly green garland and red and white poinsettia flowers, it was also unstaffed.

"I can go find someone, if you want—"

Natalie's request was cut short by a kind-looking woman

who looked to be in her sixties, wearing a soft pink sweater and a curious expression. "Pardon me. I don't mean to intrude. But you're here for Kenneth Sheridan, aren't you?"

Shock bounced through Natalie, and Jonah nodded. "Yes, ma'am. I'm—"

"His son, Jonah," the woman said, her Southern accent hugging the words as warmly as her smile. "Of course you are. You look just as handsome as your picture."

"I'm sorry?" Jonah asked, clearly as surprised as Natalie was.

The woman pressed a hand to the front of her sweater. "Oh, I've gotten ahead of myself. I do apologize. I'm Vivian. Your father's neighbor from across the hall."

The dots started connecting, one by one. Jonah had mentioned a neighbor calling for the ambulance. "Yes," he said, clearly having made the logic leap, as well. "His neighbor. Of course."

"He's in room 308, down the hall there. I was sitting with him, just to keep him company in case he woke up, but the doctor shooed me out a few minutes ago to do some sort of checkup," Vivian said.

Natalie's chest squeezed, but she nodded at Jonah. Routine neuro checks were good. It meant they were keeping a careful eye on his father's condition. "Do you want me to go have a nurse let Dr. Aronson know you're here?" she asked.

But Jonah shook his head. "No. Not yet. I don't want to interrupt the exam. The more he can assess, the better. This way, we'll get the most current information as soon as he's done." For another minute, Jonah said nothing, his brows creased in thought. Then he looked at Vivian and asked, "My father has a picture of me?"

To her credit, the question didn't seem to throw her,

although, *God*, it tugged at Natalie's heart. "Oh, yes," Vivian replied, nodding. "We play cards once a week with two of the other residents, and we rotate who hosts. Your father has a picture of you in his living room, front and center. From when you graduated medical school."

"I didn't even know he had one," Jonah said, and Vivian offered up a wry smile.

"Actually, he doesn't have one. He has three. You're just a lot younger in the other two. School photos, both of them. But my, there's no mistaking you. Your daddy's so very proud."

Jonah's lashes lifted and lowered in a quick succession of blinks. "Proud," he repeated. "He said that?"

"Not in a whole lot of words. That isn't really his way," Vivian said, as surely as if she were stating that A was followed by B, or that the sun set without fail in the west. "He gets a look in his eyes when he talks about you, though, and he's so excited to see you for Christmas. He told me all about it."

Her smile faded as she glanced down the hallway, and Natalie instantly recognized the regret on the older woman's face, along with the sadness that chased it. "I'm truly sorry I didn't call you myself. Everything happened so fast. I knew when Kenneth didn't join us for lunch that something wasn't right." Vivian paused for a breath, steeling her spine in a gesture that somehow managed to be both elegant and tough at the same time. "But I knew you were his emergency contact, and that they'd call you right away. I just wish I'd had the staff at Rosebriar open up to check on him sooner."

"You did the right thing, Vivian," Natalie said, refusing to think what would've happened if Vivian hadn't had them check when they did. *Glass half full*, she reminded herself.

Jonah's father was here, now, being cared for. That's what mattered.

Vivian reclaimed a tiny bit of her smile. "Well, I sure am glad you're here," she said, reaching out to squeeze Jonah's hand. "It will bring your father peace of mind."

Jonah opened his mouth—to protest, if his expression was any indication—but a door opened halfway down the well-lit corridor, a dark-haired doctor stepping out of the room and murmuring to a younger woman in scrubs, who Natalie guessed was a resident.

"Dr. Aronson?" Jonah asked, striding forward just in time for the man to look up. "Jonah Sheridan. We spoke on the phone."

"Ah, yes," Dr. Aronson said, shaking both Jonah's and Natalie's hands and introducing his resident, Dr. Lee, to them both. "Your father is stable right now. He's in and out of consciousness, but we've sedated him so he can rest."

Jonah indicated the electronic chart in the man's hands. "May I?"

"Of course," Dr. Aronson said, handing it over. "Your father was altered when he arrived in the emergency department, his speech noticeably slurred and his left side showing moderate weakness."

These were things he'd told Jonah earlier, of course, but the doctor was no dummy. Family members, even those who were surgeons, could blank on facts in the shock of a moment.

Aronson continued, "The symptoms, along with your father's vitals, were concerning, so Dr. Reyes called us for a consult, and Dr. Lee immediately ordered a head CT." He indicated the chart, but Jonah had already pulled up the images. "There's no bleed, which is good news. But if you look right here—"

Damn it. "There's a blood clot," Natalie said, her eyes on the scan.

"It's fairly small, but yes," Dr. Aronson agreed. "That's what's causing the symptoms. We did a number of additional scans to determine the source, since obviously, proper treatment depends on that knowledge. Your father's cerebral artery looks clear, but ultrasound shows a moderate narrowing of the carotid artery. It seems the most likely source of the clot."

Jonah nodded, his eyes still firmly fixed on the images in the chart. He asked, "So, do you think we're looking at a full-blown stroke or a TIA?"

Hope sprang into Natalie's chest. A TIA wasn't ideal by any stretch. A third of the time, they were just a precursor to a bigger, more serious strokes. But two thirds of the time, they weren't, and patients could show significant improvements over the course of hours, if given the proper treatment.

Glass half full, glass half full, glass...

"It's still difficult to tell at this point," Aronson said, not ruling it in but also not ruling it out. "Your father's vitals *have* stabilized with the anticoagulants. He's regaining some left-side motor function, but he's still altered, which is why we chose to sedate him. We don't want his brain working any harder than it has to right now, and it's equally crucial that we keep his heart rate and blood pressure stable."

"Agreed," Jonah said, handing the chart to Dr. Lee. "What's the prognosis?"

Aronson paused, but only long enough for Natalie's breath to catch in her throat. "The next twenty-four hours are going to be critical," he said. "While it's possible this stroke was an isolated event, it's also possible that he'll have another, potentially bigger one, within the next day. We'll continue to treat him with IV meds to do our best to prevent that from happening, and monitor him very closely to make sure he continues to improve. I know that wait-and-see isn't ideal," Aronson said kindly. "But it really is the best thing we can do right now while we let those anticoagulants do their job."

Jonah shook his head, his voice quiet but unwavering. "No, I understand."

"Of course, you're welcome to go in and see him," Aronson offered, gesturing to the door. "But given the circumstances, it's not likely that he'll wake until morning. Once he does, we'll do another assessment, and then we'll go from there."

"Right. Thank you, Dr. Aronson." Jonah reached out to shake the man's hand and nodded his thanks at the resident, both doctors offering polite smiles to him and Natalie before they headed toward the nurses' station. A deep thread of emotion flickered across Jonah's stare as he turned to look at the door to his father's room, and even though it had disappeared by the time Natalie had registered it, her heart still jerked all the same.

"I can go in with you, if you want," she offered, making sure that her tone marked the words as a true offer, one that was entirely up to him if he wanted privacy instead. She reached out to slide her fingers around his, and although she'd meant the gesture to be a quick squeeze-and-release of comfort, Jonah grabbed her hand tightly enough to make her breath hitch.

"I..." For a second, he simply stood there, clutching her fingers like a lifeline, emotion rolling off of him in waves. But then, he straightened his shoulders and let go.

"That's okay. I'll only be a minute. Like Dr. Aronson said, he'll be asleep until tomorrow, and he needs the rest. Plus, we're probably already past visiting hours. I'll just do a quick check of his vitals and we can go."

Natalie blinked. "He's your father. I'm sure they'd make an exception for visiting hours, especially since he's not in the ICU," she said. "Really, Jonah. We can—"

"No." Jonah's smile was small but affable, identical to a thousand smiles she'd seen him give to a thousand different people before. "I won't be long. I promise," he said.

And then he slipped past the door, leaving her to wonder what the hell had just happened.

23

J onah made it all the way to the door of the hotel room where he and Natalie would spend the night before realizing he'd probably screwed himself by agreeing to let her accompany him to Charleston. Not that he didn't want her here. Fuck, her calm, steady presence had been the only thing that had kept him from losing his shit more times than he could count today. But Natalie knew him better than anyone, and that familiarity had grown exponentially over the past four weeks. Keeping a lid on his emotions had been hard enough when they'd been just friends.

Now that they weren't *just* anything, and his emotions were churning through his chest like high tide in a hurricane? Yeah. He was going to have to nail that lid into place with gutter spikes if he had any prayer of getting through this intact.

Although, to be fair, he probably didn't.

You knew this would happen, his inner voice whispered, soft and insidious, and God, he couldn't even argue.

He had known. Maybe not in the literal sense—being able to predict that his father would have a life-threatening stroke just as they'd begun to bridge the decades' worth of distance between them was impossible, of course. Yet still, Jonah had known better than to try. He'd been foolish enough to think maybe, just maybe, he and his father could be the exception, the new leaf, the fresh start.

He'd been wrong.

Love didn't last.

Natalie used the keycard she'd gotten from the front desk attendant to gain entry to the hotel room, which she'd efficiently booked while Jonah had checked in on his father, steeling himself against the frailty of the old man's body, the pallor of his skin in contrast with the hospital pillow. Jonah followed her over the threshold and into the room, the well-appointed space softly lit by the one bedside lamp that had been left on to welcome them, and she lowered her overnight bag to the tasteful gray and white carpet beneath their feet.

"I know it's pretty late," Natalie said, moving toward him with just enough of a smile to weaken his defenses another notch. "But I can go see if the kitchen is still open in the restaurant downstairs. Or maybe we could get room service. You never had dinner."

Jonah shook his head. "No. Thank you," he added, smiling back. Okay, yeah. This was good. This, he knew how to do. Smile. Sweet-talk. Lie. "It's been a long day. Honestly, I think I just want to crash."

She wanted to argue. Jonah could see it on her face. Christ, he could read her like a billboard, and he knew it had to be killing her to say, "Okay."

But she did. They went through the motions of

normalcy—the brushing of teeth, the changing of clothes, pulling back the cozy down coverlet and turning out the bedside lamp—each action a new brick in the wall Jonah had carefully constructed over the course of years. He closed his eyes even though he knew he wouldn't sleep, metering his breathing to a slow, steady inhale/exhale to make Natalie think he was drifting off. For a minute, he thought he'd fooled her, guilt mixing in with everything else running amok in his rib cage.

Then she whispered, "Jonah. Talk to me."

She'd turned to her side, her knees bent so they rested an inch from his thigh, one hand tucked under her cheek. The room was essentially dark, with only a sliver of moonlight spilling through the gap in the drapes to put a silvery edge on the shadows. It should have made things easier. After all, Jonah was an expert at shoving his emotions into a hole, at hiding from the truth. The darkness should only make it so Natalie wouldn't be able to see him.

Except she did. Without light, without words—fuck, even when he used every last tool in his arsenal to keep her out, she still *saw* him. And instead of making him feel vulnerable and exposed like it damn well should have, it didn't. No. Lying here, next to Natalie in the dark, Jonah felt something he hadn't felt in far, far too long. Something he was certain he'd never feel again.

He felt safe.

"I was six when my mother left," Jonah said, his heart rising in his throat to tighten the words. "But I still have a lot of memories of her. The way she'd cut my sandwiches into triangles and tell me they tasted better that way. How she'd read me a story every night before tucking me in. The way she smelled like flowers."

"Those sound like good memories," Natalie said, and God, Jonah loved her bright-side heart, even if she was wrong about this.

"They should be, but they're not." All they did was remind him of how much he'd blindly loved his mother, believing that she loved him in return, only to be proven very, very wrong. "Do you know how she left my old man? In a *letter*."

Jonah waited out Natalie's soft inhale of confusion, then her deeper gasp of shock before continuing, the story clawing its way out of him, all sharp edges and teeth. "And not just any letter, nope. Uh-uh. My mother set the gold standard for Dear John letters by getting up just like she did every day, letting my old man kiss her on the cheek before he left and putting me on the bus to school like nothing-doing. As soon as that was done, she scrawled her goodbye on a piece of paper from the pad we kept by the phone, like it was a reminder from the dentist's office or a goddamned grocery list. Then she left it on the kitchen table, addressed to my father, packed up every last one of her belongings, and walked out the door. We never heard from her again, other than the divorce papers she had my father served with two weeks later. She signed over her parental rights without contest. Didn't even ask to visit me once a year."

He'd uncovered that little nugget years later in middle school, when he'd stumbled upon the divorce agreement in his father's desk drawer while searching for a spare folder for an English essay. How easily his mother had tossed him aside. It had been a matter of three checkmarks and a handful of signatures, and poof. She'd abandoned him without mention.

"Jonah, I'm so sorry."

Natalie's whisper was simple, the words ones Jonah had heard countless times for any number of reasons, and spoken himself countless more. Fucked up, really, that he actually felt the comfort of them now.

"I was finishing kindergarten," he said. "I had never come home to an empty house, you know? My mother was always there, *always*...until that one day she wasn't." And, of course, he remembered it like it had been a minute ago, because that was the sort of bitch fate was. "I was scared at first, but then I saw the letter. Even though it had my father's name on it, I opened it. I thought it would say where she was."

Natalie stiffened beside him, because of course she did. It was a natural reaction to the shit reality that Jonah had been the one to realize his mother had left first, and that *he'd* had to give his father the news. Then again, it had been meant for both of them. His mother had left Jonah without a backward glance, too, as if she'd never loved either of them.

For a second, his emotions threatened to swallow him, and panic rose in his rib cage, begging him to shut up. But then Natalie's hand was on his chest, splayed wide over that spot that always ached *so* fucking much before he sewed it shut, and he kept talking, letting more escape.

"I'd only just learned how to read, and even though what my mother had written didn't make sense to me, I knew something was really wrong. So, I went next door to the neighbor's house and told her I was alone, and she called my father, who came to get me. I had to give him the letter, knowing what it said. 'I'm sorry, Kenneth'," Jonah quoted, the words ash in his mouth. "'I just can't do this anymore'."

She hadn't even mentioned him in the letter. For Chrissake, he hadn't even been worthy of a goodbye.

And still, he'd been heartbroken.

"Jonah," Natalie said, her tone loaded with emotion even though she didn't say anything else, just kept her hand right where it was, the pressure steady, the contact warm.

"My mother pretended to love me and she stayed with my father for as long as she could out of obligation, but she was never going to stay forever. She'd just been biding her time," he said. "Her love was never real, and it was never meant to last. And now, with my father—"

Jonah's throat threatened to close, his heart slamming against his sternum so hard, it was nearly painful. But this was Natalie, who saw him even in the dark, her fingers pressed tightly over that pain, and the rest just tumbled out of him.

"For all those years, I pushed him away because I was scared that if I got close to him, he'd leave, too. I wasn't belligerent or mean—I could never bring myself to do that to him. But I was scared. I knew he was a quiet man, just like I knew there was a good chance he didn't know how to bridge the gap between us. I told myself the distance was smart. That it would keep me from getting hurt. That I probably reminded him of my mother, anyway, all those painful reminders, right there for him to see every day. That it was just better this way. And for years—Christ, for *decades*—it was."

"Until now," Natalie said.

Jonah kept going with his verbal vomit, both hating and being so fucking grateful for how good it felt to finally say everything out loud. "I should have known better than to think I could be close with him, especially after all this time, without the other shoe coming crashing down. But I got so greedy for something I'd been missing for my whole fucking life that I got reckless. I let myself want that closeness. I let myself *hope*."

Natalie shook her head, her hair shushing over the pillow in the darkness. "Hope isn't a bad thing."

But Jonah shook his head right back. "Hope is a risk that will slap you in the face just as soon as she'll kiss you on the lips. I was a fool to believe that this would work between me and my father. That we could have a relationship that would last."

Natalie's eyes widened in the moonlight. "What? How can you say that?"

"Because it's true," he bit out, and here it was. The reason he never let anyone get close, spilling into the space between them, unchecked. "Don't you get it, Nat? It's not that I think all relationships are doomed, or that love always leaves. It's that love always leaves *me*."

"No," she started, but he cut her off. Right now, in this moment, her hope would be too much.

"Love has left me from the beginning, and it always does, no matter how hard I've tried to keep it," Jonah told her past his rattling pulse. "My mother. Every girlfriend I ever had in college and med school. Vanessa. All those tries, all those chances, and *every* one of them ended. I pretend it doesn't matter. I cover it all up with a smile and a wink and a one-night stand. I never let my emotions in, and I never let myself hope for more, because I know how it always ends. So, yeah." His voice broke, and he was helpless against the raw, sad truth that came with it. "I was a fool to think for one second that I could have a good relationship with my old man now, that the other shoe wouldn't eventually drop and crush me like it always fucking does. I'm not built for anything that lasts."

"No." Natalie's voice changed in an instant, and she sat up so swiftly that Jonah had no choice but to follow suit. "That's not the truth, and I'm not going to let you say that it is. Yes, you've been hurt, and yes, you are scared. You have good reason to be. Your mother did a horrible, unforgiveable thing."

The anger in Natalie's voice flickered over her face, her fierceness pinning Jonah into place as she continued. "But *she's* responsible for that. Not you. You are a good man. Maybe you haven't found the right relationship, and maybe you created distance between you and your father because you were scared, but that doesn't mean you're not built for anything that lasts. It doesn't mean you're foolish to hope, or to want to be loved."

"I am," Jonah said, the old argument so deeply stitched into his fabric that it flew out without thought. "Those things aren't for me, Nat."

Natalie shook her head, adamant and strong and so, so beautiful. "Yes, they are. Do you want to know how I know that you're made for something that lasts? Because you have me. Maybe not in the hearts-and-flowers way," she added quickly. "But I've never doubted our friendship, ever. I've never doubted that you'd have my back whenever I needed you, and I can promise that you will never turn your head and not see me standing right here next to you." She grabbed his hands and held on tight. "No matter what happens with your father. No matter what happens *ever*, Jonah. I'm here. I won't leave you. So, yes. You are made for something that lasts. You have been for years."

"I..." Jonah's heart tripped, and when he opened his mouth again, the truth emerged. "Everything I've ever loved, I've lost. I'm so fucking scared to hope."

"Then let me carry you until you're not," Natalie

whispered.

Jonah knew in that moment that he'd been wrong. Natalie's hope wasn't too much. It was a beacon. A lifeline. It was everything.

And he was falling in love with her.

24

"Okay."

Natalie had never in her life felt more relief or more emotion upon hearing one, single word. A tiny part of her told her she should stop to memorize this moment—the squeeze of Jonah's fingers wrapped around hers, the rapid flutter of her heart beating against her nightshirt. But she already knew the moment by heart because she knew *him* by heart, and she reached up to cup his face between her palms.

"Okay," she agreed.

God, her heart ached for him. All the charming smiles, all the times he closed himself off to anything other than a fling, they weren't because he was jaded or commitment-phobic, or even just looking for a good time. They were a cover-up. Jonah had been so convinced he wasn't meant to be loved that he hadn't just avoided it. He was scared to even *hope* for it.

He'd always had her back. If he couldn't hope yet, she'd hope enough for both of them.

"You should get some sleep," Natalie said quietly. It

wasn't horribly late, but the day had felt endlessly stretched, like an old rubber band. Had they really been standing outside of the oncology unit after her blood draw only five hours ago? Everything felt so different now, as if something small yet pivotal had been shifted, the subtle buzz in the air before a thunderstorm.

Jonah reached up to circle his fingers around her wrists. "I don't want to sleep."

"You don't." Her breath hitched, the involuntary arousal he inspired far more often than not flaring to life beneath her skin as he slid his hands to her elbows, then her upper arms, pulling her close.

"No. If I'm going to hope, I want to do it right. I want you, Natalie."

She stopped with her mouth just shy of his. "And if I'm going to carry you, even just for tonight, I want to do it right, too. Let me in, Jonah. Let me have *you*."

He nodded, just the slightest lift and lower of his chin, but it was enough. Natalie kissed him, and that same urge she'd felt to memorize everything earlier resurfaced. But again, she didn't have to. She knew how Jonah tasted, that the just-enough friction of his five o'clock shadow would send a sexy thrill right—*yes*—to her center. She knew the sound he'd make if she slid her teeth oh-so-gently over his bottom lip, kissed the hinge of his jaw, traced the shell of his ear with her tongue. Natalie's fingers twitched with the envious desire to join in, and she didn't deny them. She covered every inch of Jonah's exposed skin with slow, intent touches and kisses, and when he reached down to lift his shirt over his head so she could have better access, heat gathered between her legs in anticipation. His muscles were taut, fingers flexing as if he wanted to reach for her and take the lead like always.

But he didn't. He remained perfectly still, letting her touch his shoulders and chest and abs, and Natalie couldn't tell what was hotter—what she was doing, or the fact that he was letting her take control so freely.

Her fingers coasted over the flat of Jonah's chest, exploring every inch. A breath burst out of him as she grazed one nipple, and her eyes widened in surprise.

She hesitated only long enough to see the moonlight-illuminated pleasure on his face before she brushed her fingertip over him again in a slow circle.

"Yes?" Natalie asked. A pulse moved through her, something akin to pleasure, only darker. Headier.

Jonah exhaled again, leaning into her touch. "Yes."

Her pleasure became a confident, powerful thrill, fueling the urge to pleasure *him*. She experimented, reading him carefully and waiting for, wanting, that catch in his throat —"And that," she said, pressing harder with the pad of her thumb.

"Yes," he grated.

Natalie didn't stop. Pushing him back until his shoulder blades found the mattress, she straddled his hips, her hands still roaming. The shift in position brought his cock right up against her, only a few thin layers of clothing separating him from her pussy. Her muscles clenched at the contact, aching and wet, and she stole a greedy slide before returning her attention to Jonah.

"Let's find out what else you like." She tugged her nightshirt over her head, which left her in only a pair of hip-hugging panties, then hinged forward to press a kiss to his mouth.

She didn't linger, though. Traveling down his body,

Natalie kissed and licked, her nipples tightening at both the friction against Jonah's skin and the soft moans falling past his lips.

"Fuck, Natalie," he cut out as she got to his navel. She'd had to surrender her position in his lap to get there, but this? This was worth it.

She settled in beside him, pushing her knees into the mattress and one hand beside his hip. His cock pressed a hard outline against his pajama pants, and she slid her free hand over him from root to tip, pumping once, then again, before slipping her hand beneath the waistband of his boxer briefs.

"You're overdressed." Without waiting for a response, she remedied the situation, stripping off the rest of his clothes with a few quick movements. Jonah rested a hand on her shoulder, the weight of it a warm anchor to the moment, and Natalie's heart thrummed in her chest. Yes, she wanted to pleasure him, to use her hands and mouth to make him shake with want, then release, just as he'd done for her so many times—God, she'd wanted it from the first night they'd slept together. But she wanted something more than that, too. Jonah had trusted her with all of his truths, surrendered the control that he'd worn like armor for God only knew how long to let her in.

She didn't just want the pleasure. She wanted him to know just how much she meant what she'd said.

She would always have him.

"Jonah, look at me," Natalie whispered, locking eyes with him in the shadows, her fingers resting carefully on his hip. His cock jerked, maybe at her nearness, or maybe at the intensity that suddenly connected their gazes. She slid her hand up his length, even though her eyes never moved from his. "I'm here with you." She slipped a kiss over the head of his cock, the sound of his corresponding moan vibrating all the way through her. "I have you," she said. "I promise."

She parted her lips over his cock, and oh, hell, they were both lost. Natalie read Jonah's breaths, the way his fingers tightened on her shoulder when she found a motion that turned him on, or when her tongue slid over a sensitive spot as she learned her way. He was wide open with his responses, moaning encouragement at some touches and shifting his body to enhance or change others. Every sign of his pleasure set fire to her own arousal, her sex growing hot and slick as she sucked. Kissed. Licked. Jonah rocked his hips—gently, but enough to set the tempo of her motions— and she looked up at him, wanting to see the pleasure on his face.

But rather than having his head thrown back and his eyes tightly shut the way she'd expected him to, he was looking right at her. Watching every move.

Realizing she really *was* right there with him.

Keeping her eyes on his, Natalie began to move in faster, deeper strokes. His hand drifted up to her hair, his fingers knotting there, and oh God, she was so hot with need, she was sure she'd explode. Jonah's eyes blazed with the same desire she felt, and when she parted her lips and took him as far as she could, he pulled her up and rolled her to her back in one fluid motion.

They didn't speak. They didn't have to. The brief seconds it took for her to yank off her panties and for him to get a condom in place didn't detract from a single ounce of the intensity between them.

And then Jonah was between her legs, filling her pussy with one long thrust, and she wondered how she'd ever lived without this.

Jonah dropped his chin, staring at the spot where his

as buried deep. His eyes didn't move as he withdrew slightly, sliding right back home a breath later, and Natalie's heart beat faster in realization.

"I'm here," she said, lifting her hips, then lowering them. "I'm right here."

He growled out a curse, clearly fighting for control. But still, she said, "It's okay, Jonah. I have you. No matter what."

They began to move at the same time, thrusting and retreating and thrusting again. He fucked her in long, hard strokes, their bodies slapping together, his fingers gripping her hips, and oh, how it turned Natalie on like nothing else. Jonah moved with so much intensity that it stole her breath, their connection rough and primal and utterly vital. Her orgasm crashed through her, the power of it making her cry out and let go and want more, all at once.

Jonah gave it. Angling over her, he pistoned his hips, the slight change in position altering the pressure between Natalie's legs. Her pussy clenched, making him moan, and she wrapped her arms around him to hold him deep inside.

"I'm here," she whispered.

On one last thrust, Jonah's body went bowstring tight. He shuddered in the cradle of her hips, calling her name, his voice both reverent and rough. Time dropped off the clock in a way that didn't matter, possibly a minute, possibly a hundred of them. Their breathing slowed and their bodies went lax, and eventually, Jonah parted from her to slip into the bathroom. He returned silently, climbing into bed and pulling Natalie close. She held him right back, their bodies entwined and their heartbeats pressing softly together as they fell asleep in each other's arms.

～

NATALIE DRIFTED toward wakefulness in pretty much the same position in which she'd fallen asleep. The warm, perfect weight of Jonah's bare arm over her equally bare rib cage was familiar enough for her to recognize it even in her state of near-sleep. The down coverlet, the mattress that was far firmer than Jonah's, those were *not* familiar, and her brain went from confusion to catch-up as she woke more fully.

Jonah's father. The confessions Jonah had made in the dark. The life-altering sex they'd shared afterward.

The way he was still holding her like a lifeline.

Natalie opened her eyes, wide-awake now, although she didn't move. It was still dark, the clock on the bedside table reading an ugh-worthy 5:25, and despite the fact that he was quiet and still, Jonah's breaths were neither deep nor drowsy.

"How long have you been awake?" she asked, and he exhaled in a sound that might've been a laugh under better circumstances.

"A little while."

She nodded against the pillow. "The hospital didn't call. That's a really good sign." Yeah, her optimistic side might be showing, but it was also true.

"He's probably still asleep," Jonah replied, and okay, that was also true.

Still... "We can get up and go now, so you can get a full update from the night-shift attending and be there when he wakes up."

"What if"—Jonah broke off, but only for a second—"I'm scared he won't wake up."

Natalie's throat tightened, but she'd promised to carry him. So she said, "I know you are, and I hope that's a bridge you won't have to cross. But right now, your father is alive and stable. Hearing your voice might help him come around. And no matter what happens, you don't have to face it alone. I'm here for whatever you need. Okay?"

"Yeah," he said, his whisper hoarse, and he pulled her closer. "I really...yeah. I'd like to go see him. I don't want him to wake up alone."

Natalie nodded again, this time efficiently. "Then that's what we'll do. Go on and take the first shower. I'll make coffee, and we can grab breakfast later."

"Okay." Jonah kissed her temple before getting out of bed and heading directly for the bathroom. Natalie made a mental list of things to do as she set her feet to the floor and headed for the in-room coffeepot. Checking in with Remington Mem to make sure both her patients and Jonah's were all status quo headlined the list, and she'd have to touch base with Tess and Charlie, too, both of whom had texted her in concern yesterday. Getting some snacks to keep handy was probably a good idea—they'd passed a little market last night, on their way from Saint Elizabeth's. After Jonah got situated today, she could probably handle that. Oh, and she'd need to call Langston to ask him to cover a few of her shifts. Jonah was already off because of the holiday, but...

Shit. Shit, shit, shit! With how quickly everything had unfolded, Natalie had completely blanked on the fact that tonight was Christmas Eve. She eyeballed the clock, knowing that it was early as hell, but also knowing that her mother was the queen of early risers. Natalie might not get another chance to call her today, and if she were completely honest, she could really use her mother's soothing reassurance right now.

Reaching for her cell phone, she scrolled through her

contacts until her mother's smiling face popped up, then tapped the icon.

"What's the matter?" her mother asked, at the same time Natalie opened with, "I'm fine."

Natalie gave up an ironic smile at how hard old habits were to kill. "I'm fine, Mom," she repeated. "I swear."

"Then why are you calling me at the crack of dawn on Christmas Eve?" her mother asked, her tone easing by one notch and nothing more.

"Because I'm not going to make it to dinner tonight. I'm in South Carolina, with Jonah."

She got her mother up to speed with a succinct retelling of the events of the past twelve hours. Her mom listened carefully, punctuating the story with a few sympathetic murmurs and an occasional "oh, my goodness". When Natalie was done a few minutes later, her mother said, "Well, we'll miss you tonight, but it goes without saying that you're right where you should be. You and Jonah have been close for years. More like family than friends, really. Of course he needs you there with him."

The words struck with more truth than her mother probably realized. But that closeness, and all the feelings that went with it, would have to wait for another time. Right now, Jonah's father was the only thing that mattered. "Thanks, Mom. I'll miss you and Daddy tonight, but I'll make it up to you when I get back in a few days, okay?"

"Natalie," her mother said, and yep, there it was. That comfort her mother brought like a warm blanket when things went mission critical. "You don't ever have to make something like this up to us. Go, be with Jonah, and tell him we'll be thinking of him and his father very much. And keep us posted, please?"

"I will, Mom. I love you."

"I love you, too, sweetie. Be careful driving, okay?"

Natalie laughed softly. "Okay."

She pressed the button to end the call, moving to the coffeepot. The coffee wasn't good, but it wasn't the worst Natalie had ever experienced, either (hello, she worked in a *hospital*). She blew into the cardboard cup, skimming her way through her texts and voicemail messages. Danika, the surgical resident, had sent Natalie progress reports on both her own patients and Jonah's, per Natalie's request, and she reviewed both sets for anything urgent before forwarding Jonah's on to him. She could drive to Saint Elizabeth's while he checked them over, just to be sure everything was okay.

A voicemail message from an unfamiliar number caught Natalie's eye, making her brows lower. Probably a telemarketer, she thought, tapping the icon to put it on speaker while she went to her overnight bag to grab her clothes.

The voice that filled the air sent her pulse back into shit, shit, shit territory.

"Hello, Dr. Kendrick." Harlow Davenport could probably cause a citywide freeze warning with her tone if she really put her back into it. "I understand that you're away until after Christmas. If you come to a decision regarding the director's position at the clinic between now and then, please do reach out sooner rather than later so we can proceed. I'll be working over the holiday."

Natalie blinked at her phone. She was all for a bulletproof work ethic—she had one herself—but was this woman really working in what was sure to be an empty office through the *entire* holiday?

"Additionally," Harlow continued, her voice taking on a softer quality that Natalie had never known existed, let alone heard the woman use. "Dr. Langston mentioned that Dr. Sheridan had a family emergency, and that's why you're unavailable. I know you two are close, and...well, I just want to say I hope everything turns out alright. Please let me know if there's anything I can do."

"Wow," Jonah said from the doorway, bringing Natalie back to the hotel room in less than a second. "That's interesting. I mean, not the part where she's working over Christmas. *That* doesn't shock me. But do you think it's possible she actually has a heart lurking beneath all those power suits?"

"I don't know," Natalie said, quieting her phone and scooping up her clothes. "It sure did sound like it—at least, for a second. But she's going to have to wait on a decision from me."

Jonah scrubbed at his damp hair with a towel, his jeans already slung over the lean frame of his hips. "You haven't given her offer any more thought?"

"No, and I'm not going to for the next couple of days."

His stare became serious. "Nat, I—"

"Nope. No arguing," she said, gently enough to keep any heat from her words but firm enough to make it clear she wasn't budging. "I'm where I need to be. What's going on with you and your dad is way more important than any job right now. Harlow can wait a few more days for me to decide."

For a second, she thought he might push, or worse, clam up and close her out.

But instead, he lowered the towel from his shoulders and stepped in to pull her close.

"Thank you for having my back."

Natalie's heart squeezed, but she didn't shy away from the emotion in his voice or in her chest as she said, "Thank you for letting me."

25

Jonah had never hated hospitals. As a kid, then a teenager, he'd never really had cause to visit enough to form a dislike for them, having only been once for a wrist he'd sprained courtesy of softball and for a post-fender bender exam courtesy of one of his dumb buddies who hadn't been paying attention when Jonah had been in the passenger seat. He'd known fairly early in his college career that he'd wanted to be a doctor, which made hospitals more of a place to be than a place to avoid. But as he walked through the spotless automatic doors of Saint Elizabeth's hospital, he realized he hated this one.

Please, God, don't let my old man die.

"I won't ask if you're okay, because I know you're not," Natalie said quietly. "But are you ready?"

She reached out to brush the side of her hand against his, and Christ, the simple contact was enough to smooth over Jonah's frayed nerves.

He needed to believe that his father would wake up. And he definitely needed to be there when it happened.

He needed to stop being scared to hope.

"Yeah."

"Good." Natalie smiled, gesturing to the elevators in the deserted main lobby. "Let's head upstairs and check in with the charge nurse and the night-shift attending. Then, in a little while, I can go hunt up some breakfast."

She was going to insist that he eat, no matter how far food was from his mind—and to be fair, Jonah would've made her throw a banana or a bowl of Cheerios down the hatch if the shoe were on the other foot, here—so he said, "Sounds like a plan."

The elevator ride was only a couple of floors, and it simultaneously took forever and not long enough. A brunette decked out in light blue scrubs sat behind the nurses' station desk, her eyes fixed on the computer screen in front of her. She looked up as they approached, a kind but surprised smile moving over her face.

"Early birds. Can't say we see too many like y'all around here, especially on Christmas Eve morning."

Jonah's heart tripped against his sternum. But he was here, and Natalie was right here with him. He could do this. "I'm Jonah Sheridan. Kenneth Sheridan's son."

"Oh! Room 308." The nurse's smile brightened. That was a good sign, right? "I'm Nora, one of the nurses who took care of your father last night. Ian's here, too, but right now, he's with a patient."

"Thank you," Jonah said, knowing far better than to ever underestimate the power of a good nurse. "We were hoping to get an update."

"Of course." Nora exited the screen she'd been working on, mouse-clicking her way through the hospital's system. "Your father was still sleeping when I checked in on him about thirty minutes ago, but that's very common for patients who are being treated with the type of medicine Dr. Aronson ordered."

Jonah managed a tiny smile and tilted his head toward Natalie. "Actually, we're both surgeons, if you want to just..."

"Skip to the good parts?" Nora asked with a laugh. "You got it. We've been monitoring your father's vitals closely, and he's stable. His blood pressure is a little higher than we'd like, but he's been through a lot." She read off the numbers, and while Jonah didn't love them, they also weren't ringing any huge alarm bells. "Once he wakes up, Dr. Aronson will do a full evaluation. But for now, your father is responding to the anticoagulants."

"Okay." Jonah let go of his exhale, although only half-way. "Can we sit with him until he wakes up?"

Nora nodded and stood. "Of course. Hearing familiar voices, even under sedation, can be a big comfort to patients who are trying to heal. I'm a big believer that having loved ones close is always soothing."

Jonah smiled politely and followed her down the hall-way. He hadn't been the best son. Just because he'd had deep-seated reasons for creating distance didn't keep it from being the truth. But his father had still clearly loved him, enough to display photos and brag to his neighbors about the visit they'd planned, and Jonah loved him, too. So, yeah, he wasn't perfect, and yeah, he was still really fucking scared.

But he would be here to comfort his old man. He'd be right beside him when he woke up.

He *would* wake up.

"Alrighty," Nora half-whispered, leading the way past the closed door. Jonah reached out for Natalie's hand, finding it immediately and holding it tight as Nora continued. "The call button is right there on the wall, and Ian and I will be here for a few more hours until we change shifts. Dr. Aronson usually rounds at about nine, give or take. But if your father wakes up before then, just let me know so I can page him."

"Thank you," Natalie said, and Nora slipped to the door.

"No problem. I'm right down the hall if you need anything."

Jonah took a deep breath and scanned the low-lit room. His father looked much the same as he had last night, oddly frail despite his larger-than-average frame. His chest rose and fell in shallow yet rhythmic breaths, the pale green blanket tucked around his body moving with each one. His dark blond lashes created shadows beneath his closed eyes, the IVs on either side of the bed hooked up to one arm and the opposite hand, and Jonah's throat knotted involuntarily.

Natalie was right there, as promised. "Why don't we put the chair over here so you can hold his hand if you'd like?" she murmured, indicating the side of the bed with the IV-free hand. The small task hammered Jonah's focus into place, calming him, and he nodded.

"Yeah, that's a great idea." Together, they arranged the two chairs in the room side-by-side, and Jonah settled into the one closer to the head of the hospital bed.

"Would you like some privacy so you can talk to him?" Natalie asked, standing in front of the other chair.

He didn't even think before shaking his head. He wanted her here. Plain and simple. "No, I don't need privacy. I just... I'm not really sure what to say." Jonah didn't want to get all emotional, because A) if his father woke to that, he might get emotional, too, which would be bad for his vitals, and B) it wasn't how their relationship worked. Spilling their feelings by a campfire just wasn't what they did—to push it now wouldn't feel genuine. "It's a little odd to talk to him when he can't talk back."

"Hmm. Well, I guess you don't have to talk directly to him if you feel like it'll be uncomfortable." Natalie sat beside him. "The whole point is for him to hear your voice, right? So, if you want, you and I can talk and we'll include him in the conversation."

Jonah's brows lifted. But the more he thought about it, the smarter it seemed. "Okay."

"Great," Natalie said. "What should we talk about? Work?"

"Ugh, no. I love my job, but hearing about chest wall stabilization and emergency tracheostomies is not calming stuff."

Natalie laughed, and God, Jonah loved that sound. She looked from him to his father. "I don't know, Mr. Sheridan. I think your son is giving trauma surgery a bad rap. I mean, who doesn't love hearing about a good, old-fashioned chest wall stabilization?"

His father remained still, eyes closed and breathing even, but Jonah answered without a second thought. "You'll have to excuse Natalie, Dad. She's a total workaholic."

"Oh my God, really?" She swung a sassy glance in Jonah's direction. "Jonah, the pot *and* the kettle are both giving you major side-eye right now. Major. Side-eye."

That launched a conversation about several cases they'd each worked (Natalie'd just *had* to bring up the ten-hour surgery he'd done on a woman who had sustained three life-threatening injuries in a car wreck last year), what they did to relax (he'd made a mental note to accompany her to her next yoga class, where she would be, hello, wearing yoga *pants*), and—in a weird segue—landed them back on the *Die Hard* as a Christmas movie debate.

"Come on!" Jonah said to his father, even though the man was still sedated. "Dad, really. Think about it. *Die Hard* has it all. Perfect holiday soundtrack, epic office Christmas party. And the villain is even nastier than the Grinch. What better evidence do you need?"

"*It's a Wonderful Life* is a Christmas movie," Natalie argued past a soft laugh. "*A Christmas Carol* is a Christmas movie. How are you even going to compare 'God bless us, everyone' with yippy-ki—"

His father moved. Just a shift of his hand, but it was enough to make Jonah's heart climb his windpipe. "Dad?" He grabbed his hand and squeezed. God, the old man's fingers were so cold. "Dad, can you hear me?"

His father's fingers fluttered, his eyes following suit. "Unh."

Jonah dug deep and called on every ounce of medical training he owned to keep his adrenaline from filling the room. "Hey, Dad. It's me. I'm here."

"Forget the call button. I'm going to go get Nora," Natalie murmured, slipping from the room before Jonah had even finished nodding.

He held his father's hand tightly. *Please, please...*

"J—Jo...nah." His smile was weak, but oh, God, it was there.

His father was awake. He could speak.

He recognized him.

Relief crashed through Jonah's chest, pulling an involuntary laugh out of him by way of an exhale. "Yeah, Dad, it's me. I'm right here. Try to take it easy, okay? You gave us a bit of a scare." He paused. He didn't want to upset his father with the news that he'd suffered a stroke, but the old man's blinks of confusion were becoming more panicked by the second. Better to parcel out a little bit of truth and reassure him.

"You're at Saint Elizabeth's," Jonah said. "You had a stroke, but you're in great hands, and I'm here. I promise. You've had a lot of medication, and it's going to make you feel pretty fuzzy. That's normal, so don't worry."

His father's fingers curled around his, and some of the fear in his eyes slipped into understanding. "All...right."

"Are you experiencing any pain?" Jonah asked, and oh, how you could take the doctor out of the hospital, but not the hospital out of the doctor. "Does anything hurt?"

"Mmmm," his father said. But he didn't get to elaborate before the door opened, and Dr. Aronson appeared with Nora, Dr. Lee, and Natalie in tow.

"Mr. Sheridan. It's great to see you awake. I'm Dr. Aronson. I treated you when you arrived last night." He stepped in to perform a quick assessment as Dr. Lee collected a fresh set of vitals and read them off to Nora, who recorded them with care. "Can you tell me where you are?"

"H-hospital," Jonah's father said. "Saint E's."

"Good. You're here because you suffered a stroke, but the good news is, you're responding very well to the treatment protocol." He did a few cognitive tests, what year is it, who's the President, that sort of thing, then some motor function assessments, and more relief spilled through Jonah's veins at the results.

"Well, you look very good, but let's get to the important part," Aronson said. "How are you feeling, Mr. Sheridan? Any pain?"

"No. A little foggy." His speech seemed to be getting stronger with every word, although it wasn't close to his regular volume or cadence yet. "My head...aches some. But it's not bad."

"Can you rate it on a scale of one to ten?" Aronson asked. "Three."

Jonah tamped down the urge to give up an ironic smile. Ah, but his father was a tough old guy.

"Okay, that's a pretty good sign," Aronson said, and both Jonah and Natalie nodded in agreement. He did a more comprehensive exam, explaining his findings to everyone in the room and asking Dr. Lee some questions about the specifics as they went. Some of the strength and fine motor responses were still a little shaky—damn it!—but there were some encouraging results, too. Finally, Aronson stepped back to loop his stethoscope around his neck, splitting a glance between Jonah and his father.

"Based on everything I'm seeing and how well you've regained speech and motor function, Mr. Sheridan, I feel confident in diagnosing this as a TIA. We sometimes call them mini-strokes."

He went on to explain to Jonah's father how a clot had formed in his carotid artery and traveled to his brain, blocking off the blood flow and interrupting his normal brain function. Not that Jonah heard much of it, really. He was too busy grabbing Natalie's hand and thanking every deity he could think of.

"I don't see any reason to alter the course of treatment right now, since you're responding nicely. But just because this wasn't a full-blown event doesn't mean it's not serious," Aronson said. "There is some significant narrowing in that artery, and we're going to have to keep a close eye on it. That said, considering the improvements you've made over the last fourteen hours, I also think we're looking at a very good prognosis overall."

"So, you think he'll make a full recovery?" Jonah asked. *Please, please...*

Aronson smiled. "We may not be all the way out of the woods, but I think we can definitely see the tree-line from here. There's always a risk of residual effects, but a full recovery is certainly within reach. We'll talk about a longer-term plan to keep your risk factors for a repeat stroke as low as possible later, Mr. Sheridan. Medication, changes to diet and exercise, things like that. For now, your only job is to rest."

"Thanks...Doc," his father said.

Jonah thanked both doctors and Nora as they all moved toward the door, and Nora promised to return for a vitals check in a little bit. Natalie hung back a little, and Jonah could tell she was torn between wanting to offer support and wanting to give them privacy, just as she had been before. But Jonah wanted her next to him just as much as she'd wanted to be there this whole time, so he cleared his throat and said, "Dad, this is Natalie."

"Ah." His father's eyes brightened. "The...lady doctor," he said, the words slow but even. "Jonah's told me about you."

Natalie's brows flew upward. "Oh. Well, we're, um, good friends, and we've worked together for a long time," she said politely.

"That, too, I s'pose," his father said with a smile, and ohhhkay, time to save face while he still could.

"I told him about your bathtub, and how you needed a place to stay," Jonah said. He'd told his father at least a half dozen stories that featured or included Natalie in some way over the past couple of weeks. If the fact that the corners of his father's mouth were still lifted was any indication, he was going to share that little nugget if Jonah didn't take action. "So, do you want some water or anything, Dad? Or I might be able to scrounge up some juice."

His father nodded. "Now that you mention...it, my throat is a bit dry."

"No problem." Jonah grabbed the plastic pitcher from the bedside tray. He knew far better than to fill it with tap water, which would be lukewarm, at best. "I'll ask Nora where to get some ice. I'm sure they've got a lounge up here or something."

Of course, he realized his tactical error too late. Specifically, when he returned two minutes later to find Natalie sitting at his father's bedside, both of them laughing like old friends.

"Hand to God, Mr. Sheridan. I have the pictures right here," Natalie said, eagerly flipping through her phone.

"You have pictures of what?" Jonah asked warily.

Natalie's grin went full-on mischief. "A certain princess tea party with a certain eight-year-old girl and a stuffed fox."

Well, fuck. "How on earth did you two even get on that topic?"

Natalie passed her phone over to Jonah's dad, letting him wrap a hand over hers so she could keep the display steady, and Jonah's heart squeezed at the sight of her helping the old man while still letting him do what he could.

"Your dad asked how Annabelle was doing, so I told him a few stories," Natalie said to Jonah. To his dad, she murmured, "See? She talked him into wearing the Prince Charming crown and everything."

Oh, my God, Jonah couldn't tell if he wanted to kiss her or throw her phone into the nearest biohazard bag. "Really, Nat, I don't think my dad wants—"

His father lifted a graying brow in the ultimate parental signal to stop talking, which Jonah did. "Handsome," he said, his wry smile turning almost charming as he looked at Natalie. "He gets that from me."

Jonah's jaw unhinged at the same time Natalie laughed. Since when had his father grown a spirited side?

"I couldn't agree more, Mr. Sheridan."

In that moment, Jonah knew he could save his pride, and possibly his heart, and insist that his father rest. But the happiness in the old man's eyes far outweighed the weariness, and Jonah was tired of hiding who he was. What he wanted.

And what he wanted was not just to rebuild his relationship with his father, but to take his relationship with Natalie to a whole different level. He wanted to turn his hope into having.

So he said, "What Natalie is failing to tell you, Dad, is that she also attended said party in a feather boa and sparkly pink lip gloss." Pulling out his own phone, he tossed her a wink. "And I have the photos to prove it."

26

Natalie's butt was numb and her sides hurt, but she couldn't care less. Hospital chairs had never been comfortable—there had to be some sort of weird, unspoken rule between manufacturers or something—and, anyway, the pain in her sides was a byproduct of the best thing she could've hoped for out of this day.

Laughter.

"I'm just saying, there are clear and valid arguments to be made in favor of *Die Hard* being a Christmas movie," Jonah said, looking to his father for solidarity. "It's a classic."

"If you say so," Natalie said. In truth, while she didn't think she'd ever hop on board that train and ride it all the way to the station, she'd also enjoyed watching the movie (repeatedly) with Jonah.

God, she didn't want to go back to her apartment in a couple of weeks.

Her chin snapped up at the thought, and she stuffed it away. This was hardly the time or place to think about her feelings for Jonah, even if it was true. They'd agreed to keep things casual.

You might've been okay with casual when you agreed to it, but that's not what you really want now.

"Well," she said, her smile feeling one setting too tight. "As much as I'm enjoying this conversation, we have been chatting for a while. You should probably follow doctor's orders and rest, Mr. Sheridan."

The man nodded, seeming happy but worn out. "I suppose you're right."

"And you"—Natalie looked at Jonah—"need to eat something."

He nodded, but looked at his father hesitantly, as if he knew she was right but didn't want to leave the older man's side.

Not that Natalie could blame him. "Why don't I head down to the cafeteria and grab something to go? I'll also ask Nora and Ian to order a tray for your dad. Then we can all eat together." A walk would probably help clear her head, and anyway, they *did* need to eat.

"Okay, yeah. That sounds great. Thank you," Jonah said, and she pushed out another smile.

"Of course."

Natalie made her way down the hall and asked Nora for Mr. Sheridan's breakfast, then for directions to the cafeteria. Nora directed her to the main level, so Natalie thanked her and turned toward the elevators. A lone figure in the small waiting area caught her eye before she could make the trip, though, and wait...

"Vivian?" Natalie's boots clattered to a stop on the linoleum, and sure enough, Mr. Sheridan's neighbor was sitting in one of the chairs, her blouse and pants neatly pressed and her hands folded tightly in her lap. "What are you doing here?"

"Oh! I do apologize," she said with a pause, and Natalie

realized that in all of last night's rush, she hadn't introduced herself.

"Natalie," she said, reaching out to shake the woman's hand.

She smiled, albeit hesitantly. "Natalie. I'm sorry to just turn up again. I certainly don't want to impose."

Natalie replayed their conversation in her head, starting with what she'd asked the woman a minute ago, and immediately shook her head. "Oh, no. I didn't mean what are you doing at the hospital. I was just wondering what you're doing out *here*. Why you didn't come down to say hello?"

The woman had sat with Mr. Sheridan for a little while last night. Surely now that he was awake and visiting hours had started, the nurses wouldn't turn her away.

"Well, you and Jonah are family. I didn't want to intrude," Vivian said. The words rattled through Natalie, but she tucked the feeling aside. The woman clearly needed a little comfort, and it was going to take a whole lot more time than she had right now to parse through the jumble of *so-much-more-than-friends* emotions she was feeling for Jonah right now.

"That's kind of you, but I don't think you'd be intruding if you wanted to stop in to say a quick hello."

"If you're sure," she said, her gaze growing hopeful, and she gestured to a cellophane bag topped with pretty red and green ribbons. "I made Kenneth some candied pecans. They're his favorite. I know it's silly, but I was so worried last night, and I didn't know what else to do. Kenneth is..." Vivian pressed her lips together. "Well, he's a dear friend."

Something about the way her voice caught made Natalie realize that Vivian and Mr. Sheridan were more than friends, and whoa, talk about something she hadn't seen coming.

Still, she went with the truth. "Actually, I don't think that's silly at all."

"You don't?" Vivian asked.

"No, ma'am. As it turns out, I know a little something about dear friends, and I'm sure yours would love to see you. I'm headed downstairs to get some breakfast, but why don't you go say hello? I'll bring some extra food if you'd like to join us."

Tears sprang to the woman's eyes. "I'd like that very much. Thank you, Natalie."

"Of course." Natalie's smile was bittersweet as she watched Vivian move down the hallway.

Now if she could just figure out her feelings for *her* dear friend so easily.

Now that he was finally allowing himself to feel them, Jonah was shocked at how many emotions he could jam into the span of eight hours. Between the fear, then relief over his father's prognosis, the surprise of discovering his old man had a "lady friend" (his phrase, not Jonah's), and how purely right he'd felt with Natalie at his side all day—hell, all month, really—he was pretty sure he'd run the gamut from end to end.

God, he felt right with Natalie. And the crazy part was, that didn't feel crazy at all.

It felt like hope.

"Hmmm." His father shifted out of the nap he'd started a couple hours ago, and Jonah looked up from the chair at his bedside.

"Hey, you're awake." Closing his laptop, he set the thing

aside and reached out to pour some fresh water into the cup on the rolling tray.

His father took a long draw before sinking back against the pillow. "I didn't mean to scare everyone else off."

Jonah looked around the otherwise empty room and let go of a soft laugh. "Vivian wanted to let you rest, although she said she'd check in on you after she went to the Christmas Eve service at her church. Natalie ran out to grab some snacks for the next couple of days. I was just catching up on a little work."

"Always knew you'd be an excellent doctor," his father said, and Jonah laughed again.

"I'm glad *you* knew it." Medical school exams, his internship and residency. His boards. Christ, there had been more than a few times when Jonah himself had doubted he'd make it.

His father nodded. "I should've told you before now, though."

Surprise mingled with the hard shot of regret in Jonah's belly. "I didn't make it easy for you *to* tell me."

He didn't want to upset his father—God knew they'd all had a long-ass day, and it wasn't even over yet. But it was past time for them to have this conversation, and *far* past time for Jonah to offer an apology. "Dad, I know we haven't been as close as we could be. Should be," he corrected. "But it's my fault."

"Jonah," his father began, but he shook his head, adamant.

"It is, Dad, and it's time I said so. You're my only parent. I spent a lot of time being scared about what could happen if we were close and I lost you that I didn't stop to think about what we'd have if we were and I *didn't*. I gave in to that fear and pushed you away, and..." Jonah broke off for a breath. "I shouldn't have. You raised me on your own. You were always there. You deserve better, and I'm so sorry."

For a minute, nothing passed between them except for silence, his father seeming to process the words. Jonah's pulse pumped heavy in his ears, moving even faster as his father finally answered.

"You might have pushed me away, but I didn't press the issue. I knew there was distance between us. I'd have to have been blind not to see it." He stopped for a breath, and Jonah was tempted, not a little, to interrupt so the old man wouldn't get riled up. But he wasn't upset—on the contrary, he looked as if a weight were lifting off his shoulders—so Jonah kept quiet and let him continue.

"I didn't know why, or how to fix it," his father said. "Talking about my feelings has never been my strong suit. But I was there, same as you. I could've tried to bridge the gap. I could've pushed, and I didn't. I suppose I was scared, too."

"You were?" Shock took over Jonah's rib cage. "Of what?"

His father exhaled. "Your mother left because she didn't love me. I'm quite sure she never did. I've moved past that now, but for a lot of years, there was...deep hurt there. I guess I was scared that if I tried to get close to you, you wouldn't care for me, either."

Jonah opened his mouth to say that was crazy—of course he loved his old man—but then he closed it. They'd both had irrational feelings with roots that had run deep. They might not be able to change that or get back the time they'd lost, but they could sure as hell start to repair it now.

"I've always cared for you, but I'd like to get to know you better," Jonah said instead. "I can't promise I'm going to always get things right. Talking about my feelings isn't really my strong suit, either. Guess that's another thing I get from you." He let out a tiny smile. "But I've missed you, Dad. I'd really like it if we could be closer."

"I'd like that, too."

Jonah leaned in, hugging his father as tightly as he could while still being cognizant of the IVs and the man's current state of exhaustion. His father did look lighter, the shadows beneath his eyes easing just a notch as he smiled at Jonah with more of that newfound mischief Jonah had never really seen.

"Now that we've got that settled, let's talk about your girl."

Well, shit. He'd just been blindsided by his old man. "I'm not sure what you mean," Jonah said, trying—and epically failing, thanks—to dodge the topic.

His father scoffed. "You know exactly what I mean. You like her."

Annnnd they were going there. "I do," Jonah admitted, because saying otherwise would be a big, fat lie. "We're good friends. Best friends."

"Looks to me like you're a lot more than that," his father said, lifting his hands at what had to be a look of pure WTF on Jonah's face. "What? I'm old, not blind. And for what it's worth, she likes you, too. Anyone with half a brain could see that."

Jonah blinked, but truly, after what Natalie had said to him last night, after how she'd had his back so unconditionally, he couldn't deny what his father had said. "I suppose she does."

"Well, I'm glad you found her." His father smiled. "Just do yourself a favor and hold on to her, would you? Someone like that is..."

"I know, Dad," Jonah said, and for the first time in his life, he really did. "I know."

27

Natalie brushed her teeth, her head and heart locked in a heated battle over which could drive her around the bend first. Her head kept reminding her that now that Jonah's father was stable, she really did need to give Harlow's job offer some serious thought. She didn't want to give up surgery, and she wasn't sure if she was as made for the job as Harlow seemed to believe. She had no true business experience to speak of, and certainly nothing in the corporate realm. The mere thought of all those budget meetings and policy committees made her dizzier than a sideshow carnival ride. But taking the director's position would be a huge step for her career, not to mention a huge boost financially. If she said yes, she'd definitely be secure enough to pay off the last of her medical school loans, and maybe even put a down payment on a house.

A house she wanted so she could move forward with finding someone to be with in the long-term and eventually adopt a couple (or more) kids, and welcome to her heart's side of this battle royale.

She wanted that someone to be Jonah.

Her heart slapped against her sternum, and she looked at the bathroom door that separated them. Their friendship had definitely changed over the past month, and even though they'd agreed to keep things casual, there was no way Jonah wasn't feeling at least some version of what she was feeling. Natalie knew him like she knew the reflection she was staring at right this second, for God's sake. He'd confided in her and held her close, literally *and* figuratively, just as she'd done with him. They'd both meant the things they'd said, and she couldn't deny the truth any longer.

Her feelings might be bigger than she'd expected them to become, and yeah, that was scary considering that wasn't what she'd promised him a few weeks ago. But this was Jonah. Her best friend. The man she was falling in love with.

She needed to tell him how she felt.

Finishing up with her nightly routine, Natalie changed into her nightshirt, the boat neck falling off one shoulder like it always did. The white cotton swished just above her knees as she turned toward the door and killed the bathroom lights, surprise filling her chest when she stepped into the hotel room to find it bathed in a soft, golden glow.

"What...?" Natalie's surprise coasted into laughter when she saw that Jonah had turned on the TV, somehow managing to find one of those stations that broadcast a cozily lit fireplace. The rest of the room was dark, and Jonah sat in the middle of the bed in his T-shirt and pajama pants.

"Sorry there's no tree," he said with a half-grin. "I know how much you love Christmas. But this was the best I could do under the circumstances."

The unease that had squeezed Natalie's heart only a few minutes before turned into something decidedly different as she shook her head and moved over to the bed to sit down next to him. "No, this is perfect."

"Well, I'm glad you think so." He reached for the bedside table, sliding a box adorned with a satiny red bow from the shadows. "I got you a present."

Natalie's lips parted, her brows winging up. When on earth would he have had the time to do that? They'd spent all day at the hospital, keeping his father company until after dinner, then sitting down to discuss a follow-up care plan and long-term medications with Dr. Aronson.

"I have a present for you, too, but it's back at the apartment." She thought of the photo she'd had professionally matted and framed, a candid that Rachel had taken of the two of them at the hospital, both of them laughing.

"That's okay. You should still open yours now," Jonah said, placing the box on the coverlet. It was small and flat, the sort that might hold a wallet or something similar, and Natalie's curiosity sparked. She tugged at the bow, which was the only "wrapping" on the box itself, pulling it away and lifting the lid to reveal—

"It's a key." Natalie took it from the thin layer of tissue paper inside the box, slightly confused.

Jonah smiled, arching a brow at her through the soft light. "Yes, but it's not just any key. It goes to my apartment, and I know you already have one, but I'm giving you *this* one because I was kind of hoping you'd want to keep it so you can use it every day...when you come home."

All the breath left her lungs in a gasp. "Are you asking me to move in with you? Like, change of address, pack up boxes, hang my bras on the shower curtain rod, move *in* with you?"

"Yep. I sure am," Jonah said, his expression turning suddenly serious. "I know this might be a lot. We said we'd keep things casual. But that's not how it feels to me anymore. It feels—"

"Right," she whispered, her heart beginning to beat faster. *Like two wholes making something bigger.* "It feels right."

He lifted a hand to cup her face, and oh, God, she was in love with him. "I know there are no guarantees, and I know we're going to make mistakes and have fights. But I've waited a long time to have hope, and I'm done being scared to take the risk. So, yes. I am asking you and your boxes and bras to move in with me."

"Yes. Yes, yes, yes," Natalie said, throwing her arms around his shoulders to kiss him.

Jonah laughed, his lips against hers. "You sure you don't want to think about it?"

"Well, normally, I would consult my boxes and bras, but under the circumstances, I think I can speak for us all when I say that this is the best Christmas present we've ever gotten."

"Oh, I'm not done," Jonah said, shifting to reach for the TV remote. A click of a button had the fireplace disappearing, replaced by a black and white storybook and a familiar, old-timey musical score.

"You're going to let me watch *It's a Wonderful Life*?" she asked, a pop of laughter flying out of her.

"Nope. I'm going to watch it *with* you," he said, kissing her one more time before pulling back the coverlet and pulling her in close to his side. "You ready?"

Yeah, she thought, holding Jonah as tightly as he held her. Life was definitely wonderful.

"Looks like someone had a very Merry Christmas," Tess sing-songed across the lounge in the ED two days later. Natalie had been back at work for exactly—she checked her watch—twelve minutes, and even though she'd texted both Tess and Charlie a fairly detailed update yesterday, she'd known far better than to think they wouldn't both want the full rundown now that she was physically back in the building.

She turned her gaze around the lounge, which was empty except for the three of them, and headed for the coffeepot. God, the last couple of days had taken it out of her. Even with their good outcome.

"Yeah, we really did. It was kind of quiet, since we spent it at the hospital with Jonah's dad and Vivian. But it was still great." They'd been able to catch *A Christmas Carol* on an old movie channel, then share some eggnog and fruitcake as football took center stage. In between Mr. Sheridan's naps, of course.

"I'm glad Jonah's dad is recovering nicely," Tess said. "But I meant *you*, specifically. You're all humming and smiling over there, like you've got happiness squishing right out of you—"

"Even more than usual," Charlie chimed in, and Tess tilted her head in nonverbal agreement.

"It would be gross if it wasn't so cute, plus, you used the W-word."

Natalie took a sip of coffee to A) bury her smile, and B) try to shake some of this exhaustion. "The W-word?"

"We," Charlie said with a grin. "And not the royal *we*, either. You, my friend, have it bad for The Orgasm Whisperer."

Thank God Jonah had decided to stay in Charleston for a few more days to help his dad with the transition home, although, really, he could probably see Natalie's blush from here.

And her happiness. "I might." She bit her lip, but really, there was no sense in holding back. She and Jonah were going to box up the rest of her stuff and move it to his place —*their* place—as soon as he got back from South Carolina. The fact that they'd ditched friends-with-benefits was going to become really obvious, really fast. She might as well spill the beans. "So, um, Jonah asked me to move in with him."

Tess's mouth fell open. "Shut the fuck up."

"Are you serious?" Charlie asked past her laughter. "That's wonderful!"

Natalie nodded, unable to keep from laughing, too. "He asked me on Christmas Eve."

"One of these days, we're going to teach you to lead with the good bits," Tess said, sitting down on the couch and waving Natalie over. "Although, I suppose we have to find a different nickname for him, because now...anyway." She waved a hand through the air. "Spill. And remember, I *am* living vicariously here. The only romance I have in my life is the novel on my bedside table, so don't leave out any details unless they're R-rated."

"Okay," Natalie said. She gave Charlie and Tess a basic version of what had happened, although she kept the personal details of Jonah's past and the conversation they'd had the night before Christmas Eve to herself. That wasn't her story to tell. But it was all too easy to recount how she and Jonah had grown closer over the past month, and to admit the truth.

She had hope. Jonah had hope. And they'd taken that leap together.

"So, you rented a car and came back last night?" Charlie asked, and Natalie nodded. Before she could continue, though, Parker opened the door to the lounge and came sauntering in.

"Dr. Michaelson, I've got a patient in curtain three with..." His dark eyes went wide as he looked up from the chart in his hands. "You know what, I will find Dr. Tanaka and ask her because this is not urgent and you are going to kill me if I don't leave this room right now."

"Your fiancé is very smart," Tess said to Charlie, who grinned and mouthed *I love you* in Parker's direction.

Parker laughed and turned to duck back through the door, and Tess called out, "If you can't find Tanaka, text me, Drake! God, it's never a dull moment, I swear."

The truth of it sent a pang through Natalie's belly. Tess wasn't wrong by any stretch, she still loved the bustle of treating patients. She'd *missed* it, even after only a few days.

Clearing her throat, she returned to Charlie's question. "Yeah, I wanted to give Jonah some one-on-one time with his dad, plus, I have some surgeries scheduled that I didn't want to bump. Mr. Sheridan should be released from the hospital later today, tomorrow at the latest, and Jonah's going to stick around until the home health aide and the occupational therapist are all set." With each of them scheduled for twice-weekly visits, plus Vivian there for daily assistance, things were truly moving forward.

"Wow." Tess shook her head, her ponytail brushing the shoulders of her doctor's coat. "On the one hand, I want to be shocked that Jonah Sheridan is off the market. On the other..."

"They're totally perfect for each other and it's about damned time?" Charlie supplied.

Tess pointed at her best friend with both index fingers. "That."

"I'm never going to live this down, am I?" Natalie asked, her grin breaking free for the billionth time.

"You showed The Orgasm Whisperer the light," Tess said, arching a brow. But her smile put a happy edge to the words. "No. You are never going to live this down. In fact, I'm going to be forever convinced that you're part unicorn beneath that perky, smart-girl exterior."

The conversation dissolved into laughter, and they parted ways a minute later, Tess going to follow up with Parker on the patient in curtain three and Charlie heading upstairs with Boldin for rounds. Natalie found Vasquez, her intern du jour, at the nurses' station, standing between Connor and Mallory and looking thoroughly put out.

"Good morning," Natalie said cheerily, but it barely put a dent in Vasquez's frown.

"Morning, Dr. Kendrick," she mumbled.

"I'm afraid Dr. Vasquez's bad mood is my fault," Mallory said, and funny, he didn't look the least bit apologetic about that, his pleasant smile on full display.

Vasquez snorted. "I'm not in a bad mood."

Connor tried to hide his laughter in a poorly constructed cough. "If this is you happy, I'd hate to see a *real* bad mood." His laughter died at Vasquez's frosty stare. "But you know what, I have labs to go check on for Dr. Brooks. Like, right this second. Bye!"

For a huge guy, Connor sure could hustle when the occasion called for it. Natalie turned back to Mallory and Vasquez. She didn't know what was going on between the two of them, but right now, she didn't have time to run interference. "Well, you're on my service today, Dr. Vasquez, and I'm about to make your day."

Natalie scooped up a tablet from the charging station

and tapped through a handful of screens until she reached the chart she was looking for. "Tell me what I'm looking at."

"Abdominal scans of a juvenile patient who looks like..." Vasquez's eyes narrowed over the scans. "That's an appy. No question. The inflammation is obvious, his history says his temp is elevated, and the notes list right-side guarding upon examination." She hesitated, but her curiosity seemed to get the better of her. "That one wasn't even close to hard. No disrespect, but how are you making my day?"

"Because I want you to book an OR, then go get Billy here from exam five and take him upstairs. Prep him for surgery, and I'll meet you up there. We're going to see how good your surgical skills are."

"Yes, Dr. Kendrick." The intern's entire demeanor changed in a breath, and she clutched the chart to her chest and smiled. "You won't be sorry!"

"That'll go right to her head, you know," Mallory said as soon as Vasquez had disappeared around the corner, practically skipping.

Natalie shrugged. He might not be wrong, but still. "Do I even want to know what's going on between the two of you?"

"It's strictly professional," he said, so adamantly that she believed him. "But Vasquez has got some sort of weird hate thing for ortho. I might've implied that it was because the specialty is her weak spot." Now Mallory looked a little sheepish. "I did it to light a fire in her because she's competitive as fuck, and she needs to learn like all the other interns, but yeah. Let's just say she's not my biggest fan."

"Hmm." Not necessarily the tactic Natalie would've picked, but honestly, maybe not a bad one to motivate Vasquez to learn. Even if it did also motivate her to hate Mallory. "Well, hopefully it'll inspire her and not make her try to throttle you."

"Always with the bright side, Kendrick. Always with the bright side."

Natalie laughed. She wanted to check in with Jonah to see how his dad was doing this morning before she headed into the OR, so she said a quick goodbye to Mallory and headed for the elevator. She'd taken a tablet with her so she could review Billy's chart one more time, scanning his ultrasound images and making mental notes on her way down the hallway toward the surgical unit. She was so lost in thought that she didn't hear the voice behind her until the person belonging to it had caught up to her at a near-run and whoa.

"Natalie! God, I'm so glad I found you."

Her brows popped. Jeffrey Wells looked like he'd sprinted the entire way from his office in the oncology unit just to flag her down.

"Hey, Jeff. I was just running to remove a pissed-off appy from a nine-year-old's belly. What's up?"

For all the man's rushing to catch her, he hesitated at her question, and okay, *that* was weird. "I need to talk to you about something. It's pretty urgent."

They'd collaborated on a handful of cases together over the time Natalie had worked at Remington Mem, but Jeff usually didn't handle peds patients. In fact, Hoover took all of those cases, now that Natalie thought about it. But whatever he wanted to talk to her about must be pretty serious, judging by the look on his face, so she nodded.

"Okay, sure."

"Great." There were three small, private waiting rooms along the wall to their right, the sort where they usually let the families of gravely injured patients stay to have privacy, and he led her into the closest one and shut the door. He sat down in one of the chairs, and Natalie sat across from him automatically, unease trickling into her belly.

"Really, Jeff, is everything okay?"

"Actually, I'm afraid it's not." He looked down at the printout that Natalie just realized he'd been holding, then back at her. "Your lab results came in a little while ago."

"My..."

She trailed off before she understood that Jeff wasn't talking about a patient's workup. He was talking about *her* lab results, personally. With everything that had happened directly after her appointment, she'd completely forgotten she'd had her blood drawn a few days ago for her re-check.

Oh. God.

Natalie's blood turned to ice in her veins, realization slapping her directly across the face. She knew the tone in Jeff's voice, calm, yet serious. Knew the look on his face, because she'd given it to other people more times than she wanted to count. Hell, she'd probably *gotten* that look twenty-two years ago from the first doctor who had diagnosed her with leukemia.

Oh, God. Oh, God, oh, *God*.

Jeff didn't have to say it. Natalie didn't *want* him to say it.

Her eighteen-year streak of perfectly normal results was about to end.

Jeff looked at her. "There are some red flags with your test results. I ran them twice, the second time myself, to be sure, but—"

"Let me see."

He blinked. "Natalie, I don't think that's the best idea. It's one test, and it's not conclusive of anything until we can—"

For the second time in as many minutes, she cut him off, even though she knew it was less than polite. But she needed to think, to process and find the bright side so she could figure out how to be okay, and she couldn't do that without facts.

"I'm a board certified surgeon, not an untrained patient who won't understand what she's looking at, and I am *asking* you for my lab results. Please."

His hesitation filled the room like a boulder, but it only lasted for a beat before he said, "Of course."

Natalie forced herself to remain calm as she sought out every positive sign on the sheet. Between her white cell count and her platelets, there were damn few of them.

Which meant they needed more facts. "Can we do the biopsy today?"

She knew it was the next step, and it wouldn't be her first, or even her fourth, bone marrow biopsy. The procedure was painful, yes, but it was possible that she was anemic, or had some other sort of infection. She didn't have any weird bruises, like when she'd been diagnosed with cancer as a child, and she'd had no fever or abnormal bleeding. Yeah, she'd been tired lately, but that was normal.

It was normal. She was fine.

She had to be fine.

Thankfully, Jeff decided that treating her with kid gloves was no longer his tactic of choice. "We can do the biopsy today, although I'd like to repeat your CBC and do a full workup with blood chemistry studies first. Get all of our ducks in a row so we'll know for sure what we're dealing with. You'll be off your feet for a couple of days," he said apologetically. "But I'll rush the results, and I'll have the head of hematology read them herself. Anonymously, of course."

"Okay." This was a plan. Plans were good. God, why couldn't she breathe? "Let me pass my surgery off to a resident and clear my schedule for the rest of the day. I'd like to just tell Dr. Langston I'm not feeling well and leave it at that, if you don't mind?"

"Of course," Jeff said. "We can do everything in the oncology unit, and it shouldn't take too long at all. You'll need someone to take you home, though. You won't be able to drive after the procedure. Can I call someone for you? A partner or a family member? A friend?"

Jonah's name formed in her mouth, pushed upward by her heart, but she bit down on it before it could emerge. If Jonah knew about this, he'd worry—*not* a little—and he'd already been overloaded with stress this week. Plus, he was helping his father get back on his feet after a stroke, for God's sake. Natalie couldn't justify calling him home early over a tiny little blip on her health radar, no matter how badly she wanted comfort. Even Tess and Charlie might be tempted to worry, or worse yet, say something to Jonah, if she asked for one of them to help her home, and anyway, they had people to care for here at the hospital.

"No, that's okay. I've had biopsies before, so I know what to expect. I'll take an Uber home. But in the meantime, I'd like to get this over-with, if that's okay?"

Jeff nodded. "We can get started as soon as you're ready."

Natalie's brain spun, her fear bubbling up in a sudden rush, but she shook her head. Jeff was right. Nothing was definitive yet. She shouldn't worry until there was anything to worry *about*.

She needed to hope, now more than ever.

28

N atalie stared at her phone as if it might explode at any second. Or maybe that was just her that might explode, she thought, pushing up from the couch gingerly even though her hip throbbed in time with her heartbeat, thump-*THUMP*, thump-*THUMP*, thump-*THUMP*. Even now, forty-eight hours after the procedure, she was still sore, having sprouted one hell of a Technicolor bruise at the incision site. Jeff had assured her that everything had gone well and that he'd call her as soon as he got the comprehensive results.

For the first day and a half, she'd been able to remain hopeful, sleeping off the pain and telling herself there was nothing to worry about. She'd still erred on the side of caution and dodged actual phone calls with Jonah, telling him via text what she'd told everyone else—that she'd come down with a nasty case of the flu and was spending the bulk of her time in bed. Natalie hated to lie—especially to him— but he knew her far too well, and she had a consummately shitty game face. If he so much as got a whiff that she wasn't one hundred percent fine, he'd come hauling back to Remington.

She had to be fine. She had to be.

She'd promised Jonah she'd never leave him.

She could *not* have cancer.

Her phone vibrated over the coffee table, startling her shitless and making her cut out a curse. Her pulse turned her veins into live wires, but she scraped in a breath and looked at the caller ID.

Remington Memorial Hospital.

"Hello?" Natalie said, forcing herself to inhale. She had to have hope. She had to find the bright side.

"Hi, Natalie. It's Jeff. I've got your biopsy results." The silence over the line was deafening in the two-second pause. "I'm afraid I've got some bad news. Your biopsy showed atypical cells consistent with acute lymphoblastic leukemia. I'm so sorry, but your cancer is no longer in remission."

He gave the news a second to sink in—it was an age-old strategy designed not to overwhelm the patient. But for fuck's sake, she had cancer *again*. The news didn't so much sink in as it stabbed her in the heart.

"I...how bad is it?" she heard herself ask, still grasping for something, anything that wouldn't crush her.

No luck. "We'll need to have you come in as soon as possible for an MRI and some other tests to determine that for sure. You're not exhibiting a lot of symptoms, which is good. If we've caught it early and it hasn't traveled to your spinal cord, we may not have to rely on longer, more aggressive treatments."

The thought made Natalie's stomach drop and fill with dread. "And if we haven't?" She might like her glass half full, but she liked facts even better. Oh, God, this couldn't be happening.

What Jeff said was, "Why don't we cross that bridge if we get to it?", but Natalie knew what he meant. Chemo. Radiation. Maybe even stem cell transplants, and yeah, Natalie was going to be sick. "You responded incredibly well to cancer treatments last time," Jeff was saying, and she forced herself to focus on his voice. "And with the therapies available in some clinical trials now, I feel confident that we'll find a strong plan of care. We have a lot of good options, and a lot of advances have been made since the last time you fought this disease."

Again, there was the unspoken "but". The one Natalie never, ever said to patients—hell, the one she never even allowed herself to think.

She was thinking it now.

Despite all that great medicine, you could still die.

Natalie realized Jeff had gone quiet, and she cleared her throat. She had to hold it together. She had to be strong. Optimistic. "I understand. Can I come in first thing tomorrow for the MRI?"

"Of course. We can sit down with the results and go from there." He paused. "I'm so sorry, Natalie. I'll see you in the morning, okay?"

"Thanks, Jeff."

She lowered her phone to her lap, her head swimming so fast, it nearly knocked her sideways.

Her cancer was back.

Tears formed, hot and fast in her eyes, and her heart slammed so rapidly, she grew short of breath. She inhaled deeply to counter it, logically knowing that she was within millimeters of a panic attack that wouldn't help her in any way. Good luck telling that to the rest of her, of course. She might as well be trying to nail Jell-O to a tree.

This could *not* be happening.

"Okay. Okay, okay, okay." Natalie chanted the word over and over until it blended into one sound. She had to focus here. She had to do...something other than freak out. Her brain darted to work, and okay, yes. Yes. Work always calmed her. She could figure this out. She *could*.

She was going to have to take a leave of absence—being around sick patients when her own immune system was compromised would be out of the question. She could probably—maybe?—still work when she felt up to it, though, she reasoned, grasping at the bright side like a champ. Langston might be willing to let her do research on behalf of the hospital, or...God, something. The job with Harlow was out of the question now, but Natalie was oddly not upset about that. In truth, she'd been leaning toward not taking it anyway. She had always kind of felt as if that position was made for someone with far more business sense than she owned.

Of course, Natalie was assuming she'd be able to work at all. If this cancer had spread to her spinal cord, she'd have to do God knew how many rounds of chemo and radiation, and they'd be brutal. Just because she'd responded to treatments when she'd been younger didn't mean the process hadn't been physically grueling. It also didn't mean they'd *work* this time, but no. No, no, no, no, no, she had to stay positive. A cancer diagnosis wasn't a death sentence. Natalie said this to patients all the time.

Damn, she was full of shit.

Tears threatened again, this time with more power. Yes, there were options, and yes, she was alive in this very minute, which was what counted. But the obstacles seemed suddenly huge and very, very different than when she'd faced them as a kid. Then, she'd had her parents...

Oh, God. Her parents.

Jonah.

All the hope Natalie had tried to hold on to disappeared like smoke in a gust of wind. Jonah's biggest fear, the one that had controlled him for decades of his life and kept him from having any sort of close relationships, was that love didn't last. She had sworn to him that it could, that it *did*. She'd promised him she was there, and that the risk was worth taking. She'd sworn she'd never leave him.

What if that had been a lie?

The realization ripped through her, carving a path through her chest. Yes, Natalie loved him—so much that she felt it in her blood and in her bones. But her blood and bones had cancer, and as much as she wanted to find the bright side and silver lining, she couldn't.

She couldn't do this to him. Jonah hadn't said it, but Natalie knew he loved her. He'd asked her to move in with him, for Chrissake, a step no one, including him, thought he'd ever take again. She was the only person he'd let past all his defenses. Natalie had told him she would always be there, and he'd *believed* her. The way he'd believed his mother would always be there, too.

Tears began to slide down her face, opening up a torrent of sobs that echoed off the apartment walls. She'd made a promise she could no longer keep, no matter how badly she wanted to. She couldn't look Jonah right in those beautiful baby blues and swear to him that she'd never leave, that she wouldn't crush the very hope she'd fostered. That Natalie wouldn't *mean* to hurt him was of little consequence—the pain didn't have to be intentional in order to devastate someone, and there was no guarantee that this cancer wouldn't get worse and kill her, making her leave him like everyone else he'd ever cared about.

She couldn't risk his heart. Even if it broke hers.

JONAH BALANCED the grocery bag he'd filled with chicken noodle soup, Saltines, and Gatorade on one hip, riffling through his keys to single out the one to his apartment. Getting his father situated back at home had taken a day longer than Jonah had anticipated, but it had been time well spent. They'd been able to set up a schedule for follow-up appointments and review prescriptions, plus meet with a nutritionist to start making some healthier changes to the old man's diet. Vivian had been a huge help, and it took a load off Jonah's mind knowing that someone was there, caring for his father.

Now *he* needed to take care of Nat. He'd barely spoken to her over the past four days. The flu was no joke, and they were deep in the heart of the season. He'd take his chances, though, because no way was he not going to tuck her in on the couch and fix her a bowl of soup. He might even let her pick the movie, although he'd probably regret it a tiny bit. They'd have to figure out some kind of system now that they were living together.

Jonah's grin was so sweet and so good, he could practically taste it. Christ, he loved her. Rom coms and all.

And he wanted to tell her.

Maneuvering his key into the lock, he flipped the deadbolt and made his way inside. The lights were on in the apartment, and even though the living room and kitchen were empty, he could hear movement in the bedroom, signaling that Natalie was awake.

"Hey! I'm home," Jonah called out, heading to the kitchen to drop the bag on the counter before moving back to the living room. "How are you feeling? I brought you some..."

The rest of his words stopped cold as he caught sight of Natalie, standing in the living room entryway. Although she was fully dressed in jeans and a sweatshirt (weird), she looked like hell, her face drawn and pale and shadows framing her reddened eyes.

"Oh, babe, this flu is really knocking you down, isn't it?" Jonah asked. He took a step toward her, confusion prickling through him as she countered with a step back.

"I don't have the flu."

His brows flew upward. "What?"

"I..." She bit her lip, which already looked worse for wear, as if she'd been doing it a lot lately. "We need to talk."

The look on Natalie's face was so serious that he immediately said, "Okay. What's the matter?"

She didn't answer, but walked into the living room instead. She sat down in the single chair in the room, the one that barely ever got used because they always sat tangled together on the couch, and what the *hell* was going on?

"Nat, you're kind of scaring me, here," Jonah said. He sat at the end of the couch closest to her, reaching for her hands.

But again, she pulled away from him. "I got my test results back."

His thoughts stuttered. "Your blood test?" No, no. No, she had to be talking about something else. She couldn't mean—

"Yes. My cancer is back, Jonah."

The bottom dropped out of his belly, and he tried—desperately—to process what she'd said. His brain automatically vaulted to the medicine, desperately trying to put the variables in order.

"Okay, but that's one blood test. It's not even close to

definitive. You could have an infection, or something else. It could be a lot of things that aren't cancer," Jonah argued. "You need more tests, that's all."

Natalie shook her head. "I've already had them."

Shock bloomed in his belly, a sharp thread of anger hot on its heels. "You've already *had* them? When?"

Her hesitation told him he wasn't going to like her reply, and hell if it wasn't right on the money. "A few days ago. The biopsy showed atypical cells consistent with acute lymphoblastic leukemia. The MRI and lumbar puncture confirmed that the cancer hasn't moved to my spinal cord, but the treatment plan is still aggressive. I'll be starting chemo in a couple weeks."

For the life of him, Jonah was never going to make it past the emotions crowding his brain. "You had all those tests without *telling* me?" For fuck's sake, a bone marrow biopsy was a surgical procedure. Outpatient, but still. She had to have been in pain. Not to mention terrified. How could she not have at least called to let him know this was happening?

Something that looked an awful lot like despair flashed in Natalie's eyes, filling them with tears. But she blinked them away and said, "It's not your burden to carry."

Just like that, his emotions tipped over.

"Bullshit, Natalie!" Jonah's voice rose without his permission, but right now, he didn't care. He might not have been a long-haul guy for a long-ass time, but she had to know this was different. *She* was different. "After everything we've been through, after everything I've told you and everything you've told me, how can you say that?"

Natalie closed her eyes and dropped her chin toward her chest. But when she opened them again, they didn't waver, and neither did her words.

"Because it can't be your burden, Jonah. It's not that I

don't think you'd carry it for me," she added quickly, squashing his rising protest. "God, I know you would, and that's exactly the point. You'd carry all of this for me even if it hurt you beyond repair." She paused, her gaze becoming a plea. "But I can't let that happen. I made you a promise, and I have to keep it."

Jonah's chin whipped up. No. No. Not fucking happening. "You think you're going to die and leave me behind? That's insane, Natalie. You're not going to *die*. You're going to go through treatment. You're going to kick this cancer's ass just like you did when you were a kid, and then you're going to live a long, happy life."

With me, he added silently.

But out loud, Natalie said, "Maybe. But maybe not."

"You will," he insisted, but even then, he knew she was right.

There were no guarantees. There was a chance, even if it was small, that she could die, and oh God, he couldn't lose her.

"I hope I do, but that isn't a risk I can take. Not when I know what it would do to you if I don't go into remission again," Natalie said, and in that moment, fear gripped Jonah, good and hard.

"I don't care about me," he said, and funny, he really didn't.

Natalie's smile was small and sad, and Christ, it clawed at him, despite being fucking beautiful. "But I do. I won't put you through this. It's months, possibly years, of not knowing, all with no guarantee. And I refuse to let you hope for that long, all for a risk that might hurt you terribly. I'm sorry, Jonah. I really am. But I can't let you be a long-haul guy. Not for this."

Of all the words Natalie could have chosen, those sliced

the deepest, pinning him into place as she continued. "I had a long talk with my parents last night, and I'll be staying with them until my apartment is finished. I've got a meeting with Langston in the morning, but I'll probably be taking a leave of absence for a little while once the chemo starts."

Jonah's thoughts raced along with his pulse, and he couldn't control either. "Nat, I am asking you." He swallowed hard. "Please. Don't do this."

A flicker of emotion moved through her eyes, and for a split second, Jonah had hope.

But then she stood, placing the key he'd given her on the coffee table and walking to the door.

"I have to. Goodbye," she whispered.

And then she was gone.

29

N atalie stared at the ceiling in her childhood bedroom and tried not to cry. It was only three in the afternoon, but the second she'd gotten back from her meeting with Langston, she'd put on her rattiest pair of pajamas and slid back under the covers. Her mother had given her a surprisingly wide berth since she'd shown up last night, as promised. Her parents had taken her cancer news a little better than Natalie had expected, although they'd both been clearly shaken and just as clearly worried about her. But they hadn't insisted that she move back in permanently, nor had they lost their minds when she'd confessed to what had happened with Bathtubgate. Instead, her mother had simply made up Natalie's old bedroom while her father had fixed her a ginormous Cuban sandwich ("not as good as that gal who runs The Crooked Angel downtown, but still, not too shabby," he'd joked), both of them caring for her in exactly the way she'd needed.

The only thing Natalie had been missing were a bunch of eighties action movies and a sexy, smart-assed best friend to watch them with.

God, she missed Jonah.

A knock sounded off on the door, and Natalie pulled in a shaky breath, wiping her eyes. "Come in," she said, faking a smile as her mother poked her head into the room.

"Hi, sweetie. I didn't wake you, did I?"

"No," Natalie said, "I was just...staring at the ceiling," she confessed, and her mother came in to sit on the side of the bed.

"That makes sense, I suppose. You've had a long couple of days."

Worry filled her mother's eyes. But instead of telling her she was fine, Natalie said, "I have. Getting the news was hard, and if I'm being totally honest...I'm scared."

"You wouldn't be human if you weren't," her mother replied, and Natalie's jaw dropped open.

"You're okay with me being scared?"

Her mother laughed, and who knew the woman could be so full of surprises? "Of course I'm not okay with it. You're my daughter, and I only want for you to be happy and well. But it's perfectly understandable for you to be scared, considering what you're about to tackle, and just because you're scared, that doesn't mean you can't also be tough."

Natalie sat up, pressing her back against the pillows and staring at her mother more fully. "Since when are you so Zen about this kind of thing?"

"Oh, let me be clear, honey. I'm scared, too, and your father and I are taking this news about your health very, very seriously." The sudden glint of tears in her mother's eyes marked the words as all truth, making Natalie's gut squeeze. "But if your first round of cancer taught me anything, it's that you are so much stronger than you know."

"You think I'm strong," Natalie said dubiously. She meant no disrespect, but this *was* a woman who would have (lovingly) dressed her in head-to-toe bubble wrap just to keep her from getting bruised by a bedside table that stuck out too far.

Her mother shook her head. "No, Natalie. I know you're strong, because you showed me. Not just by beating cancer, but by becoming the adult that you are. For goodness sake, look at you! You're a surgeon. Smart. Capable. Kind. And very, very strong. But also human." Her mother took her hand. "And that means you're going to be scared, too."

"But what if I get really sick?" Natalie whispered. She hated for her mother to even think about it—she was terrified to picture it, herself. "How can I be strong then?"

Her mother paused, giving Natalie's hand a good squeeze. "Well, sweetheart, if you get really sick and can't be strong for a while, then I guess you'll have to let the people who love you carry you until you can. I know you think you always have to be okay. But the truth of it is, if you're not, you can still be loved."

Tears streamed down Natalie's face, her chest hitching as it ached. She wanted to be loved. She wanted to hope. She wanted Jonah, with his charming smiles and crazy taste in movies and slow, sweet kisses.

But all of that was over now. She still had cancer, which meant there was still a chance she could hurt him. She needed to forget it and move on.

No matter how much it hurt.

A sob worked its way up her throat, and for the first time ever, Natalie didn't try to cage it. She expected her mother to wipe away her tears and tell her not to be sad, that everything would be okay. But instead, her mother did something far more soothing.

She pulled Natalie into her arms and let her cry.

JONAH MADE it ninety-nine percent of the way through his shift before Tess, Charlie, and Connor fucking cornered him in the attendings' lounge. Connor wasn't even technically supposed to be *in* here, yet here he was, his mammoth, inked arms crossed over his equally mammoth chest as he stood next to Charlie, who was anchored in the exact same stance.

Yet, neither one of them was half as scary as Tess, who locked the door behind Jonah as soon as it bumped shut behind him, and damn it. Damn it! He knew he should've bribed the interns to distract the three of them so he could get his stuff from his locker and make a quick getaway.

Hindsight was a bitch.

"Okay, Charm School. Starting talking," Tess said, moving around him to join Charlie and Connor.

"What, you three didn't want to add Mallory for extra muscle?" Jonah grumbled, and Charlie arched an auburn brow.

"He's in surgery, otherwise we would have. And nice try, but no more stalling. What the hell is going on, Jonah? Seriously."

The woman I love has cancer and she won't let me help her fight it. My heart is in a trillion pieces on the floor. I drank enough bourbon last night to tranq a rhino. Take your pick. "I'm not sure what you mean."

Connor frowned. It was a very weird look on him. "Well, for starters, Dr. Langston sent out an email about an hour ago that said Dr. K is going on an immediate leave of absence to take care of a 'personal issue'." He slung air quotes around the words, his frown growing deeper.

Charlie picked up where he left off before Jonah could

work up any sort of deflection. "And Natalie has answered all of our texts—and believe me when I say, we each sent more than one or two—with the exact same reply. 'I'm fine'." More air quotes, and yeah, that sounded like Natalie.

Tess took the conversational baton and ran. "And you've been moping around this hospital all day long, looking like someone stole your puppy and smelling like a goddamn distillery."

"I don't smell like a distillery," Jonah argued, but oh, it was the low-hanging fruit. Also, probably not true.

"Dude," Connor said, brows arched. "You have Maker's Mark coming out of your pores. For real."

"Fine." Jonah rolled his eyes. "But I didn't treat any patients today. Just caught up on case notes."

"So, you're seriously not going to tell us what's going on with Natalie?" Tess asked. "And do not—do *not*—insult me by saying nothing is going on, or I will have to harm that very pretty face of yours."

Jonah exhaled, shoving his hands into his pockets. The three of them weren't going to stop until they had some answers. He might not be able to tell them the whole story, but he could air out enough to get them off his back. Plus, they already knew he and Natalie had been more than friends.

"She broke up with me and moved out last night," he said, the words feeling like bits of glass between his teeth.

For a second, Tess, Charlie, and Connor simply stared at him. The big man regained his wits first. "Are you kidding me?"

Jonah's laugh lacked all joy. "Do I look like I'm kidding you?"

Connor's hands went up in apology. "Fair enough. It's just that you guys are...well..."

"You," Charlie finished.

"Okay, wait," Tess said, too shrewd for her own damn good. "That only explains the moping. Why would she break up with you? She was walking around here looking like that emoji with the hearts for eyes just a couple of days ago." Her stare sharpened over Jonah. "Did you piss her off?"

"No," he said, jamming a hand through his hair. "It's...complicated."

"Complicated enough that she's taking a leave of absence?" Charlie asked. "That doesn't make any sense unless—"

Charlie's spine straightened at the same time Tess's did, the latter giving Jonah a look that said he was going to have to plead the fifth really fucking soon. "Oh, my God. Her cancer is back, isn't it?"

Jonah hesitated. As badly as he wanted to say something, if only so Natalie's friends could know enough to support her, this wasn't his story to tell. "I didn't say that."

"You didn't have to," Connor said, and Charlie nodded in agreement.

"That woman is crazy for you like I'm crazy for Parker. The only thing that would make her break up with you is something *that* drastic. Trust me. I know."

Jonah remembered what Charlie had sacrificed in order for Parker to keep his internship, and yeah. She wasn't wrong about drastic measures.

Still, he couldn't betray Natalie's confidence. When she was ready for their friends to know her cancer had returned, she'd tell them. Until then... "If you want to know about Natalie's health, you have to ask her."

Something that looked an awful lot like respect flickered through Tess's stare. "Okay, so let's talk about this breakup, then. I'm going to go out on a limb and assume it was one-sided."

"Definitely," Jonah said. At least there was one thing he could shout from the goddamn rooftops.

"And you're as crazy for her as she is for you," Charlie said, and once again, Jonah nodded.

"I really am."

"But she's pushing you away because she's doing that Natalie thing where she says she's totally fine, only this time, she's not so fine," Tess said.

It was a little too close to admitting that Natalie was sick, so Jonah arched a brow and stayed quiet, but all three of them made the logic leap well enough.

Charlie tilted her head. "So, you want her back."

"Yes," Jonah said, and God, it was a massive understatement. "I want to be with Natalie more than anything, and I think she wants to be with me, too. She's just...not used to letting anyone have her back."

"*Dude.*" Connor's face brightened, his goofy smile returning in all its glory. "You need a grand gesture!"

Jonah blinked. "I need a what, now?"

Connor heaved a twenty-pound sigh. "A grand gesture. You know, a big-deal, slightly crazy way of showing her you dig her and you want to be with her no matter how hard things get." He looked at Jonah, then Charlie and Tess, before throwing his hands into the air. "Seriously, don't any of you read the books I leave in the lounge?"

"I do!" Charlie and Tess chorused, although Tess seemed to go a little red at the question.

"Connor's right," Charlie said, turning toward Jonah. "If you want to get Natalie back, you're going to have to go all-in."

"You can't just go barging in on her, all pushy and stuff,

either," Connor said sagely. "There's a huge difference between a grand gesture and something that deserves a restraining order."

Jonah opened his mouth to tell them there was no hope. He'd already told Natalie how he felt. He'd told her he wanted to be there, to carry her when she needed strength and to help her get healthy again, and she'd left anyway.

But then he stopped. Natalie hadn't walked away because she didn't care for him. She'd walked away because she *did*. That meant there was still hope.

And if there was one thing Jonah could do, it was hope.

After all, he'd learned from the best.

"Okay," he said, his first smile in over twenty-four hours tugging at the corners of his mouth as a plan started taking shape in his head. "If a grand gesture is what I need, then a grand gesture is what I'm going to make."

30

Natalie sat in the kitchen at her parents' house, a cup of tea between her palms that she had no intention of drinking. It had made her mom feel better to brew it for her, though, so Natalie had given in when her mom had asked if she'd wanted any. She'd run out of tears a few hours ago, falling into a deep, dreamless nap after her mom had left her room.

The sleep might've helped her throbbing head and puffy eyes, but it had done jack shit for her broken heart.

"Stop," Natalie whispered, rubbing a hand over the front of her nightshirt, which she'd paired with a pair of plaid flannel pajama pants for the sake of modesty. She needed to forget about Jonah, once and for all, no matter how little she wanted to.

A buzzing sound captured her attention from the counter by the coffeepot. She'd left her cell phone down here so she could ignore it—Langston must have announced her leave of absence, which had triggered a landslide of texts and emails asking about her well-being. Her colleagues were concerned, she knew, but she wasn't ready to tell the whole universe about her cancer yet. Still, Jeff had mentioned reaching out to a couple of hospitals running clinical trials, to see if she was a good candidate for one of them. She should probably check to make sure he hadn't called.

The text that had just come in flashed across her screen, marked 9-1-1. It was from Tess.

Hey. I need you. It's urgent.

Natalie's heart pumped out a heavy dose of dread, and she answered automatically.

What's the matter? Is Jackson okay?

Tess had sworn the second her son was born that if he ever needed a surgical procedure, no one would touch him but Natalie.

He's fine, came the quick reply. **But I need you to come to the front door.**

Natalie's brows popped. **What?** How did she even know where Natalie was?

I know, I know. Just trust me. Please?

Natalie sighed. The truth was, she knew she wouldn't be able to dodge Tess and Charlie forever. Jonah had probably told them she was staying with her parents—Tess was frighteningly persuasive, and Charlie was no slouch, either. If they wanted to find her badly enough, they'd do it.

Clearly.

"Okay, okay," she said a second later when a knock sounded off on the front door. "Jeez, you guys. You didn't have to—"

She opened the door and her lips parted on a soundless gasp. Tess was there, and Charlie, too. So were Connor and Parker and Mallory.

And Jonah stood right in the middle.

"I know we're—I'm—sort of blindsiding you with all of

this." He gestured to their friends, all of whom were holding bags of various sizes and throwing Natalie for the biggest loop of her life. "And I'm sorry for that. If you really, truly don't want to see me, I'll go. But I'd really like it if you'd hear me out for just five minutes."

She didn't say anything—couldn't, really, with the way her head and her heart were both screaming two different answers—and Jonah took her silence as a sign to proceed.

"I tried to come up with the right words to tell you what you mean to me, but then I realized it would be better to actually show you. So"—he turned to Mallory, who handed over the bag he'd been holding, and Jonah pulled out a clear plastic takeout container and handed it over to her—"I want to give you the last bite of cheesecake," he said, and oh, God. Oh, God.

Sure enough, the box contained one bite-sized piece of cheesecake, and Natalie's hands began to shake.

Jonah turned toward Connor, who handed over his bag. "I want to laugh when you're happy," Jonah said, pulling out a Blu-ray copy of *When Harry Met Sally* and handing it over.

"Jonah," she whispered, her voice catching, but he shook his head.

"And I want to ache when you're sad," he added, taking the bag Charlie and Parker had handed over together and giving her the box of tissues inside.

Which was probably smart, considering the bag Tess handed over contained a small box containing a gold heart locket so beautiful, tears sprang to Natalie's eyes.

"I want to be more than two halves making a whole," Jonah said, popping the locket open, and Tess quietly stepped in to take everything out of Natalie's hands and lead the rest of the group away from the front step.

Jonah pressed the two sides of the locket back together

and held it out to her. "I want to be two wholes making something bigger. Something only the two of us can make. I want you."

"Jonah," she tried again. "I have cancer."

"I know," he said. "But you also have a strong treatment plan and the very best doctors. And you have a one hundred-percent success rate with beating this disease."

Natalie's resolve wavered. But she couldn't hurt him. She *couldn't*. "I've had all that before. It doesn't mean I'm going to beat it again."

"Oh, yes it does," he told her, stepping in until he was so close, she could feel the heat of his body, right there in front of her. "Because this time you also have me, and I have enough hope for both of us. I need you, Nat. I need to be here for you no matter what. I need you to fight and beat this cancer like we both know you're going to and live a good, long, happy life with me, because you're the only person in the world who can make me a long-haul guy. I don't care if there are risks, and I don't care if there are tough times that mix in with the good. I want you, Natalie. I love *you*."

Jonah slid his fingers over her cheek, and that was when she realized she was crying.

"Happily ever after isn't always easy. But you are my happily ever after. You are the best fucking thing about me, and I am not letting you let me go. So, if you could just let me love you, and carry me while I carry you—"

"Yes."

"Really?" he asked, blinking twice.

Natalie laughed, and oh, it felt so good. "God, yes. Did you really think I could say no to that? It's even better than a rom com ending."

"Well, I was aiming for a grand gesture, so I kinda went

big. But in case you haven't noticed, you're a tiny bit stubborn, and you don't like letting people take care of you."

"In this case, I can make an exception."

He lifted his brows, his smile growing wide. "Yeah?"

"Yeah. I'm still scared, and I'm sorry I hurt you by walking away. But I promised I'd always be here, so yes, I'll carry you while you carry me. I love you, too, Jonah. God, I love you so freaking much." She stepped into his arms as if it was the only place she'd ever belonged. "And in order to kick cancer's ass—again, like we both know I'm going to—I'm going to need a little help."

"Whatever you need, sweetheart. Name it, and it's yours."

Natalie pressed up on her toes, brushing her lips over his in a soft, sweet kiss. "Actually, that last bite of cheesecake looked pretty good."

"Done," he said, but she shook her head.

"How about we split it?"

Jonah laughed, wrapping his arms around her and pulling her close, and Natalie's chest filled with hope.

"That sounds perfect."

EPILOGUE

Three weeks later

CONNOR BRADSHAW WAS WAITING for a disaster. Which was more status-quo than stressful, considering he'd been trained to the teeth as an Air Force flight medic and worked in a Level I trauma center for the past four years, but he wasn't about to bitch, regardless. Cars crashed. People harmed each other. Health failed in dozens of different directions. Bad things happened, and as much as Connor hated that little nugget of truth, he'd learned the hard way that there was no getting around it. But if he could help people *through* the worst moments of their lives instead?

He was going to be down every single time. No matter how big the disaster, or how bloody the aftermath.

He'd survived worse.

"Listen up, cats and kittens, because this one is gonna test your stamina." Tess turned to look at the group of docs huddled against the cold in Remington Mem's ambulance bay. Jonah, Drake, Mallory, Vasquez (standing as far as possible from Mallory)...damn, whatever patients were incoming had to be in pretty rough shape for all this fire-power to be out here, waiting. Usually the nurses met the ambos for triage and handoff from paramedics—especially in January.

Connor's adrenaline tapped out the Morse code equiva-lent of hey-how-are-ya in his veins, and he pulled in a slow breath to let it know he was juuuuust fine, thanks. He was hardly a fucking rookie. No way was he going to let his phys-iology tank his ability to help the patients coming in on this call. Not when they were clearly going to need all the help they could get.

Tess elbowed her way into the trauma gown that matched the ones the rest of them had donned as they'd been pulled from various tasks to handle the incoming call. "Dispatch has multiple traumas from a car wreck headed our way, ETA five minutes. At least one thoracic crush injury, a couple of penetrating lacerations, and a traumatic leg injury—that's yours, Mallory—plus possible head and neck injuries all around," she said. "I want fast assessments and faster treatment. No one's dying on my watch today. Got it?"

"Yes, ma'am." Connor's response stuck out a little in the chorus of yeses and echoed-back "got it"s, but he was hardly apologetic. The Air Force had made a lot of things second nature in his life, and he was grateful as hell for each of them. After all, the six years he'd spent there before he'd landed at Remington Mem hadn't just taught him how to take care of people who needed it.

They'd also taught him to hide in plain sight.

Spine straightening, he stuffed the thought back into its

usual hidey hole and forced himself back into the here and now. The part of a trauma that could freak a person out the most was waiting for the patients to arrive—all that what-if, flying around and fritzing out your circuitry—so Connor decided to fill the time the best way he knew how. Christ, but humor was better than Kevlar some days.

He looked at Jonah and grinned. "Hey, man. Other than being your better half, how's Dr. K?" he asked. "You gave her my care package, right?"

JONAH'S entire demeanor changed in a blink at the mention of Natalie, his smile so big it was like a third person in the conversation. God, the dude had it so bad. It was awesome. "Romance novels and mini-Bundt cakes from *Sweetie Pies*? Really, man?"

"She loved it, didn't she?" Connor's grin broadened. The woman was going through chemo, for fuck's sake. She deserved the very best.

"She did," Jonah admitted. "Although I'm pretty sure Tess swiped that one book with your buddy on the cover. When she came to visit the other day, she and Nat were giggling over it."

Connor bit back a snort. Declan would probably shit twice and die if he heard that—dude hated the spotlight, enough that his face was rarely ever in the photos on those book covers, and Connor made a mental note to shoot the guy a text this week to check in. "So, the first round of chemo went okay?"

"Actually, it did," Jonah said with genuine enthusiasm. "She's responding even better than Wells expected, and she's keeping busy with research and ideas for future trials—"

"Go, Dr. K," Connor interjected, because she really *must* be responding well if she was able to work during treatments. Of course, Connor was sure Jonah kept close tabs on her, anyway. God, he loved a happy ending.

Jonah laughed. "Once her treatments are done and she gets a clean bill of health, she'll be back to work," he said with confidence. "It's a marathon, not a sprint, though. For now, she's spending a few days with Rachel and Annabelle. They came up for a quick visit in between Annabelle's treatments."

Connor brightened. Man, that kid was cute enough to be unfair. "Yeah? Annabelle's well enough to travel, then?"

"She is," Jonah confirmed, taking his cell phone out of his pocket and swiping his way through a couple of pictures. "There are precautions, of course. They skipped the airport and road-tripped it instead. But Annabelle is making huge strides in that clinical trial in Tampa. She wanted to come give Natalie some moral support now that she's got that first round of chemo under her belt."

Connor arched a brow at his buddy and pulled the pair of nitrile gloves he'd been holding into place while Jonah did the same. Involuntary response to the sound of sirens getting closer, he supposed. "You know, under other circumstances, I'd be jealous that you're hogging all the pretty girls for yourself."

Jonah laughed, although his expression quickly grew serious at the sight of the ambulance pulling into the bay in front of them. "I'll see if they can swing a FaceTime after our shift is over. I know Nat would love to see your goofy mug, and Annabelle still swears you're magic because you can start an IV without pinching her. One of these days, I'm going to get you to tell me all your secrets."

The word snapped through Connor, ratcheting his

pulse. That was twice in one day that his long-buried skeletons had threatened to surface. Damn, he was off his game.

"Never," Connor said, shrugging off the stiffness in his shoulders and waggling his brows at Jonah as Tess hit them both with a tart smile.

"Sorry to interrupt your bromance here, but how about we treat some trauma patients? Y'know, just for shits and giggles."

"You got it, Dr. Michaelson," Connor said. As much downtime as he spent with both Tess and Jonah, when he was on the clock, they were always "doctor". No exceptions.

Her light brown ponytail bobbed over one shoulder as she nodded and lifted her voice to address the group. "Okay. Parker, you're with Sheridan on ambo one," she said to the intern-slash-former-paramedic. "Vasquez, you're with me on two, and Connor, you're with Mallory on three. Let's go."

They all turned toward the trio of ambulances pulling into the bay, eyes alert and muscles primed for movement, and Connor took one last breath before disaster struck.

It didn't take long.

"What've we got?" Mallory asked as soon as the ambulance jerked to a stop and the rear doors flew open.

The paramedic scrambled to the head of the gurney while Connor's muscle memory had him moving to the foot to take care of the honors so Mallory could assess the patient as soon as she came into view. Easier said than done, since she was strapped to a backboard, one leg heavily splinted and her body covered with a trauma blanket from the waist down.

"Shelly   Fitzpatrick,   twenty-six-year-old   female, restrained in the driver's seat," the paramedic said, guiding the gurney wheels to the pavement with a hard clack. "GCS II. Complaining of chest and shoulder pain and left leg pain.

No apparent head or neck trauma, no LOC." He rattled off her vitals—not terrible but certainly not good enough to make Connor a happy camper—before adding, "Obvious left upper leg deformity. Pain meds were administered en route."

"Hi, Ms. Fitzpatrick, I'm Dr. Mallory, and I'm going to help you, okay? Don't try to nod. We want to keep your neck stable until we can check you out," he said, falling in beside the gurney on the right side as they moved like a symphony toward the automatic doors. "Can you tell me if you're experiencing any pain?"

"My leg. It hurts *really* bad."

"I'm just going to take a quick look," Mallory told the woman, who whimpered and tensed in response, and whoa, even with those pain meds on board, Connor could see why.

Mallory said, "Definite open femur fracture. Let's pick up the pace." Without moving his eyes from the patient, he added, "Trauma two, Connor," and without moving *his* eyes, Connor steered the gurney directly toward the trauma room, his strides growing more purpose. They crossed the threshold seconds later, going through the practiced motions of transferring the patient to a hospital gurney and preparing for a more thorough exam, and damn, they had their work cut out for them with a broadsword. But while the gruesome nature of the woman's injuries would make most people panic—or at the very least, lean toward despair—visualizing what needed to be fixed solidified the necessary steps in Connor's head.

Assess. Strategize. Act.

First things' first. Connor scanned the woman from her head down, using the exact same visual process he'd learned on day one in medic training ten years ago. The woman's face was pale, sharp lines of pain etched around her eyes and mouth. A bright yellow C-collar held her neck steady, and cuts and abrasions of mild to moderate severity peppered her face and hands. There was no way to do a full exam with her jeans and sweater in the way, so Connor grabbed a pair of trauma shears and an extra blanket, making quick work of the patient's clothing while giving her as much privacy as possible.

"Femoral and dorsal pulses both weak," Connor confirmed after a manual check, while Mallory began a more comprehensive exam. An angry purple bruise was forming across the woman's chest in a sash from left shoulder to right hip, and man, thank God for pain meds, because that leg injury was one of the worst Connor had seen.

And oh, he'd seen a *lot*.

"Alright," Mallory said after a minute. "Ms. Fitzpatrick is alert and her pupils are equal and reactive. No dizziness, no nausea. Good signs." He placed a quick squeeze on the woman's forearm before adding, "Let's clear her head and neck so we can lose this C-collar, and I want a full set of left leg, chest, and shoulder films. We need to see exactly what we're dealing with."

Connor had the portable X-ray machine ready to go before Mallory had even finished ordering the films. "Okay, Ms. Fitzpatrick. I'm going to take some X-rays with machine right here," Connor told her, his gut going tight as her eyes widened and her heart rate spiked on the monitor. "I know you're in pain. I'll be as gentle and fast as possible, I promise. Once we get these images, Dr. Mallory will be able to see your injuries more clearly, and then we can fix you right up, okay?"

"It's...really bad...isn't it?" she asked, and Connor cobbled together a big, playful smile as he shouldered into the protective apron and maneuvered the machine into place.

"You're going to have plenty of time to relax and eat ice cream while you recover." He didn't mention the rods and pins Mallory would almost certainly have to place in her leg, or the boatloads of PT she had ahead of her. For now, they needed to tackle the closest alligator to the boat; namely, keeping her calm while they figured out the extent of the damage to her leg and whether or not there would be permanent effects.

Strategize, Connor told himself. "So, what's your favorite kind?" he asked, calling out over his shoulder to let Mallory know he was shooting the first set of films on their patient's head and neck.

"W-what?"

"Of ice cream," Connor elaborated as he continued to work. "I kind of change mine according to season. Peppermint around the holidays, strawberry in the summer. But, really, I don't think you can ever go wrong with chocolate. It's a classic."

"Vanilla is better," she said after a beat, and Connor placed a hand over the front of his lead apron, calling out for the second set of films before splashing a dramatic look of mock pain over his face.

"You wound me, Ms. Fitzpatrick."

She eked out the tiniest of smiles. "Shelly."

A grunt of pain crossed her lips as Connor adjusted her leg for a different view, and he bit down on the urge to wince right along with her.

"Sorry. Just a little adjustment. You're doing great." He distracted her with the whole chocolate-versus-vanilla debate for the rest of the films, which Mallory had been reading from the computer monitor on the other side of the partition in the room as Connor had been shooting them and sending them over.

"Okay, Shelly," Mallory said, coming back into full view a few seconds later. "The good news is that your head, neck, and spine are all uninjured. You sustained some pretty moderate bruising to your chest and shoulder from the seat belt and you've got some cuts from the broken glass, but none of those injuries are serious."

"What's the bad news?" she asked, her eyes darting to Connor, then back to Mallory.

His pause was short enough for Shelly not to notice it, but long enough that Connor sure did. "Your femur—the big bone in you upper leg—is pretty badly broken. The trauma is compromising the blood flow to the lower part of your leg, and in order to fix it, you're going to need immediate surgery so we can get the bones back in place."

"You want to do surgery to move my bones? Right *now*?" she asked, her voice rising in panic, but Connor stepped into her line of vision, giving her no choice but to focus on him. *Act.*

"Hey, Shelly. We're going to take a deep breath together, me and you, and then I'm going to take this C-collar off of you'll be more comfortable, okay? Here we go." He inhaled loudly, and although her corresponding breath was far shakier, at least she followed suit. Connor made good on his promise to remove the C-collar, and bingo, a little more tension left the woman's gaze.

"I know surgery sounds pretty scary," he told her. "But if we don't do it quickly, there's a bigger risk of permanent damage to your leg, or infection, or even both. Dr. Mallory wouldn't tell you it's necessary unless it was the best way to help you get better."

The words seemed to sink in, at least a little. Her eyes

widened. "Would...would you be there during the surgery, too?"

Connor smiled at her to soften the news. "I'm afraid I'm not as cool as Dr. Mallory, here. He's got that flashy surgical license, and I'm the sort of nurse that has to stick around the emergency department in case more traumas come in. But I'll tell you what. I'll ask the surgical nurse who scrubs in with Dr. Mallory to page me when you're in recovery, and as soon as you're cleared for food, I'll use my sparkling personality to get some of the finest vanilla ice cream the cafeteria has to offer. Deal?"

Shelly nodded slowly. "Okay. Deal."

"Awesome." He gave her a gentle fist bump, hiding his relief with a grin.

"Thanks, Connor," Mallory said, his expression marking the sentiment as truly genuine. "Can you do me a favor and book an OR?" He turned toward Shelly. "We'll get you upstairs and the surgical nurse on duty will prep you for the procedure, and I can answer any questions you've got about the surgery along the way."

"Is there anyone you want me to call for you, Shelly?" Connor asked a few seconds later, after the OR had been reserved and Mallory's intern du jour, Dr. Boldin, had arrived to help with the transport.

"Oh." She blinked. "Um, sure. My mom is going to freak out, but I guess you should call her. I'd really like to have her there when I wake up."

"I'll be sure to tell her you're getting the very best ice cream after your surgery," Connor promised. He took down her mother's number and turned to make his way to the nurses' station so he could make the phone call that would give the woman some extra peace of mind. But before he could make it even halfway across the trauma room floor, Tess appeared in the doorway.

"You two okay in here?" she asked, dividing her gaze between Connor and Mallory.

"Absolutely," the doc said. "Boldin and I are headed up to the OR for a femur repair, but everything else looks stable. Did you need me for a consult?"

Tess shook her head. "Nah. Sheridan and Drake took their patient upstairs, and Charlie's doing a consult on mine for a possible splenic lac. Everyone's stable for now."

"I do love a happy ending," Connor said, waving at Shelly as Boldin wheeled her gurney past Tess and toward the bank of elevators. "Anyway, I'm going to make this call before I head back to fray."

"Not so fast, flyboy," Tess said, plucking the Post-It note with his patient's mother's contact information on it from between his fingers. "Your presence has been requested in the executive boardroom."

"What?" Shock rippled through Connor, quickly chased by a hard shot of dread. But no. His time spent in boardrooms was another lifetime ago, long dead. Still, nothing good could come from those words, even though he was one hundred percent certain his nose was Spic and Span. "Why does Langston want to see me?"

"He doesn't. I do," came an all too frosty, all too familiar voice from over Tess's shoulder, and Connor's pulse slam-banged through his veins as he turned to look at the woman in the doorway. Sleek, light blond hair pulled back into a tasteful ponytail. Crisp blue stare. Black sheath dress that cost as much as his paycheck, mile-long legs that ended in stilettos as pointed as her frown, and God damn it.

There was only one thing that Harlow Davenport, the one woman in all of Remington that he wanted to avoid like every plague that had ever existed, could want with him in a boardroom.

She knows.

WANT MORE? Preorder Connor and Harlow's standalone medical romance, BETWEEN YOU & I, right here.

WANT an exclusive look at how Jonah and Natalie are doing? Sign up for my newsletter using this special link (even if you're already signed up, click here) and you'll get a very special letter, just from Jonah to you!

AND REMEMBER THAT SEXY-AS-HELL FIREFIGHTER, Kellan Walker, from the guys' night out scene? Check out this sneak peek at SKIN DEEP, the first standalone in the Station Seventeen series (Kellan and Isabella's story):

KELLAN MADE his way up Washington Boulevard, where he'd parked yesterday morning before shift. Funny how quiet the city could be before things like rush hour and regular work-days kicked in, all soft sunlight and clean storefronts. He slid in a breath of cool air, scanning the sidewalk and the two-lane thoroughfare where Station Seventeen was situated.

He saw the woman leaning against his '68 Camaro from forty feet away.

Kellan's pulse flared even though his footsteps never faltered. Long, denim-wrapped legs leading to lean muscles and lush, sexy curves. Loose, confident stance that spoke of both awareness and strength. Long, caramel-colored hair that she tossed away from her face as soon as she saw him coming, and God *dammit*, that was the second time this week he'd been blindsided by Isabella Moreno.

"What are you doing here?" he asked, wincing inwardly as the words crossed his lips. Not that he didn't feel every inch of the attitude behind them, because after her fuck-up had put his sister's life in danger three months ago, he so did. But slapping his emotions on his sleeve wasn't on Kellan's agenda, good, bad, or extremely pissed off. Of course, Isabella already knew he was chock full of the emotion behind door number three, anyway.

She pushed herself off the Camaro's cherry red quarter panel, sliding one hand to her unnervingly voluptuous hip while the other remained wrapped around a cup of coffee. "Waiting for you."

"I got that." His tone left the what-for part of the question hanging between them, and Kellan had to hand it to her. Moreno wasn't the type to mince words.

"I need a favor. I want you to walk me through the scene of Monday's fire."

Jesus, she had a sense of humor. Also, balls the size of Jupiter. "You want me to take you back to the scene of a fire that gutted a three-story house just to give you a play by play?"

She nodded, her brown eyes narrowing against the sunlight just starting to break past the buildings around them. "That about sums it up, yeah."

"It's a little early for you to be punching the clock, isn't it?" he asked. Most people weren't even halfway to the door just shy of oh-seven-hundred on a weekday morning.

Moreno? Not most people, apparently. "What can I say? I'm feeling ambitious."

Kellan resisted the urge to launch a less-than-polite

comment about her work ethic, albeit barely. "I already told you and Sinclair everything I know."

"Okay." Her shoulders rose and fell beneath her dark gray leather jacket, easy and smooth. "So humor me and walk me through it again anyway."

His sixth sense took a jab at his gut, prompting him to give the question in his head a voice. "Is this part of the investigation?"

"Why do you ask?" she said, and yeah, that was a no.

"Because you called it a favor, and you just answered my question with a question."

Moreno paused. "I'm a cop. We do that."

Nope. No way was he buying this. Not even on her best day. "And I'm a firefighter who's not interested in putting his ass in a sling just to humor you with an unsanctioned walk-through."

The RFD might offer a little latitude on firefighters revisiting scenes—a fact Kellan would bet his left nut Moreno damn well knew—but just because he'd worked the job didn't mean he had carte blanche to prance through the place like a fucking show pony now that the fire was out.

Not that a little thing like protocol seemed to bother Isabella in the least. "Your ass will be fine. I'll take full responsibility."

"I'm pretty sure I've heard that one from you before."

The words catapulted out before Kellan could stop them. Moreno flinched, just slightly, but it was enough. "Look, I need to get back onto that scene," she said. "Are you going to help me or not?"

GRAB THE BOOK HERE!

KIMBERLY'S OTHER WORKS

Other works by Kimberly Kincaid:

The Remington Medical Contemporary Standalones:
    Back to You
    Better Than Me
    Between You & I
    Beyond Just Us (late fall 2019)

The Station Seventeen Engine series, all books stand alone:
    Deep Trouble (prequel)
    Skin Deep
    Deep Check
    Deep Burn
    In Too Deep
    Forever Deep (companion novella to Skin Deep)
    Down Deep

The Line series (all free on KU):
    Love On The Line
    Drawing The Line

Outside The Lines

Pushing The Line

All four books available in a bundle: The Line Collection

The Cross Creek series (first two titles FREE in KU):

Crossing Hearts

Crossing the Line

Crossing Promises

Crossing Hope

Stand-alones:

Something Borrowed

Play Me

And don't forget to come find Kimberly on Facebook, join her street team The Taste Testers, and follow her on Twitter, Pinterest, and Instagram!